Michael Carson was born in Merseyside just
after the Second World War. Educated at
Catholic schools, he then became a novice in a
religious order. After leaving university, he
took up a career as a teacher of English as a
foreign language and has worked in various
countries, including Saudi Arabia, Brunei and
Iran. He has written three previous novels,
Sucking Sherbet Lemons, Friends and Infidels,
and *Coming Up Roses* (also available in Black
Swan).

Author photograph by Pinsharp

Also by Michael Carson

SUCKING SHERBET LEMONS
FRIENDS AND INFIDELS
COMING UP ROSES

and published by Black Swan

Stripping Penguins Bare

Michael Carson

BLACK SWAN

STRIPPING PENGUINS BARE
A BLACK SWAN BOOK 0 552 99465 0

Originally published in Great Britain by Victor Gollancz Ltd

PRINTING HISTORY
Gollancz edition published 1991
Black Swan edition published 1992

Copyright © Michael Carson 1991

The right of Michael Carson to be identified as author of this
work has been asserted in accordance with sections 77 and 78
of the Copyright Designs and Patents Act 1988.

This book is set in 11/12pt Melior by
County Typesetters, Margate, Kent

Black Swan Books are published by Transworld Publishers Ltd.,
61–63 Uxbridge Road, Ealing, London W5 5SA, in Australia
by Transworld Publishers (Australia) Pty. Ltd., 15–23 Helles
Avenue, Moorebank, NSW 2170, and in New Zealand by
Transworld Publishers (N.Z.) Ltd., Cnr. Moselle and
Waipareira Avenues, Henderson, Auckland.

Made and printed in Great Britain by
Cox & Wyman Ltd., Reading, Berks.

For Robert Stone

'What things that young man has me saying!'

—Socrates, after reading Plato

1

The Freshers' Hop was held to welcome new students to the university. Benson arrived with a Ghanaian student who had leaned out of the window of his Morris Minor in Aberystwyth's main street to ask him where the Hop was taking place. Benson had tried too hard to give the student detailed directions and eventually the African, thoroughly confused, asked if Benson was going to the Hop too.

'Yes.'

'Well, get in and you can show me the way.'

Simeon, the Ghanaian student, said that he was looking for a steady girlfriend and the Hop was a good place to start his search. 'I suppose you are too,' he said.

'Oh, yes, of course,' replied Benson. But he was already half in love with the tiny black figure in the navy-blue Crimplene suit and the orange tie.

'What are you studying?' asked Simeon.

'Umm . . . well it's not certain yet. Philosophy and English, I think, but I don't fancy Anglo-Saxon. Maybe History too. What about you?'

'Plant-breeding.'

'That sounds interesting,' said Benson, thinking how useful plants must be in Africa, and trying to decide if Ghana was to the east or the west of Nigeria. 'Ghana used to be the Gold Coast, didn't it?' he asked, though he knew the answer.

Simeon nodded, frowned at the world outside the car, and asked Benson which way to turn.

By the time they had got into the hall and Benson had found a hanger to put his jacket on, Simeon had

9

disappeared. Benson wandered nervously to the dancefloor of the students' union, where everyone was trying to dance fast to 'You Don't Have to Say You Love Me'. There he caught sight of Simeon waltzing with a large girl who was wearing blue butterfly-frame spectacles and a pale blue gym-slip. The girl was much taller than Simeon, who was resting his neat black head on her bosom, while the large girl looked around, her eyes registering great panic and dismay.

As Benson leaned against the wall self-consciously, his hands behind his back worrying his entrance ticket to disintegration between thumb and forefinger, Simeon caught his eye, winked and smiled widely. Benson smiled back, only to be confronted by the desperate gaze of Simeon's partner.

Benson sighed and reached into his pocket for a packet of Kent. Kents were his special occasion brand. Usually he rolled Sun Valley in a cigarette machine, though he was looking forward to the day when he would be able to roll a perfect cigarette using his fingers. But for the Hop he had laid out 5/6 for the white cigarettes in their white packet with their aroma of America. He was lighting his Kent with his Imco when the intense face of a dark-haired girl appeared on the far side of his lighter flame and said, 'Light me too.'

Benson did so.

'Now dance with me.'

Again Benson did so.

'I'm Meryl,' said Meryl.

'Martin,' said Benson, wondering if he should display the precious jewel of his dancing repertoire – pelvic thrusting to Dusty Springfield – at once, or merely plod from foot to foot as if it came naturally. Simeon had now disengaged himself from the bespectacled-girl's bosom and was really starting to show how he could dance, and Benson was beginning to suffer abject humiliation. His slowly-perfected pelvic thrust took on the status of a twitch. He bobbed about, feeling hugely embarrassed, tried to Twist, but the crepe soles of his desert boots, combined with a certain stiff dogmatism in his legs, failed to twist him convincingly. He threw in a couple of rather noncommittal pelvic thrusts. It wasn't really fair to be compared to Simeon. Africans were encouraged to dance as soon as they could walk, in the same way that he had been encouraged to be polite and say 'please' and 'thank you' and kiss bourgeois aunts and uncles.

Benson let his Kent hang down from his lips, frowning as the smoke stung his eyes. Sparks flew from Meryl's cigarette when she brushed the live end of it down the back of the sports jacket of a nearby dancer. 'Bugger!' said Meryl, looking at the expiring end of her cigarette. While she blew it back to rude health, Benson helpfully stamped on all the sparks, neatly performing his fire-prevention steps as part of his dance.

'It's a nice name you've got. I haven't heard it before,' Benson shouted over the din.

'I think it makes one sound like toothpaste,' opined Meryl. 'Still, who can fathom what goes on in the brains of one's parents? I believe that my father had a wet-nurse called Meryl back in the mists of antiquity. One thing about it, you can't mess with "Meryl".'

Benson was already beginning to intimate the truth of that, and nodded.

Meryl carried on, confirming his worst imaginings. 'You ain't got much sou-u-l, have you, Martin, or do you prefer to be called "Marts"? When de good Lord was distributing de rhythm it done ran out way *way* 'fore it got to *you!*'

Benson did not make any reply. Indeed he tried to pretend that he had not heard what Meryl had said. The song was finishing and he merely stood, folding his arms across his chest, looking about him, thinking it a bit thick that a total stranger should criticize his best efforts to be rhythmical.

11

The noise of pick-up on edge of record filled the room and The Four Tops were singing 'Reach Out (And I'll be There)'.

Meryl whooped and started shaking herself about as if she were trying to get a very cold key that had been dropped down her dress to come out at the other end before it gave her a chill. Her short hair with its long fringe plopped forward over her face.

Benson wondered whether he should mention that Meryl's hair was done in the same style as Cilla Black's. She also had Cilla Black's prominent nose. But he decided not to say anything as he was not at all sure what reaction his intended compliment would receive. He threw himself around, determined to keep up with Meryl, and soon found that his new step, which consisted of banging the left heel of his Freeman Hardy and Willis desert boot with the right instep thereby flicking his whole body in a clockwise direction, then doing the same thing with the right heel, was happening *of its own accord* and he felt he could hold his head up with the blackest.

He looked round, sweat trickling from his brow. Simeon and the girl with the glasses were just behind him, but Simeon was still waltzing, his head buried in the girl's bust. She seemed to have accepted defeat and was gazing down benignly at the tight-sprung African hair.

Benson momentarily wished that he was her, and lost his step. He collided against Meryl, treading on the toe of her left foot.

Meryl stopped dead.

'You can buy me a fucking drink for that!' she said.

Benson obediently queued at the bar to buy Meryl a Snowball and himself a lemonade and lime. It took the barman ages to make the Snowball. He was a bald man, clearly out of his depth with such an exotic order. He dithered with the cocktail shaker, kept rubbing his blue chin and asking himself: 'Now, let's see, what's next?' Benson said that he thought there was egg flip in a Snowball, but the barman just shook his head and rummaged under the bar where Benson could not see. 'We'll try some of this. Can't do any harm, is it?' the barman said to himself, and added things to the cocktail shaker.

'Now, that lemonade and lime,' said the barman after he had poured the yellow liquid into a champagne glass, 'would that be for a lady?'

'No, it's for me,' replied Benson, staring gloomily at the Snowball.

The barman put Benson's lemonade and lime into a half-pint mug.

When he got back to where he had left Meryl pouting and massaging her foot, she had disappeared. Benson stood holding the two drinks in his hands, wondering what to do. He badly wanted to fold his arms in front of him to protect himself from the crowd of strangers. This being impossible, he put his weight on one leg and then placed his left desert boot on top of the right. This was almost as good as folding his arms and he stood thus, surveying the dancing multitudes.

Simeon was still dancing with the same girl, who had undergone something of a transformation. She had taken off her glasses, unbuttoned the top of the blouse under the gym-slip and was dancing with no small abandon to '(I Can't Get No) Satisfaction'. She did not move her body much as she danced. But her arms were making up for it, describing snaky arabesques, slithering syncopations, attacker-doubling elbow thrusts, paradise-pleading prayers . . . even, Benson noted, what might be interpreted as a pulling in of a loaded Ghanaian fishing-net. A cordon sanitaire had formed on the dancefloor, only crossed by a very pleased-looking Simeon who wore an expression which made it clear that he felt he had struck a rich seam. He, Benson noted, was moving very little. Still, he didn't have to. His slow bounce from leg to leg

13

was, as far as Benson was concerned, pure poetry.

Then Benson caught sight of Meryl shaking her chest about opposite a lanky man who was throwing himself around in imitation of a demented puppet with no regard to the beat at all. The man's shirt-tail had come out. Benson pursed his lips and shifted his position, thinking that he must try to disentangle himself from Meryl before she asked him to buy her another Snowball. He had already spent 7/2. He would have to go easy. If Meryl were a man they would take turns in paying. As it was, he would have to do the manly thing and buy the rounds. He felt it was a bit thick. They got the same grant money after all. Still, he thought, women had all sorts of extra expenses. They had to buy rollers and creams and potions to make themselves presentable. Not to mention suits, bras, Limmits, twin-sets, spare shoes and scent.

The song ended and was replaced by Ken Dodd singing 'Tears', the current Number One in the hit parade. A groan drowned the singer's best efforts, and almost all the dancers sighed to the sidelines. Meryl came back alone.

She snatched the glass from Benson. 'Cheers!' she said and slugged back at least 3/4 worth of her Snowball. Benson sipped his lemonade and lime, trying to make it last. He asked Meryl whether her red leather skirt was hot and Meryl said that it wasn't as hot as Crimplene trousers and a bri-nylon shirt. Then he pulled Meryl on to the dancefloor because they had ripped Ken Dodd off the turntable – to the accompaniment of many hoots and cheers – and were playing Jackie Trent singing 'Where Are You Now, My Love?', a song which Benson felt was so wonderful it could have been written by Benjamin Britten. It moved him to tears. Indeed, he had sung it to himself as his train pulled out of Woodside Station, Birkenhead en route to Aberystwyth. It brought Clitherow to mind. It was consoling to think of Clitherow, his best friend from

14

home. What would Clitherow be doing now? Was he at some Freshers' Hop at Oxford? Was Clitherow dancing with strangers? If he was, Benson decided, he would be impressing them like mad. Clitherow could twist convincingly until the cows came home. His pelvic thrust was also second to none.

'Excuse me, if you don't mind!' said Meryl, knocking on Benson's head.

'Yes?' Who did she think she was? Clitherow would have told her where to get off.

'Thank you for paying attention. For the second time: What are you going to study?' asked Meryl.

'I'm not sure. I'm supposed to be Honours English and History, but I may change.'

'Thought so.'

'Why?'

'You look like the sort who wants to do something so-called useful, like Economics or Accountancy.'

Benson felt he had to defend himself. 'Oh, no! I've no idea what I want to do when I finish here!'

'Well, that's something anyway. God, I shouldn't think the world will still be here in 1968.'

Benson nodded enthusiastically. His own thoughts entirely. 'Er . . . where are you from?' he asked.

'London.'

Benson waited to be asked but, when he wasn't, volunteered: 'I'm from Wallasey . . . where Malcolm Lowry was born.' He had only heard a week or two before that Malcolm Lowry came from his town, had been born only a few yards from Clitherow's house. The news had cheered him immensely. He had read it at the start of the Penguin edition of *Under the Volcano*, though he had only managed to get as far as page thirty-two of the novel.

However, Meryl was unimpressed and did not ooh and ahh, merely nodded.

'What brings you to Aberystwyth?' asked Benson.

'Miserable A level results. What about you?'

15

'It was my second choice on my UCCA form. Bangor was first.'

Meryl nodded as if everything were falling into place.

'It was all a bit of a surprise,' continued Benson. 'I was all set to go to teacher training college – not that I wanted to really, even though teaching is useful and my dad says it's secure – but I managed to get an E in General Studies and that made up for me not having maths or a science.'

Meryl danced over and whispered in his ear: 'Shut up, you're boring me!'

Benson's pelvic thrust quivered to a stand-still. He stared hard at Meryl, folded his arms and walked from the dancefloor. Meryl followed him. 'That's more like it! A bit of spunk!' she said over the din. Benson looked hard in the gloom for his lemonade and lime, ignoring Meryl. He found it behind a chair and started sipping it intently.

'I *like* your anger!' exclaimed Meryl, shifting her position to place herself in range of Benson's averted eyes. And she added: 'Where's that from?'

'Where's what from?' he asked sulkily.

' "I like your anger." Where's it from?'

'I haven't the foggiest idea, Meryl. And I don't care.'

Meryl looked at Benson strangely. Then she said: 'You're homosexual, aren't you?'

'None of your business,' replied Benson.

'Yes, definitely,' declared Meryl, nodding sagely. 'Don't worry, your secret is safe with me. Some of my best friends are.'

Benson wondered how Meryl had guessed. 'How did you know?' he asked, his anger forgotten, anxiety taking its place.

'The way you left the dancefloor. Something about the walk. And there's a certain something in your voice.'

'I see,' said Benson who had heard such things

16

before. He knew his voice was a bit like the characters from *Round the Horne.* He had heard it on a tape-recorder. That had come as a bit of a shock. From the vantage point of inside his head, Benson felt that his voice was very dark indeed, a bit like an English Paul Robeson. But from a tape-recorder it sounded high-pitched and whiny. Listening to himself on tape he had heard his secret ambition to be a TV journalist wither and die on the spot. How could he be on television every night with a voice like that? People would say he was just like Julian and Sandy and expect to laugh while he was trying to tell them how wicked the Americans were being in Vietnam, just like Julian Pettifer, his idol, did. But he could not for the life of him work out what was wrong with his walk. He seemed normal enough as he approached double doors and passed by shop windows. His hips were a bit big, but only a bit.

'One of these days I'll introduce you to some of them,' Meryl continued. 'Anyway, where's it from?'

'Where's what from?'

'"I like your anger."'

'I don't know.'

'*Who's Afraid of Virginia Woolf*, that's where.'

Benson nodded.

'Have you read Genet?' asked Meryl.

'Yes,' he was now on home-ground, 'but I'd much rather have Gide.'

Meryl gave Benson one of the looks which were going to become very familiar to him over the next few months. He felt a pout of pique coming on, but manfully tried to master it: 'But Khalil Gibran's my real favourite. Have you read *The Broken Wing*?'

'No,' replied Meryl, turning from him, moving to the music and staring into the mass of students for a likelier lad than Martin Benson.

Still, things had got better between him and Meryl

17

since then, he felt; they had taken to meeting almost every day at the More Utopia coffee-bar. True, she criticized him all the time. She did that to everyone. Some people gave Meryl a wide berth because of her sharp tongue. But she was full of ideas and enthusiasms. He could put up with the rest. Sometimes he even liked her making fun of him, though he did not know quite why he liked it. He did not like it when Ianto did it.

Ianto, a tall Welsh student whom Benson had become friendly with, was sitting in Benson's room one evening, a fortnight into term. He seemed about to do it again. He tapped his fingers on the chair-arm, flicked the ash from his Embassy approximately into Benson's rubbish bin, placed his long legs on the desk, oblivious to Benson's frown. 'I haven't got all bloody night,' he said.

Benson gave Ianto a look similar to the ones that Meryl kept giving Benson. He told Ianto to listen with all attention. Then he turned back to his portable Philips and dropped the pick-up arm on to 'Ballad of a Thin Man', turning again as the music started to make sure Ianto was listening.

But Benson did not follow his own advice. Instead he let memories of school rise up from the part of his brain where he had buried them, believing them dead. But they were not dead. Brother Hooper came back to haunt, to taunt, him.

At the start of this new year, boys, I want to extend a welcome to the new young vines sent for training and pruning to the Brothers. I am old in Education, boys. Ancient. Sage. Yet every year hope springs eternal that this year will be different; a year without poor behaviour, rebellious attitudes, queer manifestations of the Devil's works and pomps. So far my prayers have not been answered. Dead wood continues to progress through St Bede's on its way to the Everlasting Bonfire. And there is nothing that rots the wood more certainly than pride. And none was more proud than Benson. He left St Bede's to become a Brother, then returned as if butter wouldn't melt in his mouth, his vocation and reputation in tatters, to continue into the sixth form. And he prospered! The pearls of A Level wisdom fall on the just and the unjust alike. Four A levels he got, boys! Four! But he caused a considerable amount of disruption at the school. Let me warn any future Bensons out there: knowledge and wisdom are not the same thing . . . not the same thing at all. Bertrand Russell, for instance, for all his knowledge, is not wise. Oh, he looks wise, I'll grant you that! He looks like everything you would expect from a wise old philosopher. But, believe me, boys, he is not wise. Benson fancies himself wise now, boys! He has marched off cock-a-hoop to university – without so much as a thank you in the Brothers' direction – his head stuffed full of Bob Baez and Joan Dylan and Bertrand Russell! But no good can come of it boys. No good can come of it. Pride comes before a fall . . .

Benson had allowed his thoughts to wander. His thoughts wandered a hundred times an hour. Quite often they wandered to heaven, where he imagined Mum chatting about him to Mary as they weeded happily on a heavenly afternoon when the temperature was just right. At other times he saw himself being followed by Fyfe Robertson and a TV crew, who commented on the events occurring in Benson's life in an up-to-the-minute sort of way. Quite often, too, his thoughts took him down dark erotic lanes where the trees leaned over heavy with cheerful phalluses, complete with tempting testicles which nobody minded if you squeezed. But today in his hostel room at Aberystwyth University, with Ianto his Welsh friend, it was Brother Hooper in front of the assembled staff and students at St Bede's who distracted him. Then that thought was gone and another, far more urgent, much more compelling, took its place.

19

'Ianto, do you think he really is sincere . . . I mean, like . . . I suppose he is, but do *you* reckon he is?'

Benson had had this question on his mind for some time. It referred to Bob Dylan, whose warped and scratched *Highway 61 Revisited* was causing the pick-up of his portable Philips record-player to weave and jiggle alarmingly as it made its way along the track of 'Ballad of a Thin Man' for perhaps its three hundredth journey. The going was not getting any easier. Benson had to guide it over the last chorus or it would get hopelessly mired in 'you don't know', and have to be given a gentle push to 'do you, Mr Jones?' where it once again managed to find its footing.

'Course,' replied Ianto. 'You can bloody hear the sincerity, can't you?'

Well, that was reassuring. Benson listened and thought he could hear the sincerity if Ianto could. Ianto played the French horn in the Welsh National Youth Orchestra, after all. If anyone knew, Ianto would.

'Anyway,' continued Ianto, 'you were bloody miles away. How can you know if Bob Dylan is sincere if you don't listen to what he's bloody saying?'

By way of reply to Ianto's absurd statement, Benson rattled off the complete lyrics of 'Ballad of a Thin Man' almost without pausing for breath. While thus engaged he even had enough consciousness left over to day-dream about his tendency to daydream. It was true, he did wander off rather. Thought accumulated in his brain like dirty shirts at the bottom of his wardrobe. But that was good, wasn't it? At least he had some thoughts. Not like that nasty Ian Smith in Rhodesia who only ever had one thought in his mind, and that a prejudiced one. Ianto kept telling him to concentrate on one thing at a time. Well, he could see some sense in that. But if he did that, might he not miss *the* Thought, the one that was going to show him the way forward, perhaps show the World the way forward?

'What are you trying to prove?' asked Ianto when

Benson had finished his flawless rendering of the song. 'I mean, just because you know the words, it doesn't mean that you bloody understand them, does it? You're a Catholic, anyway.'

'Was. And what relevance does that have, may I ask?'

'Stands to reason.'

'What stands to reason?' Benson asked, wondering if Ianto had just made a *non sequitur*, but not certain enough of the meaning of the term to impress Ianto by trotting it out.

'Well, you told me last week that Catholics don't understand the meaning of all that Latin. You bloody just rabbit it out and hope it does the bloody trick upstairs.'

That was true in a way, but Benson felt that some defence was called for. 'We've switched to English now,' he said, then he added: 'Well, *they* have, I should say.'

'Well, to get back to the point, I can't see why it should worry you whether he's bloody sincere or not. If you can enjoy and take something from the songs, why get bloody bogged down in fretting about the character of the bloody singer?'

'I can take your point,' Benson replied indulgently. 'It's just that Dylan says such important things. How can you talk sincerely about the position of negroes and poor people if you're so rich? Maybe his producers did a survey and found out that we all wanted protest songs and Dylan just sat down in his penthouse and wrote them, with his negro servants bringing him lager and limes and toasted sandwiches and Penguins every five minutes.'

'That's probably how it bloody is,' said Ianto. Benson was not surprised. Ianto, he had already learnt from two weeks' acquaintance, had a cynical streak as wide as Wales. Anyway, he was doing Education Theory as one of his subjects. That was bound to turn the mind funny.

'You like Wagner, don't you?' Benson observed. He felt he had ample reason to expect the answer 'yes'. His room was directly below Ianto's at the hostel, and Ianto had a large record-player that had been the cause of his getting acquainted with Benson towards the end of their first week at university. Ianto had asked Benson for his help in carrying the huge silver and blue leatherette cabinet upstairs. Benson had often wondered since if it might not have been a good idea to lose his grip on the monster record-player. He would have been saved much Teutonic proclaiming at high volume.

'Course,' replied Ianto, walking straight into Benson's trap.

'There you are! So did Hitler! Wagner just wasn't a decent sort of person. It matters. It alloys the purity of the art.'

'You're bloody potty!'

'Think about it,' said Benson from his high intellectual plane.

'You wouldn't listen to any music, read any books, if you worried about the bloody morality of the bloody artist!' retorted Ianto.

Benson tapped Ianto on the shoulder and smiled the smile of enlightenment: 'Think about it.'

'I'm off to have a game of squash,' said Ianto.

Benson walked over to his washbasin and started washing his hands. 'Think about it,' he repeated chirpily.

'I know what I bloody think,' said Ianto, making for the door.

'Do you?' Benson asked as the door slammed.

Ianto often slammed out like that. Still, to go off in a huff was what people who did not have a leg to stand on usually did, wasn't it? Nevertheless, he would have to get some really good arguments ready for next time he saw Ianto. Even a bright Arts undergraduate had to prepare his arguments. Probably even Bertrand Russell had to prepare his arguments.

Benson had already managed to demolish Ianto on

22

several occasions. Ianto was a Welsh Nationalist and was learning Welsh in his spare time. He had told Benson, after Benson had helped him get his record-player installed, that he was only interested in meeting Welsh-speakers at university. That way his skill in the language would improve faster. Benson had told him that in his opinion the purpose of language was to help rather than hinder communication between human beings, and the sooner the Tower of Babel was flattened the better for the world. Why was Ianto going round trying to build it up again?

'I want to get back to my cultural roots. The bloody English have robbed us of them for centuries! Anyway, my girlfriend, Janet, is a Welsh-speaker. She says that she can only communicate her deepest bloody feelings through Welsh,' Ianto had replied.

'Dylan Thomas managed in English.'

'And then of course there's the struggle,' continued Ianto after dismissing Benson's riposte with a smirk.

'What struggle's that?'

'To get you bloody English out.'

What had he replied to that? He couldn't remember. Still, it had been something pithy and wise, he was certain of that. Ianto had gone off with his tail between his long legs.

Benson turned over the record and listened reverently to 'Queen Jane Approximately'. Fyfe Robertson directed his camera team to get a good shot of Benson in profile – his right – thinking hard thoughts, the current ones centring on why Dylan had used the word 'approximately' in the title. Then Fyfe in his hat and goatee beard addressed the world: *Here, in his tiny room at Pantychelyn hostel above the sleepy town of Aberystwyth, a typical student grapples with weighty matters. Bob Dylan may not be your cup of tea, viewers. I am very sure that he is not mine. However, you cannot deny that it is a hopeful sign that the younger generation is looking outside themselves,*

*considering issues such as Prejudice, the Generation
Gap, Birth Control, Poverty. Personally, I find this
sight very reassuring for the future of the country.
What is your name, young man?*

'Martin Benson,' said Benson, come to, surprised to
find himself alone. Bob Dylan was singing 'Desolation
Row'.

Meryl said that 'Desolation Row' was surreal. But
thinking of Meryl made him think of what she had said
about Bob Dylan in the More Utopia coffee-bar two
days before. He was, he felt, always thinking about
what Meryl had said. Meryl at university, like his best
friend Laurence Clitherow in the sixth form at St
Bede's, always provided Benson with so much food for
thought that he invariably left her with his brain
turning out of control. On this occasion she had
asserted, as she stirred her coffee, that she was
measuring out her life in coffee spoons, and that
Benson, though he did not take sugar, was too. Well,
Benson had not had to think about that too closely.
Meryl had said that before. That was as easy as
anything to understand and had required only a
learned nod from him. But then the blasphemy about
Bob Dylan had bubbled out in a couple of staccato
sentences, leaving him dumb, not knowing what to
think, his peace of mind shattered.

Meryl had then gone straight on, seemingly oblivious to the look of horror Benson was giving her from
his vantage point behind a glass coffee-cup, to say that
chewing nutmeg gave one a fantastic high.

Because pauses between topics were anathema to
Meryl — unless the pause explained matters more
eloquently than words could — Benson was left contemplating the heinousness of her middle utterance.
She said that she had cooked her *Another Side of Bob
Dylan* in the oven and had then banged nails and hair-
clips and other *objets* into and through it. A fab mobile
had been the result.

'Why?' Benson had asked Meryl, appalled.

Meryl thought Benson was referring to the nutmeg, though he wasn't, but would. Conversations with Meryl always left Benson with loads of questions which he had trouble synchronizing.

'Because, Martin, getting high is the highest form of the Good in the truly Platonic sense.'

Benson nodded. His usual question, 'How do you mean?' was struggling for expression, but he forced it back because for almost a year Clitherow had been telling him that 'How do you mean?' was a question that required banishment if Benson hoped to be taken seriously as an intellectual. Instead he asked, forgetting for a moment the blasphemies Meryl had committed against *Another Side of Bob Dylan*, 'Why does nutmeg give you a fantastic high?' recalling that he had never got a fantastic high from Mum's rice pudding, which had contained nutmeg.

'Chemicals,' replied Meryl darkly.

'And why did you do that to your Bob Dylan LP?'

'Because, honey child,' Meryl replied in her joint hons English/American Studies way, 'he's *such* a phony, that's why!'

'You could have given it to me,' grumbled Benson, whose own copy was practically unplayable, having had a cigarette dropped on it which had completely ruined 'Chimes of Freedom' and most of 'I Shall Be Free No. 10'.

Meryl ignored him, merely batting her black eyelashes, which set off her black eyes and eye make-up. 'Of course the nutmeg takes some chewing,' she said.

'Will the powdered stuff do?' asked Benson. But he was only being polite. His mind was depressingly attached – along with all the other *objets* – to the violated Bob Dylan record turning slowly above Meryl's Union Jack bedspread in her room at Ifor Evans hostel for women at the top of the hill.

Meryl looked at him as though he were a complete provincial. 'No, powdered most certainly will not *do*. And you can't just go and get a couple of nutmegs in a box from the Maypole either. You have to get them from the *delicatessen*.'

'The what?' asked Benson.

Meryl shook her head, took a Number 10 from a packet of ten, put it in a nine-inch long cigarette holder and popped the end of the unwieldy assembly in her mouth, aiming the holder and its small stick of tobacco towards Benson in the manner which asserted that she required lighting up.

Benson took out his Imco lighter, a present from Mrs Clitherow on her return from the Tyrol, and held it out for Meryl to light her cigarette from. He had to flick it several times before the petrol fired the wick, affording Meryl much opportunity to express her displeasure by closing her eyes and reopening them to reveal the black irises directed towards the fishing-net ceiling of the More Utopia coffee-bar.

'That lighter makes one's cigarette taste of petrol,' Meryl informed Benson.

'Tell me again where you get the nutmeg from, Meryl.'

Meryl exhaled puffs of blue smoke over him as she replied: 'Delicatessen. Noun plural. Shop selling delicacies for the table – though not to people like Martin Benson evidently – etymology: from the French *délicatesse*. QED.' And she was suddenly staring out of the window of the More Utopia, her eyes wistful as they surveyed the rolling waves on the far side of the promenade: '"But now I only hear its melancholy, long, withdrawing roar, retreating, to the breath of the night-wind, down the vast edges drear and naked shingles of the world."'

Benson decided to ignore Meryl, though he could not resist letting her know that he knew the poem she had just quoted.

'Did Matthew Arnold chew nutmeg, do you think?'

'Shouldn't think so. If he had his poems would have perked up a bit. No, anyone who could write: "Milton! Thou shouldst be living at this hour, England hath need of thee!" definitely would not chew nutmeg, or smoke pot, or eat magic mushrooms. Such a fucking bourgeois.'

Benson looked round to see if anyone had heard. Then he wondered if he should draw Meryl's attention to her mistake, but decided against it, fearing the upshot.

Being with Meryl was always a bit of a mixed blessing. One part of him loved the way she made outrageous comments. But she was unpredictable, a bit like a banger that you have lit and stood back from but which does not go off. You were still afraid to go near in case it did. Then, when you plucked up the required courage and did, it did.

Benson's first weeks at university had been a confusing time in all departments of his life. Apart from the large questions of whether or not Bob Dylan was sincere, he was also greatly taken up with trying to find three subjects to do for Part I of his university course. He had done well in History at A level and thought that History should be one of his subjects, but then, at the first lecture, he found that the lecturer was popping about the millenia like Doctor Who, finding common themes and connections with all sorts of eras and personalities that rang not the faintest bell. Benson, firmly rooted in Victorian Britain and eighteenth-century Europe, panicked and started looking round for a subject more comfortable. He kept to his ambition to study English, despite the somewhat rigorous requirement of Anglo-Saxon, and had heard early on that Philosophy was an easy option, especially if one opted for Morals rather than Logic. This he did, but the third subject still remained a problem.

Then, towards the end of his first week in Aberystwyth, Benson had gone down to the beach for a swim and got into conversation with a nice man sitting on a towel on the pebbles. The man gave his name as Dr Leptos and said that he was head of Greek and that they were very short of new people. He also said that he thought Benson a very good swimmer.

Benson had been impressed to meet a lecturer in a social setting, especially one who did not look quite English. He asked Dr Leptos whether he was from overseas, but Dr Leptos had replied that he was born in Finsbury Park in London, though his parents had been Greek.

'I'm looking for a third subject for Part I,' Benson said.

Dr Leptos smiled and soon it was all fixed.

But two weeks had passed and Benson was still struggling with the alphabet. Most of the other students had at least O level in Greek. Dr Leptos kept telling Benson that he would soon catch up, had on one occasion talked gently to him over the two-way system of the language lab, saying that all it took was effort. It made Benson feel funny to listen to this advice over the headphones, then, looking up, see Dr Leptos at the teacher's console moving his lips, the sound of which could be heard by him alone. Dr Leptos saw Benson looking at him on one occasion and winked. The wink had not helped Benson concentrate on Greek verbs.

The trouble was that much as Benson wanted to please Dr Leptos, he was having to spend much too much time on his Greek and was not able to find time to read the required English and Philosophy books. And, more importantly, all this academic work was getting in the way of his devoting every waking breath to his exalted post as Vice-President of the Aberystwyth University Overseas Students' Society.

He had been taken along to the meeting of the

Overseas Students' Society by Simeon. Simeon was in the next room but one to Benson at the Pantychelyn hostel, halfway up the hill leading out of Aberystwyth. Benson had not met Ianto then, the monster record-player not having been delivered until a week into term. Simeon had been the only friendly face in those first strange days at university. Simeon took his meals at the overseas students' table in the refectory, which was next to the exit from the kitchen line. Benson had taken to joining him at the table, and was generally the only other white face to be seen, though sometimes a graduate student called Morgan sat at that table too. Morgan was in the Christian Union and kept asking everyone if they had found Jesus. He stayed away from Benson though, because Benson had told Morgan that he had found Jesus years ago but lost Him and now that He was gone he was quite happy for Him to stay gone.

Benson did not like it when Morgan came to the table. He was far happier to be the sole representative of Britain.

The overseas students did not talk much to one another. Mealtimes were for eating as far as most of them were concerned. There were two Koreans who sat together and shared a bottle of hot sauce and another of what looked like pickled cabbage. They brought these bottles to the dining-room religiously and turned their meat and two veg festive with Union Jacks of bright red and filigrees of shredded cabbage. There were also several Africans who would nod towards Benson, but seldom say anything. And there was Simeon.

The day after the Hop, Simeon said: 'It's the first meeting of the Overseas Students' Society this after-noon. They're giving us a tea.'

'That's nice,' said Benson, wishing he was from overseas, strange and exotic and with a foreign accent to send shivers through all the ordinary British people.

'Why don't you come with me?'

'Well, I don't know ... I mean ... I'm not from overseas.'

'I've asked Angela to come,' said Simeon.

'Angela?'

'The girl from the Hop. You saw her. She danced with me all night long! You don't think I would let her get away, do you?'

'No, I suppose not. She seemed like a very nice girl.'

'Yes,' said Simeon, and he smiled widely at his baked apple and custard.

Benson was still not sure, however. 'Do you think they'll notice that I'm not from overseas?'

The meeting had been held to introduce all the overseas students to the local British Council representative and to elect officials. Of course, everyone noticed that Benson and Angela were not overseas students, but Mrs Jones, the British Council lady, said she was happy to see them there and that she wished more British students would turn out to mingle with their foreign brothers and sisters. Benson agreed that mingling was a very good thing.

'I've come to university to broaden my mind!' he told Mrs Jones earnestly.

'Jolly good! Glad to hear it!' she replied. Then she wandered off to mingle, slowed down her speech and increased her volume so that she could be heard across the room telling everyone to wrap up warm and shop at Marks & Spencer for value for money – though Benson had already noticed that Aberystwyth did not seem to possess a branch of Marks & Spencer. He was missing it because he loved their lime jellies. He ate them like sweets, thinking them vastly superior to Rowntree's Fruit Pastilles and, pound for pound, excellent value for money.

When it came to electing officials for the society, nobody seemed very interested in putting themselves forward. After much prodding an older black man from St Kitts in the West Indies, stood for President. His name was Maynard Peters, which returned Benson's thoughts to fruit jellies. Maynard was elected by a unanimous vote and his wife dissolved into peals of laughter which Benson thought somewhat out of keeping with the gravity of the proceedings, though he could not stop himself from watching the way she gave herself up completely to mirth. He wondered whether he might be able to do the same one day. If he stayed around black people long enough their laughter and rhythm might rub off on him.

Try as everyone might, no candidate came forward for the post of Vice-President. That post was left empty and candidates for Treasurer were sought. A Nigerian student in traditional dress – a loose gown down to the knee and funny tight trousers, topped with a tall cap that fell over on itself and reminded Benson of the ones worn by the French revolutionaries who had done dreadful things to Sidney Carton – whose speech from the gallows Benson was much given to reciting in front of any reflecting surface – was chosen. His name was Enoch Mohammed and Benson thought that Enoch Mohammed had his feet in two camps. Perhaps he had had a Christian mother and a Muslim father and a compromise had been reached. Well, he thought, that's what makes the world go round.

Josna, a petite girl in a sari, was chosen as Social Secretary, though she had resisted like mad, repeatedly pulling the sari back up to her shoulder nervously and moving her head about in a way that Benson immediately wanted to practise.

'And what about Vice-President? Is there *nobody* who will receive the mantle?' asked Mrs Jones melodramatically. Her eyes darted pleadingly about the room. They came to rest on Benson. They moved on. Then they moved back to him.

'As we are in Wales, England is overseas in a way,' she said, pointedly.

Simeon, who was spooning with Angela on the periphery, shouted: 'I vote for Martin Benson!'

People looked round and Benson folded his arms in front of him, placed right boot on left and worked his lips.

'Mr Benson,' asked Mrs Jones, 'are you willing to accept nomination?'

'Well, er . . . I don't, er . . . know . . .' said Benson.

Enoch Mohammed placed his black hand around Benson's right arm and led him towards his fate. Benson felt himself melting away at the touch, dissolving like caster sugar into coffee.

He stood next to Mrs Jones and looked at the floor. Then he looked up and the whole of mankind seemed to be beaming back at him. Hundreds of perfect pearly teeth, tens of brown eyes of exotic shapes and sizes, rainbows of colour from faces, hands and national dresses smiled their approval.

'You'd be useful to us, Martin. You know your way around. Will you do it?'

Benson fidgeted and blinked.

'Go on, Martin!' shouted a dark voice from somewhere at the back of the room. It was a Call from On High.

'Right,' said Mrs Jones. 'Hands up those who want Martin Benson as the Vice-President of the Aberystwyth University Overseas Students' Society?'

The world raised its hand. A psychedelic forest appeared before Benson's blue eyes. He looked out but could not bear the brightness, and gazed at his contorted boots.

'The ayes have it! Will you accept?'

Benson nodded with humility and pride. A cheer filled the room.

After the meeting broke up, Simeon and Angela were nowhere to be found. Benson did not mind. He was happy to trail up the hill back to the student hostel alone with his thoughts.

'Vice-President of the Aberystwyth University Over-seas Students' Society' – he repeated his title to himself again and again as he walked up the steep hill that led east out of Aberystwyth. Halfway home he turned and stood looking at the town at his feet. Behind the grey profile of the town a blue sea was already receiving the reflection of the late afternoon sun. 'Vice-President of the Aberystwyth University Overseas Students' Society!' he told the view again and again. And he thought of all the overseas students in their cramped abodes crouched around inadequate fires, homesick and miserable amid ex-colonial exploiters. He, Martin Benson, the Vice-President of the Overseas Students' Society, had been entrusted with the welfare of these beautiful people from all the continents of the world! Tears came to his eyes and had not the cars of late-season trippers been passing him on their way out of the town, he would have lifted his arms to bless the small university town below him.

Instead he crossed the road to a corner shop, where he bought himself a quarter of Maynard's wine gums and half an ounce of Sun Valley.

2

Benson woke up to the sound of starving students. Every morning the breakfast queue woke him up. It snaked its way out of the dining-room and down the corridor, past his room, which was located on the ground floor of Pantychelyn hostel for men. His position had its advantages. There were no tedious stairs to climb. He was handy for the dining-room. But the corridor outside his room became a raucous public domain at mealtimes. Queuing students had even been known to lean against his door, and then fall in when he opened it. When this happened Benson gave the guilty student a look. He had even thought of putting up a notice: LEANING AGAINST THIS DOOR IS NOT PERMITTED AT ANY TIME. BY ORDER, but had not so far got round to it.

He got up like a shot, gave the picture of Bob Dylan on the cover of *Highway 61 Revisited* a look similar to the one he gave students who leaned against his door, and put side one of *West Side Story* on the Philips, turning the volume almost to full. This, he thought, would serve both to wake him up, while providing entertainment and edification for the queue.

Then he set about washing himself at the sink, jiggling about to the overture. As he washed he wondered if a shower might not be a better idea, but Simeon would have been in and out of the shower-room ages ago. Anyway, he did not feel like braving the stares of fellow-students in the queue. Ianto had said that they thought he was a bit strange. When a peeved Benson asked why, Ianto said it was because he sat with the overseas students all the time and didn't

34

mix with the British. He told Ianto he did not care what other students thought, but he did rather. He was just practising at trying not to care.

As Vice-President of the Aberystwyth University Overseas Students' Society, Benson felt that he had a perfect right to sit with overseas students. He had told Ianto in no uncertain terms that the other students should be fighting and barging one another for the privilege of eating their meals along with overseas students. They could thereby give the overseas students the benefit of English practice, while learning something about what made the world go round so very satisfactorily.

It did not occur to Benson that some of the British students might find it odd to be serenaded by side one of *West Side Story* as they waited in line for their bacon, eggs and toast. So keen was Benson on the music that he felt it behoved him to share his enthusiasm with others. He had been known to take his portable Philips down to the Aberystwyth prom – charged with batteries which he could ill-afford – and lie there playing records on the sand louder than was strictly necessary. But Benson was of the opinion that it *was* strictly necessary to charm passers-by with his wonderful collection of LPs. He felt sure that he was at the very least making people's days as he treated them to the sweet cadences of *Black Orpheus, The Sermons of Martin Luther King, Odetta's Greatest Hits,* Mozart's Requiem, *Ramblin' Boy, Missa Luba* and *Joan Baez I* . . . but, more than that, perhaps, he was civilizing them too. Surely one or two would return to their humdrum homes in Wrexham, Liverpool or Birmingham, and go out in search of *Black Orpheus,* leaving their silly Connie Francis and Ken Dodd records in their sleeves where they rightfully belonged, scenting the spiced breezes of new worlds. Then, as they whizzed around the room, knocking ducks off the wall and doilies off all the wretched, dust-catching, bourgeois, horizontal surfaces, feeling the breath of that new world blowing away their lace curtains, they would muse to themselves: We didn't know we were born until that day on Aberystwyth prom! And they would pause momentarily from their gyrating pelvic thrusts, lusty thoughts of wholesome miscegenation and a smiling world, the colour of cappucino at the More Utopia, and think of that nice chap reading *A Tear and a Smile* on the beach that day, thanking him for his consideration in allowing them to listen to the music which had wrought such a spectacular sea change in their lives.

Benson finished washing and then wondered if he should shave or not. He decided that he better had because today was the day he was going to see Dr Leptos and tell him that Greek was too much for him. As he thought about what he would say, he took himself out of his pyjama bottoms and started to urinate into the sink. In only a month this had become an automatic ritual for him. He no longer felt the least pang of guilt about doing it. Being able to wee in the sink made his room self-contained. Had he to go down the corridor every time the urge came on him, his little room would no longer be the cosy nest it had become.

Benson started to dress as Larry Kert sang 'Something's Coming'. He listened to the words, sang along with them, believing them totally.

He gazed at his map of the world on the wall next to the door. He had pushed pins into the map; each pin had a piece of paper at its head, glued double, on to which Benson had written in tiny lettering the name of each overseas student over whom he vice-presided.

On his desk lay a two-and-a-half-inch to the mile Ordnance Survey map of Aberystwyth, a pot of glue, more pins, and a list of overseas students. Benson was in the process of making flags with which he could pinpoint the exact locations of homes of every overseas student in Aberystwyth. Most would be clustered around the little black rectangles of the various halls of residence, but not all. A Mr Mucktar Bilal M.Sc. (Calcutta) lived in a terraced house in the centre of the town with his Australian wife, Judith. How were they managing? Did prejudiced people crack jokes when they went out together? Did they avert their eyes and think wicked thoughts? He would have to check up. Terraced houses often had prejudice. There were no black people in *Coronation Street*, were there? Benson had seen loads of them when he had gone with the school to see a production of *Pippa Passes* at the Manchester Playhouse. Why couldn't Elsie Tanner have a nice black boyfriend? It would do wonders for race relations. But no, Granada was too afraid of getting nasty letters. Typical.

Maynard and Margaret, his pretty brown wife, lived in a flat quite a way up the hill and out of town. Was Margaret housebound? Would she like to meet up with Judith to exchange knitting patterns and talk about their husbands and how to make them happier and healthier? Also, worst of all, Enoch Mohammed was homeless, having arrived late and missed all the fun of the first week: the Hop, the lecture on the history of Aberystwyth during which everyone set off bangers and made funny noises while the lecturer, who had been doing it for decades, went doggedly on . . . All that Enoch Mohammed had missed as well as failing to find accommodation in any of the halls of residence.

Benson had thought it disgraceful that room had not been kept for Enoch Mohammed, and he had been to see the head of hostel in his role as Vice-President. The head of hostel, who was also a History lecturer – though he had the decency not to remind Benson that he was an apostate from that department – said he would see what he could do, but at the moment every available room was filled.

In the meantime Enoch Mohammed was sleeping

next door but one, on Simeon's floor. Naturally, Benson had offered his, but had been told that it was already fixed.

It was nice having two overseas students sleeping a mere two walls away. It also added a certain fillip to shower-time. Benson would open the door of the showers hoping to find either Simeon or Enoch Mohammed in a state of complete undress, but, unfortunately, so far their paths had not crossed at any really significant intersection.

The queue had shrunk to three or four by the kitchen entrance by the time Benson turned off 'Tonight' and walked towards the dining-room for breakfast. He exchanged pleasantries with the serving girls. He did not want them to think that he was a snob, even if he were an undergraduate with four A levels. He selected the second-largest bowl of cornflakes on display and a fistful of triangular pieces of cold toast, but avoided the blandishments of bacon because he had to watch his figure. He squeezed himself into the last available place on the overseas students' table opposite the two Koreans, who were finishing their meals, their plates covered by smears of red. A tangy smell surrounded them which Benson now knew came from their jars. It definitely hadn't come from anything on offer in the Pantychelyn kitchen.

They nodded to him as he sat down opposite.

Benson tucked into his cornflakes. As he munched he wondered which of the Koreans opposite he loved most. Heng-Moon, the older of the two, was a married man, and this counted against him, but he had a very spiritual face, especially when he was looking down at his book or his striped dinner. His eyes seemed to close and the short lashes formed twin hunters' moons. Then, when he opened them, they opened all of a piece and so could not open very far. He always looked to Benson as if he had smoke in his eyes. Did he see the world in the same way? Probably, thought Benson, he could concentrate on things much better because his peripheral vision was limited.

The other Korean – and he peeped at the other man as he munched his cornflakes – was younger and better developed than his companion. His name was Lee-Chun and he spoke English with an American accent. Also, he was unmarried. Benson did not know either man well, but he hoped to. Maybe in the future one or both of them would be leaders of Korea. A problem might occur. Benson would be remembered as the Good Englishman. President Lee-Chun would search high and low for Benson, eventually finding him feeding the hungry in Lima. A BOAC aeroplane would fly him to Seoul. He would offer sage advice and be loaded down with honours. Perhaps the grateful people would give him a house and a succession of comely youths . . .

'Is everything going well?' Benson asked.

'Yes?' Heng-Moon replied, trapping Benson with his narrow eyes.

Benson repeated the question thinking that 'almond eyes' might refer to almonds seen lying on their sides or cut into cross-sections.

'Everything are most wonderful, thank you very much!' replied Heng-Moon with enthusiasm, nodding. He asked, as he often did: 'Good sentence?'

'Yes, I think so. I understood it. But we usually say *everything IS*. It's only a small thing, though.'

'No. Very important. Why everything is?' asked Heng-Moon.

'Well, er . . . "thing" is sort of singular, so you follow it with "is",' tried Benson.

'But everything mean all things. I am right?'

'Er . . . yes . . . umm . . .'

'So "everything" is for more than one, is plural.'

Benson could not think up any excuse for the English language and said weakly: 'I know it doesn't make much sense but I'm pretty sure that's what we say.'

39

'Your language is very difficult for me.'

'Well, don't be disheartened,' said Benson, 'I think you are amazing to be able to learn what you have learnt so quickly. How long was your course?'

'Two months,' said Heng-Moon.

'You wouldn't find any English people who could learn that much Korean in that time,' added Benson, looking at his compatriots down the length of the dining-room disparagingly, while thinking of chapter one of *Follow Me To Greek*.

Lee-Chun started talking to Heng-Moon in Korean and Benson took the respite to wonder why 'everything' was followed by 'is' and not 'are' as he buttered his toast, spread marmalade on top and then cut each piece into little pieces in an aesthetic way he felt would appeal to Korean sensibilities. These he popped into his mouth – as carefully as any geisha at a tea ceremony – still devoting his attention to the grammatical problem.

But everything was sent flying from his brain when he spied Simeon and Enoch Mohammed heading for the kitchen to collect their breakfasts. He thought ruefully that a trip to the shower-room might not have been such a bad idea after all. He also worried about Enoch Mohammed because he was not a resident of the hostel and should not, therefore, have been taking breakfast. Still, as long as he was not found out, it would be all right. Did not Britain, who had raped Nigeria for so long and treated its people abominably, owe the sons of that country the odd free breakfast?

Simeon and Enoch Mohammed emerged unscathed from the kitchen with groaning trays and the laughter of half a dozen Welsh kitchen workers following in their wake. Enoch Mohammed wore a broad grin. He was clearly pleased with his time in the kitchen.

They sat down next to Heng-Moon and Lee-Chun.

'Good morning, my friends!' said Enoch Mohammed expansively.

'What were you saying to the ladies in the kitchen?' asked Benson, still able to hear laughter and high-pitched remarks being passed from behind the partition.

Enoch Mohammed smiled a smile that split his face wide open but said nothing.

'He proposed marriage to them all,' Simeon said.

Enoch Mohammed forked a whole rasher of bacon into his mouth, looked up at Benson and winked.

Benson went all weak. 'You're not married, then?' he asked hopefully.

'Not married, Mr Vice-President, but promised. Many promises have been made. Promises have been sown like seed. I am allowed four wives, you know.'

'Are you?' asked Benson.

Enoch Mohammed nodded, held a fat sausage on the end of his fork, surveyed it for a moment, then bit it in half with his prodigious teeth while Benson looked on helplessly.

'One wife cannot satisfy his appetite,' said Simeon.

'Enoch Mohammed can have four wives! Fancy!' Benson told Heng-Moon, trying to include him in the conversation.

Heng-Moon turned to Enoch Mohammed and smiled broadly, nodding. His eyes completely shut when he smiled. Little lines formed like a river delta spreading towards his neat ears. His ears didn't stick out like Benson's. Also both were the same. Heng-Moon's mum must have made sure that he slept with them flat against the side of his head. He wondered about his own. Had he been allowed to sleep with them all ruffled up and they had stuck like that? No, probably not. He had made a lot of faces in his time and his face had not stuck like that, had it? Perhaps it had. Still, Heng-Moon, with those narrow eyes, would have to be very careful not to smile when crossing the road. It might prove fatal to smile at a driver who had stopped for him at a zebra crossing because another car might be coming and Heng-Moon wouldn't have seen it. Benson would have to write a sad letter to Heng-Moon's poor wife in Korea.

Enoch Mohammed, licking both sides of his knife with his pink tongue, stared back at Heng-Moon, his huge black eyes wide.

'Good gracious!' said Heng-Moon suddenly. Then he nudged his companion and both made to leave the table. Benson was not sure why he had said that, but was relieved in a way for he had already become a little nervous at the way the conversation was going and wondered if the aesthetic sense of the two Koreans was being offended by all the talk. He had aimed a frown Enoch Mohammed's way when he had caught sight of him licking his knife. Mum would have given him a slap on the hand with her wooden spoon for that. He could not imagine either of the Koreans approving either. But it would be wrong to chide Enoch Mohammed. Perhaps it was good manners in Nigeria.

Oriental people were beautiful, but their senses were highly-tuned. An ill-arranged vase of flowers upset them in a way which was totally beyond the ken of the British. Likewise, their sense of smell was extremely acute and they found westerners hard to be near, though, of course, they were much too well brought-up to say so. They arranged rocks into shapes and could see things in these arrangements that less sensitive races just could not see. What, then, must they think of loose talk or licking your knife? But Benson longed for one to whisk him away into dalliance. Were that to happen, he felt that it would be a deeply spiritual experience throughout. Khalil Gibran and haiku would be recited. Strange Buddhist music would intrude, cool Himalayan breezes would blow in through the window carrying the chatter of birdsong and wind-chimes with them. He would awaken from the experience reborn to a higher incarnation. It would all be Nirvana and sensibility. Africans were the other side of the coin of attraction. They were all physicality and laughter, music, pelvic thrusts perfected over the boiling, equatorial millenia. Benson would sweat and some of their colour would rub off on him. Jungle foliage would drip coolly over him. *Black Orpheus* would pound in the background. Mosquitoes would chirp happily and there would be many sighs and groans as he sought to satisfy the enormous bulk of his friend, and leave the four wives weeping unloved in the corner of some faraway hut.

Vive la différence! thought Benson, gazing contentedly at the Treasurer of the Overseas Students' Society, massive across the table, next to Simeon, who was tiny in comparison to Enoch Mohammed.

'How's Angela?' asked Benson.

Simeon smiled. 'She's coming to see me this evening.'

'Is she?' replied Benson, once again wishing that he were that big girl with glasses. It was not that he wanted for one moment to be a girl. Well, maybe he did a bit. Being a girl would make things much easier in a way. It would be really lovely to be an object of desire. He frowned, then perked up when Enoch Mohammed said: 'It would not be polite for me to be present. Perhaps, Mr Vice-President, I can come and sleep in your room?'

Benson gulped, then wondered if the excitement could be read in his face. 'Yes, of course!' he stammered.

'Also,' said Simeon, 'do you think I can borrow your record-player?'

As Benson – over the moon to be of use – nodded assent, Enoch Mohammed winked at him again, and said: 'Music is invaluable for seduction!' which made him feel irked that he would have to entertain Enoch Mohammed in silence.

'I'll be in all evening,' he told Enoch Mohammed.

It was after nine when Benson started walking down the hill towards the old university building next to the sea where most of his lectures took place. He had an Anglo-Saxon lecture at ten. After that he would probably meet Meryl for coffee and then go and tell the dire tidings to Dr Leptos. What would he say? 'It's all Greek to me, Dr Leptos!' No, that wouldn't be very sensitive. Well, he'd think about it later. Then there was nothing on until three when he had a lecture on Morals – as everyone called Moral Philosophy. Well, he thought, by then I should have come up with a third subject to study.

He tried to concentrate on thinking up a third subject, noting that his feet were pacing one and a half paving stones with each step. The tip of his left boot started at the crack and the heel of the other one hit the ground just in front of the next crack. He had not noticed that before and wondered if Welsh paving stones were shorter. At home his paces took up exactly one paving stone. Either the paving stones were shorter or his pace was lengthening. Or, could it be that he had been taking longer strides for ages and just hadn't noticed before? And, of course, he was walking downhill, so that might make a difference too. He tried to think logically. The head of Philosophy had told everyone doing Philosophy that only logical thought could save the world, which if you asked him had reached a pretty pass, and it was all due to woolly thinking. Benson had reddened because it was one of Clitherow's constant criticisms of Benson that his thinking was woolly and that was why Benson was a Red Brick whereas he, Clitherow, was Bath Stone.

Now, let's see: I am a twenty-nine inside leg and have been for years. However, if I go to C & A Modes I am a thirty. However, if I get a thirty from Marks & Spencer, it has to go back. Now, if I am a thirty in the Platonic sense then I am taller than I used to be and perhaps the Marks & Spencer's thirty is a Platonic thirty-one. But I can't be still growing. Meryl says I peaked sexually at eighteen and everything's all downhill from now on. That doesn't make much sense. I'm sure I get excited just as much now as I did a year ago. Probably more so because there is more temptation. Yes, it must be because I am going downhill, unless, of course, the paving stones *are* shorter in Wales. The people seem shorter. Myvanwy Roberts is barely five foot, so they may make paving stones shorter in Wales. However . . . er . . .

He decided that thinking logically did not necessarily lead to firm conclusions and shifted his attention to the evening. I'd better buy a packet of Kent and something for Enoch Mohammed to drink. Africans like Guinness. I'll buy some bottles of Guinness between lectures. Then he gave active consideration to a third subject to take instead of Greek. He decided against Geography because the lectures took place up the hill and Benson just did not think he could get the energy together to walk up and down the hill twice in the course of a day. Ianto says Education Theory is easy, but it sounds disgusting. How to Become Brother Hooper in Three Easy Years! They probably have Whacking Practice and workshops in The Use of Sarcasm. No, I can't do that, even if the department is handy for the More Utopia. I'll get Meryl to make the decision for me.

Benson fidgeted through Anglo-Saxon in the company of sixty or so others. He sat at the back and, in between inking in all the 'o's on the relevant page of Sweet's *Anglo-Saxon Primer*, looked at all the heads in front of him, wondering if they were able to make any sense of what was going on.

Anthea, who was sitting next to him as she often did, was writing away. Benson wrote on his file-paper cover, next to the Oxford Camera, where Clitherow was probably deep in study at this moment: Do you understand what he's going on about? and then nudged Anthea. She looked up, read the question and wrote: Yes, then returned to her note-taking.

That was typical Anthea, Benson thought.

Some of the second year students had told Meryl – and he looked round to see if Meryl was attending, but could not see her – that the only way for a creative person to get through Anglo-Saxon was to learn all the texts in modern English while reading the Anglo-Saxon. Then, when the first year exam came along, all you had to do was recognize the bit they wanted translating and get on with it from memory. This was tedious, everyone agreed about that, but not half as tedious as the dire alternative of actually learning the language.

He decided to write a letter to Clitherow in order to make the forty minutes pass by, and he turned to a fresh page of his notebook.

Dear Laurence

This is my third letter to you but I still have not had one from you. I think this is most unfair, but have tried not to be concerned because, as Khalil Gibran says:

When you part from your friend, you grieve not. For that which you loved most in him may be clearer in his absence, as the mountain to the climber is clearer from the plain.

Well, you are very clear to me. I can see you now as clear as anything. But a letter would be much appreciated. There, now you have had my protest.

I expect Oxford is fun and there is lots to do. There is lots to do here too. As I mentioned in my last letter but one, I have been made Vice-President of the Aberystwyth University Overseas Students' Society. This is a great honour of course, and I am doing my best to make a good job of it. I have to deal with all the social problems encountered by overseas students. It can't be easy living in Wales and you have to be very vigilant to make sure that none of them are being prejudiced against with regards housing and other things. When I am with an overseas student walking through the town I am always fearful that somebody we pass will say something insulting. Nobody has yet, but if they do I am ready to hit out both verbally and physically.

I have not found the Friend as yet – well I haven't found anyone other than YOU – though I am on the look-out the whole time. You saying that Proust said that homosexuals would never find the man they really want because what they really want is a heterosexual keeps going through my head and I have tried to think up logical arguments to refute it. I only know that the way I feel now, if anybody at all gave me the least sign I would cleave to him for life. (Hint! Hint!) By the way, I cannot read Proust. I got as far as page four. I didn't manage *Under The Volcano* either. I know this will come as a disappointment to you. I'm sure you can read a hard novel between breakfast and lunch.

It is a bit hard for me to write to you when I have not heard. I hope everything is going well for you at Oxford and that you have sorted out the Great Dilemma. Of course, I know what I hope you decide. It would be really lovely if you were a homo too. I heard from your mum a couple of weeks ago. She seems well. She was full of news about her German trip. I have not heard from my dad. I only got a measly postcard from the honeymoon. Do you think they are trying to tell me something? Well, who

cares I say! Still, they must be home now. I had
better get down to writing to them, though I
don't know what to say. I am really very angry
that Dad took it into his head to remarry. I don't
know what Mum would say. And fancy him
marrying a policewoman! That's TWO in the
house! A chap doesn't stand a chance! Still
their old world is rapidly fading!!!!

Write, for crying out loud!

Your friend,

Martin

There were still some minutes remaining. The lecturer
droned on. This just wasn't what Benson had had in
mind when he put his name down for English. He
wanted to walk along the shore between the sand and
the foam taking sips from Yeats and Hopkins and Eliot
and Gibran. He wanted to catch enthusiasms from
students and lecturers alike; to learn, through literature, about the world and its infinite variety. But so far
it had all been the stuff of doodles and wandering
attention. Just like school the lecturers pushed him
towards one critic after another. Benson felt that if he
heard F.R. Leavis's name once more he would scream
and change to something else. Literature was about
wisdom, wasn't it? It was about what makes people
tick. So where did all these phony critics fit in? They
were telling us how so and so told us how he saw the
world ticking. Benson felt strongly that all his literature lectures were a bit like someone explaining what
different sorts of sweets tasted like but taking so long
about it that you never had a chance to pop around to
a shop, buy some and consume them at leisure. It
was not as if they tried to help you through difficult
texts. No, it was just what *they* thought all the
time.

He was in a somewhat recalcitrant mood when he

joined Meryl in her booth in the More Utopia for coffee.

'Calm down!' she told him, after he had vented his spleen about English lectures. 'You can't change from English. It is your one fixed point in the turning world. The other subjects are all filled with sound and fury signifying nothing,' adding airily, 'Literature holds the key.'

'Well maybe it does,' said Benson, 'but they're being dead mean with the key at this place. Still, that is not the problem today. The problem today is what am I going to do instead of Greek?'

'American Studies. I am very taken with it. Two spiffing young lecturers. I could eat them both for supper. One paces the room smoking as he lectures. Fabulous.'

'Do you think they'll take me?'

'I should think so.'

'How's everything going?'

'Not too well. I sometimes think the main qualification for males at this establishment is a low libido,' said Meryl, screwing a Number 10 into her holder.

Benson fumbled for his Imco and had it ready when Meryl's assembly approached.

'Yes, I'm not doing too well either.'

'Glad to hear it.'

'However, I live in hope.'

'There's no future in overseas students,' said Meryl flatly.

'Why do you say that? If one in twenty are, then there has to be a fair chance I'll bump into a nice one.'

But Meryl was not taken in by Benson's argument: 'One in twenty in Britain. IN BRITAIN. That doesn't mean the whole world is homosexual in those proportions. Remember we had the Victorians and all that.'

'What's that got to do with it?'

'Everything. All the people you're trying to catch had normal upbringings . . . loose clothing or none at all, a certain frankness about things sexual. I read it in Margaret Mead.'

'I had a normal upbringing,' asserted Benson, then added, 'for Merseyside. Anyway, I know the Nature-Nurture argument and I go for Nature. And if it is in my nature, it is in the nature of members of the species the whole world over.'

'Yes, but if there is a strong enough taboo against it, people will stifle their nature. Find yourself a nice English friend, Martin!'

'How can you stifle it? I spent years and years stifling it! And look at me!'

Meryl looked and crinkled her nose.

Benson blinked slowly and arched his eyebrows: 'Well, at the moment the choice doesn't arise. However, I think I've told you more than once that my attractions start at Calais and get stronger the farther away the man comes from. I can't help it. It's the way I am. I think it has something to do with seeking out what I do not have. It's no different from you liking black-haired men over six feet tall. However, as I say, it hasn't arisen. I haven't met *anybody*.'

'You are always saying "however". It sounds odd. Stop it.'

'Fuck off, Meryl!' said Benson.

Meryl raised her eyebrows, pursed her lips and looked out of the window.

Benson immediately felt bad. 'I'm sorry, Meryl,' he said, not for the first time.

'Granted,' said Meryl magnanimously.

'So what should I do?'

'I've told you: take American Studies.'

'All right, I will,' said Benson.

'So you've decided to leave us, have you?' said Dr Leptos when Benson had told him everything.

Benson frowned. 'I'm no good at languages.'

'It only takes persistence.'

'But I really can't seem to get the hang of Greek. I have tried, honestly, but it doesn't sink in. I just can't remember vocabulary. And all the letters get jumbled up in my mind.'

Dr Leptos nodded. 'Yes, perhaps I was a little over-anxious to get you into the department. We're finding it hard to recruit students for Greek. And I liked the look of you. You seemed a likely lad.'

There was something about the way Dr Leptos spoke that made Benson tingle. He shuffled about on his seat, then said: 'I'll come and see you.'

'But it isn't quite the same, is it?'

Benson gulped back a bubbling-up 'Howdoyou-mean?'. He was beginning to think that he knew exactly what was meant. He squirmed and then fought that too and sat looking at the book on Dr Leptos's desk. Then Dr Leptos put his hand on the book, opened it, and without any explanation began to read a poem in Greek.

Benson listened to the sound of the poem while taking the opportunity to appraise Dr Leptos. He had a nice face, strong and bony. But he was a bit old, perhaps in his thirties. *Is he*? Benson wondered. He tried to remember Dr Leptos as he had been that day on the beach when he had persuaded him into taking Greek. His body had been quite nice. Nothing spectacular but all right. Also he seemed quite well-built under his bathing costume. Nothing definite had showed as far as he remembered, but there had been a nice aesthetic bulge like half an orange. Also, the bathing costume was a Janson with the figure of a diving man on the side. Mum would never buy him a Janson. They were not worth the money, she had said. He always seemed to end up with a sensible one from Marks & Spencer and the people at Marks & Spencer were all so bourgeois that they had not had the good taste to put something distinctive on the outside like Janson. He returned his attention to the words still

51

coming from Dr Leptos's lips. Some were familiar to him from his studies. Dr Leptos read beautifully. It set Benson quivering. He wondered for a moment whether he should relent and have another go at Greek.

Dr Leptos finished the reading, closed the book and looked at Benson closely. 'Cavafy,' he said.

'It sounded very nice.'

Dr Leptos nodded. Then he was looking intently at Benson: 'Come and see me on Friday afternoon. Around four. I'll take you for a drive.'

'That'd be lovely. I'll be able to tell you how I get on with the American Studies department.'

'Yes,' Dr Leptos sounded sad. Benson chose to think it was because of the poem he had just read. He said goodbye and walked down the quiet corridor. Fyfe Robertson and the film crew followed him down the stairs. He imagined the reporter talking to the camera, his microphone in front of him, while trying to keep up with Benson's paving stone-consuming pace: *Our hero has just broken the sad tidings to the head of Greek. What a loss to Greek Studies! See how he strides out of the building purposefully, his whole life before him! What department will next be graced by young Benson's presence, viewers? Let's follow him and find out! Such a manly gait. Manly, yet sensitive at the same time. There he goes! It's a devil of a job to keep up with him!*

3

Benson was pushing himself back up the hill to his
room at Pantychelyn hostel just after five that afternoon. Four bottles of Guinness, along with his books
and a packet of Kent, clinked in the leather briefcase
Clitherow's mother had given him just before he left
home.

But all Benson's thoughts lay back in the town. He
had achieved a lot in the afternoon, been accepted for
American Studies without the least hesitation. The
young lecturer in the flashy tie had asked him a couple
of questions, said they could probably squeeze in
another one and given him a reading list and a
timetable of lectures, adding that American Studies
was not an easy option. Still, Benson had not been
alarmed. They all said that. If they said their subject
was an easy option then the implication would be that
it was quite easy to lecture in it too, and they wouldn't
admit that, even if it were true. He tried to formulate a
rational stance on academic integrity that would help
lift standards throughout the world of education, as the
light ebbed away westwards.

Morals had been good, quite challenging. The
lecture took place in a corner room of an old building
that looked out over the sea and along a row of
Victorian terraced houses on the prom where some of
the smaller departments – Greek included – were
located. Dr Griffiths sat at his desk, swivelling in his
swivel chair. He wore half-moon spectacles and Benson
mentally reserved himself a pair for when he was of an
age to be sage.

When all the students were seated, Dr Griffiths

gestured out of the window and swivelled in his chair so that he was watching the prom. Everybody followed his gaze.

Groups of students were walking along the prom, back towards the boarding houses and hostels. Some couples walked hand-in-hand, looking at the sea.

'The naughty world wags on,' Dr Griffiths informed the students. Then he paused to let the remark sink in.

Benson looked out at the prom. He wore his provocatively quizzical expression, which told the back of Dr Griffith's head that at least one of his students could not see anything particularly naughty about the world. True, the world outside was distinctly secular. No sign of an Our Lady procession or a Catholic Evidence Guild Meeting, like you got on the pier head in Liverpool, but it did not look particularly naughty. Benson could make out Sean O'Malley, the President of the Aberystwyth University Catholic Society, walking with Myvanwy Roberts. He was pleased to see that Myvanwy Roberts had found herself a nice boyfriend. She had a pretty face and was always pleasant to Benson, though she spoke Welsh most of the time. He had worried that she would be left on the shelf because she was so tiny. But there was, he reflected, no future in it. She was bound to be Chapel. And Sean O'Malley would never marry a Protestant.

Dr Griffiths swivelled, looking hard at his students.

'What do you think of that?' he asked. Benson worried then because Dr Griffiths seemed to be looking straight at him. He should have been thinking about Dr Griffiths's opening statement. All Dr Griffiths's statements meant more than they appeared to mean. He could well point to someone and ask whether his statement had been a priori or a posteriori? Or a false premise, perhaps? Benson was not quite sure. The naughty world wags on, he thought. Well, it's just his opinion, isn't it? It all depends on what you mean by naughty, doesn't it? I should ask him to define his terms. What precisely do you mean by: 'naughty' and 'wags'? Yes, that is what we should be told.

But Dr Griffiths did not ask anyone to answer his question. He looked out over the students and said, referring to the view in general, and the couples in particular: 'They think it's love but it's only lust.'

Sean O'Malley and Myvanwy Roberts were now mere pinpricks in the distance. Benson wondered if they had been included in the judgement from the window of the Philosophy department. It was a valued judgement if ever he had heard one. One man's love was another man's lust, wasn't it? Benson knew what a valued judgement was. It was a judgement that contained your own values. Valued judgements were not necessarily very nice, because Hitler made a valued judgement when he said that Jews weren't good people. Landladies did too when they refused accommodation to black people. You had to watch valued judgements like a hawk.

Still, Dr Griffiths had not gone on to ask anybody their opinion of his opinion. He talked about Kant's Categorical Imperative, as he was often inclined to do. Benson tried to listen and take notes, while his mind kept wandering ahead to the evening with Enoch Mohammed and Friday afternoon at four with Dr Leptos. Things were looking up. Everywhere there were signs of possibilities. Something was very definitely coming.

He just hoped that Dr Griffiths would not be looking out of the window when Friday at four rolled round and he would be visible from the Philosophy department getting into Dr Leptos's A40.

Benson had fretted a little about his date with Dr Leptos, but there had been so many other things to demand his attention that he had consigned it to a rather full drawer labelled: *To be worried about soon*. He added it to the drawer as he walked, noting that other matters already there caught his attention momentarily and robbed him of sweet anticipation. *Dad and new wife* were at the top of the pile, but Benson had been unable to face giving the slightest thought to that topic. He felt that it did not need facing until the dread day arrived when he would have to return home for the holidays. In the meantime it could be kept at bay by the odd letter. Next came: *Relationship with Clitherow.* This too contained much to make him brood. Not only had a curtain of silence descended from Clitherow at Oxford, but also their parting conversation before going their separate ways gave him grave cause for concern. Was Laurence really a homo? Sometimes he seemed to be. At other times he was saying what he would do to girls if he got the chance. Then there were all the others: *What is my Destiny? Would I actually turn out to be a heterosexual if I actually tried it with a girl? Do I have big hips? Are my lips too small? Are my motives pure regarding overseas students? Is Bob Dylan sincere?*

He slammed the drawer shut, and planned out the evening.

A nap between now and the evening meal might be a good idea in case Enoch Mohammed arrived late and . . . but he dared not articulate what was on his mind. To articulate it would be certain to make sure that it did not happen. He would, of course, insist that Enoch Mohammed took the bed. He would rough it in his sleeping-bag on the floor.

Having remade his bed carefully, he lay down on it to have a nap. The noise of students arriving for dinner along the corridor would wake him up, he thought.

Benson dreamed that a landlady had refused Enoch Mohammed accommodation. The wicked woman owned a boarding house on the prom. Benson approached the front door and rapped militantly upon it.

'Yes?' asked the landlady, who bore an uncanny resemblance to Alice, Dad's new wife.

'I am the Vice-President of the Aberystwyth

University Overseas Students' Society and I am investigating a complaint against this establishment by a Mr Enoch Mohammed,' said Benson sternly.

'The darky,' sneered the woman. 'I won't have them in my house.'

'May I ask why?'

'It's none of your business!' replied the woman. 'Now leave me alone! I've got a cup of tea poured and today's *Daily Telegraph* to read. You're just an English busybody, that's what you are!'

'I warn you', stated the Vice-President of the Overseas Students' Society, 'that we shall picket your establishment until you see the error of your ways. Good afternoon.'

The door slammed.

Benson walked away towards the More Utopia, determined to raise a protest march that very day.

But on the way there he was waylaid by a black Austin A40.

'At last! I've been looking for you everywhere!' cried Dr Leptos. ' "Come live with me and be my love and we shall all the pleasures prove!" '

'How do you mean?' asked Benson, his dream releasing him from even that inhibition.

'I mean that you are the one I have been seeking all my life. You're definitely my Mr Right. I knew it as soon as I saw you. Get in!'

Benson opened the car door, but then he caught sight of Enoch Mohammed dragging a heavy suitcase along the pavement.

'Mr Vice-President!' he called. 'I am still homeless. What shall I do?'

Benson turned back to Dr Leptos, who was looking desperate in the Austin A40. 'I cannot come with you, much as I would like to,' Benson informed Dr Leptos. 'It is not easy for me, but my duty is clear. I must succour my unfortunate fellow student and overseas brother.'

But Dr Leptos was not going to let Benson follow his destiny so easily. 'You only want to help him because he is better built than I am! You can't wait to get inside his pants! I know you, Martin Benson! You pose as a great liberal but you are, in reality, a *lover of big ones*!'

'That isn't true!' shouted Benson, and he slammed the door. He rushed over and picked up Enoch Mohammed's suitcase. 'Come to my room!'

But Enoch Mohammed held back: 'I heard what the man in the black car said. Was he speaking the truth? He wasn't, was he? You do love me for myself and not for my physical attributes, don't you?'

'Of course I do! It is true that I find you very attractive. Who wouldn't? One theory of attraction states that we are only half people, always looking for our other halves. You are, Enoch Mohammed, my other half. You contain so many of the things that I lack: dark skin, a muscular physique, rhythm and a tropical outlook. I am no Narcissus, Enoch Mohammed. I crave difference. Now let's get a bus back up to the hostel.'

But Enoch Mohammed held back: 'Beware, little Englishman, my organ of generation is prodigious. It is the cause of my undoing and may be the cause of yours also.'

'Nonsense! We need a number nine. The Borth bus.'

But Enoch Mohammed stayed rooted to the spot. He gestured to the passing trippers. 'All these people! As they pass, they think: Mighty Member! and they pass on sad, frustrated, and their frustration at not being able to *possess* me turns to hate.'

'Well, it's not true with me, Enoch Mohammed,' said Benson. 'I know that's what James Baldwin thinks, and it is true that I am homosexual and feel strongly attracted to you, but if you do not feel you can reciprocate, then it really doesn't matter.'

Just then Simeon stopped at the kerbside in his Morris Minor. 'Do you want a lift?' he asked.

After a long pause, Enoch Mohammed said: 'Yes, take us home.' And Benson lifted the heavy suitcase and Enoch Mohammed lifted Benson and carried him to the car, placing him in the back seat, while he went and sat with Simeon.

On the journey to the hostel, Enoch Mohammed kept reaching back and squeezing Benson's thigh with his huge right hand.

Benson was woken up by a banging on the door. The room was dark and he wondered if he had slept through dinner. He got up quickly, switched on the light over his wash-basin and grabbed a towel which he let hang down to cover his erection. Then he answered the door.

Simeon stood outside. He greeted Benson and asked if he had been sleeping.

'Yes, I just nodded off. What time is it, Simeon?'

'Six forty-five.'

It felt much later, but Benson was relieved that he had not slept through dinner.

'I've come to borrow the record-player.'

'Yes, of course!' And Benson, still befuddled, set about unplugging his portable Philips. He took it to Simeon. 'Do you want any records to go with it?'

'No, thank you. I've got a lot of High Life and some sentimental songs for later in the evening.'

'Well, I hope you have a good time.'

Simeon nodded and smiled the quiet smile that brought out the mother in Benson. 'Don't forget, if you need any more records . . .' Benson called to Simeon as he walked down the corridor.

He turned back to his room, noting that it looked bare without the Philips. But he could not waste time worrying about décor. He took off his clothes and put on his dressing-gown for a shower.

He carefully selected his Vosene shampoo, his Pears soap and wrapped both in his towel. Then he dithered about which cologne to put on after. Dad's new wife had given Benson a bottle of Old Spice cologne with a sponge bag and a soap-on-a-rope for his birthday. The soap-on-a-rope had become entangled with the St Martin de Porres medal he wore for old time's sake and, when Benson tried to separate them, had come off the rope. He had thought of writing to the Old Spice people, but what was the point? Any company that could sell Old Spice and think it was *worth buying* would not possibly be expected to send a rep round to view his broken soap-on-a-rope. They were just filthy capitalists, after all. His soap-on-a-rope had been left to dry out on the shelf by the U-bend below the washbasin.

Anyway, tonight was a Tabac night. He had been introduced to Tabac one evening when he went to pay a pastoral visit to a Japanese student called Shigo (third floor, room 305), to ask him why he had not attended the meeting of the Overseas Students' Society. Benson had some vague feeling that Shigo might be worried about war crimes. Of course, he had not planned to bring up the matter unless Shigo did. When Shigo answered the door, Benson had found himself confronting a room bare of any decoration. One book lay on Shigo's study-desk, a small rush mat sat lonely on the floor. But on the window ledge had been placed a bottle of Tabac. It had looked just right. A utilitarian knick-knack of a shape that would spark off meditation in orientals, and anyone else with the least sensibility.

Benson had been greatly impressed by the austerity of the room, and had decided to divest his own of chattels and place only a bottle of Tabac where there had been a Beatles poster and LP covers. He had not managed this, but he had purchased the bottle of Tabac.

Off he trotted down the corridor to the shower-room. As he approached the door he could hear the sound of gushing water and his penis, which had only been allowed to return to normal while its owner considered his toiletries, reared up again in a sudden manner which shocked even Benson, who should have been used to its quirks by now.

One never knew who one would see in the shower-room. Most of the time all he saw were indefinite shapes behind the grey-white shower curtains. But sometimes he would catch a fellow student towelling himself in full view. Once he had entered *just at the very moment* that Simeon was snapping the elastic on his underpants. Had he been just a mere five seconds earlier he would have caught Simeon in the nude. Ever since then it had been Benson's ambition to enter the shower-room at just the right time. Not too early, for then he would have to enter the shower or be suspected as a peeper for hanging around too long. Timing was everything. He wished he could think of a Patron Saint of Opportune Shower Entrances to fire a few prayers to. But in such matters, he knew, he was on his own. Destiny, or at the very least the law of averages, would make sure that his lucky number came up one day.

Peeping, boys. Benson was a notorious peeper. Ask the teachers of PT. A dirty young man seeking out dishonour. And dishonour will find him. Down he goes! said Brother Hooper. Then Fyfe Robertson was arguing the point: *Such a clean young man! Another shower! And did you know that this young man has offered to share his room with a homeless African? Truly, this lad is an example to us all*!

Trembling, Benson pushed open the door, only to be confronted by the sight of Ianto in the nude. Benson sighed inwardly. Seeing Ianto, he thought, had to be better than nothing. Ianto's penis was really quite massive, but the trouble was that it was attached to Ianto. The odd thing was that he could look at a naked Ianto and feel exactly the same as he suspected most men felt about seeing their own sex nude. There was a certain admiration for the length and girth of Ianto's

61

penis. A vague envy too. But that was about it. If the world was full of Iantos, Benson felt, then . . . well, he didn't quite know how he would feel. Life would definitely be pretty uninteresting.

'Hello, Ianto,' said Benson and he started to take off his slippers and socks.

'Hello,' Ianto replied.

'Have you had a good shower?'

'They're either too hot or too bloody cold,' said Ianto.

Benson nodded.

'Going to Film Soc tonight?' Ianto asked.

'No, I can't. What's on?'

'Some French rubbish. I'm only going because Janet wants to see it.'

Janet, Ianto's girlfriend, had a car, the horn of which she honked noisily outside Benson's window whenever she dropped in on Ianto. The car had a rampant dragon painted on the roof and slogans in Welsh on the back window. Janet also had a high-pitched laugh, and Benson had often heard her laugh late at night – long after all women should have evacuated the building – and had frowned at the ceiling.

Benson stepped into the shower and closed the curtain so that not a chink remained through which he might be observed. He turned on the shower, trying to keep out of the way of the gush until it warmed up.

'See what I mean?' said Ianto.

Suddenly the water turned scalding and Benson yowled. He turned the lever in a panic. Just as suddenly the water was icy and he gasped. But cold showers were a familiar pain. He turned his face to the source, cradled his testicles and let the water torture his soft sides and broad back.

After dinner, Benson put the finishing touches to his room. He cleaned the basin, polished the taps, shone his two Duralex glasses to high gloss, opened the sash window – despite the cold – to freshen the air, cleared his desk of everything except Frantz Fanon's *The Wretched of the Earth*, took his bottle of Tabac, and holding it like a priest holds his holy-water shaker, sent narrow jets of it spurting around the room, making two cross-lines of cologne across the coverlet of his narrow student bed.

He sat down in his easy chair to read *Persuasion*, looking up occasionally from the book to take satisfaction in the unaccustomed neatness of the room. Even the enforced silence of being without his Philips was pleasing. Only occasional footsteps passing along the corridor outside disturbed the stillness.

After an hour's reading he began to wonder when Enoch Mohammed would arrive. He had not been given a time, had not even thought to ask for one. Probably Enoch Mohammed would be working hard in the library, a vision of the new Africa he was hoping to devote his life to serving keeping him rooted to the seat, when all the while he was tempted to leave his dry books for the beckoning warmth of Benson's bed. Well, that was admirable, wasn't it? Anyway, it was early still, only nine. Benson returned to the novel.

Lady Russell in *Persuasion* was Benson's favourite character. As he read, the face of Mrs Clitherow uttered the character's words, performed her actions. He read for an hour, but then thoughts of the Clitherow family took over from the action of the novel and he found that he was turning pages without any notion of what they contained. At ten he got up out of his easy-chair and wrote a letter to Mrs Clitherow.

In the letter he thanked her again for the Imco and his leather briefcase, telling her that it had received many compliments. He wrote about the subjects he was taking and about his pastoral post. Everything was fine. But . . . Qualifications did not find their way on to the paper immediately. He held them back, wondering if he could just write his usual chatty letter and not

bring up either of the topics which were worrying him.
He searched about for harmless subjects. He found
some but they bored him in the writing. Honesty
itched the seg on his writing finger. He gripped his pen
harder.

I still miss Mum a lot. Sometimes I can't
believe that she isn't here any more. I think of
something that she would like to hear, or read a
story that I know would amuse her, and think: I
must tell Mum . . . only to stop and remember
that Mum is dead. Then I think of her cold in
the earth and wish it was me there and not her. I
got a postcard from Dad and his new wife. They
were on their honeymoon in Spain. I wrote
them a letter, but did not have the foggiest idea
what to say. It came out like a letter to strangers.
I keep feeling bad for the way I behaved at the
wedding ceremony. Dad was angry that I did
not take communion and I know I was off-hand
with Alice at the reception. It's just that I
strongly disapprove of him marrying her. I try
to be reasonable and think that Dad needs
someone to keep him company now that I am
away, but that feeling does not predominate
and at the wedding all I could see was Mum
crying. I could not join in and be happy
because I did not think that she was happy.
Then, seeing them in our home, seeing the door
of the bedroom, Mum's bedroom, close, with
Dad and Alice on the inside, I felt that
everything had come undone. All the surfaces
Mum had polished so lovingly for so many
years, all the things she had dusted and taken
care of, were now to be handed over to this
intruder. I know I am being unfair and I hate all
these nasty feelings but they bubble up in spite
of all my best intentions.

No, I have not joined the Catholic Society. You may be right when you say that I am just going through an atheistic phase. I'm not sure. Anyway, all I know is that whenever I meet a Catholic I start thinking up arguments to shoot down his beliefs. I tried going to mass here on the first Sunday and I wanted to put my hand up. The priest was going on and on about the church roof and how we all had to buy a slate for God's house. Well, I don't think God lives in churches. God is outside, shaking His head, wondering how His son's simple message of Love could have produced the Vatican and the foolish priest in the pulpit of St Winifred's.

I know I can write to you like this and you will not be shocked. While I am being so honest, I must say that I'm a bit worried about Laurence. I haven't heard from him since he left for Oxford. I've written to him THREE TIMES!! Is it that he is busy? Perhaps you are in the same boat. Maybe life is just too full of new experiences for him to come down to earth and put pen to paper. It isn't that easy for me to find the time either. Tonight, for example, I am waiting for an African student to come and stay with me for the night. He hasn't found himself any accommodation in Aberystwyth yet! That's a terrible thing, isn't it? I suspect his colour has something to do with it.

Look out at the estuary for me and give it my love. It is the part of home I miss most . . . apart from you, of course!

Love,

Martin

He sealed the letter and addressed it, using his best handwriting, making sure that each line of the address had an exact indent so that, when the address was finished, he could have held a ruler under the 'M' of Mrs and under the 'C' of Cheshire and ruled a line that touched the left edge of the first letter of each line in between. Whenever he did that he thought of Brother O'Toole, and wondered where he was. Brother O'Toole had left St Bede's during Benson's last year there. Brother Hooper had asked that all the pupils remember him in their prayers. He hoped that Brother O'Toole was all right and that someone had told him that Benson was going to study English at university. He still remembered the absent-minded Brother with affection and gratitude. He had always felt comfortable when Brother O'Toole was in the classroom. He hadn't felt fat then, nor a homo with a black, maggoty soul. Just a boy who read well and wrote – with Mum's assistance – mesmerizing compositions.

Placing the letter neatly on top of his desk, next to the picture of Mum pushing a plump baby – himself – on a swing, offering a quick prayer for the repose of her soul to the Wisdom and Spirit of the Universe – Meryl's term for the creator which seemed to Benson to be as good as any – he sat down again and read some more of *Persuasion*. He found that he just was not warming to the heroine at all. She needed to dance around to 'Something's Coming' each morning, or, better still, a side of *Black Orpheus*. Had she done that, thought Benson, then she would not have got all funny and messed up. She would not have let herself get so easily persuaded.

At eleven, Enoch Mohammed had still not put in an appearance. Everything was quiet in the hostel and Benson decided to see what Simeon was up to. He tip-toed along to Simeon's room. Light shone under the door but he could not hear anything. He returned to his room feeling slightly put out. It was not very consider-ate of Enoch Mohammed to keep him up so late. He decided that he would go to bed, leaving the door unlocked. He would take the sleeping-bag and leave the bedside light on so that Enoch Mohammed would be able to find his way to bed. He might wake up when he came in, or he might not, but he positioned the sleeping-bag strategically so that he would be in a good position to see Enoch Mohammed taking off his clothes should the occasion arise.

The floor was hard beneath the shiny material of the sleeping-bag. Benson lay inside it feeling silly, his comfortable bed only a couple of paces away. He's not coming, he thought to himself. Then: I'll never be able to sleep here. But, having arranged the top of his sleeping-bag so that it flatteringly exposed his torso, his eyes grew heavy and he fell asleep.

He did not know what time it was when he saw the figure of Enoch Mohammed standing by the bed. He had bent down to draw back the coverlet. Benson, putting on an impersonation of sleep, felt his penis rising, hoping that it would not show through the sleeping-bag. He was wide awake and watched as Enoch Mohammed took off his shirt and trousers, then turned and walked over to the wash-basin. He heard the tap turned on and the sound of teeth being brushed and face being energetically washed. He squinted at Enoch Mohammed's back. Every movement of the toothbrush caused the dark brown musculature of his back to heave, like rocks emerging from the swell of the sea, different parts being exposed, then returning under. He closed his eyes again. Please let him take off his underpants before he puts on his pyjamas, Benson prayed to the Wisdom and Spirit of the Universe. I am merely curious, you understand. I really do value Enoch Mohammed as a *human being* too, but let me see him and, if it be Your will, let him be a homo too!

Enoch Mohammed returned to his position by the bed. He raised one leg, as if about to get in with his underpants on. *Please*! He lowered the leg and, his back turned to Benson, pulled down the underpants to reveal a narrow bottom that stuck out like an apple. Benson gazed wide-eyed, but quickly squinted again as Enoch Mohammed turned . . .

Then the light was off. He must have had his finger on the switch as he turned, but for a split-second Benson had seen what he had hoped to see and the image stayed in front of his eyes in the dark as if the light were still on.

He lay on the floor wide awake. Sleep seemed like something that other people did. A mighty man was in bed only a yard away. Should he pretend to sleep-walk? Should he get up and climb into bed – it was his after all – and search for what he wanted? He would surely be able to seize hold of it before he was ejected. Would he be ejected? Perhaps he would be enfolded? Perhaps, here, now, Enoch Mohammed was inwardly sighing that Benson had been asleep when he came in! Perhaps Enoch Mohammed was as hot and bothered as he was!

That theory quickly lost credibility because Enoch Mohammed started to snore mightily. The sound did not in any way cool Benson's ardour, though it did convince him that his passion was not reciprocated. His plan of somnolent attack seemed suddenly very foolish, but he could still not rid himself of the split-second image of beauty that had turned towards him before the sudden death of the light.

Enoch Mohammed was clearly asleep. Benson took hold of himself and imagined that Enoch Mohammed had come into the room.

His fantasy echoed reality until the moment when the light had been put out. But now, in the dark, reality could be replaced by something kinder, and Enoch Mohammed turned and smiled and said: 'I know you are not asleep, Mr Vice-President! I know what you want! Come to me, my dear!' as the long black muscle inflated into the shape of a 2/- block of humbug rock and pointed straight at Benson.

'How . . . how did you know?' asked Benson.

'It takes one to know one, Mr Vice-President.'

'So you *are*!' gasped Benson. 'Oh, that's wonderful! Meryl said that Africans weren't. That's typical of Meryl. She thinks she knows everything, but she doesn't know the half of it.'

Enoch Mohammed smiled and opened his arms. Benson leapt from the sleeping-bag and jumped into the dark.

He did not get any further. He lay panting on the floor listening to the snoring, feeling his seed trickling down him, turning from hot to cold. Suddenly everything was normal again. Passion seemed as impossible as sleep had done a mere moment before. Slowly, Benson settled down, listening to the snoring. It did not annoy him. It was the price you paid for company. Before dropping off Benson saw himself rising from the floor of the hut in the mosquito-chirping morning. He took one last look at the body of his Dark Beloved on the mat, snoring and satisfied. Out he walked into the African dawn. A lion roared. Benson poured oats into a mortar and started crushing them with his pestle. He put all his energy into the labour, hoping that when his man awoke he would enjoy the porridge Benson had made for him. They had condensed milk in Africa. He would sweeten the porridge with lashings of it.

As he fell towards sleep he wondered whether, with good planning, he might be able to catch another glance at Enoch Mohammed as he got up. He prayed to the ever-obliging, all-purpose, Wisdom and Spirit of the Universe to let this come true. He did not bring up the subject of that part of the prayer which had failed to find an answer.

Benson awoke to the sound of the breakfast queue outside his door. At once his thoughts turned to Enoch Mohammed and he looked towards the bed, but it was empty. Enoch Mohammed, Benson's blue towel around him, was brushing his teeth at the wash-basin.

He must have seen Benson awake in the mirror, for he said, his mouth full of foam: 'Good morning, Mr Vice-President! I hope you slept well. You need not have surrendered your bed.'

'You were very welcome, Enoch Mohammed. I'm only sorry I was sleeping when you got back.'

'Ah, yes. I was late. I was busy at a friend's house making trunk-calls to my country.'

'Is everything all right there?'

'It seems so. The chief has arranged a Mercedes Benz for my use. I must pick it up in Germany, Mr Vice-President! And perhaps a wife shall be sent.'

'Oh, yes?' All hope was fading. He moved in the sleeping-bag and noted that he was stuck to the lining.

'Yes, so I must find myself a flat to live in.'

'Maybe I can help you find a flat,' said Benson helpfully.

Enoch Mohammed turned and let Benson see his torso. Benson could think of nothing else to say. 'Let us shower and eat breakfast.'

At once Benson was worried about how to get himself modestly out of his sleeping-bag and over to the cupboard where his dressing-gown was. He stood up in the sleeping-bag and held it like a sack in a sack race, jumping over to the cupboard.

'You English are so embarrassed,' said Enoch Mohammed.

Benson stammered that he wasn't really as he manoeuvred the door of the wardrobe open and thought that he would love to show himself off if he had a body like Enoch Mohammed. If he had he would show himself off all the time, at every possible opportunity. He'd join a Nudist Club and go to the Isle of Levant. But the less-than-ideal Benson hooked down the dressing-gown and put it on, then let the sleeping-bag fall.

'You have soap and shampoo?'

'Yes, in the cupboard there,' replied Benson, thinking suddenly of the queue. It was inevitable that he and Enoch Mohammed were about to go off to the shower together. It was destiny. Destiny also, however, that they would have to pass by the breakfast queue.

Benson had to screw up all his courage for the trip down the corridor. He followed Enoch Mohammed out of the door and locked it. As he fumbled with the key he could hear the conversation in the queue cease. Studying the label on his bottle of Vosene intently, he walked abjectly behind the betowelled Enoch Mohammed along the endless corridor.

Never did there seem to have been such a long breakfast queue. Benson could hear the thoughts of the other students and he fancied they were all coming to lascivious conclusions. *Look at that queer lad with the big hips and the funny voice! Did you see 'im come out of 'is room with that big blacky? It doesn't take much imagination to guess what they've been up to! You know, he doesn't mix with us! Always sits at the overseas table! We know what he likes! Now he's goin' to take a shower! Bet his eyes will be all over the place! Brazen! Ought not to be allowed! It isn't allowed. Bloody illegal and a good thing too*! He tried not to care. The thoughts were not coming from the students, were they? They were coming from his own nervy brain. I don't care what people think, he thought. Caring what people think messes up everything. You wouldn't do anything, just crouch in the corner and watch everyone else doing what they like! Anyway, how do I know that what I think they're thinking is what they're thinking? He made a mental note to think about that later.

In the shower-room, he breathed a sigh of relief. They were alone. He was ill-prepared when Enoch Mohammed took off his towel and, turning, standing naked and composed, asked Benson for the soap.

'It's Pears,' said Benson pointlessly, staring doggedly at Enoch Mohammed's relaxed features, while the periphery of his vision drank in the swaying muscle that formed the climax of his body. Then Enoch Mohammed hung up his towel, reached into one of the stalls and turned on the shower. His head disappeared and Benson was given the opportunity to gape at what was still visible. But then he got into the next stall, removed his dressing-gown, his heart pounding, his penis engorged, and turned on the water.

This would not do. This just would not do. He turned the gauge to the blue extremity marked 'C' and accepted the penitential stream.

'No, I will have to accept that Enoch Mohammed most certainly is not a homo. I must put aside my longings and be content to be just his friend in the Platonic sense,' Benson told his shivering, shrivelling self.

But when he had finished and darted out of the shower to put on his dressing-gown, there was Enoch Mohammed, glistening and golden and glorious, towelling. He stared in amusement as Benson fluttered and pulled himself into the inside-out dressing-gown.

'You are afraid to be late for breakfast, Mr Vice-President,' he said.

'Er . . .'

'By the way, may I avail myself of your bed this evening?'

'Yes, of course, Enoch Mohammed,' exclaimed Benson. He could almost see friendship in the Platonic sense flying, weeping bitterly, out of the window as he spoke. 'I've got some Guinness. If I happen to be asleep when you come in, just help yourself.'

'Thank you, I am very fond of Guinness,' said Enoch Mohammed, his whole face the place where smiles are sired.

4

'I'll bring your gramophone back for you after breakfast,' Simeon told Benson.

'If you're sure you don't need it any more.'

Simeon frowned. 'No, if I need it again I'll ask you.'

Benson nodded and asked Simeon to pass the marmalade, an item he had decided to give up some minutes before while surveying himself in the shower. He had resolved then that he must discipline himself and make his body hard, as much like Enoch Mohammed's as possible. Then he would not need to ogle Enoch Mohammed. He could just stand on a chair in front of his mirror, and be thrilled by his own reflection. But that line of argument had dissipated as he had dried himself and peeped abjectly at Enoch Mohammed. Perhaps he should stay a bit plump. He had heard that lots of men liked their women plump and a priori – or was it a posteriori – anyway, whatever it was, a bit of plumpness might help matters . . . or then again it might not.

He took the marmalade and spooned it on top of a buttered piece of toast. Then he placed an unbuttered piece on top of the marmaladed piece and consoled himself that he was saving calories by not putting butter and marmalade on the top half. He lifted the heavy sandwich to his lips and pulled a hunk into his mouth, as a lion pulls at the thigh of a gazelle. As he pulled and munched he looked over at Simeon who was stirring his cornflakes and looking depressed. Benson hurriedly chewed, swallowed his toast and marmalade prematurely – giving himself a sudden ache in his chest – in order to ask, 'Is everything all right, Simeon?'

Simeon continued to stir his cornflakes. He did not look up, merely shook his head slowly. Then he said that it was all over between him and Angela.

'I *am* sorry!' exclaimed Benson. 'What happened?'

Still looking down at his plate, Simeon replied: 'We were having a very gay time. I gave her a glass of sherry to drink, and showed her pictures of my family. Then, when I took her hand affectionately, she stood up, saying that she had another boyfriend!'

'So she left?'

'Yes, about half past nine. But I don't think she does have another boyfriend. I think she just used that as an excuse.'

Benson nodded sadly. He could not think for the life of him why Angela would want to use any excuse to escape seduction at the hands of Simeon. Benson felt that if he had had Long John Baldry as a boyfriend he would have left him waiting outside the Students' Union in the pouring rain for a chance to be with Simeon. Still, girls were strange. If he were a girl, he'd have overseas students lining up outside his room like the dinner queue. No he wouldn't. But if he were a girl, he wouldn't have to act at being manly all the time, keeping a stiff upper lip and stopping his hands going limp. Men spent all their time keeping their voices deep and wolf-whistling and downing pints in one gulp. It really was most trying to have to try and act like that, while fretting all the time about being caught out.

'You don't know any nice girls who are looking for a boyfriend, do you?' Simeon asked.

'Well . . . er . . .' said Benson, and he took another bite out of his toast in order to gain time to think about it. If he didn't care so much about what people thought, he would now admit to Simeon that he was a homo and was attracted to him. He could leave the rest to Simeon. Brother Hooper intruded: *Benson, boys,*

74

was a slave to his passions, a homo, a sodomite. I do not make this charge lightly, boys. On one occasion he refused to answer Brother Wood's catechism question on the subject. A homo without hope, he gave Brother Wood a brazen look! As I look down on you, boys, I can see the outrage on your outstretched faces. Righteous indignation! Hold on to that, boys. Righteous indignation is the highest form of the Good – in the truly Platonic sense . . . He started searching through his brain for a replacement for Angela. There was Meryl, but Meryl had a boyfriend. There was Anthea, an acquaintance at English lectures, as well. But he couldn't imagine Anthea and Simeon together. In fact, whenever he thought about Anthea – which was seldom – he thought about her wheeling a pram. She seemed to belong behind a pram, a big Silver Cross. The trouble with that image of Anthea's future was that he just could not imagine any of the intervening stages. She was always to be seen either studying or dancing round her handbag with Emily, who was at the Library College in Llanbadarn and had the thickest ankles Benson had ever seen, thicker even than his. He just could not imagine Simeon taking to either Anthea or Emily.

'I'll have to think about it.'

'I bet you know a lot of nice girls!'

'Not that many, no.'

'You don't have a girlfriend of your own?'

'Well, not what you'd call a girlfriend, er . . .'

'How do you mean?' asked Simeon.

Now was the time, he thought. All he had to do was heave four short words into his mouth. Well, three short words and one longer one. *I am a homo.* It was the fourth that would cause the trouble. It was a strange word, like the mooing of a cow and it made you pucker your lips as if you were kissing, expressing satisfaction, kissing again. There was nothing spiritual in the word. It was unforgiving, damning . . . 'I . . .

Well, what I mean is that I have friends who are girls but not a girlfriend, a girlfriend in the non-platonic sense, that is.'

'I shall go crazy if I do not find a girlfriend,' said Simeon.

Benson nodded understandingly, 'I'll see what I can do,' he promised, racking his brains.

Three hours later, after an American literature lecture about Hemingway and short sentences and confrontation and commitment and humiliation to humility and American witch-hunts and the Kennedy era as Camelot, Benson was sitting in the More Utopia opposite Meryl.

'Wasn't he dishy? I could have just gobbled him straight down!' said Meryl of the American literature lecturer.

Benson did not think the lecturer was particularly dishy. He was much too white and thin for Benson's taste. Also, he did not quite approve of the way he strode up and down smoking Number 10s, looking thoughtful.

'I think he's a bit phony,' said Benson.

'You would!' asserted Meryl unkindly. 'I suppose you prefer the living dead in Anglo-Saxon. Ralph is vibrant. You can see the ideas forming in his brain *as he speaks* and bubbling out fresh, like wonderfully flaky croissants out of a hot oven. I could just gobble him up!'

'What's a croissant?'

Meryl expressed not the least surprise at Benson's ignorance. 'A French breakfast pastry of great refinement that melts in the mouth,' she said in a tired tone.

'Is that his name, Ralph?'

'Yes, Ralph Wynne.'

Benson pulled a face.

'Anyway, I have other things on my mind at the moment,' said Meryl pregnantly.

'What?'

'Men.'

Benson nodded. 'How's your friend, whatsisname?'

'Whatsisname is no more,' replied Meryl. 'I saw him coming out of Janet Jenkins's room last night. It surprised me rather because whatsisname had the libido of a corpse. Still, you don't go to Janet Jenkins's room for a stimulating chat, that's for certain. Do you know what she's reading? *The Lord of the Rings* for crying out loud! Anyway, whatsisname had told me he was going to the Politics Society.' And Meryl lit her own cigarette. She did not use her holder. Then she exclaimed theatrically: 'Two timin' me like it don' count for nuthin'. Well, it does. He ain't never gonna do that to no woman agin!'

'That's the spirit!' said Benson.

'I have just quoted from which musical?' asked Meryl.

Benson hadn't the foggiest and said so.

'*Carmen Jones*. Don't you know nothin'? "Hang me high from a tree! So that soon I shall be! With my darlin', my baby, my Carmen!"' sang Meryl. 'You know sometimes I think I was negro in my past life.'

Benson nodded enthusiastically. Then he thought of Simeon.

Meryl butted into the thought, however, just as Benson was about to try it out on her, 'You're not still besotted with *West Side Story* are you?'

'Oh, yes! Was, am, always will be!'

'They're making a film of it, you know.'

'Are they?'

'Yes, but it won't transfer well.'

'Why not?' asked Benson who was somewhat in awe of Meryl in matters theatrical – and much besides.

'Hollywood. Hollywood fucks everything up. Did you see *Pride and Prejudice* on BBC2 last night?'

Benson shook his head.

'An abortion! An absolute bloody abortion! That's Hollywood for you.'

'Well, just as long as they get Carol Lawrence and Larry Kert in the film, that's the main thing.'

'More likely Charlton Heston and Jane Russell.'

'Who'll play Maria?' asked Benson.

Meryl fell about.

Benson leapt in with what was on his mind: 'So you don't have a boyfriend now?'

'No. Do you think you fit the bill?'

'No, of course not, but I know a nice man you might like.'

'He isn't Welsh, is he?' asked Meryl. 'I never go out with the Welsh, though I might make an exception in the case of Ralph Wynne.'

'No, he isn't Welsh. He's African actually.'

'Not the one you were making cow eyes at at the Freshers' Hop?'

'Yes.' He thought how perceptive Meryl could be, albeit in a nasty sort of way. She did not miss a trick.

'But he's a midget!'

Benson demurred. 'Oh, come on Meryl, he's lovely. Really cuddly. And he's very lonely.'

'Well, he ought to find someone his own size,' said Meryl.

Benson thought of Myvanwy Roberts. She would do nicely, but he remembered that he had seen her with Sean O'Malley. It would probably not last but still . . . He put further pressure on Meryl.

'Go on, Meryl! You've nothing to lose. You could come to my room for a drink. I'll invite Simeon and you can decide then. If you don't like him after we've talked for a while . . .'

Meryl interrupted Benson coldly, 'I thought you were only the Vice-President of the Overseas Students' Society. I wasn't aware that that post involved pimping as well.'

'Pimping? How do you mean?'

'What I say.'

'That's not fair, Meryl!' said Benson. 'I'm only trying—'

'To find a woman for a man. Almost a dictionary definition of a pimp, I'd say.'

'Well, just forget I mentioned it,' said Benson, resolving to look up 'pimp' in the dictionary and hit Meryl with the correct definition on their next meeting.

'What time?' Meryl asked.

'What time what?'

'What time are you giving your little soirée?'

'Er . . . say eight.'

'I like dry white wine,' said Meryl.

'Do you?' asked Benson. White wine – dry or wet – was not budgetted for.

Meryl left shortly after that, saying that she was going to put a notice up in the Students' Union offering an almost new set of Carmen Rollers for sale. She only had twenty pounds left to see her to the end of term, she said, which made Benson feel better. He had thirty-five, though he did not think he would stay solvent if he had to keep buying wine.

He sat on in his booth nursing a second cup of capuccino and reading *The Wretched of the Earth.*

He had drunk his coffee and was in a suitably wretched mood about the Earth when Sean O'Malley and Myvanwy Roberts came in and asked if they could sit next to him. Benson said yes, though he was a little embarrassed to meet Sean O'Malley after the abrupt way he had refused to join the Catholic Society. Still, Sean did not seem to be bearing any grudges. He couldn't very well, thought Benson. Not as the head of the Catholic Society. Grudges just did not go with the job.

Sean smiled at Benson: 'How are things going . . . Martin, isn't it?'

'Very well, thank you, Sean. I'm settling down nicely.'

'You haven't changed your mind about joining the

79

Catholic Society, have you? We need all the support we can get.'

'No, I haven't. Sorry.'

Myvanwy brought their coffees over and sat down. She smiled at Benson.

'So you're having trouble gaining recruits?' Benson asked, a hint of glee in his voice which he took pleasure in not stifling.

'Well, we've got more than last year, but they're a stodgy lot on the whole. They're all splitting into groups and going off to climb Cader Idris. Hearty trips were not quite what I had in mind for the society. I have a few radical plans, but I can't find anybody who'll take them seriously.'

'Like what, for instance?'

'Happenings.'

'Happenings?'

'Yes, Myvanwy and I are interested in getting something off the ground.'

'But you're Chapel, aren't you, Myvanwy?'

'I'm under instruction,' she said.

Benson nodded. So that's it! he thought. 'The catechism and that sort of thing?' he asked with the merest hint of a smirk.

'Oh, no! That's out these days Martin! Where have you been? No, Myvanwy just meets with other interested people over a sherry with Father Derbyshire up at the Abbey.'

'Yes, but you still get the dogmas drummed in, don't you?'

Sean leaned back in his seat and smiled at Myvanwy, who smiled back. Benson felt his hackles rise.

'Martin, this is 1965.'

'Well, it may be 1965, but the Catholic Church won't change. It can't.'

'Why do you think that? Good Pope John opened all the windows.'

'Not possible,' said Benson with conviction. 'The Catholic Church will never be able to face the fact of two thousand years of error. I can hardly convince myself that there is no truth in every jot and tickle of it and I only had seventeen years' indoctrination. But think of all those generations of the Catholic Dead! They lie on top of us . . . of you . . . and it is bloody impossible to get out from under all those millions. "We did it, now you bloody get on with it!" The Church will never admit to error. It is a hopelessly haunted house. Nothing left to do but just leave without baggage, lock the door and never go back.'

Sean and Myvanwy seemed a trifle befuddled by Benson's string of metaphors, as tangled as a rosary kept in the pocket too long.

'But it has changed!' managed Sean after taking a long sip of his foaming coffee. 'When did you last go to mass?'

'A year ago,' said Benson, partly to shock, partly unwilling to admit that he had darkened the doors of St Winifred's.

'Well, if you went now you'd see some changes.'

'Cosmetic. Tell me, is it still a mortal sin to miss mass on Sunday?'

'No, I don't think so. The very concept of mortal sin has undergone vast changes.'

'And masturbation? Surely masturbation is a mortal sin?'

Myvanwy giggled, but Benson ignored her.

'Personally, I don't think it ever was. A biological necessity, I'd say,' laughed Sean.

'Do you mean to say that you never thought masturbation was a sin?'

'Well, I would say that it is a failure of the ideal, but no, I never thought it was a mortal sin.'

'Well, I don't see how you can be head of the Catholic Society. You'll be telling me next that artificial methods of birth control are acceptable.'

81

'I really think it's up to individual couples. You see, Martin, it's all a matter of love. That's what morality comes down to.'

'These are all fine words, Sean, and I suppose I agree with you. But what I cannot agree with is that the Catholic Church thinks that. It's either all or nothing.'

'What a little Jansenist you are!'

'I am a little Agnostic!' snapped Benson. 'Also,' he added, aware that he was out to shock and stop Sean's sickly smile, 'also I am homosexual. There is no place for me in the Catholic Church.'

But Benson was disappointed. The smile did not fade. 'Splendid! If that is what you are that is what you are. Don't you agree, Myvanwy?'

Myvanwy nodded enthusiastically. 'Definitely,' she said.

'The Church is for everyone, Martin. Many mistakes have been made, but things are changing. Believe me.'

Benson melted towards Sean somewhat. He wanted to say that he believed him, but the temptation to do so was interfered with by the memory of his years of agonizing. The idea that just a few miles away from home, in Catholic public schools and in the swanky south of England, people had been following a very different brand of Catholicism from the one promulgated at St Bede's and enshrined in his little red catechism did not please him at all. Rather it appalled him, made him feel hugely cheated.

'You know what really makes me see red about what you're saying? There must have been millions of people who have died thinking that masturbation would damn them, ditto for missing mass and the rest. It makes me livid to imagine that suddenly the Catholic Church says: "Sorry, chaps, we were mistaken. All those things we said were mortal sins were really just a little less than the ideal!"'

'You're eaten up by anger, Martin.'

'Not usually I'm not!' Benson almost shouted. 'Only

when I get around damned Catholics! I can be quite calm and cheerful when I'm not around Catholics!'

And Benson picked up his bag and said he had to go.

Sean and Myvanwy continued to smile at him tolerantly, and Benson saw them still smiling at him through the fishing-net-draped window of the More Utopia. He scowled at them and stomped down the prom towards his Morals lecture.

Morals cheered Benson up no end and gave him much to think about as he pushed himself back up the hill with a bottle of wine, an ounce of Sun Valley and a bag of salted peanuts from the little sweet shop halfway up the hill, whose proprietress was getting to know him and called him 'Sir'.

The lecture had been based on Plato's *Republic*. Benson had a soft spot for Plato – not only because 'platonic' had become one of his favourite words – but because Plato had been a homo. At least that was Benson's impression. Also, the word Plato was a nickname in Greek which meant broad-shouldered. Benson was broad-shouldered. Plato had been clever too with his three ideas of the Good. He tried to sort out what the lecturer had said. There were three versions of the Good. The first was like going into a cave and having a look at the view outside; the second when you saw the shadow of the view on the wall . . . but then what was the highest form of the Good? He had missed that somehow. Perhaps it was when you were in a cave and a boulder had been rolled over the entrance and you couldn't see a thing, and were left to your own devices. He would have to sit down and read *The Republic.* He would also have to read *The Phaedrus* and *The Symposium*. Such a lot to read! Then there was all that American Studies to do, the Anglo-Saxon to be learnt by heart! It was clear that he would have to curtail all those hours spent in the More Utopia with

Meryl, all those argumentative evenings at the hostel with Ianto, and really get down to work.

After a hurried dinner during which he did not see Simeon, Benson penned an invitation to him for eight that evening, slipped it under his door and sat down in his easy chair to finish *Persuasion*.

He had decided by the time he finished the novel that his initial impression of Lady Russell was incorrect. She wasn't a patch on Mrs Clitherow and neither was *Persuasion* a patch on *The Good Earth*, which Mrs Clitherow had lent him just before he left home. Benson knew that *Persuasion* must have something to recommend it. It was on the course, after all. Great critical tomes had been written about it. Scholars had spent their whole lives trying to sort it all out! Still, he had found it a pretty dull tale and was pleased to be able to finish it, bang it shut, and send it whizzing from his hand on to the bed.

Next he picked up *The Republic*. He gave his hardback edition a reverent kiss before opening its pages. The introduction took ages, almost the first third of the book, and Benson gave up on it, though he knew he would feel guilty later. He had developed a need to read every word of a book, from the date and place of printing to all the bits of information on the back like the price it would have cost him if he had bought it in New Zealand, and how the edition wasn't, for copyright reasons, for sale in the United States of America.

The Republic kept him on the edge of his seat for half an hour, and he thought he was beginning to understand the three levels of the Good. He had also, he felt, mastered Plato's idea of heaven. Heaven involved a contemplation of the essence of the circle. Nothing was truly circular until you got to heaven. Heaven did not go on forever. After a decent period had been spent in contemplating what circular and other things *really* meant, then you were allowed back to Earth, your head buzzing with all the *essences* you had experienced in heaven. The priest who came to speak to Benson in the sixth form – the one whom Benson had demolished in argument on occasions past computation – had said that the good Catholic spent heaven in rapt contemplation of the Godhead. There would have to be an awful lot to contemplate if it were going to take up all that time. Benson's enquiry about whether there would be breaks for Kit-Kats and tea had been dismissed as levity. Heaven, he was told, was not this Vale of Tears. There would be no need of sustenance or 'breaks'. He would have put Kit-Kats behind him. But the nuns at the convent had allowed into heaven all the sweets and sensual experiences that could possibly be thought up by a class of six-year-olds. Now, if there was a heaven, and Benson still rather hoped that there would be, it would have to include free access to Enoch Mohammed's nether regions. He could understand a heaven like that, full of nude, smiling Clitherows and Africans. Eternity would pass in the blinking of an eye!

In the light of this it was less clear what relevance Plato's three levels of the Good and of heaven, had to his own life. It looked as if Plato had reserved the top bit of the Good for the upper classes too.

His eyelids were becoming heavy but he fought the temptation to drop off. He got up and rinsed his face, then went over to the desk and considered his map of Aberystwyth and its little flags. It was incumbent upon him in his role as Vice-President of the Overseas Students' Society to visit everyone. He would have to make a start. He worried a bit about knocking on doors unannounced, but then reasoned that it could be no worse than doing house-to-house collections for Fr McCarthy's babies, and that it would be like a trip around the world. He set about planning his itinerary.

Eight o'clock came and Benson put on side two of *Black Orpheus*, turned off the overhead light to create the right ambiance, tidied his textbooks away on to the window-ledge, flicked some Tabac around and combed his hair in front of the mirror. He pouted. I am a ho-m-o, he told his reflection. With time, he thought, he might get to like the word. He had had no trouble informing Myvanwy and Sean of the fact that he was a homo. Maybe one day he would let it trip off his tongue as easily as a comment on the weather being much as expected for the time of year.

At half past eight Meryl arrived. She produced a stem wine-glass from her bag saying that she could not possibly drink wine from a tooth-mug which she was sure – correctly – was what Benson would try to serve the wine in. She slugged back a glass very quickly, leaving Benson to look at the level of the bottle and attempt to compute how many more glasses it was good for.

'Where is he then?' asked Meryl, after Benson had poured her her second glass.

'Search me. I put a note under his door. I didn't see him at dinner.'

Benson filled in the time by telling Meryl about Plato's idea of the Good, and Meryl remarked that she did not think the wine that Benson had bought would reach even the bottom stage.

'You know,' said Benson daringly, 'you might find Simeon a bit much for you. Are you sure you want to go through with it?'

'How do you mean "a bit much for me"?' asked Meryl.

'Come on, Meryl! You must know!'

'Know what?'

'Well, you must have seen those Armand and Michaela Dennis films about African tribes!'

'Yes?'

'Well, then.'

'I suppose in your usual dishonest and pimping sort of way you are referring to the sexual endowment of

Africans. It's a fiction. My father was in the colonial service in Uganda for much of his career. The judiciary. He says that Africans are the same size tumescent as they are when quiescent. It's a racial characteristic. Whites have penises like concertinas. It's a climatic thing. The penis retreats in the cold. In Africa it is seldom cold and the penis does not need to retreat to protect itself.'

Benson could not decide whether to be more astounded by the theory Meryl was so flatly expounding, or the fact that her father had discussed such a topic with her.

'Did your dad really tell you that?'

'My father and I discuss everything.'

Benson nodded, trying to hide his confusion. Is that what parents and children talked about in London? And was it true? If it were true – and Benson had never seen an African tumescent – then that would put a whole different slant on things. If it were true then he might find that there wasn't much of a difference. Perhaps he would be as big as they were. Still, he thought, Meryl's father probably only said that in order to make himself feel better. Yes, that was it. These gin-swilling colonial types just could not give the African credit for any superior attributes, physical or otherwise.

He was wondering whether he should articulate anything of what he was thinking to Meryl when Simeon arrived and shook hands with Meryl. He sat down on the very edge of Benson's bed, placing his hands underneath his narrow buttocks. There he sat, appraising Meryl across the room, rocking a little back and forth. When Benson took him his Guinness he could hear Simeon humming quietly to himself.

'I saw you at the Hop,' Meryl said to Simeon in a gentle tone of voice, one Benson had never heard from her before.

Simeon nodded and smiled, but did not say anything.

Benson waited a decent interval, but neither said anything further. He decided to put a new record on. He chose Oscar Peterson's *Canadiana Suite*, thinking it bridged the gulf between black and white rather well. Benson liked 'Wheatlands' best, but he put the record on at the beginning, resolving to put off pleasure. He would have to do rather a lot of that if he were ever to make himself as hard and strong as Enoch Mohammed.

'You are from Ghana, aren't you?' Meryl asked Simeon.

'Yes I am, but I've lived in London for ten years.'

'Oh, have you? What part?'

'Notting Hill.'

'I'm from London. Hampstead.'

'It is beautiful there,' said Simeon.

'I've never been to London,' Benson told them.

'No? You should,' said Meryl in more familiar tones, and she shook her glass to show Benson that it was empty. He had known, had watched her chucking back his liquefied grant money and had thought to postpone refilling her glass. But this was clearly not going to work. He poured Meryl a glassful and Meryl twitched her lips by way of thanks before spreading them in a bright smile towards Simeon.

'Do you like Aberystwyth?' she asked Simeon.

'Yes, it is a very nice and quiet place.'

Meryl nodded and sighed. 'Yes, it is so *very* nice and so *very, very* quiet.'

'You do not like it so much then?'

'No, not so much. It's so far from everywhere. I can't imagine a more remote or provincial place. My ex-boyfriend is even unhappier about being here than I am. Do you know what he does when he feels too cut off?'

Simeon, Benson saw, was still humming to himself, rocking back and forth on his hands, which must have gone to sleep by now, and smiling serenely at Meryl.

But he did not seem to have heard a word of what Meryl had said.

'No, what does he do?' Benson asked, as it was obvious Simeon wouldn't. What was wrong with Simeon tonight? Benson felt like giving him a good shake.

Meryl replied to Simeon as if it were he who had asked. 'He goes to the station and he sits on the platform watching the trains coming in and going out. He took me with him once. We took a picnic and just sat there looking at the people getting off and getting on – especially getting on – and thinking: those lucky sods will be in Shrewsbury in a few hours. And after Shrewsbury it's the world!'

'Well, I think it's a nice place,' said Benson, thinking it a bit thick that Meryl should be sowing depression among overseas students. 'It isn't London or Oxford of course, but there's lovely countryside all around and then there's the sea and the chance of getting to know people much better than you would in a big city.'

Meryl deigned to look in Benson's direction then, and he knew that he was about to be subject to one of her barbs. But just as she opened her mouth there was a knock at the door and before Benson could say 'Come in!' Enoch Mohammed stood resplendent, completely filling the place where the door had been a short moment before.

'Oh . . . er . . . it's you, Enoch Mohammed. Meryl, this is Enoch Mohammed. Enoch Mohammed, this is Meryl. Simeon you know, I think.'

But Enoch Mohammed took not the slightest notice of Benson's careful introductions. He stared hard at Meryl through slit eyes that formed two equal signs, matching as they did the horizontal scars along his cheekbones. 'A lady!' he said with a voice that seemed to emanate from a cave rather than a mouth. ' "O, she doth teach the torches to burn bright!" '

' "It seems she hangs upon the cheek of night as a

rich jewel in an Ethiop's ear . . .'' *Romeo and Juliet*. Very neat,' said Meryl.

'''A hit. A very palpable hit!''' added Enoch Mohammed, flicking the cavernous sleeves of his robe with a deft flick of his arm that caused both sleeves to roll themselves up.

Benson looked hard at the cuffs of his Marks & Spencer bri-nylon shirt and said *Hamlet* to himself.

'*Hamlet*,' said Meryl. 'Get this bard a drink, Martin.'

'What would you like?' asked Benson as Enoch Mohammed sat cross-legged beside Meryl. 'I've got Guinness or wine. At least I think there's enough wine. I . . .'

'Guinness! It isn't Export Guinness, is it?'

Benson looked at the label. 'No, I don't think it is. Does it matter?'

'Give me some!' said Enoch Mohammed, rather imperiously, Benson thought. 'The Guinness in Nigeria! They make it especially strong for us!'

'You like Guinness, do you?' asked Meryl.

'Ah, yes. It is good for you,' replied Enoch Mohammed. 'It makes us strong,' he added, taking the foaming toothmug from Benson's hand, and toasting Meryl.

The two started to talk earnestly and quietly and Benson went over and sat on the bed next to Simeon and tried to make polite conversation.

But Simeon did not appear to be listening. He had removed his hands from under his buttocks and was staring at them idle on his lap. Benson talked about Guinness in Ghana, venturing his opinion that if Nigerians were fond of it then Ghanaians probably were too, and did they have the strong export stuff as well?

But, getting no response, he joined Simeon in looking at Simeon's hands.

Benson was thinking how beautiful Simeon's hands were. The cuticles of his nails especially impressed him and the place where the back met the palm and suddenly lost its pigmentation. He could see that heavy thumb pushing sprouted seeds into dark African earth and making the whole country bloom. Simeon would probably invent a new strain of wheat while he was at Aberystwyth that would make the continent of Africa the breadbasket of the world. He, Benson, would look back on his time at Aberystwyth, proud to be able to tell his grandchildren – well somebody – that he had once known that famous plant-breeder and had even then seen the mark of greatness stamped upon him.

'Nigerians,' whispered Simeon into Benson's ear.

Benson was quite startled to be pulled back from his reverie. 'Yes?' he asked.

'Nigerians. They are all bad people,' whispered Simeon.

'Surely not?' Benson whispered back. 'I mean, there are good and bad everywhere, is that what you mean?' He knew that Simeon had not meant that, but he did not want to consider what he had meant. He was a little irked with Simeon for the remark. It did not seem nice that fellow overseas students should insult one another. There were enough wicked landladies behind lace curtains to do that as it was.

Simeon did not say anything else. He accepted another glass of Guinness, then just wrapped his hands around the glass and stared hard into the foam, hunched on the edge of the bed.

Benson gave up with Simeon. He knew what was behind his anger. It was clear that Meryl and Enoch Mohammed were hitting it off. Still, in a way it was Simeon's own fault. If he liked Meryl, why had he not acted more enthusiastically towards her before Enoch Mohammed came in? Benson kept hearing Meryl saying: 'God, yes. Oh, yes! God, that's right!' and he could see that her eyes were the largest he had ever seen them and that they looked upwards into Enoch Mohammed's and fluttered more often than required.

'Is everything all right?' Benson asked the pair.

'Where did you find her, Mr Vice-President?' asked Enoch Mohammed. 'She is not only the barn where all beauty is stored but also of formidable intelligence. You English are generally so ignorant about African affairs. But Meryl, she has read Camara Laye, Chinua Achebe and Wole Soyinka!'

'Has she?' asked Benson, who hadn't, though he was in some ways consoled to catch sight of *The Wretched of the Earth* displayed prominently on his desk. He also wondered whether Meryl would take to being compared to a barn. Looking at her, she seemed to be quite taken by the idea.

'Clarence in *The Radiance of the King*', said Meryl, 'is the archetypal spineless white. The book is a powerful tale of a race in decline.'

'Have you read *The Fire Next Time*?' asked Benson.

'Who hasn't? But what Enoch Mohammed and I are talking about, Martin, is the fire *this* time.'

'Have you read many African writers, Simeon?' Benson asked, desperately trying to get Simeon into the conversation.

'Yes,' replied Simeon.

Everyone except Enoch Mohammed, who kept staring at Meryl, looked towards Simeon to see what would come next. But nothing did. Benson let his mind wander to worrying about whether Enoch Mohammed and Simeon were the same tumescent as quiescent.

The evening wore on with Benson becoming increasingly aware that it had been a failure as far as fixing Simeon up with Meryl was concerned.

At eleven, Meryl announced that she had to go, and Enoch Mohammed insisted on walking her up the hill to Ifor Evans. Just as she was leaving, Meryl offered her cheek for Benson to kiss, something she had never done before. As he withdrew, smelling her scent, Meryl gave Benson a slow wink. Then she strode out, Enoch Mohammed standing back for her to pass.

Benson was left with Simeon who stayed long enough to finish the last bottle of Guinness, then, still monosyllabic and depressed, he started walking hunched back to his room. Half way along the corridor, he turned and looked at Benson, whose heart jumped up hopefully for a moment. Then Simeon said: 'Enoch Mohammed is no good. He borrows money and does not repay it.' Then he continued on towards his room without another word.

Benson wished he could offer Simeon some consolation, though he felt in need of some himself. What did Simeon mean? If it was true, then it might explain why he had been so silent and morose. But he was more saddened because of the failure of his split-second hope. As Simeon turned, Benson had felt that perhaps he was going to say something to the effect that, as he was not going to find a girlfriend, then Benson would do. If he had tried to heave the words *I am a homo* out of his mouth, would Simeon have smiled and come back? Probably not, but possibly yes. Still, if he was honest, it was plain to see that he did not have anything that Simeon wanted.

He set about preparing himself for another night on the floor. Perhaps, he thought, Enoch Mohammed would come back fired up with lust. But that tumescent thought fell down flaccid at once. Any lust he had was in all probability going to be slaked in room 433 of Ifor Evans hostel. Perhaps Meryl's Union Jack bedspread would put him off. Perhaps the mobile would alert him to what an odd girl Meryl was and convince him that he was better off in room 112 at Pantychelyn with a Vosene and Pears shower to look forward to in the morning.

Eaten up by lust, boys! He thinks he is kind and generous, but lechery lies behind it all, boys! I only thank God that he did not stay with the Brothers, boys! Imagine the trouble he would have been in the missions! The scandal! Better a millstone be tied around his neck and he be drowned in the depths of the sea!

Benson sighed and shook himself. He cleared up, brushed his teeth, left the bedside lamp on for Enoch Mohammed and arranged his sleeping-bag strategically. Then he got into it, said a prayer for Mum, another for Simeon and Clitherow, worried a bit about the meeting with Dr Leptos, had a short dialogue with himself about mixed motives, stroked himself, remained flaccid, pulled a face and fell asleep.

5

He woke the next day to a very noisy queue outside his
door. His eyes focused on the empty bed, the top sheet
still turned back artistically to welcome Enoch
Mohammed to its seductive warmth. He lay back in his
sleeping-bag, and thought of Meryl's slow wink. He
pouted. Then he was aware of a scratching sound at
his door. Doubtless some lazy, leaning student was
messing up the paintwork with the stud on a pair of
jeans. Then he heard loud laughter from the queue.
Really, he thought, it was too much. He was surrounded by insensitive morons who were only fit to
attend night-schools and do sandwich courses! The
high tone that should exist at a university was not
being maintained. Far from it! He lay, letting his ire
rise towards the low ceiling. No, it was too much. He
would put up a notice, that's what he would do. This
was stretching tolerance to intolerable lengths. Wasn't
it enough that students came in from the pubs of
Aberystwyth at all hours and made a dreadful din?
Was his sleep to be disturbed at both ends? None of the
British students took the smallest interest in overseas
students. They were blind, blind and daft, that's what
they were! Then he saw Meryl wink again.

  He tried to simmer down, got up and brushed his teeth
as though they were to blame. He felt very let down.
Why hadn't Enoch Mohammed come back? It had been
nice to have someone to share his room. It had been
novel. He had always had his own room (except when
he had been at St Finbars). It would have been nice if
Enoch Mohammed had graced his room a second time.
He could have snored all night if he had wanted to.

Some students at Pantychelyn hostel shared rooms. Benson would like to have shared with Enoch Mohammed on a permanent basis. And the possibility of sex was not the only reason. Sex would have been nice – more than nice – but, much better than that even, it would have been wonderful to grow familiar with him, to be easy in his presence, to have to fit in with someone else. To be with somebody meant feeling different. Self-regarding thought stopped. That was a wonderful thing. To stop thought. Here, now, with Enoch Mohammed nearby getting ready for breakfast, he would not be seething with the anger he was now feeling. The noisy queue outside would just be a noisy queue, not a personal insult. As it was, he was 'Angry of Aberystwyth', railing against the irresponsibility of youth.

That morning he resolved once and for all to put all hope of a sexual relationship with Enoch Mohammed out of his mind for good. It was a lost cause anyway. Seeing the way Enoch Mohammed was different when Meryl was in the room had shown him that. In the freezing shower he made resolutions not to think about Enoch Mohammed, not to seek out opportunities to spot him in the nude, but to try and see him in the same way as he saw Ianto.

Only when he was unlocking the door of his room did Benson notice that someone had scrawled HOMO on his door. He looked at it hard as he fiddled with the key. Then he let himself in and closed the door behind him.

He remembered the scratching and the laughter. Some nasty person in the queue – the queue he generously tolerated each and every morning – had written HOMO on his door. What shall I do? he thought. Do I go to the Head of Hall and demand that it be repainted forthwith? No, he could not see himself doing that. Perhaps he should cover it with a notice. But that would only give the wicked scribblers an easier surface to write on. What, then? He had to do something about it, didn't he? Did he?

When they had called him 'homo' at school, had he done anything? No, he could imagine the reaction if he had. It would be the same now, wouldn't it? He got dressed and decided that he would leave the scratched scrawl as it was. Just as overseas students got prejudiced against, so he was receiving a bit of the same. He would just have to be stoical. I shall just not worry about it, he told himself resolutely.

He worried about it over breakfast and down the hill into Aberystwyth. *Your sin shall find you out, boys! Even in this world the sinner feels the vinegar of remorse, the loss of reputation* preached Brother Hooper. His voice was vanquished by Fyfe Robertson: *A peaceful town, this. Or so one might be forgiven for thinking, but come with me. In this room lives an example to British youth. He is the Vice-President of the Overseas Students' Society and devotes himself night and day to those exiled from their homes. But look, viewers, look what someone has written on this good lad's door! It makes one ashamed.*

Suitably distracted by lectures, comforted by a coffee and a Penguin biscuit, Benson sat opposite Meryl at the More Utopia, trying to find out what had transpired between her and Enoch Mohammed the night before.

Meryl refused to recount anything at all of her time with Enoch Mohammed, and greeted his enquiries with arched replies about the right to privacy. Still, that in itself had been enough to convince Benson that something had been going on.

'When are you meeting him again, Meryl?'

'He has gone off to pick up his Mercedes. Won't be back for a week or so. He had nothing but praise for you, said you were the nicest Englishman he had met. I had to bite my lip.'

'Oh?'

97

'Well, as I believe I have mentioned before, I can see beneath your liberal façade, Martin.'

'I don't know what you mean. It's true, I find him very attractive, but that isn't the only reason I'm nice to him.'

Meryl nodded patronizingly.

'Anyway, it was supposed to be Simeon that you got friendly with.'

'He doesn't have much to say for himself, does he?'

'Silence is golden,' said Benson.

'You'll be telling me next that nice things come in small packages.'

That was true. It had been on the tip of his tongue. He swallowed. 'But Enoch Mohammed is obviously committed to another woman. Did he tell you his dad is sending him a wife?'

'We didn't have time for mundane chatter,' said Meryl. She smiled broadly and winked again.

'I do wish you wouldn't do that, Meryl,' Benson told her.

'Why not?'

'It's common.'

'Here comes the cat.'

Benson wondered what Meryl was getting at, but he was soon informed as the resident ginger tom at the More Utopia jumped up on to the seat next to Benson's, and then stepped tentatively on to his lap, making a squeak like a rubber toy as it settled down.

The cat had got into the habit of making straight for Benson, and usually Benson welcomed its attentions. He had never had a cat or a dog at home. It was nice that the cat came straight for him. It made him feel like St Francis. Of course, it would have been much more impressive if birds had hovered round his head in the street, but this was almost as good. An elderly couple, doubtless late trippers, were giving him a smile. To be chosen by the More Utopia cat conferred virtue on him.

'It hasn't been neutered,' Meryl told him.

'What's that got to do with anything?'

Meryl did not reply, but looked out at the busy street. 'There's Ralph Wynne!' she said.

'Well, is it true?' Benson asked.

'Is what true?'

'Tumescent and quiescent.'

'Wouldn't you like to know!'

Benson concentrated on scratching the cat under the chin to make him purr.

'Well, I will say this,' continued Meryl, 'the experience was – how shall I put it – cathartic.'

Benson wished that Meryl had described the experience in another way that did not necessitate a trip to his Collins Gem. The trouble was that all the hard words he was being bombarded with on a daily basis were sorely testing his Collins Gem. Several had not been listed. He could see himself having to lash out on something larger. More expense! Was there no end to it?

Meryl left for the library soon after, volunteering no further snippets of information. He carefully manoeuvred his dictionary out of the briefcase and read: carthartic; purgative. Well, that didn't help. He looked up 'purgative' and read: strongly laxative, purifying effect. That was a funny way to describe dalliance with Enoch Mohammed. Meryl had clearly misused the word. Probably Meryl wasn't as bright as she made out.

While replacing the dictionary in his briefcase the cat nipped him for fidgeting, squeaked and jumped off his lap, upsetting his coffee-cup. The old couple gave him a funny look. Did they think he had hurt the cat? He frowned, got up and, brushing cat hairs off his anorak, walked out of the More Utopia.

Apart from lectures, reading and pumping Meryl to no effect, Benson filled in the following days by visiting a number of overseas students at home. He knocked at six doors and introduced himself. It had been a whole different world, a world with exotic spices in the air, stiff photographs of families, hand-woven cloths. At each of the houses he visited, Benson had been treated well, sat down to cake and sweet tea by the rather bemused hosts.

He asked them if they were having any problems and all except a single Sudanese student said that they weren't. The Sudanese, whose name was Omar, said he was missing his family and feeling the cold. Benson commiserated about the former and recommended string vests for the latter. He also resolved to visit the Sudanese student again, once the hump of Friday had been scaled.

Omar was a taller, willowy version of Enoch Mohammed. So thin were his wrists that the silver bracelet on his watch slipped down over his long hands. His English was excellent, but he did not have Enoch Mohammed's energy, his joy of life. He paused before making replies to Benson's questions. But these quieter qualities were impressive in their own way.

He left the last house on Thursday evening, wondering if everything were as rosy as it appeared. Could it be that the students were suffering dreadful harassment, but were afraid to mention the problem to an Englishman? He tried to put himself in their position. Would he complain about his hosts if he were studying in Calcutta? Probably not. Still, perhaps they weren't having any problems. If that were indeed the case then it was good news, wasn't it? It would certainly make his job as Vice-President of the Overseas Students' Society a good deal less onerous than it otherwise might have been.

Benson decided to put aside his worries about his foreign charges for the time being. He would return to his visiting in time. Then, perhaps, the truth would come bursting forth. The saried lady would break into sudden tears over her peculiar pastries, admitting that she had her voice imitated by the girls in the Welsh Wool Shop; the Kenyan couple would complain of the landlord; Omar would reveal that unruly youths taunted him on the late-night streets and did black and white minstrel impersonations. It was just a question of gaining their trust. Perhaps he ought to place an Overseas Students' Complaints Box somewhere strategic so that they could write down the prejudice they were encountering anonymously. But that wouldn't help, he thought. If they remained anonymous, how could he help them?

At four on Friday, Benson was shuffling from foot to foot outside the Greek department. He could see Dr Leptos's Austin A40 parked across the road. Part of him hoped that Dr Leptos would have forgotten their appointment. He cast a wary eye up the road to the Philosophy department, but the low sun was shining directly into the window and he could not tell whether Dr Griffiths was looking out and passing judgement on goings-on on Aberystwyth prom. Benson tried not to care.

'Oh, there you are, Martin!' said Dr Leptos, leaving the Greek department, a shabby briefcase bulging with books and files in one hand, a Thermos-flask in the other. 'I thought you would come and knock at my office door.'

Dr Leptos put his spare arm around Benson's shoulder and led him across he road towards the car. Benson felt himself go crimson, and could imagine what Dr Griffiths would be saying. He wanted to shuffle out of range of the hand. Still, he thought, perhaps people passing would think that Dr Leptos was his father, though Dr Griffiths would know better.

'I didn't like to. I might have interrupted a class or something.'

'No classes on Friday afternoon, and not that many at any other time, truth to tell, Martin. You haven't decided to come back to us, I suppose?'

'No, I haven't. It really was too hard for me.'

'It would have got easier, and it is a wonderful language.'

Benson nodded and waited on the passenger side of the car for the door to be unlocked for him. When he got in he noticed that the car smelled strongly of cigarettes. It reminded him of Mum.

'Do you drive?' Dr Leptos asked.

'No, Dr . . .'

'My name's Andreas, Martin. My friends call me Andy. Why don't you call me that?'

Benson nodded but he did not fancy calling Dr Leptos Andy. It doubled his worries straight away because Andy had been the name of the man who had seduced him in the cemetery at home two years before. Every time he called Dr Leptos Andy he would see the old Andy working his lips knowingly. And that Andy had let him down . . .

'Right, where shall we go? I live in a cottage near Devil's Bridge. I'll take you on a short tour round. If you haven't got a car, you won't have seen the countryside. It is very beautiful in parts.' He looked over at Benson, who nodded enthusiastically. 'Then we'll go to my place.'

Benson still did not know for certain whether Dr Leptos – Andy – was a homo or not, but he had a feeling that he probably was. Otherwise why would he be asking a first year undergraduate out for a drive? But he rather hoped that Dr Leptos wasn't. He did not feel particularly attracted to him. Dr Leptos had a nice face. You could tell that he wasn't English, even though he had English colouring. His hair was dark – almost like Heng-Moon's – and fell lank on to a great steppe of a forehead. The nose was high and straight. It did occur to Benson, however, that probably a man like Dr Leptos was exactly the sort of man he should be seeking. He could learn a lot from such a man. He must be chock-full of wisdom to be a Greek lecturer.

Probably knew all of Plato off by heart in the original.

They climbed up the hill out of Aberystwyth, past Pantychelyn, where the girls would be laying the table for dinner, past Maynard's house at the top of the hill and out into the country.

Perhaps he would learn to love Dr Leptos. It might just take time to see his attractions. He probably had them even though they were by no means as obvious as Enoch Mohammed's. Yes, perhaps he should give Dr Leptos a try. What did he have to lose?

'"The trees are in their Autumn beauty",' quoted Benson, to show Dr Leptos that, though Greek had been too much for him, he was not a complete illiterate.

'Certainly are!' replied Dr Leptos, not seeming to get the reference.

'You have a long drive to work every day, don't you?'

'Yes, but my wife works in Lampeter, so it's a good compromise. Anyway, it's nice to live a bit away from work I always think.'

'Yes. How long have you been married?' asked Benson, who had used a considerable pause to re-adjust his perception of his relationship with Dr Leptos rather in the way he might adjust his story were a bully like Eddie Rudge to sidle over to him in the play-ground – Benson convinced that he wanted money for ice-cream – only to say that he wanted to buy Benson one. He was immensely relieved. If Dr Leptos was married that must mean that he couldn't possibly be a homo! Ninety per cent of Benson was thrilled and contemplated an evening ahead with cake, and Benson telling Dr Leptos and his intellectual wife all about the plight of overseas students and Plato's idea of the Good, while he ate and then helped Mrs Leptos to wash up and was told how well brought up he was. Only a peculiar ten per cent of him felt let down that there would be no tension in the air.

'Too bloody long!' replied Dr Leptos. 'Eight years! Still, there's no need for you to worry about that, Martin!' And Dr Leptos let his hand stray from the gear stick to pat Benson's knee.

Benson looked at the hand on his knee, as confused by it as by Plato's idea of the Good. What does he mean there's no need for me to worry? he thought. He looked out of the window and worried like mad.

They arrived at Dr Leptos's cottage, parked the car in front and then walked round to the back door because Dr Leptos said they never used the front door.

At the back there was a conservatory. Dr Leptos ushered Benson ahead of him through that door and Benson, smelling the smell of humus and home, wondered about Dad. Then he saw a family of little wellington boots in a neat line along the path leading to the door into the house proper. On the door was pinned a note which Dr Leptos pulled off and read.

'Victoria – that's my wife – has taken the kids off to Ludlow to stay the weekend with friends. She wants me to make sure to get in plenty of milk for Sunday.'

Benson said: 'That's nice.' He then wanted to take back what he had said because it sounded as if he wanted Victoria to be away, which he didn't. On the contrary, he wanted Victoria to be here, keeping order.

'I'll put on the kettle for a nice cup of tea,' said Dr Leptos. 'Then we can walk down into the village for a couple of pints. They serve good food there. You can even get bortsch there some nights.'

'Can you?' asked Benson, biting his lip.

'You will stay the night, won't you, Martin?'

'Well, er . . . I didn't think . . .'

'Go on! You might as well! If I have to drive you back tonight I won't be able to have a few drinks at the Druid's Head. I love my Friday night pints.'

'I haven't brought anything that I need, Mr, er . . .'

'Andy. You don't *need* anything, I'm sure we can

104

rustle up a toothbrush. And a fine young chap like you doesn't wear pyjamas.'

'No, but . . .'

'And there's no young female waiting for you, is there?'

He wondered if he should lie. Perhaps he could use Meryl as an excuse. But he should have used Meryl as an excuse ages ago if he were going to use her. 'Er . . .' he said.

He sat down on an easy chair in the living-room while Dr Leptos was in the kitchen putting on the kettle, laying a tray. He returned briefly and put a record on a turntable, then went out again. Benson watched the pick-up arm jerking noisily on to the record.

A strange sound filled the room, a single deep voice intoning what might be plainchant, but then followed by a gust, a sudden storm of voices: boys and men. The sound came from two speakers. Benson did not think he had ever heard recorded sound like it. Had he been at home, he would have had two worries in his head: Dad and the neighbours. But here there was no dad and there weren't any neighbours for miles and miles. No, he was in a sophisticated environment that would make Home gasp.

He flicked through a copy of *The Spectator* on the table by his armchair, but nothing struck him as interesting, and he flicked it back on to the pile as he felt Julian Pettifer or David Frost might. He thought of Clitherow. What would Clitherow think? What would Clitherow do? Clitherow had said that he must experience everything, hadn't he? He could almost hear Clitherow telling him not to be a twerp and to just relax and enjoy what the evening would bring. The trouble was . . . What was the trouble? Think logically! he told himself.

The trouble is that Andy is married. That's the trouble. Adultery is a sin. He could already hear

Clitherow laughing at that: *Look Martin, homosexuality is a sin! If you accept your homosexuality you are already a sexual outlaw! Why should you worry about puny little sins like adultery?* Well, yes. There is that. But surely, just because I'm homosexual that doesn't mean that I am free to go with somebody who is committed to somebody else. I have to have moral standards, don't I? By marrying, Dr Leptos – Andy – has forfeited any rights he might otherwise have had to me. *You make yourself sound like third prize in the egg and spoon race* countered Clitherow. *Sex is first and foremost fun*! Yes, but I'm not even sure I'm attracted to him. I'm not sure he's me at all. Clitherow had no answer to that, but one came from inside Benson which totally confused him: You only want to give yourself to people who are beautiful and ideal and exotic! Where's your Christian charity? The over thirties need love too! Think how you'll hurt his feelings if you say no to him!

Dr Leptos arrived, carrying a tray.

Look at all the trouble he's going to, he thought. How mean you are! Your so-called *chastity* is just another form of selfishness. Now if Andy were Enoch Mohammed, that would be another matter entirely.

'Do you like the music?' asked Dr Leptos.

'Yes, it's lovely. What is it?'

'Heinrich Schütz. His Symphony Sacrae.'

'It sounds like a mass.'

'No, it's sections from the Old Testament mainly. This is called "Pater".'

'I've only got a little Philips,' said Benson, thinking that heaven would now have to include stereo speakers and a house with no neighbours. Only when he had these and all the rest as well would he be able to concentrate on adoring the Wisdom and Spirit of the Universe.

'I only play it when Victoria isn't here. She says loud music gets on her nerves.'

106

Benson nodded, asked how long Dr Leptos had owned the cottage but didn't listen to the answer, trying as he was to think rationally about why a man with the intelligence of Dr Leptos should saddle himself with a wife who could not appreciate music. Then he thought that when they were married there were only 78s and nothing that could produce volume. Still, there must have been ways for him to sound her out!

'And how many children have you got?'

'Three at the last count, but the oldest, Thomas, is mine from a former marriage. The twins, Susan and Andrew, are seven.'

'Did your first wife . . . er . . . pass away?'

'Heavens, no!' replied Dr Leptos. 'She's married to a lecturer in the Philosophy department.'

'That must be a bit embarrassing,' opined Benson, wondering who the guilty lecturer in the Philosophy department might be.

'No, not at all. We're good friends.'

Again Benson was nodding, though he did not feel like nodding. Dr Leptos was not only married, but a divorcee. He wondered if he had been mistaking the signals. How could he be a homo if he had made the same mistake twice? It just did not make any sense. But if he was one, and if he had designs on him, then not only would Benson be committing a queer form of adultery were he to give in, he would also be committing adultery with a divorced person. And divorced people were . . .

But a voice came back at him: You don't believe in that any more!

Dr Leptos turned over the record while Benson tucked into scones made by Victoria. The jar had written on it: *Victoria's strawberry jam, August 16th, 1965*.

'I know exactly what I was doing on August 16th!' said Benson, drawing Dr Leptos's attention to the jam label.

'What?'

'I was at school picking up my A level results. August 16th is St Joachim's Day by the way.'

'So it was a nerve-wracking day for you?'

'Well, it was up until ten thirty, no quarter to eleven. After that, it was a lovely day. You see, I only expected to scrape through two A levels, but I got four. I got an E asterisk for General Studies.'

'What was the asterisk for?'

'Well, I did Spanish at O level because I wasn't thought bright enough to do French. Anyway, when I opened the General Studies paper I found that Spanish wasn't included in the choice of translations. Of course, I complained to the teachers and wrote a stern note on the paper. So they gave me E asterix. If I hadn't passed the General Studies Paper I wouldn't be sitting with you now, because, you see, I didn't get any Maths or a Science. I thought I'd failed English. If I had, it would have been completely my own fault. One of the questions was: Compare the Characters of Hamlet and Laertes. It should have been a doddle, but I compared the characters of Hamlet and Leontes!'

'Who's Leontes?' asked Dr Leptos.

'He's the king in *The Winter's Tale*, married to Hermione,' Benson informed Dr Leptos, 'but you see that was the other play on the syllabus. I noticed about fifteen minutes from the end what I'd done and frantically started answering the question properly. But there wasn't enough time.'

Dr Leptos was nodding politely. The room had become dark around them. He switched on a lamp with a big red shade, and Benson thought how nice he looked. Had he failed to see it before, or was it the light? Perhaps that was what happened when women said 'I learnt to love him'. Maybe it just took time to see the chap they didn't fancy at first in just the right light.

'Still, I'm boring you, I think. It's only that the jam reminded me.'

'No, you're not boring me, Martin. I'm interested in everything you want to tell me. What else did you do on August 16th?'

'I was really chuffed when I got my results. I thought to myself that perhaps the UCCA people would let me in to university. I'd been accepted by a training college but I really wanted to go to university. But, as I say, I didn't have any Maths or a Science. However, the General Studies had taken care of that. I was very happy and was walking down the lower corridor of the main school building with my friend. However, I should add that I'd grown a beard during the holidays. Anyway, along comes Brother Hooper the headmaster and says something nice to Clitherow, the chap who was with me. Brother Hooper liked Clitherow because he's terribly intelligent and his dad's a Knight of St Columba. Then he turned to me and I thought he was going to congratulate me, but instead he took the tip of my chin between his thumb and forefinger and turned my head first one way and then the other. "A beard, I see! I'd have expected that from you, Benson!" he said. And he walked away.'

Benson stopped and looked down at his cup and saucer on his lap.

'So what did you do?'

'Well, what could I do? I had wanted him to say well done or something. I mean it was a surprise. It was far from expected that I would do well. I had wanted to say goodbye and to thank him for everything. Also I had wanted to say I was sorry for the trouble I had caused him over the years. I was rather rebellious in the sixth form. But all he did was congratulate my friend. As he walked down the corridor, I gave his back a V-sign, a double V-sign with both hands. I know I'll never see him again. As soon as I'd made the V-signs I thought how childish it was. Every time teachers turned to the blackboard right the way through schooldays we would make V-signs at them,

109

then stop when they started to turn. And that is all I could think of as a final gesture, a farewell to school.'

'Yes, but a V-sign can mean victory, can't it?'

'It does if you do it this way,' and Benson made a Churchillian gesture, 'but this way it means – well, you know – and that is how I meant it.'

'It sounds as if he deserved it.'

Benson shook his head. 'Not really. The headmaster wasn't a friendly person, but he has given his whole life to the gratuitous instruction of youth.'

'What does that mean?'

'The brothers take vows. They don't get paid for what they do.'

'Maybe they'd behave better if they were.'

'Yes, I often think they were frustrated.'

'Are you frustrated?' Dr Leptos asked.

'How do you mean?'

'Sexually frustrated.'

'I suppose so. I mean, I don't have a girlfriend or anything.'

'Do you want a girlfriend?' asked Dr Leptos. He was looking unblinkingly into Benson's eyes. His eyes reminded Benson of Peter O'Toole's in *Lawrence of Arabia*.

'No, not much,' replied Benson, looking at the floor.

'So what do you want?'

'Well, I . . . er . . . think I'm . . . er . . . probably homosexual.' He said it in the way he thought Clitherow might say it, but it did not come out properly.

Dr Leptos nodded. Then he smiled and said 'Let's go to the pub.'

In the pub Dr Leptos ordered two pints of bitter before Benson could tell him that he usually only drank lime and lemonade.

When he was on his second pint he told Dr Leptos why he didn't drink.

'On my eighteenth birthday Laurence Clitherow – he's my best friend at home, the one Brother Hooper liked – took me for my first legal drink at a pub. I was pleased when we went in because they queried Laurence's age but not mine. Anyway, we drank draft Guinness all evening. On the way home I was terribly sick and I haven't drunk anything stronger than a shandy since.'

'Oh, dear! I hope this won't make you ill.'

'Well, I'd better go careful, but I feel wonderful at the moment, thank you very much. I'll just drink slowly from now on, though.'

They ate a meat pie and salad. Dr Leptos insisted on paying for everything.

Towards the end of the evening, Benson accepted a third pint.

'You've got quite a capacity!' said Dr Leptos as they headed back from the Druid's Head to the cottage. They crossed a narrow bridge. Benson looked down, listening to the invisible waterfall far below.

'"The cataracts blow their trumpets from the steep,"' said Benson.

'There's a story attached to this bridge,' said Dr Leptos. Once again he had failed to take up a quote. That was odd. They were all pretty elementary, Benson thought.

'What's the story?'

'Well, young man, you are walking over three bridges. All is not as it seems.'

You can say that again, thought Benson. Yes, that would make a good motto: *All Is Definitely Not As It Seems* written artistically below a winking black eye. It said it all. It explained the wellington boots in the hall, Dad remarrying, Clitherow's silence, Victoria in Ludlow, tumescent and quiescent, Catholic missions, everything really. Yes, he thought, I must remember that. 'Yes, but the story?'

They were standing on the bridge. Dr Leptos looked

down at the waterfall as he spoke. 'Well, there was once an old woman who lived near the river here. There was no bridge then. One day her cow wandered off across the river and, because of the deep gorge, she wasn't able to get it back. The Devil appeared and said that he would build her a bridge, but he wanted to have the first living thing that crossed it for himself. The old woman agreed. The Devil thought that the old woman would cross first in order to fetch her cow. But she was too clever for him. She threw a piece of meat across the bridge and her dog ran across the bridge to eat it. So the Devil got the dog and the old lady got her cow back.'

Benson nodded. He joined Dr Leptos in looking down at the pluming water. Me and Mum could have come up with a better one than that between tea and *Criss-Cross Quiz*, he thought.

'Are you OK?' Dr Leptos was looking at him strangely.

'Yes, thank you,' replied Benson jauntily, trying to think why he might not be. Then remembering. Then realizing that, though he appeared jaunty, he was not. Yes! True! All Is Definitely Not As It Seems!

'I'm really enjoying my time with you,' said Dr Leptos. 'It's such a change to be with someone so young. What you said about Plato was really interesting.'

That was too good to miss and Benson said: 'Thank you. It's all about appearances and reality really. Things are never quite what they seem.'

'Yes, what is the point of anything, Martin? Tell me that. When you get to my age you will realize that everything after twenty-five is lies, prevarications and compromise.'

'How do you mean?'

'Take marriage for instance. To tell you the truth, Martin, I should never have married. I really wasn't made for it. Until I was twenty-five I vowed I never would. Then I got tired of aunts and uncles asking me when I was going to name the day. I just caved in. The biggest mistake I've ever made.'

Benson knew that Dr Leptos was telling him something. 'But you've done it twice, Andy!' he said as they passed a Bethel Chapel with a wayside pulpit in Welsh. Benson thought they ought to put in an English translation. Did they only want to save Welsh-speaking sinners? Ianto would have been as pleased as anything.

'Yes, I know,' Dr Leptos was saying, 'but that's what I mean . . . lies, prevarications and compromise.'

He's a Greek lecturer. He's got a car, a lovely house, a stereo, a wife and children, but he can't tell Stork from butter, Benson thought to himself. 'So why do you think you weren't made for marriage?' he asked Dr Leptos.

'You mean you don't know?'

Benson, if there had been any doubt at all in his mind, was suddenly very sure that he knew.

'Yes, I suppose I know,' he said.

'Will you sleep with me?' asked Dr Leptos outside the sweet shop.

'Er . . . Well, I don't know . . .' He was confused by the straight question and also by a row of moral scruples that kept marching across his attention like the line of sweets in jars in the sweet-shop window. They centred on adultery, Enoch Mohammed, wellingtons in the conservatory and the fact that he did not feel particularly attracted to Dr Leptos. The last one he shot down in flames first: Well, how mean! How mean you are! He is attracted to you! He has a Ph.D. and it is surely a great honour that a person whose head is crammed full of wisdom and the hard-to-learn Greek alphabet should see something in you worth liking! Are you going to say no to him because he is less than the Ideal? That would be a sin against Charity. Oh yes, your precious chastity would remain intact but that is a

113

pretty sterile virtue. St Paul said that the greatest of these is Charity. Be charitable. Anyway you can always avoid passing the Greek department in future and go along the main street instead . . .

He spoke his other worry: 'But you're married now.'

'Martin, all the Greek boy-lovers were married! The great Socrates was married! I thought you had slewed off all the petty Judeo-Christian proscriptions!'

'Well, I suppose I have,' sending St Paul scuttling away with a toss of his head, his scrolls and strictures under his arm.

He walked alongside Dr Leptos, thinking. Then, as they passed the butchers, he said: 'Yes, I'll sleep with you.'

I'm never going to be able to manage this, thought Benson, as Dr Leptos attempted penetration, an hour or so later.

Things had gone quite nicely up to that moment. Benson had stripped down without much shame, quite proud of the remains of his summer tan and of his flat tummy. He had lain naked on the candlewick bedspread and watched as Dr Leptos took off his clothes. He gripped himself, stroked his erection as he watched, knowing as he did so that this was not like him, but then thinking that if he was doing it then it must be like him in the Platonic sense of like him. Dr Leptos looked down as he unbuttoned his cavalry twills and pulled them off, then looking hard at Benson, took off his underpants.

Even in a semi-erect state, Dr Leptos, Benson knew, was bigger than Benson. He did not know why, had never known why, but this was important. Clitherow had been bigger than he was. So had Bruno. Both had stayed in Benson's mind partly for that reason alone. And now he saw that Dr Leptos, though his body was soft, his white skin not particularly attractive, was big. His size would make him take charge. It was like a

114

badge saying PREFECT at school. It proved you were a big boy capable of commanding respect. At school you had to obey anyone wearing that insignia.

Dr Leptos lay down beside him, and then rolled over on top of him. He put his tongue down Benson's throat and played tag with Benson's in the padded cell of his mouth. He sucked on Benson's tongue until Benson wanted to tell him to go easy, but found that the organ with which he had been going to give the instruction was all tied up in Dr Leptos's embrace. Then he thought to himself: D.H. Lawrence would not approve of all these thoughts going on in my head. Sex should be in the body. And he tried not to think, but to simply feel like a good Lawrentian hero. But it was no good. Everyone he had ever known crowded round the bed with questioning expressions that demanded hard answers.

After ten minutes of French kissing that was becoming a trifle trying, Benson felt it was time to start exploring.

Brother Hooper railed. Even Fyfe Robertson found it hard to look on the bright side and say something nice. He winced into the camera.

Benson felt very self-conscious about groping towards the penis. While kissing and sighing and playing with his nipples it was possible to believe that Dr Leptos thought he was interested in him *as a person* – which he was of course – though some bits were very much more interesting than others. But once he let his hand wander down to the penis to squeeze and compare shaft and balls, then Dr Leptos would know that his soul was forgotten, and that *it* had taken its place.

Benson had not been slow to show Dr Leptos what he knew, and worked his way down his body, trying not to neglect the bits that were not particularly attractive to him, giving them equal attention so that they would not feel left out. He kissed the nipples and

115

passed his tongue across them until they stood up erect. Dr Leptos moaned to show Benson that he was pleased, but Benson did not think much of nipples, neither his own nor others. They simply marked the route. He kissed Dr Leptos's navel reverently. Then continued on down to what he really wanted.

'I want to please you,' he told the erect penis as if it were something completely separate from its tense owner. And he kissed the end of Dr Leptos's penis and then suddenly swallowed the lot. And as he did this the thought came: Once you've felt this, the soul is pretty thin beer. The soul takes effort to know . . . while this . . . Stop it!

Dr Leptos's whole body jerked upwards with the shock of Benson's surprise move. Then Benson set to work, kneeling over him.

Sucking on Dr Leptos was nice. Since the first time he had done it – to Clitherow – the act had entered his repertoire, in the theory of masturbation at any rate. Now that it was happening, he could hardly perceive the reality of it. But neither could he keep away thought: What must I look like? Was Mum watching him and shaking her head? Was this perverse or was it part of the rich human pageant? Benson had seen people doing it on Greek vases, and this gave it a certain amount of respectability in his eyes. After all Thames and Hudson wouldn't put illustrations of it in their book on Greek Art if it wasn't respectable, would they? The aesthetics were dubious, though. Little children put peculiar things in their mouths and were told off for it: 'It's dirty!' If the adults had thought bits of coal and pipes and the corner of *The Sunday Express* dirty, what would they make of what he was doing? How would he be able to sit in front of Dr Griffiths taking morals to bits when he had had Dr Leptos's penis in his mouth and half-way down his throat? Still, Meryl said that girls did it to boys and boys did the same to girls. That was consoling. If girls did it to boys it probably meant it had always been done and that the mouth had evolved in order to be a suitable love-making tool. The idea of doing it to girls, however, struck Benson as the very pinnacle of perversity. He could not see how anyone could manage to do the necessary to a girl. Anyone who did that deserved a medal or a Plenary Indulgence. Still, he must not be judgemental. Perhaps the tongue had evolved in order to pleasure penises and vaginas. Benson felt that his tongue was now definitely the flapping point of his turning world . . . then D.H. Lawrence was back, stroking his little ginger beard and telling Benson not to think but to feel. Benson tried and concentrated on a rhythmic movement.

Dr Leptos seemed to be getting more and more excited. Then quite suddenly he pulled Benson's head away.

'I was very close,' he gasped.

'Were you?' asked Benson, his mouth aching, thinking it a bit thick that after all that work Dr Leptos had not done the decent thing.

'I want to fuck you,' said Dr Leptos.

'You don't, do you?' asked Benson forlornly.

If the aesthetics of fellatio still preyed on Benson's mind, he had hardly allowed himself to consider the prospect of the other thing. The idea had never appealed to him in the least. He could not think of a worse part of him to be used for the expression of love, lust, or anything else much for that matter. It was, he felt, a rather large leap in imagination to go from an attraction to men to a need to avail oneself of that particular orifice. It was not a leap he felt inclined to take. Clitherow had tried to do it to him once and had been told in no uncertain terms where to get off. Clitherow had not let the matter drop, but kept telling him about things he had read in the works of Sir Richard Burton and the poetry of Verlaine, not to mention the oft-quoted Genet, whom Benson had read

117

with little enthusiasm except for a couple of good bits. But even Clitherow's attempts had fallen on deaf ears, and Benson had kept his portals tightly pouted.

Now he knew he was on the edge of the chasm. One side of him felt mean. Another side felt curious. Yet another worried that he would have to return to fellatio if he refused, and his jaw was aching rather . . . But there was not one iota of him that relished the prospect. But it seemed easier to at least have a go than to say no. If he said no, perhaps Dr Leptos would say he was mean and cowardly. He might even ask for his beer and pie money back.

Dr Leptos told Benson that there was a bidet in the bathroom. Benson nodded and made for the door, trying not to give Dr Leptos a full-rear view of his bottom, which, he felt, was not his best feature by a long chalk. He looked around in the bathroom for anything that might say bidet on it. He read all the bottles and boxes in the medicine cabinet, but found nothing. Instead he distracted himself by wondering what the low thing next to the toilet was. It had taps on it and looked like it might be a child's toilet, but then he thought it wouldn't be much good except for number one because there did not seem to be any-where for number two to go. He looked at himself in the mirror and thought: I am a harlot, then he dabbed some cologne on his chest and returned to Dr Leptos who was smoking a cigarette in bed, looking nonchalant.

He clasped his hands behind his head and looked at Benson as he darted to the bed, all the time taking puffs from the cigarette.

Then Dr Leptos went into the bathroom, returning with a tube. He lay on the bed and smeared what looked like Trugel on to himself. 'Hold out a finger,' he told Benson. Benson did so and then looked at the Trugel sitting on the end of his left index finger.

'Well, put it in,' said Dr Leptos.

118

Benson did not much like the bossy way Dr Leptos said that, but he obediently applied the Trugel and waited for the worst to happen.

Dr Leptos knelt on the bed and lifted Benson's legs on to his shoulders. 'Just relax,' he said. Benson gave Dr Leptos a weak smile and Dr Leptos went ahead and tried to push himself into Benson. But Benson closed himself up in a pucker that mirrored the tight one on his face. This is a physical impossibility. Then he thought: This is the sin of Sodom. And all the exiled angels were back weeping in droves all around the black and white beamed ceiling. Benson thought of Victoria. Victoria was designed for this kind of thing. Then he suddenly had the distinct impression that someone was in the doorway that led to the landing. He looked hard and saw that it was a dressing-gown, hung on the door by a hook.

'Have you ever done this before?' asked Dr Leptos, panting.

'No, I haven't,' lied Benson, 'and I'm really not sure I'm . . . er . . .'

He hoped that that would make Dr Leptos stop, but all he said was, 'Try to relax,' and moved his position slightly.

The situation seemed hopeless. At last, Benson, realizing that Dr Leptos was not going to give up, decided that he had better try to make things easier. 'I think it might be better if you let me hold you and take my own time. Perhaps that will work.'

And he felt under and grasped Dr Leptos's erect penis and aimed the head towards himself. The feel of Dr Leptos's flesh excited him a bit, and slowly the will not to be penetrated was replaced by a desire to know what it would be like. The touch at once set off sparks of uncaring. Thought ebbed away. He rubbed the head against his puckered portal, and willed it to relax around it.

Benson gasped when the first lubricated inch moved

119

past his sphincter. 'Can you hold it there for a mo please?' he asked. 'It takes some getting used to.' Dr Leptos was far away above him and in a way Benson was not speaking to him at all but to the urgent organ which was trying to go where by rights it had no business going. He pushed down and pulled up. He tried to get used to the presence and then Dr Leptos started pushing and an odd shiver ran through Benson as he felt the rest of the shaft disappear.

Dr Leptos pushed Benson's legs back until his toes were locked against the back of the headboard of the bed. Again Benson saw himself for a moment, all his dignity gone. It could not be a pretty sight and everyone he conjured up looking down on him looked down on him.

Dr Leptos started to move against him, back and forth. The bed creaked and pain came in waves. Benson screwed up his features, trying to communicate the pain, but Dr Leptos carried on regardless.

'Excuse me, but could you go a bit easy?' Benson asked.

'Just try to relax. That's the key.'

Benson tried to relax. He thought of an apple but thinking of apples – something recommended in a meditation book he had looked at in Smiths – led on to serpents with apples in their mouths being crushed by the feet of Our Lady who was looking down, and was displeased. Then he tried to push, to open himself. This worked better and when the pain had subsided he was able to feel the queer sensation of Dr Leptos moving inside him. A man is inside me. A man is doing me! His own penis, limp through the preparations and false starts, hardened and looked back at him from his doubled-back position. He reached down and manipulated himself in rhythm to Dr Leptos's thrusts. He had thought about it in theory often enough but here it was happening. And he tightened himself round Dr Leptos, tried to narrow the channel of his movement still further and this caused Andy to moan. 'I'm coming!' he said.

But Benson was not listening. Suddenly he felt very much in charge. He let his sphincter relax its grip on Dr Leptos, stroked himself less frantically, made Dr Leptos work harder. He did this several times until he began to feel an edge of soreness.

Was he enjoying it? He felt he was rather. Physically, the mixture of pain and pleasure was alarming. He had the feeling that something dreadful was going to happen at any minute, a terrible agony poised to engulf him. But at the same time he felt peaceful and in exactly the right place.

The final part contained great swathes of pleasure and pain, combined in an odd combination. Benson saw Enoch Mohammed doing this to him. Then Simeon. Then the two Koreans. Then, feeling guilty about letting his mind wander, was happy to observe Dr Leptos sweating above him.

He felt completely relaxed and took time to stroke Dr Leptos's hair. There, there is a man and here am I. Then passivity was replaced by equal labour.

'I'm going to come!'

'Me too.'

Dr Leptos went off to the bathroom. It was only as Benson lifted himself up off the bed a few minutes later that it collapsed. Something snapped and the high, carved hardwood headboard banged down on the top part of it. Benson looked back at where he had just been lying, and wondered whether to be pleased that they had wrecked a good, solid bed, or whether it was a sign.

'What happened?' asked Dr Leptos, coming through the bathroom door, a red toothbrush sticking out of his mouth.

'The bed collapsed,' said Benson.

'Not again!' said Dr Leptos, and he disappeared back into the bathroom.

Benson stood and looked back at the wreck of the bed. I have been done! he thought to himself happily. Now I know everything! Then he stared at himself, tousled and tired in the mirror. He winked at his reflection. Then he frowned.

6

All the following week, Benson trailed round
Aberystwyth feeling hurt and chastened. Three more
sessions with Dr Leptos had left him raw and used up.
In fact the second time Dr Leptos penetrated him on
Saturday night he had taken so long, been so rough,
that Benson had been crying into the pillow by the
end. He had, in fact, decided that he must not be a
homo after all; Dr Leptos seemed to be enjoying
himself, but Benson most decidedly was not. He was
irked by the way Dr Leptos had assumed that Benson
was to be on the bottom all the time. He had not had
the courtesy to ask whether Benson might like a go too.
Perhaps the first two times were his by right. He was
older and bigger after all, but it seemed odd that he
wouldn't at least ask. Benson would probably have
said no and suggested that they just cuddle instead,
had he felt free. But he had felt like the guest, the
undergraduate to the lecturer, and could not heave his
thoughts into his mouth. Benson's period of pillow-
biting made him aware that the attraction which
seemed like the most natural thing in the world most of
the time, could also, in the wrong circumstances, be
totally unnatural and absurd.

Dr Leptos drove Benson back to Aberystwyth on
Sunday morning, having tidied up around the cottage
so that Victoria would not guess that anything had
been happening. Dr Leptos had become strange,
nervous and a bit bad-tempered. They had not talked
much in the car. Benson was feeling uncomfortable,
and not only that but pangs of guilt – easily banished
when he had been in the middle of discovery and

enjoyment – had returned to further oppress him.

By Monday Benson was having trouble walking about. The pain in his bottom kept reminding him of what he had done and was echoed by a psychic pain which would not be banished either.

Right, he told himself as he waited for the bus to take him down to lectures. Right, that's it! No more of that! I am going to be chaste from now on! The pain in my bottom is clearly a sign from the Wisdom and Spirit of the Universe that I have done wrong. Probably if I had just done it with a single man I wouldn't be feeling bad now, but I did it with a married man – and a divorced married man as well! That is why I am in pain. I had no business doing what I did and Dr Leptos had no business asking me to do what I did.

He took great trouble, even availing himself of his strategic overseas students' map of Aberystwyth, to vary his route around the town so as to avoid meeting Dr Leptos again.

Benson worked hard that week. He sat on soft seats in the library, read and took notes, only returning to Pantychelyn hostel in time for dinner. After dinner, he sat quietly in his room and read some more, taking breaks to make himself coffee with the communal kettle, and roll himself slim Sun Valley cigarettes. No-one knocked at the door of his room, and he was happy about that. He was at university to acquire knowledge, after all. Company, conversation, even the Overseas Students' Society, were just incidental to the real point, weren't they? Anyway, he had wounds which required a good licking.

Enoch Mohammed was nowhere to be seen, having gone away to collect his things – and, most importantly, his Mercedes Benz. Benson hardly missed him. It had been a difficult week, steering a course through the town which avoided both the Greek department and the main street.

Almost his only social act of the week had occurred

in the Maypole where he had bumped into Mrs Jones, the British Council lady. Benson had been wondering whether or not he could afford to buy a jar of Marmite when Mrs Jones came up behind him and reached across for a jar of Chivers Olde English marmalade, saying 'Excuse me, young man' as she did so. She did not recognize him even when he asked her how she was. Then he pointed her towards a tin of Mamade and said that she could make her own marmalade at home much more cheaply. His mum always had, he said, and it was as good as Chivers, probably better in fact. Mrs Jones said that she didn't have the time.

Benson could tell that Mrs Jones was trying to remember where she had seen him before. They had not met since the meeting of the overseas students at the beginning of term. He introduced himself and Mrs Jones asked him if he would like to have a cup of tea with her.

'I hear that you are taking your post very seriously,' she said offering him a cake at the posh hotel on the prom she had taken him to.

'I enjoy it,' he told her.

'That's good. Any problems?'

Benson munched a custard slice and, while emptying his mouth, tried to think of problems. 'Enoch Mohammed doesn't have anywhere to live,' he said. 'He's not here at the moment, but when he comes back he's going to have to sleep on the floor in Pantychelyn hostel.'

'That's terrible. I didn't know that. I wonder how that happened?' asked Mrs Jones.

She promised that she would see what she could do for Enoch Mohammed, and offered Benson the top half of her custard slice because she said she did not like the icing.

'Are you sure?'

'Perfectly.'

Benson bit into the flaky pastry topped with pink

125

icing. Fancy not liking the icing! He wanted to sup some tea through the sweet mixture in his mouth, but thought that it might offend Mrs Jones's sensibilities, and refrained.

'Are you working hard?' she asked him, looking at her watch and gathering her handbag and gloves together.

Benson said he was. He walked Mrs Jones to her car. She told him that she would not forget about Enoch Mohammed's problem and thanked him for bringing the matter to her attention.

He waved until the car was out of sight. Then he returned to the library, his mouth full of sweetness.

By Friday evening Benson was feeling that he had turned into a complete intellectual. *The Republic* had been finished and, as far as he could see, mastered. He now understood all there was to understand about *The Crucible* and its relationship to McCarthyism. *Who's Afraid of Virginia Woolf?* was really about Existentialism and Existentialism was about Sartre. Well, he knew about Sartre, didn't he? Sartre kept saying that Benson had to confront reality and, having confronted it, leap into the dark. But he felt that he had leapt into the dark of Dr Leptos's bed rather too readily. How had that happened? It had happened, he decided at last, because he had not first given the matter enough consideration. Existentialism insisted on careful thought before actions were embarked upon. You sat over endless cups of coffee in a Paris café, listened to Juliette Greco and thought the matter through. He should have spent far longer meditating on the implications of his action. All those children's wellingtons in the hall; Victoria in Ludlow; Dr Leptos's first wife remarried to a philosopher. It all screamed WRONG! at him. Devil's Bridge was well named, he decided. The story of the bridge, told to him by Dr Leptos was also just right. A myth, perhaps, but one that fitted perfectly.

Dr Leptos had intimidated him, got him drunk, robbed him of the requisite time. That was mean of him. He couldn't help it if he was young, attractive and vulnerable, could he? During the week he looked at himself in the mirror a lot. His lips suck forth my soul! he told himself. He also told the youth in front of him that he was rudderless. Bertrand Russell was right. Religion was a poor basis for morality because when the religion was dropped the morality followed and people were left with no sure footing. Yes, he was a fragile bark floating about without direction. Any old wave of passion could flood his little leaky vessel and send him down into the depths of depravity. True, he had a tendency to knee-jerk his Catholic morality all the time. But then the other voice, the cynical voice – always Clitherow's, never his own – came back to say: *You don't believe in that any more*! or to criticize him for being woolly.

On Friday night Benson sat reading in his room, hearing the students leaving for the pubs of Aberystwyth. They sounded carefree enough. They would return around eleven – those who were not otherwise occupied in one of the girls' hostels – and noisily wander off to one another's rooms for more drink, coffee and talk. Benson looked at the door. Perhaps he should go with them. Perhaps it was what he needed, to get drunk and be surrounded by good fellowship. They might accept him. He hadn't tried. He felt that his difference was somehow visible, but that was only his opinion. It was not particularly a priori. He should not take too seriously what Meryl had said. But then he thought of the word HOMO scratched on his door. No, there was no fellowship to be had in the pubs of Aberystwyth. British People could spot him a mile off. His overseas students did not seem to notice.

As it was, the only person he had spoken to that day was Ianto, and that conversation had further confused him. Ianto had offered to walk with him up the hill

127

back to Pantychelyn. Benson had been going to say that he wanted to take the bus, but decided to walk with Ianto instead. He had to get back to walking at some point.

'What are you doing tonight, Martin?' Ianto asked him.

'Work. I've still got a lot of catching up to do. What about you? Are you going out with Janet?'

'No. We're going up to North Wales.'

'Why?'

'Can't bloody tell you.'

'Suit yourself.'

But Ianto obviously wanted to tell him. After a pause he said: 'Did you know I was a Welsh Nationalist?'

'Yes. What of it?'

'Well that's why I'm bloody going to North Wales.'

Benson nodded without enthusiasm. Nationalism was something of which he disapproved. He wanted a world without borders, full of happy, coffee-coloured people. If the people of the British Isles couldn't manage to get on together, then what chance was there for the other, less happy, tribes?

'So what has your trip to North Wales got to do with Welsh Nationalism?' Benson asked.

'Plenty. We're going to take direct political bloody action.'

'Are you?' Benson yawned ostentatiously.

'Yes, we're going to turn round the bloody signposts so that they face in the opposite direction.'

Benson looked at Ianto uncomprehendingly.

'They're not in Welsh, you see,' Ianto added, by way of explanation.

'But you don't speak Welsh!'

'I'm bloody learning, aren't I?' replied Ianto defensively.

Benson cheered up no end at the prospect of having someone else's moral dilemma to deal with. 'But what's the point of turning round the signposts?'

'It's bloody obvious, isn't it? So people get lost. We did a trial run last weekend. Just a simple operation, mind. We turned the sign to Borth round so that it faced towards Machynlleth. If you stand on a chair and push the top of the sign hard, it's bloody easy to turn the pole.'

'And you're going to do that in North Wales this weekend?' asked Benson rhetorically.

'That's right.'

'But what if some poor woman about to give birth takes the wrong turn and instead of arriving at Bangor Hospital comes to Llanberis?'

'Well, it's her hard bloody luck, isn't it?' said Ianto unkindly.

'I would not have expected that of you, Ianto,' replied Benson, though in truth he had never really known quite what he should expect from Ianto. 'I wonder if you have really gone into the moral implications of your actions thoroughly enough. It is incumbent upon you so to do. You know that, don't you? Have you really considered all the ramifications of this plot?'

'We had a bloody meeting about it . . .'

'Well, I suppose that is better than nothing.' Benson had completely forgotten the pain in his bottom as he engaged in his ad hoc Socratic dialogue with Ianto. 'But is "a meeting" enough? Did you, for example, consider the universal implications of your proposed action?'

'How do you mean?' asked Ianto.

'What I mean is that perhaps you should consider what would happen if everyone turned signposts round in the opposite direction? I think that is a good yardstick by which to measure your morality. It is Kant's Categorical Imperative basically. There may be little upset if a couple of Welsh Nationalists turn round a few notices, but what if everyone did it?'

Ianto was silent for a moment, then he said: 'Almost

everyone has spent a bloody weekend in Devil's Bridge with Dr Leptos.'

Benson wondered if he had heard correctly. He had a sudden spasm of pain and felt the need to stop pounding up the hill.

'What did you say, Ianto? And could you slow down a bit please? We don't all have legs like yours.'

'Not important. It's just that people in bloody glasshouses . . .'

'Repeat what you said before,' demanded Benson, stopping in the middle of the pavement.

'Well, a couple of fellows from the orchestra saw you in the pub in Devil's Bridge with Dr Leptos last Friday.'

'So?'

'So he's bloody famous in Aberystwyth.'

'Famous for what, may I ask?'

Ianto closed up then, having forgotten the utterance of Benson which had caused him to produce his dagger-twisting riposte.

'Famous for what, Ianto?' Benson repeated.

'I don't like to say,' said Ianto sulkily.

'Force yourself!'

'Well, he's always doing it . . . I mean asking students to go with him for the weekend. Then, when they do, he . . . well you know . . .'

'How do you expect me to know?'

'Well, you've been. He did, didn't he?'

Benson looked hard at Ianto and then started walking at a fast pace away from him, up the hill. Ianto followed.

'Well, didn't he? I mean, didn't he try? He always bloody tries. He tried with that fat chap, Brian, the one with the bloody birthmark. He's famous for it. Brian had to run away, didn't he? Had to hitch all the way from Devil's Bridge to Aber in the middle of the night! It gave him a real bloody turn. He's not been the same since.'

Benson pretended to take no notice of Ianto. He was

in great pain. All this untoward exertion was upsetting the physical healing process. Mentally, he felt, he was beyond repair. How could Dr Leptos have seen anything in Brian? He must be a very sick man indeed! A very devil!

'Silence signifies assent,' Ianto called, unexpectedly legalistic, further twisting the dagger in Benson's bowels.

Benson felt he had to extricate himself from this bind. He screwed up all his courage, turned on Ianto and said quietly, 'Yes, he did, if you want the truth.'

That silenced Ianto. He stopped on the pavement, and Benson found himself walking away from him, backwards, facing the dusk sea in the distance and the twinkling lights of the town – the town he knew he was definitely the talk of. Would the news have reached his overseas students? Would they refuse to allow him into their flats to enquire about prejudiced landladies? Had his action of the past weekend destroyed any chance he might have had to be of assistance as Vice-President of the Overseas Students' Society? Would people start banging at his door at the hostel shouting 'Homo'? Would they bash him up?

But Ianto was not silent for long. 'So there you are then, isn't it?'

Benson, knowing exactly what Ianto meant, said that he did not have the slightest idea what Ianto meant.

'Well, I mean, there you are, a bloody homosexual. What if everyone did it? You think it is all right for you, but what if the whole world took it up?'

'Well, there's very little likelihood of that, isn't there?' responded Benson, who felt that he had good reason to know.

'Yes, but that isn't the point. You were saying that if something is wrong for all it is wrong for one. Everyone in the world isn't going to turn bloody signposts round!'

Benson searched around frantically for a hole in

Ianto's argument. To gain time, he said: 'It's just not the same thing.'

'Oh? Tell me how it's different?'

Benson started his reply without the vaguest notion of how it was going to end. 'Well ... er ... first ... turning signposts back to front is agreed to be anti-social and illegal ... er ... and—'

'Just like homosexuality.'

'Well, homosexuality is illegal in this benighted land, but I would dispute that it is anti-social. If you ask me, in the present state of the world, with lots of people camped out on rubbish dumps outside Lima, and famines in India, society ought to be paying homosexuals a weekly stipend at the post-office for not having children. Ergo:' he added, using a word he had picked up from Polonius, but only got round to looking up after a History of Philosophy lecture the day before, 'homosexuality is not anti-social in the way that turning signs round is anti-social.'

'But Dr Leptos is married with kids!' said Ianto.

There was no answer to that, and Benson knew it. He decided to muddy the waters: 'Well, you can talk! What would Janet's mum and dad think if they knew that she stays in your room all night!'

'That's different. It's natural.'

'Well, homosexuality is natural ... to me.' Benson rapped back, suddenly picturing himself in a most unnatural position on Dr Leptos's bed, crying into the pillow, being unceremoniously rubbed raw.

Both walked silently on up the hill for a while, trying to see how the argument had found its way from turning signposts the wrong way round to the natural-ness of Benson's proclivities.

They arrived at the hostel. As Benson was unlocking his door, he looked hard at Ianto and said, 'However, I think you should think very carefully before you embark on this course of action.'

Then he disappeared into his room and shut the door.

Yes, you had to think hard. The trouble was that the more you thought the more complicated everything became. Appearances were deceptive. He saw Meryl's black eye wink.

Benson opened Sweet's *Anglo-Saxon Primer* and tried to learn all the different ways to say 'this' in Anglo-Saxon. It was strange to think that such an ignorant group of people as his forebears should have so many ways of saying 'this'. The poor things hadn't had the chances he had to learn and make sense of the world. They were dependent on the priests to tell them what to think. Anything that contradicted the priests' view of the world was suppressed. In those days you couldn't put your hand up and say: Hang on a minute. They'd have come down on you like a ton of Greek lecturers, hanged you in a minute. Still, at least the Anglo-Saxons knew where they stood. Life might have been nasty, brutish and short, but he could not imagine an Anglo-Saxon having the sort of conversation with Ianto that he had just had. Was that good or bad? Dr Griffiths said that progress was a myth, but then Dr Griffiths said a lot of strange things. He felt sure that progress was a good thing. It was just that it was so confusing. Anyway, what was Dr Griffiths doing in the Philosophy department filling everyone's head with conflicting philosophies of life? Shouldn't he be testing the catechism like nasty old Brother Wood? Of course, there was no money in that. Dr Leptos had said that people over twenty-five were dishonest. That was probably the truest thing he had said all that weekend. What was he doing now? Probably spooning on the same bed with Victoria and telling her she was the only one for him. Until her next trip to Ludlow. Dr Griffiths, he decided, was probably a phony. Much more likely to be a phony than Bob Dylan. Bob Dylan was as confused as Benson was. That was consoling. Bob Dylan would never stop searching, would never accept any tired old catechism. But Bob Dylan's records cost 32/6 – and were probably going to go up to 37/6. He made money out of his confusion, didn't he? And look at the Rolling Stones! All over the country girls were leaving home, going to London and coming to bad ends – encouraged by the songs of those so-called heroes! Was that good?

He had tired himself out with his wonderings as he repeated the rude-sounding words the Anglo-Saxons had used for 'this'.

Daydreaming, Benson imagined himself at the slave market in Rome. All his words for 'this' had not saved him from being brought manacled and in chains to the Eternal City. It was not nice being sold into slavery, especially as he was a good Catholic just like the Romans. Still, here he was, and he had better just make the best of it. Perhaps somebody nice like Marcellus from *The Robe* would buy him and be nicer to him than Dr Leptos had been.

Just then the Pope came along the street and came up to Benson. He was a saintly-looking man who gave his name as Gregory. He looked Benson up and down for a long moment, pinched him gently in soft spots once or twice, and then asked the slave-driver where Benson was from.

'He is an Angle, from Angleland – far away to the north, your Holiness!'

Pope Gregory smiled a quiet beatific smile at Benson and said: 'Not Angles, but angels!'

Benson's reverie over Sweet's *Anglo-Saxon Primer* had turned into a dream. He awoke with saliva all over the page, something which upset him rather because it would lower the price of the book when the time came to sell it to the Union – a time he hoped would be not far away. He got up and rubbed the book on his towel, then looked at his bleary face in the mirror: not Angles but angels. He pulled a face. A pity Enoch Mohammed had not had that thought when he had first clapped eyes on Benson. If Pope Gregory could see it, why couldn't Enoch Mohammed?

Benson was halfway through urinating in the sink when there was a loud knock on the door. Quickly, he pushed himself back into his trousers, the sudden cutting-off of the flow giving him a pain.

'Er . . . come in!' he called.

The door opened and Laurence Clitherow was standing in the open doorway. He was holding a grip-bag in his hand. On his back was the army-surplus rucksack he had used for school, with: BEYOND YOUR COMMAND inked in blue biro on the flap.

'Laurence!' Benson cried, and he ushered him into his room, relieving him of the rucksack. 'What a surprise! I thought you'd forgotten me! How did you get here?'

'Hitched,' replied Clitherow, sitting down on the bed with a long sigh.

'Hitched all the way from Oxford? That must have taken ages.'

'Six hours.'

'Gosh! Your hair's longer than it was, Laurence! Why haven't you written to me? I've written to you three times without getting a thing back. I've been worried about you.'

Clitherow keeled over on the bed, as if he had been shot.

'It's a long story, Martin. I'm sorry. A whole new scene. You don't have a coffee, do you?'

'Of course I do! I've got Guinness too. I must have known you were coming!'

Benson uncapped the bottle of Guinness and handed it across to Clitherow.

'Now I'll go and get you a coffee. Won't be a mo.'

Clitherow held up the black bottle from his recumbent position on Benson's bed. He toasted Benson with it. Benson smiled back at Clitherow and made for the door.

'Back in a mo!' he repeated.

Benson trotted down the hall to the small room where the kettle was kept, chained to the draining-board next to the sink. He filled it with water, searched around for his mugs and coffee in the cupboard and set about making a good, strong cup for Clitherow. He smiled as he did the task. He thought of his best friend lying on the bed in his room. They would drink many cups of coffee and talk and talk. He wished, though, that Clitherow had given him some notice of his visit. He did not have anything for him to eat. He must be famished.

Benson returned to his room with the coffees. He opened the door. Clitherow was lying where Benson had left him, but the room was full of smoke that floated in great undulating waves in the light of the desk lamp, and a sweet smell filled the air.

'Here's your coffee, Laurence. What are you smoking? It smells very strange.'

'Marijuana, Martin. I don't suppose you get it here.'

'It isn't, is it?' asked Benson.

Clitherow was inhaling when Benson spoke. He burst out laughing, laughing rather more than Benson thought his remark justified. A cloud of smoke was exhaled over Benson, who was suddenly worried that the smell might leak out of the room.

'You're going to have to try it, Martin,' said Clitherow.

'I'm not sure I fancy it very much, thank you very much all the same.'

'"I'm not sure I fancy it,"' Clitherow mimicked Benson. 'You're just the same, Martin! You don't change. "I'm not sure I fancy it very much!" That's typical Benson. Yes, distinctly Bensonesque!' He held out the untidy, thick joint towards Benson, 'Come on, have a drag! It's good stuff! Moroccan!'

'I've got my coffee, thanks.'

'Oh, come *on*, Martin! So bloody bourgeois! God,

you wouldn't last at Oxford two minutes! You'd be a laughing-stock!'

'Well, I think it's a bit mean of you to come here and straight away start getting high. Between my leaving the room and coming back you've become a stranger! If it's bourgeois to want to chat to you normally after all this time then I am bloody bourgeois. Anyway, I've never taken marijuana before. I've been bloody worried about you, Laurence. I can't say that what you are doing now is making me feel any easier.'

Clitherow had covered his eyes. 'Oh God, Martin, stop it will you? I just can't take this in. Turn off that desk lamp, would you? It's hurting my eyes. You know, you've really got to have a few puffs of this joint with me. You don't need to take much. I don't take it all the time, honestly. I've had a hard day and I wanted to relax. But you must join me. Don't take much. It's not hard stuff. When you are on my wavelength then I can talk to you. Come on, Martin!'

'Where did you get that American accent?' asked Benson accusingly.

'I haven't got an American accent.'

'Yes, you have.'

Once again Clitherow covered his eyes and said 'God'. He wrinkled his face and pulled himself up on the bed, taking the mug of coffee that Benson held out.

'Thanks.'

'You must be hungry. Are you? I could get us some fish and chips. It won't take long.'

'No fish and chips.'

'But did you eat anything on the way?'

'I had a sandwich and a Crunchie in Hereford.'

'You still like Crunchies, then? It's a pity you couldn't stick to Crunchies!'

Clitherow started to laugh again and flopped back down on the bed. Benson rescued his mug of coffee from him before he could spill it.

'Come and lie here next to me, Martin, but before

137

you do, lock the door and make that desk lamp shine somewhere else. It's right in my eyes.'

'Oh, all right.'

A minute later they were lying beside one another on the narrow bed.

'I've missed you,' Benson said.

'Are you ready to try some now?'

'I'm not sure.'

' "How beastly the bourgeois is!" Go on. Trust me.'

'All right,' sighed Benson.

Clitherow relit the joint and handed it to Benson, who dragged on it and inhaled.

'Not too much . . . go easy until you know how it makes you feel. I don't want you acting all weird on me. Well, maybe I should say "more weird than usual".' And he started to giggle.

'Thank you very much!'

'Don't mention it!'

The taste of the marijuana smoke was really quite nice, rather nicer than Sun Valley in fact. Benson inhaled gingerly. 'You know, Laurence, you've really got to do something about the way you're speaking. You sound like one of those blokes on Radio Caroline. I thought Oxford was supposed to make you go all posh.'

Clitherow giggled: 'Well, I'm becoming posh underneath. My brain is simply crammed with upper class notions. I'm doing PPE, for your information.'

Benson took another pull at the popping, sparking reefer. 'I know what PE is. It doesn't sound like you. But what's the other P stand for?'

'PPE', replied Clitherow archly, his accent suddenly very posh, 'is short for Politics, Philosophy and Economics.'

'I'm doing ASPE,' said Benson, after a pause to consider.

'What's that when it's at home? Is it what killed Cleopatra?'

'American Studies, Philosophy and English, but I don't enjoy English much.'

'How's the sex life?'

Benson handed the joint back to Clitherow, but did not say anything.

'Are you feeling any different?' Clitherow asked.

Benson shrugged. 'I was done last week,' he said.

' "How beastly the bourgeois is!" Are you feeling any different?' Clitherow repeated, while blowing on the end of the now-stumpy joint, making it glow red.

'How do you mean? And I do wish you wouldn't quote Lawrence at me, Laurence! I don't like Lawrence. If you ask me, he was a real phony. His head was full of sex. Otherwise, how could he write about it like he did? Also, he was pretty bourgeois. Meryl, a friend of mine, says he had a house in Hampstead where she comes from, and she's dead bourgeois. Anyway, I cannot see what's wrong with being bourgeois. I've tried, but I just can't see the problem.'

Clitherow started laughing in a manic way which was not like him, Benson thought. 'There you go again! You know, whenever I think of you in Oxford – more often than you probably think – I see you crinkling up your nose and asking "How do you mean?" and wittering on.'

Benson was not sure whether to be flattered or angry or confused enough to repeat the question in question. 'No, but you asked me if I felt any different, and I was wondering to what you were referring, whether I felt any different as a consequence of my having been done, or whether I felt any different because of the marijuana. With regards the former I feel very different. With regards the latter, no, it hasn't done a thing.'

Clitherow giggled: 'Well, I've not heard you speak in that sort of register before! That's different. Have you been listening to the Third Programme.'

What did that mean? Benson wondered, but he did

not say anything. The design in the Welsh handloom quilt had begun to intrigue him in a way that it never had before. He looked at it closely, amazed at how the green disappeared for inches at a time and then reappeared and melted into the yellow. How could anyone get the amount of concentration together to work out the design? Then the red dragon shapes that ran all the way down the quilt. How had that been achieved? It was amazing really. To think that Anglo-Saxons had been able to do things like that!

'Are you there?' asked Clitherow, banging – rather rudely, Benson thought – on Benson's head.

'Yes, thank you very much. Why didn't you write, Laurence?'

'I kept meaning to. Honestly. I intended to.'

'The road to hell is paved with . . .'

'Knickers!' exclaimed Clitherow, and he giggled again.

'Good intentions. You might have the politeness to allow me to finish. Or do I ask too much?' continued Benson, himself now aware of the fact that Clitherow found what he was saying funny, and enjoying his friend laughing at him just as he had laughed at him before on occasions past counting. He brought out his Brother Hooper impersonation to add to the mirth: 'You, Clitherow, I am surprised at! With a brain like yours, your father a doctor and a knight of St Columba, hanging around with that mediocrity Benson! How can you do it, son? You'll catch his fleas, boy, you'll catch his fleas!' He seized Clitherow's ear and twisted it: 'Tell me! What will you catch?' he demanded.

'His fleas, Brother!'

'Again!'

'His fucking fleas, Brother!'

They rolled about on the bed. Benson seized Clitherow's balls and squeezed. Clitherow yelped. 'Gerroff!'

'That's more like it!' Benson told him. 'You sounded

like yourself just then. A chip off the old block.'

Clitherow became suddenly very serious. He frowned and said quite sanely, in an accent that reminded Benson of Malcolm Muggeridge: 'Please, Martin, no clichés. If one speaks in clichés one's whole life becomes one.' Then back to his normal self, 'Look, Martin, I have not had an easy time at Oxford. I've had all sorts of things to sort out and to come to terms with.'

'Well I've had lots to get used to too! I wrote to you!'

'I've become a Marxist, by the way.'

'Have you? And Marxists don't write letters to the bourgeois, I suppose! Is that all?'

'No, it isn't all. I'm engaged to be married!'

It was now Benson's turn to laugh at Clitherow, and he seized it with alacrity: 'You, engaged! Well, that's bourgeois!'

'It is a bit, isn't it? She's the daughter of a Conservative MP as well.'

Clitherow spluttered with laughter again.

'Have you told your folks?' asked Benson, thinking of Mrs Clitherow's reaction, trying not to think of his own.

'No, I haven't. To tell you the truth, I'm not sure I've done the right thing, but Amanda – that's my fiancée – insisted that we make a commitment before she would sleep with me.'

'So you've slept with her?' asked Benson, suddenly knowing his reaction exactly, feeling peeved and betrayed, like a man who has had a foothold he had hoped was firm casually ripped from under him. Clitherow had definitely gone over to the opposition.

He had begun to feel a pang of desire for Clitherow, was covering his erection with his left hand and remembering their times together and the feeling of Clitherow's body against his, but when the news of Clitherow's heinous lapse with Amanda had been so casually dropped on him, it made him retreat.

'Yes, but I didn't like it much. I keep thinking I'll get to like it more. Amanda is trying to get me to make it public. She wants to take me to see her parents.' He seemed to be trying to put back the firm ground and inviting him to stand on it.

'And you don't want to?'

'Well, I . . . I . . . don't know.'

'She isn't pregnant, is she?' Benson asked, suddenly all practical, safe again.

'She says she's on the pill.'

'Well, it seems to me that you will just have to tell her you have made a mistake. It's far too early for you to even contemplate sacrificing your freedom. You're certainly a fast worker, aren't you? You've hardly been there a term and there you are up to your neck in dramas. Have you managed to find time to study?'

'Not really. Still, I think I'll be all right. No, it's Amanda that is the problem. You see, I really like her a lot. Sometimes I think I love her too, but when we make love it is all a bit bland somehow. I'm not really with her one hundred per cent.'

'Where are you?'

'I think of us a bit.'

'Do you?' asked Benson, immensely pleased, stamping around, testing the ground beneath him, finding it steady as a rock and glinting with diamonds.

'Yes.'

'Well, that's a surprise. It wasn't just a lark for you, something that would "do" until you found the real thing?'

'Why did you think that?'

Benson didn't like to say, but he knew why. For a start, Clitherow had always wanted Benson to do things for him, but never offered to do the same for Benson. He did not think he was being legalistic. But time after time the same thing had happened. Clitherow had kissed him and hugged him but had never been carried away enough to do anything

142

difficult. Benson had always been left to masturbate himself after he had satisfied Clitherow.

'Why do you think that?' Clitherow repeated.

'I don't like to say.'

'Go on!'

'No, I'd rather not.'

'I insist!'

'Well, if you really want to know, it was always me who had to do things to make you happy. You held back and never reciprocated. Now, it's not that I really minded. I loved doing what I did. It is part of me. It comes quite naturally. Still, the fact that you never took me into your mouth and sucked on me, showed me that you were not really . . . really . . . a homo. I mean, I could have been a woman.'

'No. Amanda won't do that!'

'Well, Amanda has a tailor-made part for making love. I don't. I have to make it up.'

'But you never asked! You kept covering yourself!'

'You should have insisted! If you were really a homo you would have done it naturally.'

'That's nonsense! How legalistic you are!'

'Let's talk about something else,' said Benson.

Clitherow, without giving Benson any warning, reached down and opened Benson's trousers. With difficulty he disentangled him from his underpants and pulled out his erect penis. He moved his head to a position where he was staring down at Benson on the bed. He looked at him until Benson had to blink and then moved himself down, taking Benson into his mouth, sucking on him hard.

Benson gasped. He wanted to ask Clitherow if he was absolutely sure he wanted to. He really didn't have to.

Clitherow swallowed Benson and withdrew, swallowed and withdrew. He sighed and pulled Benson's trousers down with his hands. Benson stopped worrying then and stroked Clitherow's hair,

143

telling him that he loved him. *They think it's love but it's only lust*! No, you're bloody well wrong, Benson thought. And then he stopped thinking.

Benson came, and Clitherow did not withdraw.

He was smiling as he returned to his position lying next to Benson.

'There you are,' he said.

'Thank you, Laurence. That was really lovely.'

'Think nothing of it.'

Then Benson had a cruel thought: perhaps it was the marijuana that had allowed Clitherow to do what he had just done? But he did not articulate the thought. Probably the marijuana had just released Clitherow's inhibitions and allowed him to behave naturally.

Benson got up and staggered over to his Philips. He groped around for *West Side Story* and put side one on the turntable. Then he searched for the last track. The pick-up plonked itself down exactly on the space between the tracks. 'There! I can do it when I don't think about it too much!' And Carol Lawrence was singing 'One Hand, One Heart'. Benson lay back down on the bed and forced Clitherow to listen, holding on to his hand.

'I'm famished!' said Clitherow, as soon as the song was finished.

'Oh, dear! Are you? I don't have anything. We can't go out as we are, can we?' Benson was wiping away the tears from his eyes.

'Why not?'

Benson shrugged and shambled about, pulling his trousers back on. He found himself wondering if he might be healed enough to let Clitherow do to him what Dr Leptos had done. Well, he wouldn't think about that now. It would be nice, though. It would cement things, help to unglue Clitherow from the wicked Amanda.

They walked past the National Library and down to

144

Llanbadarn. Clitherow did not enthuse over the National Library of Wales, which formed the pinnacle of Aberystwyth's architecture. Benson did not press the point, though he was very fond of the building and wished he could swallow its contents whole.

It was almost midnight. On the Llanbadarn road, they passed groups of students wandering home. One swaying man barged Benson as he passed and Benson said sorry. The student shouted something at them in Welsh.

'What a common bunch they are!' observed Clitherow.

'Yes,' replied Benson, though he was taken up with closely observing the way the streetlamps were reflected in the windows of the houses. He wished he could catch the effect on paper or film. The trees by the road, he noticed, were busily tossing off their leaves. It was sad in a way. Then he had a thought. Perhaps he should take photographs of the trees in autumn. Then take other photographs in winter, spring and summer. Each photograph would be identical, like the cover on his Golden Guinea recording of *The Four Seasons.* If he took the same scene at different seasons, he might be able to have postcards made and sell them. That would help to eke out his grant money. Why, it might also be a career. He could take photographs of people's houses throughout the year. Then, with the photographs mounted in a frame, he would go to the house and offer them to the householders. They would be bound to buy them. The important thing was that he caught all the seasonal changes in the houses he chose. They would have to be big, expensive houses with trees around them. Without trees there would be no change. But then he thought that he might be able to catch the houses at different times of day. Yes, if he carried through the idea he might be quite a rich student. As it was, he was worried about even buying two helpings of haddock and chips. But would such an

145

occupation be Business or Art? Such photographs might be taken seriously. It would be nice to be asked to photograph Buckingham Palace in sunshine and snow. His reputation would grow. He would journey to Lima and take moving pictures of the rubbish dumps which would stir the conscience of the rich countries and make people sell their spare possessions to help the poor. In the end he would get a Nobel Prize. What would he say when he accepted it? Well, he would definitely say something wise, something that people would write down on the fly leaf of their favourite books. But what? He didn't have to think about it yet. There would be plenty of time. First he would have to get a decent camera. His Brownie 127 had a crack in the back.

Then he found himself listening to the sound made by his feet wading through the dead leaves on the pavement. They crackled like waves breaking on a shore. Exactly like that. He kept listening.

'Listen to that!' he told Laurence.

'What?'

'The sound of the leaves. What does it remind you of?'

'High as a kite,' said Laurence.

'Think!'

'Crisps shaken in a bag?'

'No, it's much more wonderful than that. Listen. It *is* the sound I'm thinking of.'

'Waves breaking on a pebbly beach,' said Laurence.

Benson stopped and hugged Laurence. 'That's it! That's it!' and he started to skip along the pavement filling himself up with the sound, storing it away in his memory.

The fish and chip shop was about to close when Benson and Clitherow went inside. Both ordered haddock and chips but the man said he only had one piece of cod and one steak pie left. Benson asked Clitherow which he would prefer. Clitherow chose the cod. The man in the shop pushed some chips into the fat-fryer. He was almost bald but had pulled stray wisps of hair growing round his ears across the dome of his skull. As he pushed the chips around in the fat, the wisps came unstuck from the top of his head and flew off wildly, blown by the oily breeze rising from the fat. Clitherow looked at Benson and both started to giggle.

'Had a good night then?' asked the man amiably.

'Yes, thank you,' said Clitherow. Benson frowned at Clitherow because he was imitating the man's Welsh accent.

'Make the most of it. You're only young once. Just the once,' said the man.

'Don't worry, we will!'

Benson trod on Clitherow's shoe affectionately and pushed himself against him.

'Are you trying to get off with me, young man?' asked Clitherow archly.

Benson did not reply. He moved away, watching the reaction of the man frying up the chips. The man smiled at Benson, then he winked.

'You two friends, are you?' asked the man.

He must be one too! thought Benson. We're everywhere. Just a matter of looking, that's all!

'Yes,' said Clitherow.

'There's lovely,' said the man in his gentle Welsh voice.

Benson smiled at the man, wanting to ask him if he had a friend too, hoping that he would say yes. But then he looked again and saw the man looking at him and Clitherow, and looking sad. He gathered his wisps of hair together and smoothed them back across his head.

'There's lovely,' he repeated. Then he lowered his arm again. It hung at his side for a moment, dangling like a puppet whose string has broken.

'They look like super chips,' said Benson, trying to cheer up the man.

The man nodded without enthusiasm. 'The salt and vinegar's over there,' he said, still sad.

Clitherow had started to hum 'Desolation Row' and it was left to Benson to thank the man, pay and say good night to him.

They sat on a bench in front of the National Library and ate their chips.

'So what's your news?' Clitherow asked.

'Well, you've had most of it in my letters. But I've been violated by the head of the Greek department.'

'So you said. And you didn't like it?'

'I did at first but it just went on too long. And the man's married. I don't think I should have done it with him. I was just intimidated rather. It happened at Devil's Bridge.'

'Nonsense! Grist to the mill. Where's Devil's Bridge?'

'You probably passed it on your way here. It's on the Rheidol River. There's a waterfall there. I could hear it from the bedroom. There's a small bridge over the river, not much of a bridge. You wouldn't look twice at it normally. It's not hump-backed or anything. Just a roadway with railings. But the view down is wonderful. Frightening too. And there are three bridges, at least that's what Andy said.'

'Andy?'

'Dr Leptos. He pointed down and said that you could see three layers of bridges. The ugly modern bridge – nineteenth century apparently – and below it an arched bridge. Below that there was a stone bridge that monks had built, though the legend says that the Devil built it. Every time you cross the top bridge you are also crossing the other two layers.'

'Three in one and one in three,' said Clitherow.

'Yes, I suppose so.'

'What's the legend?' Clitherow asked, then he yawned mightily.

Benson told Clitherow the story Dr Leptos had told him.

'Well, it brings in the tourists, I suppose,' said Clitherow.

'Yes,' agreed Benson. 'I suppose the fact that it was probably built by monks is not particularly romantic. I expect the parish council got together at some point and asked one another how they could get tourists into the place.'

'Like Lourdes.'

'Do you think that about Lourdes?'

'Yes, it's obvious, isn't it?' said Clitherow. 'Look at all the tourists they've got as a result. The people of Lourdes looked around at other shrines and decided to get a slice of the cake.'

'But you can't deny that people have been cured at Lourdes.'

'Says who?'

'Say lots of doctors. I read about an atheist doctor who went to Lourdes and encountered so many miracles that he became a Catholic.'

'Propaganda. Are you still watching *The Magic Roundabout* by the way?' Clitherow asked.

'No, the television room is full of rough types. They have commercial television on all the time.'

Clitherow nodded. 'It sounds horrific. I watch it every night in Oxford. Everybody does.'

Benson nodded and ate his last chip. Clitherow still had lots left. Benson frowned at them, wanting them. He was still hungry.

'There's a chocolate machine at the bottom of the hill,' he said.

'So?' asked Clitherow, holding a bundle of chips over his mouth like a bunch of grapes, and then plunging them in.

'So I'm still famished.'

'That's the pot.'

'Is it?' Benson had forgotten about the marijuana. When he remembered he said: 'It didn't do anything for me.'

149

'It's doing a lot for you, Martin. It might be an idea for you to take it up on a daily basis. A great improvement. It makes an honest man of you.'

'I'm always honest!' Benson said, conveniently passing over scenes of dishonesty like layer upon layer of the bridge.

'You would never have told me what you told me in your room if you hadn't been high.'

That was true.

'You wouldn't have been so camp in the chip shop if you hadn't been high,' Clitherow continued.

'What does "camp" mean?' sighed Benson. 'All these new words. There isn't a day goes by without people bombarding me with new words! I wish people talked like they used to.'

'Well, I don't know much about that. It's all part of the educative process. But I would have thought that you of all people would know what "camp" meant!'

Benson lifted his eyebrows and blinked slowly.

'That's camp!' exclaimed Clitherow, throwing his chip paper on to the grass.

'You shouldn't do that, Laurence!' And Benson stood up and picked up the paper, putting it in his pocket.

'That's camp too! You're a walking definition of camp!'

'I'm sorry, I just don't understand.'

'Of course, Mick Jagger is camp as well, but in a different way.'

'Yes, but what does it mean?'

'Let's go and find that chocolate machine,' said Clitherow. He put his arm round Benson's shoulder, and together they walked back down the hill towards the sleeping town.

7

Despite Benson's pleadings, Clitherow left Aberystwyth late on Sunday morning. He had to go to a concert with Amanda in Oxford that evening, he said. Benson told him to ring Amanda and cancel it, even offering to pay for the call. But Clitherow refused. Benson, feeling a bit let down, stood beside him on the hill, on hand to wave until he was out of sight.

He still tended to get tearful over goodbyes. He spent much time by the side of the road trying to keep his upper lip stiff. This was supposed to do the trick and keep the tears at bay, but it was not working very well during the protracted leavetaking with Clitherow. One side of him was relieved whenever a car passed, not giving his friend a ride. But it also felt like an insult to his guest and reflected badly on the taste and discernment of the Sunday drivers. He aimed looks of derision after the mean cars, even going so far as to give his famous double V-sign to the single occupant of a Rolls Royce.

'Now, when you get back to Oxford, I want you to do two things, Laurence. Laurence? Are you listening to me?' Clitherow was looking forlornly back down the hill for the advent of promising transport while whistling 'It's Alright Ma (I'm Only Bleeding)' between his teeth. He nodded. 'I want you to start working hard, and I want you to tell Amanda how things stand.'

'How's that?'

'How do you mean?'

'How do things stand?'

'Well, you tell me. I thought we had agreed that it is much too early for you to get engaged. What if you decided after marriage that you were a complete homo

151

after all? Think how hurt Amanda would be! Also, I just can't imagine what your mum and dad would say. No, you'd better make up your mind while you're still free, otherwise you're liable to end up like Dr Leptos.'

'Yes, yes, I know,' replied Clitherow, a bit impatiently, Benson thought. He had put up the hood of his duffle coat as though he wanted not to see Benson. 'I think you're stopping me getting a lift, Martin. The drivers think they have to pick up two.' Then he glanced over at Benson's woeful look, the grotesquely stiff lip, the quivering chin, and added: 'And they might be a bit alarmed by the sight of you.'

So Benson said he would cross the road and sit on the verge. This would make it clear that he was not going to hitch with Clitherow while at the same time allowing him to be near enough to wave. He seized Clitherow's hitching hand with his right hand, punched him affectionately in the duffle coat with his left and ran across the road. He scarcely had time to sit himself down on the opposite verge before a lorry pulled up, blocking Clitherow from view. Benson stood up, trying to see his friend. The lorry started up and the driver glanced at Benson, wondering what was so fascinating about his cab. The lorry slowly picked up speed, but he could not make out Clitherow at all. He waved once and a couple of tears came to his eyes, dropped down his cheek, and on to his university scarf. Fyfe Robertson ordered the cameras to close in on the tears on Benson's newly-sanctified scarf and told the viewers that university scarves soaked up a lot of different experiences. Benson stared miserably into the camera lens. In times to come he would be able to look at the scarf and remember his university life in its stains. He had already used it to blot his pen on.

The lorry disappeared and depression fell over him, caught him like a heavy wet net. There was something incomplete. Something had not been finished. When you said goodbye to people you waved until they had disappeared. That was the rule. The weekend with Clitherow had shown him just how lacking he was in real friends, soulmates, at Aberystwyth. They were all pale imitations of Clitherow, to whom he could say anything, anything at all.

Benson turned and started walking the few yards back down the hill to the gate of the hostel. Just as he was about to turn into the entrance, a white Mercedes Benz passed, going up the hill. Benson stared after it. He was sure the driver was Enoch Mohammed. He lifted his arm to wave, wondering if Enoch Mohammed would come to his room to stay the night. But the car did not slow down. What would Meryl say? Would she be pleased?

The passing Mercedes distracted Benson from his gloomy meditations. Lunch would be in full swing and he made straight for the dining-room. Sunday was a slack day in the hostel, many of the students having gone out for the day. But Simeon was there, eating his meat and vegetables by himself on the overseas students' table.

'Where have you been?' asked Simeon. 'I haven't seen you for a long time. Are you avoiding me?'

'How could you think that, Simeon!' Benson replied, dimly aware that he was treading on eggshells. Overseas students must see prejudice everywhere, even where it did not exist; even, perhaps, where quite contrary emotions existed.

'I think I've just seen Enoch Mohammed,' said Benson.

Simeon said nothing.

'He was driving a white Mercedes Benz up the hill.'

Still Simeon said nothing.

'He did mention that he was going to pick up his Mercedes. I wonder if he'll be staying with us again.'

'He won't be staying with me,' said Simeon darkly.

'You don't like Enoch Mohammed very much, do you Simeon?'

'He is a rapacious man,' replied Simeon.

'Yes, but I am sure he's very nice underneath. How's Angela?'

Simeon looked at Benson hard and with some hostility, Benson thought. Then he remembered that he knew how Angela was, no longer going out with Simeon. 'I'm sorry, Simeon. I'm a bit distracted at the moment. To tell you the truth I'd forgotten. Have you managed to find another girlfriend?'

'No.'

'Are you trying hard enough?'

'I go down to the Angel every night, but nobody will talk to me.'

Benson nodded. He was sure that it was true, but then Simeon was not the easiest person to talk to. Benson wondered if he should give Simeon some hints on how to carry on a basic conversation, a few ice-breaking topics. But then he thought that ice so thick as the types who frequented the Angel would not be at all amenable to Simeon's warm approaches. Drunken bigots just did not melt.

'Is there anything I can do?' he asked Simeon, without hope.

Simeon, a remote capital of Sadness, just shook his head and returned to his lunch.

Benson decided to think about Simeon later and turned his attention to thoughts of the weekend with Clitherow. He had not liked much that he had heard. Clitherow seemed to be hanging about with a bad crew in Oxford. They were all rich and feckless. They drank champagne in punts. They drove a Morris Minor with an open top down the Kings Road while drinking bitter from big tins, and took drugs. Amanda had the use of her father's flat in Victoria. The goings-on there seemed somewhat less than wholesome by Clitherow's accounts. For people doing PPE it seemed a bit of a falling below the ideal.

The trouble was that although the Clitherow family

had more money than the Bensons, they still would not be able to afford to subsidize Clitherow in the way which Oxford seemed to require. Clitherow said that he had already run out of his grant money and was living on an overdraft. And there were still six weeks of term to go. But perhaps Amanda would subsidize him from her cornucopia just as Benson had had to that weekend.

That returned his thoughts to his own situation. The weekend had swallowed up £6 17s 11d. Where had it gone? He would have to go very easy or he would be cashing naughty red cheques in a couple of weeks and dreading being hauled in to have an interview with the bank manager. Benson had communicated his fears to Clitherow, but Clitherow had just told him not to be bourgeois.

That afternoon Benson tried to study but could not concentrate. He kept slamming books shut and opening others, only to discard those after a few minutes of fruitless jittery reading. The trouble was the return to the single state after a couple of days of company. The trouble was also Sunday. Sunday was always miserable, especially after lunch. It had been the same at home. Once Billy Cotton and *Round the Horne* were over Sunday had nowhere to go but downhill into regions of grey gloom. It was irritating to find that this feeling had outlasted his schooldays and come with him to university. There was, after all, nothing to worry about here. Ralph Wynne wasn't going to strap him or humiliate him in front of everyone, was he?

Benson tried to sleep but could not manage it. He got up and mooned around the room. There was nothing, absolutely nothing, that he fancied doing. Perhaps, he thought, he should just sit down and wallow in existential gloom, confront ultimate despair. But maybe it wasn't real despair at all. Maybe he was irregular like the girl in the syrup of figs advertisement. Maybe he was hung-over from the marijuana. He decided that wallowing was not a good idea. He could not think of a better idea offhand, so jumped up and down on the spot for a few moments. Then he stopped and glared at himself in the mirror. I have nothing to be gloomy about! I am not on a Lima rubbish dump. He squeezed a blackhead. Clitherow was his friend and his Friend. Clitherow was going back to Oxford to break things off with Amanda. He had promised to write every week and to get down to serious study. Things couldn't be better there, could they? But still Benson was unhappy.

He decided to take a long walk. He put on his desert boots and his anorak. He put some Tabac on his cheeks and winced as it stung him. Outside the hostel he dithered about which way to go, up or down. He decided on down and walked a hundred yards, but then changed his mind and, cursing himself, walked up the hill instead. At the top of the hill he saw a sign saying Clarach and turned down a narrow lane with high hedgerows and few houses. His mood was lifting from a heavy depression to a sweet melancholy and he searched around in his mind for pieces of poetry to recite. He tried 'To be or not to be' but lost it after six lines. Then he tried Polonius's speech to Laertes, got as far as 'Neither a borrower nor a lender be' but found himself once again stumped.

He was not stumped for long and started whistling his way through the soundtrack of *West Side Story* as the last autumn leaves fell from the trees, and the crows in the stripped fields wheeled and cried woefully.

The road twisted down to the sea through woods. When he reached the coast he gave the petit bourgeois caravan sites a severe look, and turned south, climbing a track up to cliffs that would bring him back to Aberystwyth over Constitution Hill. The track rose steeply, penitentially. Benson had to stop himself offering up his coming sufferings for the Holy Souls. Then he thought: Why am I refusing to offer it up? It may do some good. You never know. He smiled at the truth of that. Meryl would say that 'you never know' was a cliché. But it was true! You never did. How could you tell the truth without clichés? If you spent all your time trying to avoid them, where would you end up? Being clever and shallow in the back of an open Morris Minor bound for nowhere, that's where. He resolved to startle Meryl with that argument. In the meantime he addressed the darkening, slate sky. 'I offer up this climb – which will cause me no end of travail – for anyone suffering in the world; Simeon, for instance.' He commenced his Via Dolorosa.

He climbed without stopping until he reached the crest of the track. It moved easily now along the clifftop. Ahead of him, partly obscured by the outcrop of Constitution Hill, he could make out the town of Aberystwyth. Some lights were already twinkling. The sight of them panicked him and he set off along the path speedily, thinking that it would not do to get caught out in the dark.

In no time at all he was descending the seaward side of Constitution Hill, the outcrop that stopped Aberystwyth dead in its tracks. To his right there was a rocky bay and he could see a man just above the water-line. He was sitting on the stones, his knees drawn up to his chin, his arms banding his legs. It was strange that a man should sit like that in the cold with night about to fall. But then Benson thought that that was just the sort of thing he himself might do. It buoyed him up momentarily. Perhaps he was not the only one who liked to sit between the sand and the foam and empty the endless ocean into the tiny pool of his head. There was a story there somewhere. A saint had been on a beach, and a child . . .

The man must have noticed that night was falling. It was growing cold. Benson, despite his exertions, was regretting not having put on his blue jumper before setting out.

He was now level with the man, who was about twenty-five yards away from him across the pebbly beach. But Benson did not stop, merely kept walking slowly down, past him towards the deserted promenade. Then, just as the path turned to take him out of sight of the beach, he saw that the man had stood up and was walking into the sea. He did not seem to be in any hurry, but took regular, slow steps through the breaking waves, holding his arms out to steady himself.

Benson looked around to see if there was anyone who could help him. The side of Constitution Hill was empty, as was the gloomy promenade ahead. He ran along the track, sliding dangerously on the slope, and then across the beach towards the man. The water had reached the man's neck and the swell took him off his feet, before replacing him on the bottom. Benson reached the shoreline and over the breaking waves could hear the man moaning, crying out. The cry was almost like the mew of a cat.

'Are you all right?' Benson shouted to the man. He was wearing a cloth cap. Strange, he thought. But he did not seem to hear Benson and it was obvious that he was not all right. As he watched, the man launched himself into the sea, gave himself to it, lying on his front, holding his head underwater.

'I say . . . er . . . you oughtn't . . .' shouted Benson. A wave covered his desert boots and shocked him with its cold. He took a couple of paces back, looking down at his soaked lower leg. Then he looked out towards the man and the light seemed to have changed, ebbed away from the earth in the split second since he had last looked. The man's body was prone in the water, his arms, only his arms and the white, spidery hands at the end of them, quivered and fisted and shivered.

Benson said a prayer and threw himself into the water. The freezing water took his clothes and filled them up, making him gasp with the pain of it, weighing him down. He swam out wildly to the man and seized him round the neck, pulling his head up out of the water. Then, grasping the man's clothes, he started swimming back towards the shore, while the man fought him and swore and kicked. He got hold of Benson with both arms and pushed him under.

'Stop it this minute!' But his cry made no difference to the man, and Benson let go of him and went down under the water with no breath inside him. He felt that he was drowning, but he was much too angry to drown. He pushed himself upwards and shouted at the man, who once again was trying to pull the ocean up over his head, moaning and mewing with frustration. Benson made a lunge, caught him by the scruff of the neck and started swimming towards the shore again. The man went limp then, which was just as well because Benson had been preparing himself to punch him in the mouth. But he continued to moan and, in the midst of his effort, Benson was already wondering what he was going to do after they finally got to the beach.

This was easier thought than achieved. An undertow kept them from reaching their depth and Benson was becoming tired, and convinced that he was not going to be able to keep up the struggle much longer. Then he touched the bottom and pushed himself on tip-boot up the pebbles until the next swell pulled him up in the water and out of touch with the bottom, but the next time he touched he had established leverage on the pebbles and was able to tug his heavy load further up. One more effort and he was lying with the man in the breaking waves – the darkness pulsing deeper – chilled to the bone.

Benson hauled the man across the pebbles, out of range of the waves. He no longer struggled, had gone completely limp and did not render Benson the least assistance. Benson lay him down on his front and started artificial respiration, thinking as he pressed and lifted, pressed and lifted, of the hours at the swimming pool preparing for his Bronze Medallion, a Bronze Medallion he had not stayed around St Bede's long enough to obtain. After a few minutes, the man said in a flat Welsh voice: 'You can stop that. I'm OK.'

'Well, that's good. Why did you have to go and do that?'

Perhaps the man shrugged an answer. Benson could not tell. Neither could he see the man's face when he slowly sat up.

'Christ, it's cold!' the man observed.

'We'd better get you back to Aber straight away. Come on, stand up,' said Benson in his district-nurse voice.

'You're a bugger,' said the man. 'I could have been dead by now.'

Benson felt greatly peeved to be given this piece of information, but said nothing. He pulled the man to his feet and aimed him back towards the track, across the pebbles.

'It took me hours to pluck up the courage to do it and then you come along,' said the man, his teeth chattering.

Still Benson said nothing. He could not think of a thing to say. His mind was completely taken up with the prospect of what to do when they reached the prom.

'I'll only do it some other time,' continued the man.

'No, you will not!'

'Why not?'

'It's a sin, that's why not!' said Benson automatically. He tried to change the subject. 'My name's Martin. What's yours?'

'Gareth.'

Benson thought there was something familiar about Gareth. Did he work at the hostel? Was he someone he had met in Aberystwyth?

'Christ, it's cold!' Gareth said again. 'I spent most of

the afternoon up there,' he pointed towards the rocks of Constitution Hill, 'but I just couldn't step off.'

'I should hope not indeed! Look, we must get somewhere warm.'

But, holding on to Gareth's jacket to bring him along with him, Benson's left foot got sandwiched between two large stones and he turned his ankle painfully.

Limping, Benson pushed his lost sheep across the beach towards the twinkling prom in the cold dark. Once Gareth stopped and would not proceed. He slapped Benson's hand off his jacket and looked back towards the sea, his teeth chattering. He started to cry quietly.

'Now look . . .' said Benson taking Gareth's sleeve again. Gareth twisted his arm out of Benson's grasp and started walking.

They reached the bar at the end of the prom which generations of Aberystwyth students kicked whenever they came to it, though Benson could not think for the life of him why, and had never once taken part in the ritual himself. Both were catatonic with cold and Benson wondered what he ought to do now. The women's hostel was nearby and he tried to think of someone he could contact there. Did Anthea from his Anglo-Saxon class have a room there, or was she in digs? He made for the door, encouraging Gareth to follow him. But Gareth held back, 'I'm not going in there! You'll tell everyone!'

Benson had not had it in mind to tell anyone. He had thought that his condition would speak for itself. He would not have minded in the least if someone realized that he was a hero. In fact, as they walked back, Benson had felt rather put out that there had been no witnesses to his act of bravery. It would have warmed him to receive some applause. But then he had thought that that would rob him of treasure in heaven. Then, 'What heaven?' he had asked of the blackness above the track.

'All right. What do you want to do?'

'You *know* what I want to do!' said the man.

'Well, you'll just have to think of something else! You can't do that!' rapped back Benson impatiently.

Benson looked into the man's face, now illuminated by the lights on the promenade. He was ancient – forty plus – pale, unhealthy-looking. He still had the feeling that he had seen the face before, but he could not think where.

'No, I mean apart from that. You can't do that. Don't you have any family?'

'None that I care about.'

'No wife?'

The man smirked.

'Well, you must at least have a home in Aberystwyth. I know you are from here because your face is familiar. What's your name?'

'I've already told you my name, Gareth.'

'Ah, yes. I forgot. Sorry.'

'Don't mention it. You just leave me here. I'll make my own way home.'

'No. I can't do that. You might try to do something silly again.'

'So you're going to hang about me like some fucking guardian angel all my life, are you?'

Benson did not think he was, but just said 'er . . .'

'So there you are then.'

'Look, where do you live?' asked Benson.

'Aberystwyth. About a mile away.'

'Look I tell you what I'll do: I'll go into the hostel and ask the porter to get us a taxi. Then I'll take you home.'

The man nodded: 'No police mind,' he said.

'No, of course not. What do you take me for?'

Benson strode boldly into the foyer of Alexandra hostel for women. A few women stopped to look at the apparition, but Benson – though proud – took no apparent notice of all the stares, went over to the porter's booth and asked him to call a taxi.

'It's a bit of an emergency,' Benson told him.

The porter could see that and stifling barbed comments about what wet Benson was doing to his nice parquet floor, telephoned for a taxi. He told Benson it would arrive in five minutes. Then he added, rather unkindly Benson thought, that he would prefer him to wait outside and stop dripping everywhere. He showed not the least curiosity about Benson's exploits. Benson was tempted to say: 'Do you realize that I have just saved somebody from drowning? I would have thought that a little civility might be in order! Parquet can easily be perked up. What about me?' But he saw all the jewels dropping off his heavenly crown. He pursed his lips and turned on his heel, making a strange, embarrassing squishing noise on the parquet.

Benson went outside to tell Gareth about the taxi. But Gareth had disappeared. Under the streetlight there was just a wet place on the pavement where they had stood, and some footprints leading towards the railings of the promenade. A cold wind was blowing off the sea, whose sound reached him like a sad walk through dead leaves.

Back at the hostel, Benson fetched a towel, soap and shampoo and made straight for the showers. There he stripped off his sopping-wet clothes and stood under the shower for fifteen minutes. At first it did not seem that the hot water would make any difference. His skin warmed up nicely, but the centre of him felt like a block of ice. And his feet were numb, his ankle throbbing, as though he had spent the night sleeping awkwardly.

In his head, however, Benson was livid. What had happened to Gareth? Had he wandered off on to the dark beach by the prom – the same stretch of beach where Benson had met Dr Leptos – and completed the job that Benson had interrupted? Maybe he had just slunk off home, thinking that Benson was going to turn him in to the police.

As it was Benson had told the taxi-driver to take him to the police station, not considering in his anxiety how long all the formalities were going to take, how much it was going to cost. The police took ages, made him a cup of tea while the taxi clicked outside. Finally, Benson went and told the taxi-driver to go, paying him with a sodden 10/- note, and not counting his change.

Half an hour later the police drove him back to Pantychelyn. They had given him a red blanket and the policeman sitting next to the driver had helped him put it round his shoulders and smiled. Neither did they ask for it back when they dropped him at the hostel. That was something, anyway. He would put it on his bed as a conversation piece that would easily outdo Meryl's Union Jack by a million miles.

He liked the police. It was not really proper to like them, but he had never suffered anything dreadful at their hands. Meryl would probably have screamed obscenities at them if they had tried putting a red blanket round her shoulders. But then Meryl was a veteran of anti-UDI-in-Rhodesia marches. And, of course, Meryl did not have any of her kith and kin in the police force.

He dried himself off and darted back to his room. Straight away he got into bed. He lay there for a while, but could not sleep. I might well die as a result of this, he thought. I wouldn't be in the least surprised if this chill just got worse and worse. Then, when I die, the whole story will be printed in *The Western Mail* and Aberystwyth University will realize – too late – what a hero they had in their midst. They might get Henry Moore to do a statue of me and put it on the prom. They'll have Benson Walks to show where all the significant acts of my student career have taken place. 'Here Benson saved a man from drowning. If you look carefully you will notice that the sand in this cove is a

164

different colour from that anywhere else on this coastline. Geologists cannot find any explanation for the perfect white colour of the sand, and swear that it was not like that before. And here is his room. Note the maps on the wall. Benson spent much of his free time ministering to overseas students. Yes, madam, there is a distinct perfume of roses. I notice it every time I come in . . .' His fame would spread. The Catholic hierarchy would send people to investigate his life to see if he were a candidate for beatification. Yes, a martyr, that's what he'd be! He died as a direct result of saving someone from death.

Greater love than this, viewers, no man hath than he who lays down his life for a friend. And poor, dear, departed Benson died for a stranger, viewers, a stranger! Surely he is more blessed than the most blessed! In the opinion of your humble reporter, Benson's action beats a Nobel Prize by a scotch mile! But, he mused, if the hierarchy sent investigators, they would also send a Devil's advocate. And the Devil's advocate would be bound to find out about Devil's Bridge. If Dr Leptos kept quiet, Ianto would spill the beans. On second thoughts, he decided, it might be better if he didn't die.

Don't be fooled, boys, don't be fooled! An automatic act has no virtue in it. Benson is praising himself for saving a man's life. What is that in the Lord's eyes? I'll tell you what it is, boys. Nothing. Unless the motives are pure, no act can have the aroma of virtue about it. Benson performed a good act by chance. The very worst of us can do that, boys. It may give the sinner a cup of tepid water in hell, boys. Nothing more. Nothing more.

He shook himself and returned his thoughts to Gareth, wondering where he had seen him before. Surely, he wouldn't be able to pluck up the courage to do it again, would he? He couldn't in one day twice bear the pain of the freezing sea? No, he would probably wander off home. Would he have a bath to soak in? Would there be someone there to ask questions? Who was he? The sound of the dinner queue outside, combined with his fruitless attempts to remember where he had seen Gareth before, finally got him sighing and getting up. He put on more clothes and joined the line, which, fortuitously, had come to an end exactly outside his door. The one good thing in an otherwise desperate day, he thought.

Benson saw Ianto coming out of the kitchen with a full tray as he was going in with an empty one. When he came out himself, he made for Ianto, though he was not sitting at the overseas students' table.

'What happened to you?' asked Ianto. 'Your face is all scratched.'

Benson told Ianto what had happened.

'You should have bloody left him to it,' said Ianto. 'He obviously wanted to go.'

'But suicide is wrong!' exclaimed Benson, thinking as he spoke of the eternal punishment that awaited suicides . . . then dismissing the idea. If there was no God, then there was no hell and what was wrong with suicide? Was there no God? If no God, no jewels in his crown either. He sighed inwardly. You couldn't win.

'I suppose you would have reached over and pulled the bloody hemlock out of the mouth of your precious Socrates, would you?' asked Ianto.

'That was different,' replied Benson, though he could not for the life of him work out just how it was different.

'How was it different?' asked Ianto.

'Er . . .' Inspiration flashed. 'Socrates didn't have any choice. They were going to execute him anyway.'

'Well, maybe your Gareth didn't have any choice either. Maybe he has cancer and was trying to save the bloody National Health all the trouble.'

Benson was silent. He had been expecting some

166

congratulation, though he felt bad for wanting congratulation. If Ianto were a reasonable sort of chap he
would be leaving his steaming dinner, banging a fork
on a glass to attract the assembled students' attention,
then telling the entire hostel what Benson had just
done. How ashamed the wicked student who had
scribbled HOMO on his door would be then! He'd
probably come up to Benson, get down on his knees
and ask for forgiveness: 'I forgive you right readily!' he
would reply magnanimously . . . and in the morning
the door would have AN HEROIC HOMO written on it. But
not a bit of it. Just criticism. It did not seem fair at all.
There was just no justice on this side of paradise.
But . . .

But then Benson recalled what Ianto had been doing
to fill his own weekend. That should serve to divert
matters satisfactorily.

'Turn around any good signs?' Benson asked.

'Not so loud!' whispered Ianto.

'Well, did you?'

'We managed a couple, but the main ones were set
into concrete. Anyway, the others were a bit of a
bloody let down. They kept wanting to find pubs and
get bloody drunk.'

'But there aren't any pubs open on a Sunday where
you've been!'

'Don't you believe it!'

'I think I've seen the man before.'

'Where?'

'If I knew that I wouldn't just think, would I?' replied
Benson.

'What are you doing tonight?'

'I'm going straight to bed with a book. I feel chilled
to the marrow, and I must say, Ianto, that your less-
than-enthusiastic attitude to my heroic action – I mean,
I could have been killed – is something of a disappointment to me.'

'Congratulations!' said Ianto sarcastically.

'Thank you very much,' replied Benson, picking up his tray with an arch flourish which caused the Duralex tumbler to spin and fall off, bouncing on to the floor of the dining-room. The room went hushed as the students looked at him accusingly. Benson picked up the tumbler, put the tray back on the table and walked out of the dining-room back to his room. The kitchen staff could collect the tray. That was what they were paid for after all.

Benson slept well and did not wake up with the chill he had half hoped would excuse him from hoofing it down into Aberystwyth for lectures. He had an American literature lecture to attend and took his place at the back of the lecture theatre. He did not particularly want to talk to anyone, and started reading *Invisible Man*.

The sound of rubbing PVC approaching should have warned him that Meryl had spotted him. She sat down on the next seat.

'Where have you been, Martin? I haven't seen you for ages. Have you been avoiding me?' She parked a huge plastic bag on the ledge in front of her.

'No, Meryl. All last week I was studying like mad. I'm still very behind, in fact,' replied Benson defensively.

'I was looking for you.'

'Well, you've found me. How's life?'

'Everything is absolutely fantastic apart from one thing.'

'What's that?'

'I'm late.'

'What for?'

'My period. Honestly, Martin, you are dense.'

'How late are you?'

'A week or so.'

'Well, that's nothing, is it?'

'I'm usually as regular as clockwork.'

168

'And . . . er . . . who's the father?' asked Benson, suddenly filled with forebodings.

But Meryl looked at Benson oddly. 'I said I was late, Martin. I did not say that I was pregnant.'

'Yes, but you're worried about it, aren't you?'

Meryl nodded, and quite suddenly a tear sprang from her left eye and landed on her black PVC coat.

Benson had not thought Meryl capable of tears. It upset him greatly and he did not have the least idea how to react. The young lecturer had come into the room and was standing looking out of the window at the sea, lighting his first Number 10.

He reached down and squeezed Meryl's knee. Meryl looked down at Benson's hand and another tear joined the first on her coat.

Day after day, our hero comforts and aids those in distress, viewers! said Fyfe Robertson.

'Don't worry, Meryl!' whispered Benson. 'I'm sure everything is going to be all right. We'll talk later. I've got news, by the way,' he added, hoping to distract Meryl from her problem, while revaluing his own currency upwards. 'I saved a man from drowning yesterday!'

' "Thou mettest with things dying, I with things new-born." Funny, isn't it?' said Meryl sadly.

'That's from *The Winter's Tale*, isn't it? Gosh, you are well-read, Meryl.'

The lecturer had stepped up to the lectern, was turning the pages of his notes and looking out at the assembled students, the cigarette held artistically between his teeth, frowning at the smoke rising into his eyes; a frown that also served to silence the assembled students.

'Edward Albee could be said to fit into the movement known as "The Theatre of Cruelty". We have seen how George and Martha, through a succession of brawls and mutual cruelty, strip away the façades, the pretences, from their relationship, until at the conclusion of the play, at what appears to be the darkest moment, the total humiliation they are both reduced to forces them into a position where neither has anywhere to go but up. Today I would like to discuss *The Zoo Story*, an earlier play by Albee, but one which states Albee's position most succinctly . . .'

Benson wrote 'The Theatre of Cruelty' at the top of the page in jagged italic writing. He then inserted a dagger into the T of 'The', aimed a revolver at the word 'Cruelty' from above, and underlined what he had written with a barbed-wire line. He made to show his artistic achievement to Meryl, but she was writing notes devoutly.

Benson set about imitating Meryl's good example. Beneath the title he wrote: 'Relationships are important.' Then he wrote: 'Albee makes Jerry try to form a relationship with a dog. One has to start somewhere.' After that he wrote: 'It's probably tension that is holding up your period, Meryl!' and showed it to her. Meryl nodded and returned to her note-taking. She was once again under the thrall of the American literature lecturer, was writing great screeds of notes. Benson continued trying to emulate her. He wrote: 'The death of Jerry on the bench – and the bench is made of wood – is surely a reference to the crucifixion. This imagery is emphasized by Jerry's forgiveness of Peter after the knifing. "Forgive them, Father, for they know not what they do!" Peter, unlike Jerry, is mired in ignorance. Even after the act of murder, he shouts: "What have I done?" Jerry, on the contrary, has attained wisdom, and has, perhaps, saved Peter.' Well, that was all very well, but it did strike Benson as a bit distasteful on the whole.

The hour passed slowly, though Meryl was writing away like mad. Benson had noticed this before about Meryl. She was single-minded at lectures, and even today, when by rights she should be as distracted as Benson was, she was scribbling away as if her life depended on it.

Benson wished he had read *The Zoo Story*. At the end of the lecture some students at the front were having a lively question and answer session with the lecturer. Meryl asked a question which the lecturer said showed great insight. Benson searched around furiously for one, but just could not think of a thing to ask.

Part of him felt that the lecturer before finishing should announce that he had something rather special to tell everyone. Did they know that one of their number was just like a hero in a good, old-fashioned play where everything ended happily? Did they not know that silent and modest Benson had saved a man from drowning without caring about his own safety or the condition of his desert boots?

But nothing of the sort happened. The lecturer left the room, lighting another Number 10 – his fourth – as he went. Well, he was obviously not trying to make his grant money last.

Benson and Meryl strolled up to the More Utopia for a coffee.

'He is dishy, though, isn't he?' said Meryl.

'Who?'

'Ralph. And I'm sure he wouldn't insist on one being a virgin.'

'I bet you he would!' replied Benson. 'These men don't mind sleeping with a girl who isn't a virgin, but they always want to marry one.'

Meryl gave Benson a dark look.

'Still,' he decided to be conciliatory to Meryl, 'if I were in the running, which I'm not of course, I would insist on not marrying a virgin. The idea of learning how to do it on your honeymoon doesn't sound very nice at all. There are risks in not marrying one, of course, but on the whole—'

Meryl interrupted: 'What risks, may I ask, Dr Spock?'

Benson did not get the reference, but was learning to

ignore anything he wasn't sure of. 'What I mean is that someone with experience will compare all the time. I think that is the origin of the insistence on virginity. It is rather prevalent throughout the world, you know. I mean, men don't want their wives to be thinking how much more potent her lovers had been compared to her husband.'

'I don't understand.'

'Well, I don't see how I can make it any simpler, Meryl,' said Benson, relishing Meryl's lostness. 'You of all people must know that men come in different sizes, small, medium and large. Wouldn't it be terrible to end up married to someone who was so small he could not make friction against the sides? What I am saying applies to pre-marital sex too. It is obviously essential that the couple know that they are compatible. I mean, imagine Myvanwy Roberts married to a massively-built man who just won't fit! What do they do then? All the wedding presents would have to go back.'

'Martin, I have long thought that you had some peculiar notions, but the ones you are now spewing out have to be the peculiarest. You can't imagine that women are as obsessed with anything as mundane as size. What about love, tenderness, kindness, meeting of minds and the rest?'

'Well, yes, I know these are important, but if things just won't fit together. Surely that's the *sine qua non*?'

'*Non*,' replied Meryl. 'Physicality has its place, but not high up on the pantheon of qualities that go to make a successful relationship.'

There was a sweet reasonableness in Meryl which was most untoward. Perhaps she really was pregnant. Perhaps hormones of tenderness were coursing through her body and making her motherly, even motherly towards Benson. But what Meryl said next banished that thought from his mind: 'Well, if I am pregnant, I'll just have to go and have an abortion.'

Benson was speechless.

'Buy me a Wagon Wheel, there's a pet,' Meryl said.

Benson stood up without protest and, his hand ferreting in his pocket for coins, made his way to the counter of the More Utopia.

In Ancient Greece, he knew, they had left unwanted children – girls usually – outside until they died. Lots of tribes practised abortion to this very day. The Russians and the Japanese did it all the time. But he would hate to think that Meryl would do it – assuming she was pregnant. Maybe it wasn't murder, but it would surely leave a permanent hole in the heart. He bought two Wagon Wheels and took them back to Meryl, noting with a frown that Wagon Wheels seemed to have got smaller since the last time he had bought one. The whole world was going mad. Did the manufacturers of Wagon Wheels not know that their honour lay in maintaining the quality and value for money of their product? Didn't they care? It was a smack in the face for the shopper to find himself holding a Wagon Wheel which was but a shadow of its former self. If he went into a shop and was treated badly, not given a smile and basic politeness in return for his custom, he would never go back to that shop again, would he? Well, it was the same with Wagon Wheels.

'They've got smaller since I last bought them!' Meryl was informed as Benson placed a Wagon Wheel in front of her.

'Everything's size with you,' replied Meryl. 'Is that why you wear such loose trousers, by the way?' she continued.

'How do you mean?'

'Well, most men around here have started wearing tight trousers which show everything they've got. According to your rather eccentric morality I'd have thought tight trousers would be positively virtuous. It would allow us females to size you up without committing ourselves too deeply. Myvanwy Roberts could see straight away if a chap was beyond her capacity and scuttle off to find something more mouse-like. But your pants don't give a thing away. Not a thing. You could be built like a bull or a beaver. Nobody would know. And that just isn't fair, is it?'

Benson kept looking round the More Utopia anxiously. Meryl's voice insisted on rising in decibels in direct proportion to the outrageousness of its content. It was as if she took great delight in making him squirm.

'Have you seen Enoch Mohammed since that night?'

'No,' replied Meryl tentatively.

'Was it true?'

'Was what true?'

'Your father's theory.'

'Martin, you are really disgusting!'

Benson felt that he was, a bit. It was just that he wanted to know. 'Well, I'm just interested from an anthropological point of view,' he lied. 'Is quiescent and tumescent about the same?'

Meryl looked at him hard. He felt that he had opened himself up to her more than was safe. He wondered about himself too. Why did he want to know? It was knowledge that nobody seemed to have any curiosity about. That must mean that it wasn't important. Well, maybe it wasn't, but he still wanted to know. If Meryl said that Enoch Mohammed was only average, would he be consoled or disappointed? If she said he was absolutely massive and had to employ a crane and a wheelbarrow to get himself to the bed, how would that make him feel?

'White trash in the South share your obsession, Martin. Whenever they lynch – and they lynch with frightful frequency – the pinnacle of their beastliness is to castrate the victim. Read Baldwin's *Going to Meet the Man*.'

'I'm only curious, Meryl!'

'Curiosity killed the cracker!' replied Meryl, deadly serious.

He did not know where to put himself. 'I'm sorry, Meryl. Let's talk about something else,' he said quietly.

Strangely, Meryl changed the subject without the least protest. 'So tell me about this man you saved.'

'I was walking back towards Aberystwyth from Clarach along the coast. There's a path and there was this man sitting on the sand just above the watermark. I didn't think anything of it . . .' And suddenly Benson saw Gareth sitting by the sea and he knew where he had seen him before.

'Yes, go on!'

'Well, I . . . Will you excuse me, Meryl? I've just realized something. I've got to go!'

'Well, suit yourself!' said Meryl. He smiled at her lamely, picked up his things and left the More Utopia, trotted down the main street, past the Midland bank where his fast-diminishing grant money was kept in a safe, and along the wide, blank street that led up to the hostel. He did not take the road up the hill, but went along the Llanbadarn Road instead. He looked at his Kienzle watch. It was still going, though the glass had a scratch on it as a result of yesterday's exploits. Only eleven thirty. It might not be open yet, he thought. Still, it might be.

Benson reached the shop next to the fish and chip shop. It was a tobacconist's and he looked through the window at the array of sweets in bottles. He read the labels: *Mint Crisps, Chocolate Limes, Lemonade Powder, Aniseed Balls, Cough Candy, Everton Mints, Nuttall's Mintoes, Sherbert Lemons, Chocolate Eclairs.* As he read each label and looked at the solid stacks of sweetness in each huge bottle, he was able to conjure up the taste and texture of each and every sweet. On a day like today, he thought, a bag of cough candy would go down nicely and keep any cold bugs at bay. Gingerly, he took a few paces past the window, until he was able to look into the window of the fish and chip shop. The long Formica counter was empty, no sign of the man. Only a neat row of soldier-like salt, pepper and vinegar bottles and a greasy advertisement for mid-Wales.

He went up to the door and saw the CLOSED sign. Then he read the opening times. There was still half an hour before the shop was due to open. His anxiety rose. If the shop was due to open in half an hour then the man should be getting everything set up: Please God, let him open up on time! Please! prayed Benson. He recalled himself but did not recall himself. Right now he needed God. Jean-Paul Sartre was behind him, laughing up his French sleeve. Bertrand Russell was frowning and shaking his wise, white head. But neither could help him now. Only God could. Please, God!

Benson returned to surveying the sweets in the shop next door. In the half hour before the fish and chip shop opened – and it would open, it must! – he would buy a quarter of cough candy and go up to the bench by the National Library where he had sat with Clitherow on Friday night. There he would eat the cough candy, study philosophy and bask in sweet poetic melancholy. He might recite a poem or two from *A Shropshire Lad*, and think about Clitherow on the bench on Friday night, but not on the bench on Monday lunchtime. After that he would return to see if the shop had opened. What would he do if it didn't? He would have to go and tell the police what he knew. But that wouldn't happen. He decided to bring in Mary and aimed a Hail Mary in her direction. He imagined his Hail Mary landing at her feet like a bag full of rubbish. His sins would cause a horrible stink to Our Lady's nostrils. Still, he thought, she must be used to that. All those bloated plutocrats in Rolls Royces aiming prayers at her; all those prostitutes on Lima rubbish dumps, all those unbelievers in a crisis. She

176

must be quite used to searching through the rubbish for the single rose of pleading.

He was about to walk into the sweet shop. His left boot was on the doorstep. He could see the woman in the shop putting aside her *Western Mail*, about to get up to serve him. He stepped back a pace. I will do without the cough candy to help my prayer have more effect! he thought. I will offer up my lack of cough candy for the intention of Gareth opening the fish and chip shop. Then he remembered his half-eaten Wagon Wheel back at the More Utopia, and added that to the bouquet zooming heavenwards. But then he had to ask for the Wagon Wheel back. Meryl would have been bound to eat it. She couldn't resist them.

The wind blew into Benson's face when he had seated himself on the bench. Everything except the grass in front of him was the colour of slate. He opened up his book: *The Essential Thoughts of One Hundred Great Philosophers* – a book which he felt sure would contain everything he needed to get him through his first year course – and started reading about Kant.

Benson could not understand Kant very well. The only really interesting thing about Kant was that he was really punctual, so punctual you could set a clock by him. His book condensed Kant into four dense pages, but they were not easy pages, and Benson finished the survey little wiser than he had begun. I am not clever enough for university! he thought. I should be welcoming customers at Marks & Spencer or helping old ladies across the road in my policeman's uniform. Maybe I should compere *Ready! Steady! Go!*, read the news or something easy like that. He had another go at the piece on Kant. 'The things we intuit are not in themselves what we intuit them as being, nor are their relations so constituted in themselves as they appear to us. As appearances they cannot exist in themselves, but only in us. What objects may be in themselves and apart from all this receptivity of our sensibility, remains completely unknown to us.' Benson made a face and aimed a blank look at grey Aberystwyth. Then he looked at his watch. Ten minutes to go. He read the piece again and thought he detected Plato's idea of appearances in it. The chap in the book said that Kant had been awoken from 'dogmatic slumber' by Hume, and Hume had said that Causality was *not necessarily* true, whatever Causality was. Did that mean that, if Benson went down and found that the fish and chip shop was open, that it was *not necessarily* open? If he saw Gareth happily frying chips, that Gareth was *not necessarily* frying chips? Did Dr Leptos's ex-wife have to listen to her new husband wondering what it all meant over breakfast? Did philosophy lecturers really *understand* all this? Surely not. But then how could they become philosophy lecturers if they didn't? If they didn't they should give it up and become trainee shop managers and fish and chip shop owners. He let the text go blurred, and then closed the book. He opened *Invisible Man* instead and read happily until ten past twelve.

He prayed his way down the hillside back to the Llanbadarn Road. He kept his eyes on the pavement, not wanting any advanced warning as to whether the fish and chip shop was open. He crossed the road, staring intently at the sweet shop next door. The cough candy beckoned and he thought that, but for his self-denial, some of those pieces would have been in his tummy by now. Finally, he repeated his approach to the fish and chip shop, gazing past the green-painted window frame into the interior of the shop.

Gareth was inside pushing potatoes through a chipping machine. The white snowballs went in. Gareth pulled a lever and the chips dropped through into a steel pan. He did not look miserable. He did not look happy either. He looked neutral, probably still hopelessly sunk in *dogmatic slumber*, Benson thought. Still, it was a relief to see him there at all.

Thanking God and Mary, Benson retreated to the sweet-shop window to think. Should he make himself known to Gareth or walk away quietly? He was more inclined to walk away. After all, it would be terribly embarrassing for Gareth to see him again, wouldn't it? And he had felt that Gareth must be a homo when he had served him and Clitherow on Friday night. If he was right, if Gareth really was a homo too, then he might expect Benson to comfort him physically. And Benson did not think Gareth was very attractive. Gareth made Dr Leptos seem like Sidney Poitier.

He started to walk away, back towards the town centre. But his conscience pricked him. He thought that appearances according to Kant and Hume could be deceptive; that, though Gareth appeared to be all right, he very well might not be. Yes, wasn't that what Kant was really saying? Appearances are deceptive, all is not as it seems. Who knows? Benson wondered if people had Hume and Kant to thank for that piece of folk wisdom. On the strength of it, grateful that he had managed to come up with an easy hook to hang Kant's heavy coat on, he turned around. He did not want to turn round and go back. Rather he wanted to return to the More Utopia and eat a toasted cheese and onion sandwich. But he knew how he would feel if he did that. He would be worried about Gareth. It was going to be untidy to return and confront Gareth. But confrontation and commitment were important, weren't they?

Benson, trying not to think about it, found himself entering the chip shop. He was relieved to see that it was empty.

'What can I do for you?' Gareth asked in his sing-song voice.

'A six of chips, please,' said Benson.

Gareth nodded, then glanced up at Benson. He looked a bit embarrassed, but only for a moment. He looked down again.

Benson smiled at Gareth: 'How are you doing?' he asked.

'Can't complain,' Gareth replied, lifting his arm to smooth back the errant wisps of hair. 'The chips won't take long. You're my first customer.'

'You make good chips. Do you remember I came in with my friend on Friday?'

'Yes, I remember,' said Gareth. 'You were a bit drunk as I recollect. Still, it's the ones who aren't drunk of a Friday that you notice. I thought you were a nice couple of lads.'

'Thanks.' Benson wanted to say more, wanted to ask Gareth what had happened to him the previous evening; how he had got home; how he was feeling. But Gareth did not seem to want to talk about it. Well, that was all right too. 'My friend, his name's Laurence, has gone back to Oxford now. I miss him. We went to school together.'

'There's lovely,' said Gareth, and he smiled.

'Have you got a friend?'

Gareth's smile did not fade, but the spirit of the smile died, and it just stayed stuck to his face like an autumn leaf to a winter tree.

'Not what you'd call a friend.'

'I get lonely too,' said Benson truthfully.

Gareth nodded. 'Salt and vinegar?'

'Yes, please. Lots of salt!'

Gareth's smile came alive again. He added the salt out of sight of Benson's gaze and wrapped up the chips in newspaper. He handed it across to Benson and Benson gave him his sixpence.

'Thank you,' said Gareth.

'I'll come and see you again soon,' said Benson. Then he added: 'Now I've found the best chips in Aber, I mean.'

Gareth nodded. 'Yes, come back any time, I'll be here.'

'That's good,' Benson waved and left the shop.

Benson thought it rather common to eat chips in the street, but he could not resist the hot parcel in his hand. He unwrapped the newspaper carefully. Lying on top of the largest six of chips that he had ever seen – like a gold bar on a cushion – was a huge, fresh fillet of fried haddock. The steam rose from the bubbly golden batter and Benson salivated at the sight. Then he smiled at the slate sky.

8

Benson finished dialling, held a shilling over the slot and breathed deeply. There were some clicks, then a ringing tone. He put the ball of his thumb against the shilling, ready to push. He imagined the telephone ringing in the hall at home. Dad would be standing up from the dinner table and making for the phone. He would be passing the grandfather clock now, stepping on the creaky board at the bottom of the stairs, perhaps passing his hand over the shiny wooden knob at the bottom of the banisters . . .

The telephone was picked up. A woman's voice gave the Bensons' telephone number and added 'good evening'. Benson pushed the shilling into the slot as the pips sounded urgently. He had time to think how disgusting it was to have to part with a shilling. Why, he remembered the time when telephone boxes took pennies, had button A and button B, which made a lovely clicking sound for free whenever you pressed it. Telephone boxes also had a button that could summon the fire brigade. He surveyed the grubby acoustic plasterboard covering of the Pantychelyn phone box and wondered if perhaps Dr Griffiths were right: there simply was no such thing as progress.

'Er . . . hello . . . er . . . it's Martin. How are you?'

'All the better for hearing from you, Martin. Your dad has been getting a bit worried about you,' replied Alice, Benson's stepmother.

'Didn't you get my letter?'

'Yes, Martin, but it was quite a while back. You mustn't let your dad think you're forgetting him.'

'Is he there please, er . . .?' Who was this *person*, he

wondered. What gave her the idea that she had the right to dictate to *him*?

'No, he isn't I'm afraid, Martin. He's gone off to a meeting at church. How are you?'

'Everything's all right. Is everything all right with you?'

'Yes, it is. We're looking forward to seeing you at Christmas. It's not long to go now. I've been finding out where the tree and all the decorations are kept.'

The idea of Dad's new wife searching through Mum's carefully packaged Christmas things irked him. What else was she sticking her nose into? Places where her nose did not belong, that was certain. Perhaps she was rifling his drawers, reading his diaries!

'It'll be lovely to see you. I hardly feel I know you at all, and I do want to know you, you know.'

'Er . . . yes,' replied Benson tentatively.

'We're both very busy at work. Rushed off our feet at the station. We've got a bit of news for you, but we'll get down to writing to you about it.'

'Can't you tell me now?'

'No, not really. It's not certain yet. Anyway, your dad should be here.'

'Should he?' Benson asked, feeling a remote guilt, hoping the news hadn't anything to do with him.

'Are you working hard, love?'

Benson did not like Dad's new wife calling him love, but he decided not to make an issue of it. The phone call was designed to calm everything down. He mustn't ruffle Alice's feathers again.

'Yes, I am. I've got exams at Christmas.'

'Well, I'm sure you'll do well. Your dad is very proud of you, you know.'

'Is he? Yes . . . er . . .'

'You still don't know what to call me, do you? Call me Alice for crying out loud!'

'Alice.'

'Now that didn't hurt, did it?'

'No,' replied Benson, though it had a bit.

'Nobody likes stepmothers, you know,' said Alice.

'Don't they?'

'No. Look at fairy tales. Stepmothers always had a bad time. We're thought of as a wicked bunch.'

'Look, er . . . Alice,' said Benson with difficulty, while reading Abergavenny 45423 on the acoustic plasterboard as he tried to say what was on his mind, what had been on his mind since the day it had happened, 'Alice, er . . .'

'Yes, Martin?'

'Well, I just want to say that it wasn't anything personal when I didn't take communion at your wedding. I don't take communion any more, you see. Don't tell Dad that, by the way. I really didn't mean to hurt you by it. I know that's what it must have looked like.'

'Well, it would have been nice to have taken communion like a family, and you didn't say anything beforehand.'

Benson could still see his father turning and looking at him kneeling alone in the front pew as the priest came down from the altar holding the ciborium of hosts before him. He had wanted to go and kneel beside him. Fear of sacrilege, and a lesser fear of being compromised in his lack-of-faith held him back. Dad had turned away, whispered something to Alice and prepared himself to receive the sacrament.

'Yes, I suppose so.'

'Still, let's put that behind us, shall we?'

The pips sounded.

'Yes, I've no more money!' lied Benson. 'We're going to be cut off. Love to Dad!'

'All right, son. Bye for now!'

'Bye!'

Benson put the receiver down and looked at it sitting on its cradle. 'I'm not her son,' he told it. Then he turned and faced the long corridor back to his room. It was empty so he played hopscotch along part of the

184

design of linoleum tiles. Still, he thought. It was just a way of speaking, wasn't it? Alice probably called anyone she came into contact with 'son'. As she took out the keys that opened the cell doors at the police station to an erring youth like Eddie Rudge, she probably put her uniformed arm on to the lad's shoulder and said: 'Come with me, son!' and then, when she had put Eddie Rudge behind bars, she would add: 'It's your mother I feel sorry for, son. How must she feel?' She seemed nicer than he had given her credit for. He was surprised that he had been able to say as much as he had. He would not have thought it when he pressed in the shilling. It made him feel a traitor in a way.

Still, the fact remained that Dad should not have married again. That was the worst of it. It was just not right. And so quickly too. Not right. That it should come to this! But two years dead, nay, not so much, not two. So excellent a Mum, that was, to this, Hyperion to a Satyr in a policewoman's uniform. Mum would be looking down from heaven. (Would she? Whose heaven?) Anyway she would be somewhere nice, making tea for Socrates – no, Socrates would be making tea and honey-cakes for Mum if there was any justice and wisdom in the Wisdom and Spirit of the Universe – and looking down on *them.* For Benson felt that just as he prayed for Mum in his own way – talked to her daily as he had once talked to Guardian Angel Tom – so Dad should be doing the same only more so. On his bicycle to work, in the patrol car, in the greenhouse, everywhere, he should be communing with Mum. How could he do that with a new wife at his side? Before going to sleep how could he talk to Mum? As he honeyed and made love with Alice, how was it possible that he keep lines of communication open with Mum? Would not Mum turn away sad? Would not the conversation she was having with Plato dry up on her tongue? Surely she would look down and

185

see the disgusting things happening. O Insupportable!

Benson got back to his room in a state. He locked the door, lay facedown on the bed and wept into it. He wept for Mum as he often did. Tears brought him a strange solace. He imagined his mother's hand stroking his hair as he lay there. But then odd thoughts came into consciousness. Behind a smiling Mum stroking his hair, was the television camera and boom microphone recording the scene with Fyfe Robertson speaking into the camera: *Was there ever such sorrow like unto this young man's sorrow? A young man without a Mum. It is a common occurrence in this vale of tears we call our lives, but how hard it is for those so afflicted. And how much harder for a sensitive soul such as Benson, unacknowledged as a hero, with* HOMO *scrawled on his door! Well I for one think it's scandalous in this day and age*!

He pushed the TV film crew out of the room and returned to Mum. He thought of her saying 'Have a good time, son!' as he had left her that day to meet up with Clitherow. He thought of the too-quick peck on the cheek he had given her. Then he thought of Mum with the tubes coming out of her nose and mouth in the hospital ward. The tears gushed with renewed vigour, and he felt sweet melancholy spreading like oil over the choppy waters of his depression.

The tears abating, he sought to bring them back with sad pictures from Vietnam and Lima rubbish dumps. So many Mums looking down on their children! His grief was pretty minor when placed against the huge ones of those born in exploited colonies and in wicked South Africa. He got up and put Mozart's Requiem on to his Philips. The music started and he bawled for a minute or so. Then he stopped.

The thought that his sorrows were on a lesser plain altogether than those of others around the world, eventually made it to his tearducts. What was his psychological pain in comparison to their physical agonies? Cold, hunger, thirst, discomfort of all sorts, were surely much worse than his petty worries and sorrows? He lifted himself up to look at the damp pillow. He had made a most satisfactory stain. Then he went over to the mirror to see what ravages his tears had brought about to his strong good looks. His eyes were red. His cheeks were damp. Books said that faces which had just wept looked puffy too. Well, his didn't look puffy. Not in the least. More lies!

He wondered what he could recite in front of the mirror: '"Oh that this too, too sullied flesh . . ." "O pour the wine and in the fire of spring, the Winter Garment of repentance fling . . ." "Earth has not anything to show more fair! Dull would . . ." "When I play on my fiddle in Dooney, Folk dance like . . ." Well, I'm glad you asked me that question, Mr Pettifer. I suppose it all depends what one means by existential . . .' No, nothing suited the mood.

He turned away from the mirror, took his handkerchief out and blew hard into it. He searched for his Palgrave *Golden Treasury*. It was a suitable time for him to play Random Poetry.

The idea of Random Poetry was that you opened the book at random to find something that was appropriate. Benson had substituted his poetry book for his bible. The Wisdom and Spirit of the Universe guided his hand, rather than Yahweh or Guardian Angel Tom. But the rules had not changed. Benson was still only allowed one go.

Benson closed his eyes and placed his thumb into the book. He thought of Mum. Then he opened the book and placed his finger on the right-hand page and opened his eyes. The very end of his finger-nail touched the 'R' of the title of a poem called 'Remember'. Benson read:

Remember me when I am gone away,
　　Gone far away into the silent land;

When you can no more hold me by the hand,
Nor I half turn to go yet turning stay.
Remember me when no more day by day
    You tell me of our future that you planned:
    Only remember me; you understand
It will be late to counsel then or pray.

Yet if you should forget me for a while
    And afterwards remember, do not grieve:
    For if the darkness and corruption leave
    A vestige of the thoughts that once I had,
Better by far you should forget and smile
    Than that you should remember and be sad.

He pulled his sleeve across his face after the first
reading, sat down on the bed and read the poem again.
It had worked! Mum was talking to him and telling
him to be happy. It was so like her. She might not have
put it in just those words, but the poem spoke
everything he could imagine her saying from the
invisible country beyond the grave where the Lord of
Socrates, of the Moabs and the Muhammadans and the
Strung-Out and the Poor presided. And it occurred to
him too that Mum might also have said these things to
Dad. Maybe Dad had heard 'Remember', or maybe, if
he hadn't read it, he had intuited it and its meaning.
Dad had moped his way through the year following
Mum's death. He and Benson had been unable to talk
about her at all, though Benson had really wanted to.
Mum had joined all the other secrets he kept under his
hat and which gave him a severe headache sometimes
with their weight. He had thought that perhaps Dad
was trying to forget, and Benson had resented that. But
the poem said otherwise. The poem to which his game
of Random Poetry had led him was exactly the one he
needed. It made him feel much better. He wrote down
the poem in his notebook, resolving to learn it by heart
as he made a further pastoral foray among the overseas
students in their flats and furnished rooms.

*

Benson rang the bell of 4A Merthyr Terrace where his sad Sudanese student lived. It had taken Benson weeks to visit him again, but then he had had other things on his mind, still had other things on his mind. Meryl was very much on his mind, though he had not seen her for almost a week. Enoch Mohammed too impinged and was one of the culprits whom he felt might be responsible for Meryl's present fix – if indeed it proved to be a fix. And then there was Gareth. He felt responsible for Gareth too, wanted to visit him, but didn't want to at the same time. What if Gareth decided that Benson was his Mr Right? that would be terrible. Then, if Benson said no to Gareth, he might go off and try to kill himself again.

Maynard, the President of the Overseas Students' Society, had given Benson brochures to hand out. Although he felt that he was being spread rather thinly one way and another, he still had a responsibility to see to the needs of the alienated strangers in his midst.

He rang again. It was eight in the evening and Benson could not imagine where Omar could be. Perhaps he was at the library. Perhaps he was out with friends. That would be nice, in a way.

But then a light went on, and Benson heard footsteps coming down the stairs. Omar opened the door a foot or so, and then fully when he saw Benson standing there.

'Ah, it's you, my friend!' called out Omar, as if Benson were standing across the road.

'Yes, it's me, Omar. I just thought I'd call to see how you were.'

'Very kind of you. Will you come in and have a cup of tea or coffee? Alcohol I cannot offer because I am a Muslim.'

'I understand. A cup of tea would be really nice. It's cold, isn't it?'

Omar led Benson up three flights of stairs to his attic

189

room. The corridors were bare and chilly – how mean landladies were. If he were a landlady he would put up lots of posters to brighten things up. But once inside Omar's room Benson immediately felt he must take off his anorak. A gas fire with all three sections lit sent out a fierce heat into the room. A Baby Belling, its oven door open, stood in the corner on a table covered in oil-cloth. Benson wondered if the oven was on too. Gosh, if Omar was this cold in November, what would happen come February?

The room was a bit bare for Benson's taste. Also there was an odd smell. It wasn't unpleasant, more like the smell he got when he passed farms on his walks. Apart from family pictures on the desk next to an anglepoise, there was little in the way of knick-knacks or gadgetry. Omar's soap and shaving things were placed in a tidy row on the coffee-table. The narrow single bed under the high attic window was neatly made, covered with a white counterpane.

Omar placed the kettle on one of the rings of the Belling and then sat down across the coffee-table from him.

'How are you settling in?' Benson asked Omar solicitously.

'Oh, very well. I am working hard. There are many books to read and this is a little difficult. But, yes, I am content. My research work is very interesting.'

'What are you researching?'

'Goats. We are experimenting with different feed-stuffs.'

'Yes? That sounds interesting.'

'Very interesting, but also very dirty work. I have to weigh their droppings every day. And also measure them. People say that I always smell of goat.'

'No, I'm sure you don't,' said Benson. He felt that Omar's work must be very useful for the Sudan. He must not be put off by the thought that it was causing him to smell funny.

'You can't smell anything?'

'No, nothing,' lied Benson, 'the atmosphere in this room is very fresh.'

Omar looked round the room, smiled and said: 'Good.'

'No problems?' asked Benson, now very aware of the goat smell whenever he inhaled. Still, it wasn't so bad.

'I told you on your last visit that I am missing my family. This does not change.'

'No, I suppose not, but you are making friends, aren't you?'

'I do not have much time for making friends. My work comes first. Perhaps later on when I know the work.'

'Yes, but all work and no play . . .' began Benson.

'Yes?'

'Well, you must have some recreation too! You can't work all the time.'

Omar nodded. Then he smiled, 'I am not working now! I am talking with my new English friend!'

'Yes, that's right!' replied Benson, the old thoughts returning to tempt him, the thoughts which he had hoped he had sent packing after his frustrating time with Enoch Mohammed. Omar was a bit like Enoch Mohammed; not as bulky, but as tall. He also had scars on his face. Benson loved scars on black faces. Get thee behind me, temptation! he told himself.

'How did you get your scars?' he asked Omar. Then he added: 'I hope you don't think I'm being cheeky.'

'No, not at all. Well, I've told you that I'm Muslim. My marks do not have anything to do with religion. They are a custom of my tribe going further back than our religion. The scars are made at the same time as we are circumcised. They are an outward sign of our manhood.'

Benson nodded. 'I saw a programme on television, Armand and Michaela Dennis. They went to a puberty ceremony in Kenya. The poor boys had to lie still and not flinch while they were circumcised.'

Omar nodded and smiled: 'It is amazing how much pain you can endure when your friends and family expect it of you.'

Benson was not sure that he agreed. He saw himself, Eric and Bruno lying naked at the bottom of the cul-de-sac while Mrs Brown chanted and danced with the other neighbours. Fyfe Robertson made a film for *Tonight* and Mr Jenkins sharpened the knife. Eric would have howled like mad. 'I suppose it makes adolescence easier,' he ventured.

'What is adolescence? I have heard it mentioned but do not understand it.'

Benson felt that he was a very good example of adolescence, a walking definition, but he could not expect Omar to see that, and did his best to tell him what it was: 'Well, it's the in-between stage. You're not a child and you're not a man. All your hormones are changing and your attitudes are in a state of flux.'

'How is it different from puberty?'

'Well, I'm not sure really. I'm not a psychologist or anything. I suppose I'm an adolescent. Puberty is long behind, but puberty is only the physical side. The emotional results, putting aside childish things and taking on a man's role is more difficult. Takes years and years.'

'I think adolescence is something western. We in the Sudan are taught to grow up quickly. From a very early age we are doing manly things. Circumcision and markings are the completion of the process . . .'

'That's nice,' said Benson.

'Not so nice, really. You are very lucky. You can take your time in becoming a man. We do not have the time. We have to make ourselves useful immediately. When I was sixteen my father died and I had to take responsibility for the family. I did not even think about it.'

192

'My mother died two years ago, but my father has remarried.'

Omar nodded as if both events were the most natural things in the world. He got up and removed the boiling kettle from the glowing hob. Benson watched him. He felt very soft and silly next to Omar. There was a quiet confidence in Omar, an aura of maturity. He was like a big brother might be. The thought struck him that it would have been wonderful to have had Omar as a big brother. Omar would have put everything into perspective for him. With Omar standing above him with that beautiful face, he could have borne the blade of circumcision without complaint. He would have just stared steadily into that magical face, and not flinched. With Omar around all the torture he had been put through – and put himself through – might never have taken place. No, he thought, I'd have found a way to make it all take place . . .

'Tell me about your religion, Omar,' Benson said, as Omar came back to the coffee table, carrying a tray with a tea-pot and two dainty cups and saucers.

Omar laughed: 'No, you ask me how many brothers and sisters I have!'

'Why?'

'It's what I am always being asked. English people sense I come from a large family and they ask me so they can be surprised when I say twelve brothers and ten sisters. But I surprise them more by saying that I just have two sisters, who are much older than I am.'

'I see.' He wondered if, as Omar did not have a brother, he might fit the bill. Omar poured the tea and Benson considered this. To have a big brother always by his side, and best of all a big brother who was black and strong and full of mysterious lore and culture, a brother who spent his days improving goats. The idea excited him. Perhaps that was what he had been lacking. Maybe a big brother – why had the thought not occurred to him before? – yes, a big brother was just what he needed. This notion of the Friend was just a substitute for what he really wanted. Perhaps Omar would like a smaller brother. Perhaps asking Omar about his brothers and sisters was not such a cliché of a question to be asked at all. Perhaps – at a subconscious level, where all the really good things happened – all the people who asked Omar whether he had brothers and sisters were thinking how much they would like Omar as a big brother. He wanted to go and think about it deeply between the sand and the foam, and he did not immediately notice that Omar was holding out a cup of unmilked tea for him.

He took the cup from the long black hand of his big brother elect, noting the podgy thick grey hand which was taking the saucer, the contrast, the lack of pigment and grace in his hand when compared with Omar's. He put the tea on the table and sat on his hands.

'Are you cold?' Omar asked.

'No, er . . . I was still wondering about your religion. I don't know anything about it really. Don't you want to talk about it?'

'It's just that it is a very large subject. It is not so easy to talk about. I would have to say many things. It would take much time.'

'Am I taking up too much of your time? I don't want to do that.'

'No, you are my guest. I am glad to see you.'

'You are Muslim and your book is the Koran,' prompted Benson.

'Yes . . .'

'And you can have more than one wife.'

'Yes, in theory, but the Holy Prophet Muhammad made it very difficult for Muslims to have more than one. You see we have to treat each one equally. We must love them the same, give them equal amounts of worldly goods. When you think about it, this is almost impossible. If you can't manage it, then you shouldn't have more than one. Most Muslims only have one

194

wife. My father only ever had my mother. I think we children would have felt very unhappy if he had taken another one.'

Benson nodded agreement. His big brother echoed his views exactly. 'Have you been to Mecca?'

'No, not yet. My father died in Mecca, however. He is buried there.'

'Why?'

'Well, when he felt himself growing old, he told my mother that he was going on the hadj, and he left the village with a camel train. They got to Port Sudan and the difficulties of the journey made my father sick. Still, he got a sailing boat across the Red Sea and then walked from Jeddah to Mecca. But the journey was too much for him. He collapsed and died during the procession around al-Ka'bah. His companions buried him there.'

'What a terrible thing to happen!'

'No, we do not see it like that. It is a great blessing to die on the pilgrimage. Many people do. It is a guarantee of paradise for people to die while engaged in a holy work.'

Benson wondered if he would feel the same if Dad went off to Lourdes and died, but did not think he would. He would try to sue Quo Vadis tours if such a thing happened. He would shake his fist at God.

Omar did not volunteer any further information. Benson knew he would have to go and find some information on Omar's religion. Then, when he knew something, they could have a fuller discussion.

'Drink your tea before it gets cold.'

Benson took his hand out from under his bottom, and obediently picked up the cup. He aimed a wide smile at Omar, who smiled widely back. Then he noticed the backs of his hands had been wrinkled by the corduroy trousers he was wearing. The tea, still hot, tasted sweet, but there was an extra herby taste to it. He remarked on this to Omar.

'Na-Na. Mint. We always put mint in tea.'

'We put it on roast lamb. It's very good in tea, though.'

'On lamb? I must try it.'

'What you do is, you chop the mint and then add six spoons of vinegar and a teaspoon of sugar. It bucks up the lamb no end,' said Benson, thinking of how Mum had taught him how to make it, suddenly thinking of the smell of Yorkshire pudding and roasting meat, happy to be able to discuss cultural variations over a cup of tea opposite a nice overseas student. But then he reminded himself that he was visiting Omar for a reason.

'Have you somewhere to go for Christmas?' Benson asked.

'I think I am staying here. Christmas will give me time to work,' he replied.

'There are some holidays arranged for overseas students,' said Benson, and he handed Omar a sheaf of papers. Then an idea struck him. He uttered it straight away, did not give himself any time to think of the implications, 'But if you don't fancy any of those holidays, you might think about coming home with me instead. We've room at home and it would be lovely for us to be able to have an overseas student to stay.'

'That's very kind, I . . .'

'You don't have to tell me now. Tell me when you next see me. There's only Dad and my stepmother at home. There's plenty of room.' He was already imagining himself giving Omar tours of Liverpool, being sure to omit the chains on the docks where slaves had been tied up before being shipped out of Liverpool to America. Or perhaps he would not omit them.

'Where are you from?'

'From Wallasey. It's across the river from Liverpool.'

'I live in Omdurman, it's across the Nile from Khartoum.'

'How do you travel across the river?'

196

'By ferry.'

'We have ferries too. I'll take you on the ferry. We can feed the birds. I can show you The Cavern where the Beatles started.'

'What religion are you?'

'I haven't got one any more. I was brought up a Catholic, but I don't believe in it at all now.'

'Why's that?'

'It's a long story,' replied Benson looking at his watch. 'Still, although I've lost my religion, I really am looking around for a new philosophy of life. I am searching for eternal verities.'

'For what?'

'For the Truth. The trouble is that there seem to be so many of them. Once you have thrown away the religion you were born with, it's a problem choosing. It's as if you'd been brought up on fish and chips and then suddenly discover a well-stocked, sophisticated delicatessen. Lots of philosophies have good things in them, but none of them really answer all the problems. Still, I'm very new in my search. I expect I'll find something to hang my hat on eventually.'

'What you are saying shocks me, Martin,' replied Omar.

What Omar said shocked Benson. 'How do you mean?'

'It seems to me that a man must remain loyal to the traditions of his family and country.'

'Why?'

'Because if everyone decides to go down their own road, the society would break up. Also, with regards families, it is a terrible thing for a father and mother to see their children departing from the ways they have been taught.'

'Yes, but if you can't believe it . . .'

'I think', replied Omar, 'that there is a case for living your life within the religion you were born with even if you do not believe it.'

197

'But that's hypocrisy! You've got to follow your own drummer, even if the sound seems measured, distant and confusing!' replied Benson, thoroughly mangling Thoreau.

'Even if your search will divide the society? I am a scientist, Martin. I look down a microscope and think that things are, perhaps, more complicated than I was taught. We Muslims believe that God made man from clots of blood, but scientifically it does not seem to be the case. Still, if you leave the beliefs of your childhood and embark on your search, do you think you will arrive at any closer approximation to the Truth? Every answer breeds more questions unless you have faith. Also, you are not only an individual, you are a person who must function within society. In Britain you have a consensus based on your Christian heritage. I, as a Muslim, can admire that and even fit into it. We may disagree about details, but when it comes down to the important things we agree. I fear for the country where everyone believes something different. Home would cease to be home if I could not rely on my neighbour having a roughly similar set of beliefs to myself.'

Benson was wondering if a big brother was such a good idea after all. 'But something is either true or untrue! And if it is untrue I have a duty not to follow it, to seek out what is true. Anyway, I am not suggesting that because I am no longer a Catholic my actions will change.' Benson's face reddened as he thought of Dr Leptos.

'Yes, but you no longer have the anchor. Now you are young, the teachings of your religion are still fresh in your mind. But what will happen in twenty years? I think there is such a thing as too much knowledge. Knowledge is sometimes dangerous. Maybe ignorance is better – and a simple faith.'

Benson had not the vaguest notion what would happen in twenty years. Like Meryl, he half thought that the world would cease to exist in twenty years what with the bomb, Vietnam and everything. A simple faith? Well, that was not much use, was it? If there was a God, what had he given us our heads for? Brother Hooper had often said that he admired the simple faith of poor Irish widows, but then poor Irish widows thought people like Brother Hooper were wonderful and gave them lots to drink whenever they visited.

'Maybe,' continued Omar, 'maybe it is better to live your life as if you believed in your religion. I have my doubts but I do not think any journey I undertook to search for truth would leave me any the wiser. When I came to Britain and went to the National Library for the first time I was dizzy with all the books up there. How could I ever read them all? And where would I be at the end of my reading, assuming that I managed it? I think I would be a very confused old man. Probably I would throw all my studies up in the air and collapse back into my religion. I do not know if I'm speaking the truth. It is just a theory. But we do have the example of many intellectuals. This searching for truth is a long voyage alone in a small boat. There is no guarantee of reaching land.'

The smell of goat seemed to be getting stronger. Benson's thoughts wandered from what Omar was saying to a consideration of what he might be able to do to rid the room of the smell. Probably Omar was used to it by now, but it might be a bit off-putting in the lounge at home. Dad wouldn't mind it because he often sniffed manure and said how nice it was. But Alice would really take exception to the smell. Good.

He also wished that Meryl were here. If Meryl were here she would have shot Omar and his arguments down in flames. He would have been a weeping wreck on the floor by now with Meryl standing triumphant, holding the flame of Truth aloft over Omar's cowering, charred frame. But all Benson could do was frown, nod and run his right index finger around the rim of his empty teacup.

He was wondering if inviting Omar home for the holidays had been such a good idea after all. With Omar and Dad together they would have him back to the altar rails and lighting candles in front of St Joseph statues before he had time to say 'different drummer'.

'Are you really interested in my work with goats?' Omar asked Benson as he was leaving.

'Yes, very interested.'

'One Saturday I'll take you to see what I do.'

Benson left Omar at eleven, promising to call round the following Saturday. He walked through the quiet town wondering whether he should visit Gareth on his way back to the hostel. He took the Llanbadarn Road and as he walked tried to think of answers to Omar's arguments. Perhaps the trouble was that he had only been a free-thinker for a couple of years. If he, like Meryl, had been brought up to think and question instead of having everything pumped into him pre-digested, he would be able to argue with Omar better. But from the sound of it, Omar had had a very restricted upbringing, not to say a deprived one. How was he able to argue like that? Perhaps he's just bright and I'm thick, he thought.

Gosh, it would be terrible if he really were thick. Perhaps all his hopes of becoming a great intellectual were houses built on poor-quality sawdust! Perhaps he was not university material at all. It was Kant, wasn't it, who had said that before you act you had to consider what the world would look like if everyone did it? Or was it the park-keeper: *If everyone dropped toffee-papers, what would the park look like*? If everyone was a homo, what would the world look like? But that was a valued judgement and possibly a posteriori too. Anyway, whatever it was, it didn't hold water in his bucket. It was patently obvious that the whole world would never want to do what he wanted to do. He was a homo, one in twenty, though at the moment the proportion seemed to be much less. Very few homos indeed had plucked up the courage to take the train across the Welsh mountains to Aberystwyth. There was Gareth and Andy and Clitherow (maybe) and Oscar Wilde and James Baldwin and people in Mary Renault books and the ones who drew pictures on the walls of the convenience at Kings Hall corner on the prom. But the whole world? The whole world looked askance! Omar would probably look askance.

Anyway, Benson was not sure that he disbelieved in Christianity. It was just that he still felt Jesus to be a friend who had let him down badly. All those years of black sin and white virtue and then no help when he needed it most! All that dogma and then – if Myvanwy and Sean were to be believed – everything had been turned on its head. What had been sinful was no longer sinful. That was as shocking to him as much as his homosexuality being inherently sinful. If dogmas could change then anything could change. Omar was wrong. For a cradle Catholic the roads had already diverged. They led off in all kinds of directions. He would have to be dead – or in a monastery – to be whole. No, dead.

Benson was getting near the chip shop where Gareth worked. He had decided to go in, having enough money in his pocket for a six of chips and a small bottle of Tizer. But, just as he was within sight of it, a car stopped and four loud men got out and went into the chip shop. He passed the sweet shop, its window too dark to allow him to see any friendly bottles of sweets. He peered around the chip shop window, saw that Gareth was behind the counter chatting with the men and spooning chips into newspaper. He was all right then. Reassured, Benson walked back to the hostel thinking up all kinds of wonderful belated arguments to get Omar – his big brother – to admit his cardinal error.

9

'Don't you dare say another word!' said Meryl threateningly. 'It's all arranged.'

'Well, I won't then,' said Benson.

He had said everything, he thought. Was Meryl sure that abortion was not murder? — because Benson wasn't. He had said that. It all depended when the foetus became human. Was it at the moment of conception or when the baby was born? He had said that too. Then he had changed tack and tried to persuade Meryl to wait a while. But he was on weak ground there because Meryl had said that to wait meant that the foetus would become much more human. Anyway, it had to be done soon. 'You are absolutely sure you are pregnant?' he'd asked. 'Absolutely fucking positive!' Meryl had replied. Benson had thought of *A Taste of Honey*, then, a film he had just seen at the pictures. He suggested that perhaps he and Meryl could bring up the baby like Rita Tushingham and her friend. Meryl had just looked at him and he had been relieved that she hadn't taken him seriously.

Meryl said that her mother had been informed and thought abortion the best thing to do, was arranging for it to be done at the clinic owned by a friend of the family in London.

What had really stopped Benson's argument was one from Meryl that abortion was really only an emotional and practical form of miscarriage. Miscarriages, she said, were natural abortions; the way the body had of saying that the baby would not survive. Abortion was simply the bringing of reason to bear on this. The body could not have a miscarriage just because the mother was unable to give the baby the time and attention that was its due. The body did not know that the baby was not wanted, could not be looked after properly. The body was not evolved enough to respond to extraneous factors. Abortion helped the body along. It was simply a mindful miscarriage. Anyway, sperm was wasted by the trillion, eggs by the million. Why not a combination of the two?

'Have you told Enoch Mohammed?' he asked.

'No. And you must promise not to mention all this to a soul. I plan to merely disappear for a week. I'll be back before you know it.'

'Are you still seeing him?'

'Yes.'

'Well, it is your decision.' Part of him thought that that was not necessarily so either, but he did not dare say another word on the topic. If it had been theoretical, like a brawl with Ianto, he might have said a great deal more, both pro and contra. But it did not seem right to persist, given that Meryl was in the midst of the problem.

'Will you come and see me off?'

'Yes, of course. When are you going?'

'This afternoon.'

'So soon?'

Meryl nodded.

Benson made his way to his English lecture while Meryl took a bus up to Ifor Evans hostel to pack. He enjoyed the lecture. It was about Wordsworth and Pantheism. Benson thought that Pantheism was rather a nice way of looking at the world. God was in natural things. It was primitive, but seemed to say all you could say about the Godhead. He was struck for the first time by the import of Wordsworth's 'Intimations of Immortality'. He had done the poem for O level, had passed his O level partly by answering a question on the poem, but then it had not meant much to him and

203

he wondered how he had managed to please the examiner with it. Now, he felt, he understood it better. Everything he saw moved him just as it had moved Wordsworth. He cried at Paul Robeson singing 'Sometimes I Feel Like a Motherless Child'; at Martin Luther King's sermons. A sunset set him off; the moon on the Irish Sea likewise. Yet the poet said that this would fade into the light of common day. Would this happen to him? Would there come a time when he would not feel these things? It would be terrible to say along with Wordsworth: 'The things which I have seen I now can see no more.' How would that happen? What was the process? But he could see the truth of that too. When Dad came in and told him to turn down the volume of his Bob Dylan records he was clearly under the influence of the slow death of middle age. He just could not see what was obvious to Benson. Could such an erosion of sensibilities be slowed or prevented altogether? Must there pass away a glory from the earth? Did familiarity inevitably lead to contempt? He shivered at the thought. Death rather than a loss of sensibility! he told the record-shop window he was passing.

But with Dr Leptos what had been an ineffable thrill on Friday had turned into a bore by Sunday. Meryl, though she had slept with Enoch Mohammed, did not want to pack up her duffle-bag and follow him wherever his fate led him, did she? Dusty Springfield, echoing Wordsworth, sang that she wanted to return to the days when she was young enough to know the truth. But did he know the truth, let alone the Truth? No, he was completely mixed up. He did not know what was right and what was wrong any more. He distrusted his conscience because conscience was just indoctrination, wasn't it? It was not only conscience that made cowards of us all. It was uncertainty too. There were so many places to stand and fidget in life. Every perspective gave a different view. Once one left the island of dogmatism on which one had been reared, nothing from then on stayed still.

After the lecture, Benson bought himself a family-size chocolate Swiss Roll and a bottle of milk from the Maypole. This he took down to the prom. By the pier he went down the steps and found himself a clean place to sit on the cold pebbly shore. He unwrapped the chocolate Swiss Roll and started to consume it, beginning from one end, as though it were a piece of French bread. He masticated the sweet cake and took a slug from the milk. The top of the milk and the cake combined deliciously in his mouth and he was lost in ecstasy for a brief moment. But then the moment had gone. He surveyed the cake and the milk. In five minutes it would be gone and he would be sitting on the cold beach with a Swiss Roll and a pint of milk inside him. Then what? Omar Khayyam was right. Nothing lasted.

He thought of the other Omar in his life. Omar, it seemed, was a still point in the turning world. Omar would have had an answer for Meryl. He would have taken his answer from his stock of answers, from what tradition and family expectations demanded. Lucky Omar, he thought he thought.

An hour later Benson – a chocolate Swiss Roll and a pint of milk inside him – was waiting for Meryl at Aberystwyth Station. The train was in and passengers were already aboard, but there was no sign of Meryl. Benson had bought a platform ticket, but was waiting anxiously near the booking office for her to turn up.

He fidgeted, read the advertisement for Beautiful Borth and surveyed the dusty pipes and tins of tobacco in the kiosk display case. Perhaps he should take up a pipe. If he smoked a pipe while talking perhaps people would listen. It seemed to work for Harold Wilson after all. Bertrand Russell too.

Benson saw the sign GENTLEMEN. Then he saw a gentleman going in. Benson wondered whether he needed to go. He pushed on his bladder. Maybe he did. It was hard to tell. Would he have thought of going if he hadn't seen someone going in? Probably not. But if he did go, he would be going for a practical reason. It was rather like seeing someone smoking and then wanting to have a cigarette too. He did not feel in the least bit tempted sexually. He had Meryl to minister to. The man who had gone in before him did not strike him as being particularly attractive. He walked towards the entrance.

Entering the toilet, he turned a sharp left and collided with the man he had seen coming in, who was on his way out. Benson said sorry, but he thought he had probably said it so quietly that the man did not hear. He decided that he must learn to project his voice farther. There were three urinals and Benson stood in front of the one on the right. The porcelain had 'Armitage-Shanks' written on it. It had often made him wonder about porcelain manufacturers. How could they want their names urinated on all the time? Wouldn't it make them shiver in their Staffordshire mansions thinking that a million times every day someone somewhere was urinating on their name? They should call urinals 'Hitler' or 'Ian Smith' or 'George Wallace' or 'Adolph Eichmann', then people could wee on the names to their heart's content. It would probably help the flow too. He should write a letter to the manufacturers.

Benson managed to get a meagre flow going but this abruptly stopped as the man he had collided with came and stood next to him. Benson was surprised at first. Then, without a thought in his head, his penis started to stiffen, strangling any hopes he might have had of finishing the operation for which he had ostensibly entered the toilet. He tried to pull himself away from the urinal, but he couldn't. The man stared down doggedly at himself. Benson watched him out of the corner of his eye, though he did not turn his head one iota. The man moved back from the urinal and Benson knew that if he looked he would see the man's penis. But to turn his head even ever so slightly would show the man that he was interested. As of this moment, so hunched was he over the urinal, that the man would not be able to see the erection which had grown on Benson. At this moment he would think that Benson was just taking a long time. No, already he had taken far too long. Why not just glance? Benson thought. A quick look won't hurt. It isn't an irrevocable commitment, is it? Benson turned his head towards the man and looked down at him. But it was an irrevocable step. The man was erect, was waggling his penis about obscenely to left and right. Benson looked up into the man's face and the eyes met his gaze. Helpless, he stared back at himself, pulsing, almost gasping, above the yellow river four feet below.

'Come on after,' whispered the man. He had stepped further away from the urinal and was putting himself away. Benson did not say anything, did not nod or shake his head, though he knew that he was going to follow the man. He heard the footsteps leaving the toilet, then he went over and washed his shaking hands.

When he got outside, the man was standing under the clock. Benson, looking left and right for Meryl and witnesses, walked over to him and as he came up to him the man was lighting a cigarette and offered Benson one. Benson took the cigarette and the man lit it.

'Want to come with me?' asked the man in a strong Welsh accent, looking nervously around.

He seemed quite old, at least thirty-five, and Benson was surprised that he was a homo. He did not look like one. He looked more like a farmer or a builder.

'Yes,' said Benson, dragging on his cigarette. 'But I'm supposed to . . .'

'I've got a place we can go,' the man whispered,

smoke pluming from his mouth as he spoke. 'I've got a car too.' And to prove it he took his car keys out.

'That's nice,' said Benson.

'Come on,' said the man.

And where is Benson now, boys? I wonder, I often wonder. Somewhere between here and hell. And on that broad easy road, he does not know he is heading for perdition. No, the Devil has filled his head with filthy lusts that blind him to the truth. He has lost all direction, boys.

Benson followed the man out of the station and along the road. A cream-coloured Vauxhall Viva was parked next to a building which said 'Education Department Annexe' on it. The man unlocked the door and got in, leaning across to unlock the front passenger door. Benson looked round once more to see if he could spot Meryl, then he got in.

'It's a lovely car,' said Benson.

The man started up. '0 to 50m.p.h. in 13.3 seconds,' he said.

'Gosh!'

'All-syncro gears and a twenty-nine-foot turning circle,' added the man.

'Really? That's nice. And four doors too.'

'It's not mine, though.'

'No, well . . . I don't have a car either.'

'It cost £500.'

'Did it?'

'But it's not worth the money.'

'Mmm.' Benson knew that he should not be sitting in this Vauxhall Viva talking boring man-talk. He should be at the station waiting for Meryl. Still, it was too late now. And the man had such a whopper. It made Benson giddy just to remember it. The man had fished him out of the water with a living Swiss Roll as bait. The car ash-tray was full. Benson wondered for about the millionth time why he was so abjectly attracted to other men's penises. He had one, didn't he? Wasn't that enough? What was the source of the attraction that propelled him hopelessly, giddily, towards those of other men? But the thought did not lodge. There was no answer to that either, unless he listened to Brother Hooper. The man drove on in silence, taking the road south out of Aberystwyth along the coast towards Cardigan.

What would he say to Meryl?

He bit his lower lip hard, thinking there was something else that he would have to pay for later. Then the man said: 'Come on, show us yours,' and nodded down to Benson's fly.

'Here? I really don't think it . . .'

'Yes, why not? We're out in the country. No-one can see. Look, I'll show you mine.'

'Do you think you ought? I mean, the cab of a lorry is much higher than us and the driver might . . .'

But the man undid the buttons on his pants and heaved out his penis, half erect and nodding upwards, weaving itself under the steering-wheel. Benson looked at it, frowning, biting his lower lip.

'Go on, your turn,' said the man.

Benson looked mournfully to left and right, then undid himself and with some difficulty took out his own penis, but returned his gaze to the man's.

The man smiled but did not say anything. Then he reached over and squeezed Benson. His hands were rough, the nails dirty. He returned the hand to the steering-wheel.

They drove on for some minutes in silence. Benson watched the man's erection doggedly. The man looked over once or twice then said at last: 'Go on, you can touch it if you want. It won't bite. Not just yet anyway.'

Benson reached over, thinking that that was an odd way of putting it. He put his hand round it, noting at once that his thumb could not connect with his index finger, no matter how hard he pressed. Gosh, it was immense, he thought, at once comparing it – unfavourably – with his own.

'Go easy!' said the man.

Benson stroked the man then, as if his penis were a bird or a kitten. A smile came to his face, a smile completely unselfconscious in origin.

'You'll have some fun with that!' said the man.

'Er . . .' said Benson. There was no answer to that either. Benson wondered if he would ever be able to say something like that to someone else. No, he wouldn't. Even if he thought it he would not say it. He just would not be able to heave such a crimsonly-revealing statement out of his mouth.

'Have you got a nice pair of bollocks?'

'Well . . . er . . . I suppose average, maybe a bit better than average. Er . . . I've never had any complaints!' replied Benson, who was rather proud of the size of his testicles and wished the other bit had kept pace with them.

'What do you like to do?'

'I don't know really.'

'I like a man who knows his mind,' said the man sarcastically. 'I like to fuck young lads. That's what I like.'

'Yes, that's nice,' said Benson accommodatingly. He was beginning to lose his erection.

'Will you suck it?' asked the man, gesturing to his penis.

Benson felt there was nothing he would like better, but it seemed like cheating to ask like that. He was positive John Wayne would never have said such a thing to Maureen O'Hara. If he had, he could imagine Maureen O'Hara's reaction. But the question itself made his penis rear up. Answering the question was, however, another matter entirely.

'Er . . . It's a long way, isn't it?' said Benson. 'Nice countryside though. I've never come this way before.'

'Was that a joke?' asked the man.

'Was it? What do you do?'

'Farming, sheep.'

'I'm a student,' said Benson. 'What's your name, by the way?'

'That doesn't matter.'

'Doesn't it? My name's Martin.'

The man nodded but did not seem particularly interested. Benson's attempt at polite conversation seemed to have a bromidic effect on him. He scowled and pumped on his penis to bring it up to erection again.

After several more miles the man turned left off the main road, along a single lane track, bending this way and that, undulating across rough pastureland. The man had to concentrate on his driving and Benson noticed that his erection was flagging again, his phallus bowing over on itself, forgotten for the time being – except by Benson. Well, he thought, it must get hard to keep an erection at his age. A final turn to the left and a black and white sheepdog was barking at the car as it drew up beside a tiny farmhouse surrounded by untrained yew hedging.

'Here we are!' said the man. He got out of the car, took the dog by the scruff of the neck and led it away around the building. Benson got out and looked around. The wind was blowing strongly off the sea. Dragon-shaped clouds scudded across the sky. The stunted trees all about were permanently bowed, pointing towards the clouds' destination.

The man came back. His penis was lolling outside his trousers and Benson felt giddy again. He had put his own away when the car stopped.

'It's just a small place, mind,' said the man, leading him inside the house.

'It's very nice,' said Benson, suddenly reminded of the Queen visiting a council house.

'I don't need much.'

Benson thought he was going to be asked to sit down in one of the armchairs by the grate, perhaps offered a cup of tea, but it was not to be. The man began to take off his clothes and motioned to Benson to do the same.

Benson looked round the room: 'Nobody will come, will they?' he asked.

The man laughed, and sat down to pull off his trousers. 'No worry there,' he said. Then he stood up and took off his vest and underpants as Benson watched, somewhat behind in the operation.

It was a bit much not being offered a cup of tea or anything. If the situation had been reversed Benson felt that he would have searched high and low for little morsels with which to entertain his guest. He slowly removed his clothes, watching the man out of the corner of his eye.

He was lost in admiration for the man's body. It was totally unexpected. He was lean and hairy, his stomach was flat and muscled, his arms and legs wiry and strong. He thought his face let the rest of him down a bit, though. His chin had started to sag. He still had a few years to go before it was as bad as Auntie Muriel's, but the process had started all right. There were deep wrinkles extending around his throat to his ears, as if many years ago he had been cut there several times by a knife.

The man stepped over to Benson and helped him off with the underpants he had been keeping on for decorum's sake. He pulled at them a bit roughly. Did he think underpants grew on trees?

'Here we are then,' he said.

'Yes,' said Benson.

He raised his eyebrows and pointed with his eyes down to where his penis pointed rudely towards Benson.

Benson knew that the man wanted him to make the first move. He knew exactly what was expected and he knew just as certainly that he wanted more than anything to do what was expected of him. But his body would not work. The man put his arms on Benson's

212

shoulders: 'Go on, say hello to it,' he said, and he pushed Benson down on to his knees.

'Er . . . Hello . . . I . . .' said Benson as he passed the man's navel.

'You're a shy one,' said the man. 'Go on, get down there and give it a kiss. You know that's what you want. I know you. Go on, kiss it.' He placed his penis an inch from Benson's mouth, then pushed the tip against his lips. Benson frowned, tried to think of a cutting riposte, but the man moved forward slightly and he found his pouting lips up against him. The pout turned into a kiss and the man insinuated his penis through the kiss and told him to suck on it. Benson did so, still wanting to say something, though he was not sure what. He felt a need to establish that he was human. Would a verse from Wordsworth help? A catechism answer? The man moved in on him, forcing Benson to swallow him.

Benson was not at all sure that he was going to be able to manage half of it, let alone all of it. But he tried to allow the man's penis further back down his throat. The man pulled back then enveloped him again, making him want to gag. He did this a number of times until Benson had become used to the motion, had got his breathing right and had opened his eyes to watch the phallus approaching and retreating. The man hissed and took hold of Benson by the ears and changed the movement so that Benson's head was moved on to his penis while he stayed still. Benson was aware of the tight grip on his ears and a part of him felt like protesting, but another part was happy to be so controlled and he groaned and gulped and swallowed.

'I'm going to come,' said the man matter-of-factly.

But Benson was too taken up with trying to breathe to worry.

The man pushed and pulled on Benson's ears and then gripped him round the back of the head, pushing himself into him, still hissing between his teeth.

Benson felt the spasm, tried to pull back but was not allowed to and only managed not to retch with the greatest difficulty. The man withdrew.

He was left on his knees, and the man was already half way across the room. He swallowed and gulped and rubbed his ears. The man disappeared. Benson heard the sound of running water. He hoped he might be making the tea.

When he came back Benson was still on his knees. He had considered getting up but did not think he ought to until the man told him to. Why he thought this he did not know himself. He sat back on his haunches like an oriental wife, and the man smiled when he saw him there. He lit a cigarette, though he did not offer Benson one. Then he sat down in the armchair.

'I'll soon be ready again. We'll go upstairs for the next one. I've got a good solid bed up there. You'll like that, won't you?'

Benson nodded and smiled. He hoped it would be returned. It wasn't, and this troubled him. But it thrilled him too. This worried him.

'What are you kneeling down there for? Go and sit on that chair.'

Obediently, Benson did so.

The man smoked and played with himself with his spare hand. Benson did not conceal his own erection when he was sitting down, just watched him. He could just not understand the man. He could not understand how he could be so brazen about everything. He could never be like that, so frank about his desires. He could never have done to someone what had just been done to him. But was that true? He remembered the orgy he had gone to with Clitherow two years before, and how he had felt about the man below him. Yes, perhaps he could understand. Perhaps now he could also understand Andy's pleasure in the cemetery. Thought stopped during the act. He felt – and it was another peculiar by-road – that he was where he belonged. He wondered if the man were nicer to him whether he would be feeling like this. Carmen Jones, he thought.

The tension did not ebb. At no time did the man treat him as a guest. He was here for sex and was not allowed to forget it for a moment.

The man stubbed out his cigarette in an old grey shell. Then he snapped his fingers, stood up and opened a small door behind him, a door which Benson had thought might lead to the bathroom. In fact a narrow flight of stairs climbed steeply. He snapped his fingers and Benson walked over to the stairs and started climbing, wanting to cover his bottom from the man's stare, but knowing it was not the thing to do. Instead he tried to tread on his shame as he trod the bare-wood steps. The man closed the door and followed him up.

'It's a nice bottom. Could be a girl's,' he said and he slapped him.

Benson turned: 'A bit fat, I'm afraid. I was a fat kid.'

'Prime,' said the man.

'Thanks.'

The stairs led straight into the tiny bedroom. It had once been papered with a flock wallpaper but this had been painted over with white paint. A picture in a heavy wooden frame of Christ knocking at the door hung on the wall opposite the bed. The bed had a brass frame in need of a good go with Brasso, Benson thought. Behind the bed, a small window looked on to outhouses and a field with some sheep in it. A couple of colour pictures of nude women had been tacked to one of the other walls.

The man lay down on the bed while Benson pretended to be admiring the pictures on the wall.

'Give us a bit of a suck,' he said, holding himself out.

Benson knelt between the man's legs and did as requested.

After a couple of minutes of this the man got up and

215

told Benson to kneel on the bed with his bottom out. He told him to stick it right out so that he could get a good look at it. Benson did so. He did not even think to argue the point. It did not enter his head. He might have been obeying a doctor. The man knelt behind him and ran his hands over Benson's lower back and bottom. He pinched him there hard, then slapped him.

'Just like a girl, there's lovely!' he said. And he started to push his finger into him.

'Ow, that hurts.'

The man said nothing.

Benson tried to pull back, but the man's finger followed him.

'Tell me what you want!'

'How do you mean?'

'Tell me!' And he slapped him hard.

'I didn't come here to be hurt and in . . . ?'

'Tell me what you want!' And the finger was pushing and twisting painfully inside him.

'I want you to . . . er . . . fuck me,' replied Benson tentatively, in a resentful whisper.

'I can't hear you! Tell me what you want!' More slaps while the finger kept pushing.

'What do you mean?' moaned Benson. 'I've already said it.'

'Say it loud. Tell me you want me to fuck you.'

Benson did not want to, but did so.

'Stick your bum out!'

Again, Benson did so.

But as he did so, the man sprung up off the bed and came round in front of him. He didn't say anything, but seized Benson's chin, turned his face round and with his fingers pressed to the sides of his mouth as if he were a rough father opening a baby's mouth to get at what the child has concealed, pushed his erect phallus into his mouth and rammed it home. *Benson, I would have expected that of you!*

'Suck on it,' he said.

Benson did his best without protest.

Again the man returned to his position behind him, and spat. Benson felt the man's spittle applied, tickling. He tried to remember what to do, what he had done when Dr Leptos had done it to him in Devil's Bridge. But then it had not been like this. The man spread Benson's cheeks and pushed against him hard. Benson reached behind to try to control the thrust but the man knocked his hands away.

Benson did his best to untense and he felt the phallus edging into him.

'Stick your bum out farther!' said the man.

He pushed relentlessly into him and Benson collapsed upon the bed. He thought he would get into trouble for this but the man lay on top of him and did not seem to mind the change of position.

Benson felt the warmth of the man's whole body covering him and the moving penis inside him.

The man started to ride him and as he rode he called him names. He said that Benson was a soft girl who belonged under a real man and could not get enough. Benson was made for this. He was bloody no good for anything else but to have a stiff cock stuck up him. He asked how it felt? He knew Benson, he said, knew him through and through. What Benson wanted was a big cock like his pushing through him and coming out at his mouth so that he could suck it while he was being fucked. That was right, wasn't it? He was like a girl with his big, soft bottom and his sissy voice, what he wanted was what he was getting. That's what he wanted. Wasn't it?

Benson replied in the affirmative – though a part of him wanted to enter into a Socratic dialogue about some of the points – aware that he was going to come. He tried to hold off, to concentrate on the pain, but the pain when he looked for it was not there. Or, rather, it was there but had become something to which he could not put a name. His head buzzed and jangled

217

with it. Far away he could hear the bed creaking loudly and the man's obscenities as he rode him like a horse or like a woman or like a no-good thing of no value.

'You're right,' Benson told the man.

The man seized him by the hair and lifted his head to kiss his mouth, but when he reached the mouth he bit the lips and hung on to them and hissed: 'I know you! I'm going to spurt into you! That's what you want!'

Benson whimpered and came and his spasms convulsed through him and brought the man on. With a couple of plunges which made Benson cry out, the man came too, still holding on to Benson's lips with his teeth.

'I'm sorry but I came on your sheet,' said Benson, as they were disentangling themselves from one another.

'Take it down to the kitchen and rinse the bit under the tap. Then put it by the fire to dry,' the man said.

Benson gathered the sheet off the bed, frowning at the mattress, and followed the man back downstairs. He stood behind him, envying him his muscular bottom as he stood on tip-toe to wash himself at the kitchen sink. Then, when he had finished, Benson washed a part of the sheet using a pink tablet of soap. The sheet became soaked across a wider diameter than he would have thought, but he remembered that that always happened.

The man took the sheet from him as he came back into the living-room and draped it over a chair by the fire. He had already put on his clothes. Benson struggled into his.

'I'll take you back now,' said the man, jangling his car keys.

'Can I have your address?' asked Benson.

'There's no address. Nor telephone neither. Where are you in Aberystwyth? I'll come and see you if I need you.'

Benson gave the man his room number and address.

They drove back in silence to Aberystwyth. The man

took him to Pantychelyn, leaving him at the roadside. He nodded when Benson said goodbye.

Benson watched the red tail lights of the man's Vauxhall Viva disappearing down the hill.

10

'And where were you?' asked Meryl.

Benson knew perfectly well where he had been, of course; had had loads of time to consider every second of his movements on that confusing afternoon a fortnight before. But he did not feel that he could in all conscience burden Meryl with his exploits on the day of her departure, and replied, 'I don't know how I missed you.'

'I don't believe you even bothered to turn up,' Meryl observed, looking out of the window of the More Utopia.

'The train had three carriages, and there was a man with a guide-dog on it.'

Meryl shrugged. 'Well, I wept all the way to Shrewsbury. The fellow opposite thought it was the book I was reading, but it wasn't. Nobody's going to be able to wring a tear from Sweet's *Anglo-Saxon Primer*. No, Martin, I felt bereft of friends and support.'

'I really am sorry, Meryl.'

He was too. His failure to say goodbye to Meryl had caused him a great deal of soul-searching. On the one hand it seemed like a good act to say goodbye to a friend; a bad act to go into a toilet. But the scales had been weighted with all sorts of confusing ingredients. The good of goodbye weighed less heavy because of Meryl's lateness and, if he were honest, her reason for going. The bad action of going into the toilet weighed the lighter for thoughts of the spectacular sensations of the afternoon. That had been marvellous, hadn't it? Had it? The man had not been a very nice person, not particularly well brought up. Either that or he had forgotten how to behave. Yet why had he been so excited by it? Often since, he had thought of himself kneeling in the room and not getting up because he thought the man would be angry. Why had he been like that? Why had it excited him so? It excited him still. The man had called him names which would normally have caused him to rise up and strike back — or at least leave in a huff – why not then?

'Do you feel all right in yourself?' he asked Meryl.

Meryl accused Benson of committing tautology and Benson did not ask for an explanation. He felt that he should humour Meryl as much as possible. After all, Meryl was probably carrying a great weight of guilt. Not that she would admit it for a minute. No, she would never do that. She was Meryl Magdalen all right. Probably the Meryl at the well as well. The trouble was that she did not see it that way, at least would not admit to seeing it that way.

'You haven't breathed this to a soul, have you?' Meryl asked him.

'No.'

'No, I don't suppose you have. I doubt you care enough to talk about it. After all, I'm just a woman.'

'Do you want to talk about it?'

'Well, I was about to but now you come to mention it, I think I'll save it for another time. What have you been up to?'

Benson told Meryl about his adventure with the farmer, though he changed dates and locations to protect the guilty. Himself.

'You've clearly got masochistic tendencies,' said Meryl after Benson had finished his tale.

Well, Benson thought, at least she shut up while I was telling her. That was a tribute to his powers of story-telling for a start. It hardly mattered if at the end of it Meryl came out and told him that he had tendencies the nature of which he would have to rush to the dictionary to discover. That was two words he

221

would have to file away from today. He tried to think of the other, but couldn't.

'And your chum is a sadist if you ask me. God, if a man tried to treat me like that I'd give him a mouthful.'

Benson knew what a sadist was. 'I don't think he was really a sadist. He didn't beat me. He was just a bit . . . well, uncouth.'

'No, Martin. You can be uncouth and yet tender where it counts. What seems strange to me is that you enjoyed the experience.'

'Yes, that's been bothering me.'

'Well, you're not unique. Lots of women like being abused. I have several friends who live with real bastards.'

'Have you?'

'Yes. How's your fish and chip shop friend by the way?'

'He's all right.' Benson knew that Gareth was all right because he had peeped through the window the previous night, though he had not gone in. As a matter of routine he now returned to Pantychelyn along the Llanbadarn Road just to make sure Gareth was all right. He did not always venture inside. He felt that if he went inside too often he might be drawn deeper into Gareth's life. If he did the charitable thing and went to bed with Gareth out of pity then Gareth might want to make it a regular thing, and Benson might get stuck with the most boring sex imaginable. He might even end up working in the fish and chip shop! How Brother Hooper would laugh! He'd use him as an object lesson at Assembly or arrange special school trips so that boys could watch wicked Benson slaving over the hot vats. *During the summer, boys, I was on a motoring holiday with Father Mahon in Wales. One lunchtime in Aberystwyth we happened to stop at a fish and chip shop for a bite. Don't laugh boys. I am quite partial to fish and chips, in moderation naturally. However, my weakness for fish and chips is not* the point of this salutary tale, boys. I have often told you about a wicked boy called Benson. Of course, I knew he would come to a bad end. He surprised us all by obtaining four A levels. When I last saw him he was sporting a beard. Now that was ten years ago, boys. I want you to imagine my surprise when, upon entering the fish and chip shop, I found myself confronted by this arrogant errant ex-pupil of St Bede's. He was shovelling chips into bags, boys! Ah, but he was greatly changed, I can tell you. His face pasty from a life of chips and unnatural acts. Boys, I can assure you that it took all my Christian charity not to say to him: 'I told you so!' You will be pleased to know that I did not say such a thing. I simply ordered and watched him as he looked up from the greasy vats – I might almost say hell-like – vats of boiling oil, and recognized me. It was a sweet moment boys. It capped by a long chalk my having cause to complain to O'Gorman about mer-chandise bought at British Home Stores, whence O'Gorman, as I believe I told you last week, has found his vocation as Deputy Manager. Now, be silent, boys, and think on Benson's fate. A thick boy deluded by the world and too many Bob Baez records. Then he chided himself for these thoughts on several counts. Why did he rush ahead of things so much? Gareth had not even ever said that he was a homo. Of course, Benson was sure that he was. It was as clear as Kant.

'Coo, look at those two!' exclaimed Benson, pointing out of the window of the More Utopia at Sean and Myvanwy. 'What do they think they look like?'

Meryl looked. Myvanwy had a tray of flags around her neck, and Sean was shaking a donations box. Both were dressed oddly. Myvanwy had on a plain white smock over a long black skirt. Her bare feet were encased in sandals. Sean wore a pair of jeans with patches all over them, a thin tartan shirt with a tear and one blue sock and one green sock, with similar sandals to Myvanwy. Both wore coolie-hats.

'They're collecting for something,' said Meryl.

'Well, that's obvious, but what are they wearing?'

'It's all part of the show,' said Meryl.

'How do you mean?'

'You mean you haven't noticed them before? They've become quite famous for their happenings. A couple of weeks ago they stood outside the cinema where *Lawrence of Arabia* was playing, wearing Arab garb and notices around their necks which said: "Homeless Palestinians". They just stood there all abject as everyone queued for the evening show. They were still there when we came out.'

'Why?'

'Well, it's obvious, isn't it? They're trying to draw attention to the plight of these people. Sean told me that at Christmas he's going to lead Myvanwy round the town on a donkey and ask for accommodation. He says that it will bring home the real message of Christmas. It's all part of their radical approach to religion apparently.'

Benson had expected Meryl to show some contempt for the pair. He had been ready to agree with her contempt and add a little of his own for good measure. But Meryl did not add anything to what she said. She just stared at them, a smile on her face. Then, as Benson was about to ask what they were collecting for, she said: 'It takes guts to do it.'

'What else have they done?'

'What haven't they done?' replied Meryl. 'Sean gets on a soap-box on Saturday and tub thumps for Catholic doctrine. He gets heckled like mad but it doesn't stop him. I can't understand how you haven't seen them before! You've probably been too busy getting picked up by farmers.'

Benson might have said something to Meryl at that point, but his heart was busy sinking as he saw Sean and Myvanwy making for the door of the More Utopia.

'They're coming in,' he told her, fidgeting on his seat. Meryl stared back at Benson frostily.

He could hear the collection box being rattled and Myvanwy saying: 'Give till it hurts!'

Sean kept repeating: 'Thank you! God bless you!' and his voice was getting louder as he came nearer.

'Hello Martin!' he said. 'We're collecting for Vietnamese orphans and we demand a contribution!'

Meryl put a half crown into the collection box without a word. Benson reached into the pocket of his anorak and found what he hoped was a selection of pennies and halfpennies. He took these out and pushed them nervously into the slot, only noticing when it was too late that there was a florin hidden in the pile.

'Thank you! God bless you!' said Sean.

'Yes, thank you very much!' added Myvanwy, taking two flags from her box and sticking them into Meryl and Benson's fronts.

'Have a coffee,' said Meryl, moving over in the booth to make room.

'No, thanks all the same. We have work to do,' replied Sean. And they continued on through the More Utopia. Benson heard the till open and the owner pushing money into the collection box.

Then he watched them leave the coffee-bar, feeling a familiar ache, and yet resenting the pair at the same time.

'I envy them in a way,' Meryl said.

Benson knew exactly what Meryl meant but he asked her what she meant in any case.

'They're so certain about everything. And I've never seen them looking miserable, unless looking miserable is part of a happening they're engaged in. Myvanwy lives on my floor at Ifor Evans. She's generous. Always ready to listen.'

'Yes, maybe,' replied Benson, 'but imagine what she would think of you if she knew.'

'What would she think of me?'

225

'Well, I mean . . .' began Benson.

'Let me tell you, Martin, I'd rather have Myvanwy's judgement than yours any day of the week. I think she'd be quite understanding. She might well think I was a sinner. I don't mind that. I'd at least know where we stood. No, it's people like you who don't know shit from shinola that would worry me more. You're liable to change with every wind that blows.'

'That's not fair, Meryl!'

'It bloody well is fair! Before I went away, I was getting so fucking fed up with all the nonsense the girls at the hostel were coming out with. "It's your body"; "It's just a form of birth control". Well, I knew all that! Even my precious parents went on like that. A load of trendy rubbish. Not one of them breathed the thought: Babykiller! But all of them were thinking it. You were thinking it and you're a liar if you say otherwise. How could you not think it? But no-one came out and said it. It would have been far too embarrassing. It would have spotted their liberal credentials to give that side of things an airing.'

Benson felt a bit irritated, because he distinctly remembered coming out with how wrong abortion might be. He had couched it tactfully, of course. But he could imagine the reaction if he had been less tactful. What did Meryl want, to be stoned in the street? There was just no pleasing women.

'Let's change the subject, Meryl,' he said.

'I think I'll have a Wagon Wheel,' said Meryl.

'Penguins are better value,' opined Benson.

Meryl mimed 'Wagon Wheel' then pursed her lips and Benson stood up and bought her one. For himself he bought a Penguin reasoning that he might be able to convert Meryl to a better class of biscuit by taking longer to eat it.

Meryl held her Wagon Wheel in both hands and set about nibbling it intently. She was greatly absorbed by this and hardly seemed to notice Benson stripping the

226

silver paper off his Penguin and then prising open the two pieces of biscuit to reveal the chocolate cream in the centre stuck to one of the slabs. He took the piece with the cream on and rubbed it down his lower front teeth, thereby detaching the cream and liquefying it with great chomping sounds. Then he started licking the chocolate off until the light-brown biscuit stood revealed in his chocolate-stained fingers. He laid aside this piece and picked up the other chocolate-enrobed piece. He sucked off the chocolate.

Meryl had finished her Wagon Wheel by this time and was regarding Benson. Benson grinned at her and lay the second stripped biscuit down on the silver wrapper next to the first.

'There you are!' he said.

'Yes?'

'Well, you've finished your Wagon Wheel while I've got two quite substantial biscuits still to look forward to! And I bet you I've enjoyed my Penguin just as much as you enjoyed your Wagon Wheel! Maybe I'll just fold these two pieces away and eat them when I'm next peckish.' And Benson – as good as his word – folded the silver paper round his bare Penguin.

'You're disgusting, Martin,' said Meryl.

There was something in the way Meryl said it that reminded him of other matters: of toilets and remote farmhouses and him kneeling on the floor.

'You don't think I am, do you?'

'Are?'

'Disgusting. I mean really. I sometimes think I am. You don't think I am?'

'No, it was a joke,' said Meryl.

'You see,' he continued, unwrapping the foil on the Penguin and pushing one of the biscuits into his mouth, 'I feel I am becoming a bit of a mess. I'm getting mixed up again. Before – of course I was mixed up then too – I always thought I knew where I stood. There was an answer for everything. Usually they

227

weren't answers that I liked much, but they were definite. Now everything is a question and when I try to answer I keep thinking of buts and howevers and anyways and on the other hands. I didn't know it would be like this.'

'I don't get you.'

'When I decided I didn't believe in the Church any more I thought it would all become so easy and straightforward. But it hasn't been. I feel that with every passing day I understand less and less about everything.'

'I shouldn't let that worry you too much if I were you. You've joined the human race, that's all.'

'But you just said you admired Sean and Myvanwy. I know exactly what you mean. Part of me does too. Also, there's an overseas student I visited the other day, a man from Sudan. He talked to me about his religion and his certainties make him so reliable, straight, untwisted. Next to him I feel, well, disgusting, is as good a word as any.'

'I'm not going to coddle you, Martin,' said Meryl lighting her own Number 10. 'I'm the one who should be getting the comfort. However, I must say that even if I were in a better mood I would still have to state that there is nothing to be done about your confusion. It is the human condition. The search is everything.'

'Yes, I suppose so. But I just don't seem to be able to make any sense of things. I don't think there will ever be a time when I will be able to make sense of things. Jesus, Mary, Joseph, Kant, Plato, Bertrand Russell, Bob Dylan, Jean-Paul Sartre. What is Love? Can I love? Is friendship compatible with sexual satisfaction? It all just goes round and round.'

Meryl nodded.

'I think I'll have another Wagon Wheel. I hear that Penguins contain chemicals which cause neuroses. Now let's talk about something else.'

They talked about Ianto's trip to North Wales to turn

the signs the wrong way round. It was only later that Benson remembered that he had promised Ianto that he would not tell a soul.

The next day, Enoch Mohammed nearly bumped into Benson in his Mercedes. Benson was walking along the main street out of Aberystwyth in the afternoon, back towards the hostel. He had been trying to decide whether to check on Gareth, had almost decided not to, rather to buy himself a quarter of wine-gums and study quietly in his room until dinner, when he had started a rather tentative crossing of the road, at an obtuse angle. He heard brakes scream and fearing the worst, tried to break into a trot. The car stopped about a foot from his foot. Benson watched the fly whisk on the front nodding its plumage, its reflection shining in the white bodywork of the Mercedes.

He walked round to the driver's window, but finding that Enoch Mohammed was driving on the near-side, he scurried round there. 'I'm terribly sorry, Enoch Mohammed, it was completely my fault.'

'Think nothing of it, Mr Vice-President. I was driving with due care and attention. Get in, I'm going to the garage to check my tyre pressure.'

'That's nice.'

Benson got in. He sat next to Enoch Mohammed on the seat where in English cars he would have been the driver. Enoch Mohammed started up and proceeded at speed along the road, turned left, ignoring a lollipop lady with her sign up on a children's crossing as he did so. Benson looked alarmed for the benefit of the startled lollipop lady but Enoch Mohammed just accelerated away from the scene.

'I am glad to see you again after this long time. I will show you my new flat. I believe that you were instrumental in obtaining it for me.'

'Not really. I just mentioned that you didn't have a place. Mrs Jones did the rest,' said Benson, clutching the dashboard with both hands and wondering if Enoch Mohammed would take kindly to being asked to slow down. He felt extremely vulnerable sitting where the driver should be sitting, much too close to cars passing in the opposite direction. Is this how drivers on normal cars felt all the time? It must be a good training for death, he thought. Every other second Death seemed about to scythe him down.

'It's a very nice car,' Benson observed.

'Yes, it is beautiful. It is German.'

Enoch Mohammed suddenly turned left. The brakes screamed. Benson was sure Enoch Mohammed had not indicated his intentions.

'Power steering,' said Enoch Mohammed.

'Really?' The Man had been interested in the attributes of his car too. Were all the men he found attractive going to be car fanatics? Perhaps he should take out a subscription to *Motor* and cancel *The Listener*.

The car was brought to a sudden halt in a garage forecourt. Enoch Mohammed honked the loud horn three times and Benson saw a man in the workshop looking towards them with a frown on his face. Still, mechanics always frowned like that. It seemed to be part of the job. Mr Bentley at Benson's bike shop frowned like that whenever he had taken his bike in. 'What have you done now, sonny Jim?' he'd ask him. Now, Benson averted his gaze and looked doggedly at the dashboard, like an innocent bystander of some scene in which he is powerless to intervene.

Enoch Mohammed got out of the car and then spoke to Benson through the open door. He was wearing a suit that shone as if made of fish scales. 'I have a little task for you to do, Mr Vice-President. I am besieged by work at the moment. I have stolen too much time from my studies and am having to burn the candles at all ends.' He reached inside the car and honked the horn again.

'Yes?' asked Benson. He pulled his bag off the floor and on to his lap. Then he saw the garage owner approaching, wiping his hands on his overalls. He looked much more stern than Mr Bentley ever had.

'There is the matter of the overseas students' Christmas dinner-dance. I am hiring the Pier Ballroom on December 18th. It is all in hand. Invitations have been printed. It only remains to collect the money from our overseas brothers and sisters. Normally I would volunteer to do this onerous task myself. But I was wondering if perhaps – because of the difficult circumstances – you might do this work for me.'

'Yes, of course,' replied Benson helpfully. 'I quite understand. How much do you want me to collect?'

'Thirty-five shillings from each student.'

'That's rather a lot. Do you think they'll be able to afford it?' Benson's heart was sinking, both at the thought of having to pay out thirty-five shillings at the very end of term, and at his view of the garage mechanic.

'It is really very reasonable. We shall be subsidizing each ticket to the amount of fifteen shillings. There will be an excellent dinner and a dance with a band. It will be a night to remember!'

'But do you think they will all want to come?'

'You must use all your powers of persuasion, Mr Vice-President.'

'Well, I'll do my best,' said Benson. He could see the garage mechanic standing nearby looking daggers at Enoch Mohammed. 'Er . . . I think he wants to . . . The garage man is here, Enoch Mohammed!'

Enoch Mohammed did not seem to care. He kept talking to Benson. 'That's A-1. I have the tickets back at the flat. I'll give them to you today.'

Then Enoch Mohammed had straightened up, turned away and was speaking to the garage mechanic. They started walking together towards the garage. Then they stopped. Benson saw Enoch Mohammed put his hand on the man's shoulder and the man shrug it away, turn and start wagging his finger at Enoch Mohammed. Benson wondered whether he should get out and try to mediate, but then he saw that a group of schoolgirls were making their way across the fore-court, giggling at the fly whisk on the front of the car bonnet. Enoch Mohammed saw them and shouted something that Benson could not hear. Whatever it was it sent the girls into whoops of laughter.

The girls, he thought, saw Enoch Mohammed as rather special. Well, he was. They probably thought he was like Cuddly Dudley on *Oh Boy*. Cuddly Dudley had been the one bright spot on *Oh Boy* as far as Benson was concerned. He didn't sing very memor-able songs, but Benson loved it when he was talking on the telephone to his girlfriend and said sexily: 'But, baby, you knows what I likes!' He would then go off into a rather unintelligible song that did not fulfil the preamble of the sexy telephone conversation, but he definitely made *Oh Boy* worth watching. Benson could just about sit through that silly Cherry Wayner playing her padded electric organ with her daft dog on the top. Why did it never cock its leg? He knew that millions of viewers all over the country were waiting for Cherry Wayner's dog to do something disgusting. That would have wiped the sickly smile from her silly South African face! Marty Wilde was all right too, though he didn't move about much and earn his money by putting his whole heart and soul into his songs, but it was Cuddly Dudley that made the programme worth a look-in. However, Benson wondered why they never did anything really worthwhile on *Oh Boy*. Could they not have Peter Pears singing 'In Darkness Let Me Dwell'? Like *Ready, Steady, Go,* it was narrow in its appeal.

When Benson came to himself, Enoch Mohammed and the man were still arguing. Enoch Mohammed had picked up the tyre pressure hose and was trying to pull it towards the car. The garage mechanic had placed his foot on the coiled hose and would not let him do it. I am witnessing a clear case of racial discrimination, Benson thought. I must do as Sartre says and *act*!

Benson acted and got out of the car, tripping over his scarf as he did so, and walked purposefully over to Enoch Mohammed and the garage mechanic. 'What's the matter?' he asked.

'Your friend should pay his bills,' said the man. He looked nervous, but a bit relieved to see Benson. Then he addressed Enoch Mohammed in an angry but quavering voice, 'Until you pay me what you owe me you're not getting anything from me.'

'It says "Free Air",' said Enoch Mohammed, still tugging on the hose.

'I don't care what it says. It's not free to you.'

'That's no way to treat a visitor to our country!' exclaimed Benson.

The mechanic looked nonplussed for a moment. Then he asked, almost sulkily, like a guilty schoolboy, 'What do you know about it?'

Benson took in the mechanic's discomfiture, and felt his confidence rise. 'This gentleman is a friend of mine.'

'You should pick your friends more carefully. Your friend owes me sixty pounds for work I've done on his car.'

'I gave you a cheque,' said Enoch Mohammed.

'It bounced, as you well know.'

'A misunderstanding.'

'It was no misunderstanding,' said the man. 'Anyway I've informed the university. They'll sort you out.'

'I'm sure the problem can be very easily mixed up,' said Benson, who, now the mechanic had regained his manly poise, was nervous himself again, 'sorted out . . . I mean overseas students . . .'

'I'm not going to get into a discussion with you about it. Your friend knows. Now just get off my property.'

Enoch Mohammed dropped the hose. 'Let us go,' he said to Benson.

'No, you've got to stand up for your rights, Enoch Mohammed! You can't give way to prejudice!'

'It's no good.'

'I'm going to report you,' Benson told the garage mechanic, who had already turned away and was walking back to his office. He followed Enoch Mohammed back to the car, turning once or twice to aim resentful looks at the mechanic.

'It was a mix-up. The bank put the money my father sent them into the wrong account,' said Enoch Mohammed as they drove away.

'You don't have to explain anything to me, Enoch Mohammed. I know what these people are like.' He was already wondering how he could organize a group of students to picket the prejudiced garage-owner and drive him out of business.

Enoch Mohammed gunned the large car down the street, turned on to the promenade, then back the way they had already come, up the hill out of Aberystwyth. They did not speak, though Benson was desperately searching about for something comforting to say. Then Enoch Mohammed turned to Benson and said, 'Women are most difficult to control.'

'Are they?' asked Benson, wondering what that had to do with anything. Then he thought of Meryl. Was Enoch Mohammed talking about Meryl? Meryl was difficult to control all right. Then he wondered whether Enoch Mohammed knew where Meryl had been, what he had caused Meryl to do.

'Do you mean Meryl?'

Enoch Mohammed nodded but did not elaborate.

'She's a lovely girl, though.'

No acknowledgement came from Enoch Mohammed. He frowned at the gleaming windscreen.

At the top of the hill the car swerved into the lane that Benson had walked down the afternoon Clitherow had left. The trees along the road had completely lost their leaves, the branches were jagged lines in black crayon against the fuzzy grey paper of the sky. Some crows and seagulls swooped across a fallow field. Two walkers, alarmed by the sight of the car almost completely filling the narrow lane, pushed themselves against the hedge, and then aimed resentful looks at Enoch Mohammed as the car passed. Benson tried to give them a split-second, reassuring look, but could not tell whether it had registered. He hoped it had. But he looked at Enoch Mohammed then, hoping that he had not noticed his sudden partizanship. He might think him a traitor.

He thought that Enoch Mohammed should drive a little less fast for his own good. He was really giving people ammunition for their deeply engrained prejudices. All the people who had nearly been run over by Enoch Mohammed would go home thinking negative thoughts about black people. Then, when the topic of race was raised, they would think of him bearing down on them and say something nasty. Still, what must Enoch Mohammed be thinking every time he saw a white person? Benson shuddered.

The car turned off the road and along a driveway flanked by tall pines. A house came into view, a large house that Benson had not noticed during his walk along the road. Around the house were neat lawns.

'This is lovely! Do you live here?' Benson asked Enoch Mohammed.

'Yes, in the flat over the garage. This is where Mrs Jones lives. She rented the flat to me.'

'Did she? I didn't know you were living with her. I thought she had just found you a place.'

'She is also a Justice of the Peace.'

'Is she?' That might prove useful at some point, he thought.

The Mercedes came to an abrupt halt inside the garage, but it was unlike any garage in Benson's experience. The big car went nowhere near to filling the floor space. To the left a stairway led to a door half way up the wall.

Benson followed Enoch Mohammed up the staircase and into the flat. 'It's really lovely. It makes every other flat in Aber look like a real slum. Is all this furniture yours? It looks antique.'

'No, it is included in the rent. I must pay very little.'

Benson thought what a nice woman Mrs Jones was. It restored his faith in human nature somehow.

Enoch Mohammed brought Benson a large envelope full of invitations to the overseas students' Christmas dinner-dance, and offered him tea. Then he disappeared down the hall. Benson heard dialling and then loud exchanges in a strange language.

Still, perhaps loud voices were just a way of speaking. Not everyone went through life keeping their emotions in a strait-jacket like the dull old English. George and Martha in *Who's Afraid of Virginia Woolf?* fought all the time but that kept things interesting for them and helped them achieve a sense of reality and all that. Maybe it was the same for Enoch Mohammed. He was high-spirited and wore his emotions on his sleeve. No bad thing that.

After what seemed like a long time, Enoch Mohammed returned with tea. When they had drunk it, he offered to show Benson around the grounds.

These were as impressive as the house had been. Enoch Mohammed took great pride in pointing out the gazebo to Benson. They followed a track down to a small pond, completely surrounded by trees, on which some ducks were swimming. Benson kept telling Enoch Mohammed how lucky he was.

'I am an English gentleman.'

'You certainly are. I'm very happy for you. If I had a home like this I would never want to leave it.'

'The girls I bring here like it too. I tell them that I am a prince in Nigeria.'

236

'I bet Meryl didn't believe you,' said Benson.

'I have not brought Meryl.'

'So you have other girlfriends. You are lucky, Enoch Mohammed,' said Benson, thinking about Meryl.

'Your women like black men,' said Enoch Mohammed very matter-of-factly.

Benson felt he knew that already. He had read James Baldwin and Ralph Ellison after all.

'But what about you?' Benson asked.

'Me?'

'Yes. Don't you feel a bit . . . well . . . funny . . . having more than one girlfriend?'

'I have a lot of energy. Sometimes, Mr Vice-President, I think I could satisfy all the ladies of Aberystwyth!'

Benson thought that rather odd. In a way it conformed with his own viewpoint of Enoch Mohammed's powers, but it upset him to hear it from Enoch Mohammed himself. It was all very complicated and made Benson feel peculiar and a bit depressed. Enoch Mohammed was as sure of himself as the man in the farmhouse had been. He knew his power and that was part of his attraction. A part of Benson strongly disapproved of Enoch Mohammed and thought that if the world were full of Enoch Mohammeds everything solid would start giving way. Another part would have followed him around the unreliable thin skin of the planet. What was it all about?

'It sounds as if you think that English girls believe that Africans are more sexy than Englishmen,' said Benson pointedly.

'They are right to think so, Mr Vice-President.'

Benson could not stop himself. He felt greatly peeved. Even if Enoch Mohammed thought that, he might have the good manners to deny it. When Auntie Muriel had said that he was a clever lad for getting four A levels, he would not have dreamed of letting it pass. No, he had assured Auntie Muriel that he was as thick as two short planks.

Benson felt that he no longer quite liked Enoch Mohammed. It made it easier to do what he had started to conjure up in his mind. He launched himself into space. 'You know, er . . . I sometimes wonder if I am . . . well . . . big enough to satisfy a girl.'

'Have you ever tried?'

'No. Never.'

'Well, you should try. What about Meryl?'

'Meryl and I are just friends.'

'Why don't you try?'

Benson kicked some toadstools into the grass as he considered his answer. Now Enoch Mohammed seemed to be trying to push Meryl on to him, pass her on like a package in Pass the Parcel. That was mingy of him. 'I'm not really sure I'm well-enough equipped. Down there. I mean . . . what I mean is . . . I suppose I am but I often think that maybe I'm not . . . er . . . I mean you never can tell and . . .'

Enoch Mohammed nodded and started walking down a path between trees.

Benson followed. He addressed the sparkling back of Enoch Mohammed's suit: 'Remember when we were in the shower? You looked so big and I felt little beside you. Ianto's big too. I just think women might laugh at me.'

'I think there is more than what you say, Mr Vice-President. Meryl told me a story about you.'

Enoch Mohammed stopped and turned.

'She didn't, did she?' Benson asked, cursing Meryl – thinking her mingy too – then thanking her, hoping she was all right. Benson stared at the ground, then, let his eyes move up the body of Enoch Mohammed furtively. He smiled.

'I said I could not believe her. We do not have such problems in Africa.'

'It isn't a problem. It's just something that happens.'

There. It was out. Meryl and her big mouth. Still, it was out, and Enoch Mohammed wasn't running.

'Show me!'

'Here?' asked Benson, looking around. The giddiness engendered by every sexual encounter in his past seemed to come together and knock him about. He staggered. 'Can't we go to . . .'

'There is no-one to see.' And Enoch Mohammed walked off the track and stood against a tree, motioning Benson to stand beside him.

Benson was erect. Enoch Mohammed took himself out of his trousers and started to piss against the tree.

'I am hard,' Benson told him, excusing himself.

'Let me see, then I can judge about your size.'

With difficulty, Benson took himself out and waited for a reaction.

'That is it? You are hard?'

'Yes.'

Enoch Mohammed, looked to left and right, stopped pissing and began to pump at himself and Benson watched his black member, matt black along the shaft and glossed at the end, stand out straight from his flies. He looked down at his own and then across at Enoch Mohammed.

'You're bigger than me,' he said. He did not feel resentful. There was something wonderful about being able to admit the fact to Enoch Mohammed's face.

'Yes, I am. Now you know, Mr Vice-President.'

Benson nodded, though he felt he had known for a long time. Still, now he *knew*.

A minute or two later, their new knowledge safely buttoned up again, they were walking back to the house. Benson felt more embarrassed than anything. He told Enoch Mohammed that he would walk home. Enoch Mohammed went up to the flat and brought down the envelope full of invitations. Benson took them and said goodbye. He would sell every one. Then he would deliver the money to Enoch Mohammed. Then what? He thought about that for a mile along the dark lane. After that he would do everything he could to stay out of Enoch Mohammed's way. Enoch Mohammed had lost his mystery. And, though Benson had learnt something that day, Enoch Mohammed had too. In future, every time they met, wounding arrows of nasty knowledge would zoom between them. Benson did not feel that lust had softened into ease. For a moment, back in the grounds of the big house, he had thought it might. Now he knew better.

He would sell the tickets and that would be that.

'"Nymph, in thy orisons be all my sins remembered!"'
Benson muttered to himself as Dr Leptos's car passed
him and honked. It was a week later. Benson was
walking purposefully along the promenade on his way
to the library for some last-minute panic revision.

He held his breath. Was the car about to stop? The
brake light was on. A bad sign. Don't stop! Please don't
stop! Ugly hell gape not! I'll burn my books! . . . but Dr
Leptos was only braking prior to turning left by the
Philosophy department. Benson breathed again.

*See, boys, how he flees his sin! Pleasures turn to
wormwood on the tongue, boys. Benson is fast becoming
the Aberystwyth tosspot, the Mandy Rice-Davis of
mid-Wales. You all know how he tried to seduce poor
Enoch Mohammed with his bent logic and wicked
ways! Oh, he reproaches himself now! He fancies he is
repentant, boys! But it is not real repentance. His
words fly up, his thoughts remain below the belt.
Words with dirty thoughts never to heaven get sent. He
is sorry. But Judas Iscariot was sorry, boys. Sorry is
such a little word. It comes out with no effort at all,
like a dying man's last sigh. I bump into someone in
the street: 'Sorry!' I spill my tea on the nice new rug:
'Sorry!' Is our Heavenly Father going to be satisfied
with 'sorry'? Is He? Let Benson be an example to you.
He has crossed the Devil's Bridge. The widow of this
world has thrown him to the Devil. Perhaps you,
seeing his fate, may cross in safety.*

Brother Hooper had a point. Was he any nearer
towards finding Dearest Him, assuming of course that
Clitherow was not Dearest Him? No, of course

241

Clitherow wasn't. If he was there would not have been any uncertainty. He would at least have been sent a thank you note from Oxford. But if he kept on like this . . .

To help with his studies Benson had borrowed a small reel-to-reel tape-recorder from Ianto to record his Anglo-Saxon texts, and extracts from plays and poetry. Tape was, he decided, a wonderful invention. Ianto's Fuji Cherry was allowing him to get all sorts of things into his brain in a most convenient manner.

But who was Dearest Him? Dr Leptos or Enoch Mohammed? No, they weren't. They weren't even homos. His Dearest Him had to be a homo. He could not stand the idea of someone going off to a wife after being with him. What about the Man? Though Benson had waited for him to call, he hadn't called. It was him that Benson remembered most. The Man had become the raw material for his nightly fantasies. Was it possible that that man could be the Friend? He made a face. It would be all right for part of the time, that part of the time when everything went purple and rude. But what about the rest of the time? The Man would never be able to talk to him about Existentialism and the Nature of the Good. No, Benson would have to mug up on different kinds of sheep dip, try to sound enthusiastic about *Farming Today*. He'd probably have to churn butter day in day out and do hedging and ditching like Walter Gabriel. It didn't sound quite what he wanted. But the sex would be good. Or would it? No, probably he'd be tired and worn out in a week and he'd have to pretend to have a headache, like Gwen Watford.

Still, if he did meet up with the Man again, he would definitely be able to talk to him about how to test different kinds of feed on goats. He had gone with Omar to the Animal Husbandry department out in the country. There Omar held sway over a captive population of black and white goats. They were kept in a shed lit by strip lighting, and all had canvas bags over their bottoms. Omar had explained how he and his Welsh assistant had to weigh the contents of the bags each day, milk the goats, weigh the goats, measure the fat layer on each goat with a thing like a protractor and correlate all the material collected, comparing yields according to the different feeds that the goats were fed. Waste from Sudan's cotton industry was specially imported as part of the project. Omar had to put a specimen of goat droppings from each goat into a test-tube for analysis. If Omar had been a Catholic he would have offered it up for the Holy Souls. Thousands would have zoomed heavenwards each time he filled a test-tube. What he was missing!

The smell of the goat shed was similar to the one in Omar's flat, but multiplied to a point that had made Benson giddy. Still, he accepted the tour as a privilege, asked lots of questions and walked about with his hands behind his back like the Duke of Edinburgh, thinking it a pity that there was not a little machine for spraying Tabac over the goats at regular intervals.

'What'll happen to your work when you come home with me for Christmas?' Benson asked Omar.

'My assistant will do it.'

'That's good.'

Benson worried a bit that Omar would not be able to rid himself of the smell before he got home. Should he ring up ahead of time to explain that there might be a problem? It would be terrible if Dad and Alice thought it was him, or worse, Omar!

Benson opened the library door, padded quietly towards the desks that looked out over the sea. Someone was sitting at his favourite desk, but one that was almost as good was free, and he made for it.

He could see a rough winter sea beating against the pier. On the pier the overseas students' Christmas dinner-dance would take place in just over a week. By then examinations would be over and he would only

243

have the Christmas party and Omar's visit home to worry about. Omar had bought a ticket for the dinner-dance.

Dad had not put up any objection to Omar coming for Christmas. Alice had said that she would have thought he would want to bring a girlfriend home, but had not laboured the point. They would just have to start getting used to him not doing what was expected of him. It was going to go on for some considerable time.

Before starting his revision work, Benson opened the now-creased envelope given to him by Enoch Mohammed. Of the one hundred and fifty tickets he had managed to sell one hundred and forty. Every overseas student had been approached. All except Faridah (Alexandra Hall, room 606) from Mombasa had agreed to come. She was going back to Mombasa for the holidays. Some had protested at the price of the ticket but Benson replied, echoing Enoch Mohammed, that it was being subsidized and that he was sure it would be a night to remember.

He wondered whether he would be able to sell the other ten tickets. Perhaps he could ask some of the students in the hostel to go. He also knew that he would have to get the money back to Enoch Mohammed before too much longer. It was frightening to be going around the town with more than two hundred pounds in his briefcase.

That evening at dinner he managed to sell Ianto two tickets, and Ianto said that he would spread the word, though he also thought they were a bit on the pricey side. Simeon approached him and asked for another one, saying that he had a girlfriend to take. Benson asked who the lucky girl was. Simeon merely smiled.

He decided to hold back the seven remaining tickets, but drop the money he had collected into Enoch Mohammed's that evening. He did not want anything to happen with Enoch Mohammed of course. No, he didn't. Didn't he? No, he didn't. Anyway, nothing would.

Fyfe Robertson followed him down the Clarach Road, asserting that even on the darkest nights Benson was to be seen doing good. But Brother Hooper drowned him out with a very different account. Benson, he asserted, was daily walking deeper and deeper into the quicksand. He might struggle, but that would just make things worse, and Bertrand Russell wasn't going to be around to throw him a rope, unless it was a rope to hang himself with. 'You can talk all you like! I'm not going to listen to either of you!' Benson told them.

The night was cold and the stars shone clearly in a moonless sky. He started whistling alone in the dark to keep his spirits up; then he was whistling to entertain the stars. Each of them is a departed soul, he thought. Mum's star is there somewhere. He stopped whistling, stood still and looked up till he felt his eyes pushing through layer upon layer of stars, seeking to penetrate their haze and discover what lay behind. Tears came to his eyes then and he started walking again, whistling a selection from *On The Town*.

He made out lights from the house through the pines and turned down the drive. The main house was dark, but a light burnt in the garage and he saw from a distance that Enoch Mohammed's car was parked there. A faint light glowed behind heavy curtains in one of the windows of the flat.

Benson walked up the stairs and rang the bell. He saw the door being answered and Enoch Mohammed asking him in. He would be pleased to see how much money the Vice-President had managed to collect; how he had kept records of money paid so carefully. He would smile and clap him on the shoulder and appreciate just how efficient homos could be.

'Is that the taxi?' It was a woman's voice.

'No, it's me ... er ... Martin Benson. I've got something for Enoch Mohammed,' replied Benson, leaning down towards the letter-box. 'I've got the dinner-dance ticket money for him.'

The woman did not reply. Benson thought he heard footsteps retreating from the door, then a silence. He bit his lip, looked down into the garage from his position at the top of the steps, and said: '"Romeo! Romeo! Wherefore art thou, Romeo?"' to the roof of the parked Mercedes. Then he started down the stairs, feeling like a thief.

But the door opened and Enoch Mohammed was standing resplendent in a dressing-gown on the spot Benson had just been fidgeting upon.

'Mr Vice-President, it is you!' he said.

'Yes, I'm sorry to call at such an inconvenient time, but I've er ... got the donner-dunce tacket money ... the dinner-dance ticket money ... for you.'

Enoch Mohammed held out his arm, and Benson ascended the steps and placed the envelope in his hand. 'I would invite you in, Mr Vice-President, but I am engaged, you see. One of the beauties of Aberystwyth. She works in the bank I attend.'

'Yes, don't worry. I'll be off. Bye,' said Benson, and he headed down the stairs again.

The door closed and he retreated down the drive, looking back at the muted light through the heavy curtains, wondering what was going on inside.

The stars had lost their magic as he retraced his steps. 'What I need is a nice homo to snuggle up with, just as Enoch Mohammed is snuggling up with that girl. Fancy making her get a taxi home. You'd think he would have the decency to drive her himself!' He badly wanted to talk to someone, and made a small detour to Ifor Evans hostel, knocking at Meryl's door. There was no answer. He jittered about in the corridor of the women's hostel. It smelled different from Pantychelyn, a smell of perfume and clothes drying on radiators. What shall I do? he asked himself. Perhaps some fish and chips might mop up the existential gloom.

'Hello, Gareth,' said Benson.

'I thought you'd gone home for the holidays,' replied Gareth, stirring chips.

'No, not just yet.'

'You students are always on holiday. Everything all right?'

'Not bad. You?'

''bout the same. Things don't change much. What can I do for you?'

'Six of chips and a piece of cod, please.'

Gareth took the money Benson offered, piling the newspaper high.

'Is business good?' Benson asked. The state of Gareth's business had been a cause of concern to him for some time. It seemed a bit easy to catch Gareth alone in the shop.

'Can't complain.'

'But you're managing all right, are you?'

Gareth stopped in the act of wrapping Benson's fish and chips.

'You needn't worry,' he said.

'Well, I wasn't. I mean I . . .'

'I'm not going to do anything silly. I mean it wouldn't be right, would it? Not when I've got a friend who's so worried about me.'

'Who's that?'

'You, of course. I've seen you peeping in, checking on me.'

'I haven't done it much.'

Gareth set about smoothing his hair back into place. The long skein of it growing above his ears was hanging down. The first time he tried he completely missed it and his hand made the motion, smoothing nothing over his bald head. Benson had been about to tell Gareth that he had missed his hair, but immediately Gareth repeated the action and caught the hair, smoothing it across the top of his head. Benson thought he looked better bald.

'No-one loves a fairy when she's forty-four,' stated Gareth.

'I don't see why that should be,' said Benson, though he could think of several reasons straight off. 'Perhaps it all depends what you mean by love.' And Benson thought, if he knows I wish he would pass it on. I'd love to know the answer to that one.

But Gareth did not seem inclined to get embroiled in a philosophical discussion on the meaning of love. He just nodded sadly. 'You're a queer boy too, though, aren't you?'

'Yes.'

'Well, you just watch yourself, boyo. You just watch yourself!'

'Don't worry, I will.'

'It's easily said.'

'Yes, things get complicated, don't they?'

'You can say that again.'

'Things get complicated, don't they?' Benson said. But Gareth did not laugh at his joke. 'I'm going home for the holidays in a week or so. Still, I'll see you when I get back, won't I?'

'Oh, yes. A bad penny, me. No worry on that score,' said Gareth.

'That's good,' said Benson.

'But don't forget me, will you?' Gareth said anxiously. 'It's been nice to see your face darting round the window like. You're a bit of a guardian angel on the sly. Perhaps when you come back you can come back to my place for a meal. I don't mean fish and chips. I'm quite a good cook if I do say so myself. And don't worry that I'm going to pull you into bed. I'm sure you're worried about that. I always did when I met queers at your age. Some of them acted like they owned you. They'd show you a good cottage and then expect the moon. I wouldn't treat my guardian angel like that. Maybe you and I can be sisters.'

Benson frowned. He thought brothers more appropriate. Still sisters sounded harmless enough, though Benson could not help reaching into the past to see two black-clad nuns walking down the pavement together.

'Why not?' he said.

An old couple came in with hymn books under their arms. Benson wished Gareth a happy Christmas, resolved to send him a card, and noted the address of Gareth's shop. He wandered back to the hostel to eat Pro-plus and study till dawn, folding his wings neatly down – the chair-back between the feathers and his body – so the wings would not get crushed.

12

Benson had to borrow a dark suit from Ianto's friend, Brian, to allow him to attend the Overseas Students' Christmas Dinner-Dance with all the sobriety befitting his high office. The trousers did not fit very well, being a bit tight around the bottom. He had trouble pulling up the zip and noted ruefully that his penis showed through as a most unimpressive hillock, unflatteringly small. He remedied this by rolling up a sock and placing it down his trousers, inside his underpants. Women used falsies, didn't they? Anyway, it did his ego good. He did wonder what would happen if he managed to find someone and brought him home. If that happened the chap might be in for a disappointment. 'Put a sock in it!' he told his neurotic side, feeling slightly irked that there was no-one with whom he could share the joke.

In the end, Benson had invited Meryl to accompany him to the dinner-dance. He had tried to sell her one of his last seven tickets, but she said that she had had a lot of untoward expenses. Benson nodded understandingly, and offered to take her. Only later did he consider what a hopeless financial quagmire he was getting himself into. Still, with any luck he would not have to pay anything until the beginning of the following term. If he kept out of the way of Enoch Mohammed, everything would be all right.

The examinations had gone well, he thought. He had managed to write the whole time. That was something. Even Anglo-Saxon had gone better than it might have. He was sure he had recognized the places where he had had to start translating from his learning work with the tape-recorder. Naturally, Morals had been a cinch.

At six thirty on the night of the party, Benson walked up the hill to Ifor Evans hostel to pick up Meryl. He knocked at the door, but there was no answer. He looked at his watch, sighed, and walked down the corridor to the kitchen, where Myvanwy was standing in her dressing-gown waiting for a pan of milk to boil.

'Have you seen Meryl?' Benson asked Myvanwy.

'She's having a bath.'

'A bath! She's supposed to be all ready to go!'

Myvanwy shrugged and poured boiling milk into her coffee. She didn't add any water at all. She would be as round as a ball by the time she was thirty, he thought. Still, now she was a Catholic – or well on the way to becoming one – she would be putting her body behind her.

'There are going to be snacks and pre-dinner drinks. I wouldn't be at all surprised if we miss them,' Benson told Myvanwy and his ticking Kienzle watch.

Myvanwy smiled and offered him a cup of coffee.

'No, thank you all the same. It's a bit thick, though. Typical Meryl.'

'Now don't be too hard on her,' counselled Myvanwy. 'She's had a bad time, you know.'

'I know.'

'That Nigerian friend of hers picked her up this afternoon. She only came back half an hour ago. Between you and me, Martin, she looked a bit upset.'

'Enoch Mohammed? She went out with Enoch Mohammed?' asked Benson. Enoch Mohammed had not even had the courtesy to ask Meryl if she would go with him to the overseas students' dinner-dance.

But Myvanwy was, despite Benson's frown, adding too much sugar to her coffee, and just nodded with her back to him. 'You don't want to be a shepherd in our Christmas happening, I suppose?' she asked him.

'How do you mean?'

'Well, we're planning a radical Christmas happening. Haven't you seen the donkey? It's in the field by the hostel entrance.'

'No. Where did you get it?' He could dimly remember Meryl mentioning Sean and Myvanwy's Christmas plans.

'The man who does donkey rides on the beach is a Catholic.'

They're everywhere, he thought.

'What we plan to do is this: Sean will lead me down the hill. We'll both be dressed for the part. Then we'll go around asking people for accommodation. We won't get any, of course. So we'll spend Christmas in the bus-shelter on the prom. We're arranging for students to ring the police and complain about the Holy Family and the donkey in the bus-shelter. But we'll also phone television Cymru. It should cause quite a stir. The trouble is that we need shepherds to come and visit on Christmas morning. You'd have to bring hay for the donkey as well.'

'I'm taking an overseas student home for Christmas,' said Benson, trying both to keep his end up in the virtue stakes and make a convincing excuse. Then he saw a dark shape with a white turban pass the kitchen door. 'Meryl! Hurry up, will you! We'll miss the . . .'

'Go easy, Martin. There's a love,' said Myvanwy. She started sipping her coffee.

'All right,' he replied. 'I'll just go and hurry her along a bit. I know she'd hate to miss the snacks and pre-dinner drinks as much as I would.'

Myvanwy nodded and wished him happy Christmas.

'Same to you, Myvanwy.'

He retrod his route along the corridor. *Bell, Book and Candle. Candle, Book and Bell. Forward and backward to damn Benson to hell!* Fuck off! I won't tell you again . . . He knocked at Meryl's door and waited for a reply. *Though sorely threatened with the*

252

missing of snacks and pre-dinner drinks our hero observes those little decencies which have made this sceptred isle a fit place for heroic homos.

'I hope you're not going to take too long,' Benson told Meryl. 'We're going to be late. They're having snacks and pre-dinner drinks. It's not every day we have those, now is it? We've got to get our money's worth.'

'Give it a rest, Martin. I've said I'm sorry.'

Benson sat on the bed and pursed his lips. It was true, Meryl had said she was sorry, but she had not said it with much contrition in her voice. If he had been Meryl he would have been saying he was sorry all through the lengthy procedure of changing and making-up he had been forced to sit through. Anyway, who had paid for the tickets?

'It's going to be a really nice do,' he said, trying to warm the atmosphere.

'Doubtless,' replied Meryl flatly.

On the way down to the Pier Ballroom, Benson tried to engage Meryl in conversation. He asked her what she had done for the Anglo-Saxon examination.

'Translated the texts,' she said.

'Did you start your translation into English with the lines: "The land to the north is windswept and inhospitable"? I think that is where it started.'

'Maybe.'

'Well, I hope you did. As I probably told you, I learnt the texts off by heart. I just haven't been able to learn the language. You really are clever, Meryl. I expect you'll pass with flying colours. I know Anthea thinks she's done well, but she's a real worker. I know I've done well on Morals. I just couldn't stop writing, but I'm not that sure about American Studies. I tried the one on the Negro novelists, but I think I made a botch of it. I went on and on about James Baldwin and Ralph Ellison because I haven't read Richard Wright. What I did at the end was start a new paragraph and say: "We

253

now come to the important writer Richard Wright who is well-known for . . . time up.'' It's an old trick, but at least your Ralph Wynne will know I've heard the bloke's name. Still, I did a very good one on Carson McCullers even if I do say so myself.'

Meryl stopped and looked at Benson. He caught her scent and was aware that the funny clip-clop sound made by her high-heels had ceased. Women ought to wear desert boots, he thought, then rapists wouldn't know they were coming.

'Have you finished?' Meryl asked him.

'Yes, well, er, don't you think you ought to wear desert boots?'

Meryl, who had started clip-clopping again, stopped again.

Benson looked at his watch. 'I mean, I was thinking that if you wore desert boots, if all women wore desert boots—'

'They could give Martin Benson a more effective kick in the shins. Just shut up, Martin, there's a good boy.'

'All right, I will.'

And he did. All the way to the Pier Ballroom he kept his lips shut tight. He was burning to ask Meryl what was wrong, but there was obviously no point while she was in this curious mood. He concentrated on worrying about whether he and Meryl would have missed their snacks and pre-dinner drinks.

Life became even more curious when they arrived at the pier. A large number of overseas students in national dress milled round the door to the ballroom. There was also a sprinkling of Welsh people in evening dress. These people were going to the door and disappearing through it, giving the overseas students odd looks as they went. A knot of overseas students stood round a harassed-looking man who was preventing them from going into the ballroom.

Leaving Meryl on the fringe of the crowd, Benson

pushed through wondering if here he had come upon another case of racial prejudice, until he found himself opposite the doorman, who looked flustered.

'What's the matter?' Benson asked Josna, the Social Secretary.

'The manager of the ballroom says that we aren't booked in for our dinner-dance. He says that the Rotary Club are having their dinner-dance tonight.'

'Have you shown him the invitations?'

'Yes, I've seen the invitations, young man. But they have nothing to do with us. We don't have a booking for you tonight or any other night,' the man said. He looked as uneasy as the garage-mechanic had done.

Maynard, President of the Overseas Students' Society, arrived and asked what the matter was. The sad information was repeated. Benson could see Simeon standing with Anthea. He was glad to see that Simeon and Anthea had got together, sad that their first date was proving to be a let down. Was it their first? They could be married with a family for all he knew, given what a peculiar world it was.

'Have you seen Enoch Mohammed?' Maynard asked Benson.

'No, not recently. I thought he would be here.'

Mrs Jones appeared. She had on a beautiful dress. Her husband was in a dinner jacket. Maynard took her by the arm and spoke quietly to her. She nodded and looked stern. Then, hoisting her stole higher around her shoulders, as if it were armour, she marched over to the doorman and started talking to him loudly in Welsh.

Then some students on the fringe of the group, led by Ianto, started chanting 'Why are we waiting?' to the tune of Adeste Fidelis. Benson went and stood beside Meryl.

An Indian student to whom Benson had sold three tickets passed him and murmured pointedly: 'A most disgusting occurrence!'

'There seems to have been a mix-up. Enoch Mohammed hasn't arrived yet. I thought he had made all the arrangements,' Benson told Meryl, though he hoped his voice was reaching the disgruntled Indian too.

He looked over at her. He was not expecting a reply to his observation, but neither was he expecting what he saw. Meryl had opened her mouth wide and was panting like a dog. Tears were pouring down her cheeks from wide-open, unblinking eyes.

'Is everything all right, Meryl?'

Meryl looked at Benson in a way that made him flinch. He had been about to put his hand on her shoulder, but the look caused him to step back a pace. She stopped the rapid breathing and forced her breath out in a scream that was at first soundless, but which then pierced the ear and went on and on like a baby's first bout of weeping until the air in her lungs was completely exhausted. She breathed in deeply, threw her shoulder bag away as if it were a huge insect that had landed on her, and the scream turned into loud weeping. She curled up and keeled over on to the pavement.

The complaining crowd of overseas students had gone silent when they heard Meryl's scream. Some came over and watched. Maynard's wife had retrieved Meryl's bag and placed it carefully on the pavement beside her. Benson got down on to his hands and knees and tried to pull Meryl's hands down from her face. But she resisted him with all her strength. He saw that she had buried her long nails deep into her cheeks and was using them to provide leverage to stop Benson from pulling them away.

'You'd better leave her alone for a while.' It was Mrs Jones. She lifted Benson up and led him away. 'What's the matter with her, do you know?' she asked him.

Benson looked into Mrs Jones's face and wondered what to say. Perhaps not getting into the dinner-dance was just the last straw for Meryl? Perhaps it had something to do with Enoch Mohammed? But how could he say that to Mrs Jones? Anyway, it could be something completely different. Meryl could have taken something. Perhaps the nutmeg-chewing had worked at last?

Mrs Jones was waiting patiently. He looked at her and started to shrug and say 'I don't know', but before the utterance was out she said coldly: 'It's to do with Enoch Mohammed, isn't it?'

How could Mrs Jones know about Enoch Mohammed and Meryl? Benson looked at his desert boots. They did not go with the suit at all. Maybe it was just as well that the dinner-dance hadn't happened.

'It might be, yes,' he said, hoping that he had not betrayed Meryl by imparting even that amount of information. He looked towards her hunched form on the pavement and thought: I've let you down. I wasn't a good friend to you at all!

'I think it's best if I take her home in the car,' Mrs Jones said. 'If she hasn't calmed down we'll get the doctor in. I don't think there's much you can do. Perhaps women understand these things better.'

Benson nodded. Mrs Jones was amazingly calm. Apart from hitching up her stole more often than strictly necessary, she was just as she had been that day in the Maypole. He could see how she had got to be a JP. 'Anyway, you'll have your work cut out here smoothing ruffled feathers. Tell everyone not to worry. We'll have our dinner dance, even if I have to put it on at my house in the New Year.'

'Good, I'll tell them that. I'm sorry, Mrs Jones.'

Mrs Jones smiled, but there was little mirth in it. '*You*'ve got nothing to be sorry for, Martin.'

Benson smiled gratefully at Mrs Jones, though he was not sure she was right.

Meryl, still weeping, was being talked to quietly by Josna and Maynard's wife. Mrs Jones joined the group and took Meryl's hand, coaxing her up off the pavement.

Benson fled to the fringe of the crowd. He looked from the shadows cast by the Philosophy department building at the disgruntled united nations of overseas students – united, Benson felt, against *him* – talking in groups. Ianto was standing in the midst of them with Janet. Both were smoking, and the smoke rose above the group and hovered in a blue pall in the still air. Behind the angry and depressed knots of people he could hear the waves breaking against the pier's supports, sounding for all the world like a walk through dead leaves. There was no escaping it, he thought. They don't sound a bit like crisps shaken in a bag.

Benson had started to plan his escape. There was nothing but embarrassment for him here. But he strode manfully into the midst of the throng and announced in a faltering voice that everything would be sorted out and that no-one was to worry. They took little notice of him. He wondered whether he ought to try again louder, but could not face it.

'What a bloody cock up!' said Ianto.

'I'd have expected that from you, Ianto!' Benson rapped back. 'It's not my fucking fault.'

'Language!' said Ianto.

'Let's go to the pub,' said Janet.

'No, thank you,' said Benson.

'Who's bloody asking you?' said Ianto.

'He can come if he likes! Don't be so nasty, Ianto,' said Janet.

'Thank you, Janet. But I really can't. I'm very sorry for what has happened.'

Janet pulled Ianto away, and Benson pulled tongues at his tall, retreating back.

The overseas students had started to drift off, murmuring darkly. A Ugandan student whom Benson had always found a bit formidable because of his constant monologues about the evils of colonialism, passed him and gave him a nasty look. Then Simeon passed him with Anthea.

258

'It's a disappointment for us,' he said.

'I know. Same here,' said Benson.

'Where's Enoch Mohammed?'

'I don't know.'

Simeon nodded knowingly and looked at Anthea, whose face presented a stormy picture.

'What's the matter with Meryl?'

'I honestly don't know.'

Then Simeon looked down at Benson's feet. 'What's that?' he asked.

'What's what?'

'That on your shoe,' said Anthea, in her thick Preston accent.

Benson looked and saw his sock.

'It's a sock,' said Simeon.

'So it is. I wonder how that got there?' said Benson, staring balefully at his guilty sock.

He picked it up, stuffed it into his pocket. Simeon and Anthea walked on, away from the pier. Benson turned on his heel and fled back to the hostel. He found a route through previously unknown sidestreets, and he walked with his head down and his jacket covering his crotch, wondering about Meryl, praying despairingly for Meryl, pleading that the Wisdom and Spirit of the Universe would let the soul of Meryl's aborted baby out of grey limbo and into heaven, where it would be well looked after by Mum.

The following morning Benson felt the need to get out of harm's way. He did not dare present himself for breakfast, fearing that he would be attacked and asked for £1 15s 0d by every overseas student in Aberystwyth. But what to do? There were no lectures to attend.

He found Mrs Jones's number in the phone books and dialled it. Her husband answered.

'Can I speak to Mrs Jones, please, Mr Jones. It's Martin Benson.'

'Martin Benson?'

'The Vice-President of the Overseas Students' Society,' he added, thinking that he should add an 'ex' to his exalted title.

'Oh, yes, of course. I'll get her for you.'

The phone was put down and he heard a clock chime nine. Even over the phone it sounded beautiful and helped steady his nerves. He thought that he would definitely have a chiming clock when he had a place. He had often admired the ones with rotating balls in one of the jewellers of Aberystwyth. Did they chime like that? One day he might pluck up courage, go in and ask. Mum had always said that he should never go into a shop that did not have prices on everything. He would only find thieves inside.

'Hello, Martin.'

'Hello, Mrs Jones, it's Martin Benson,' replied Benson, trying to gather his wandering thoughts.

'You've rung about Meryl, have you? Well, she's here with us. She's much better now, dear. We gave her a tranquillizer. I don't think she's woken up yet.'

'Is there anything I can do?'

'No, I don't think so. I've phoned her parents and they are coming up to collect her later today. A kind friend of hers at the hostel is packing up some things for her.'

That would be Myvanwy, he thought.

'You haven't seen anything of Enoch Mohammed, have you?' Mrs Jones asked.

'No. Nothing. Isn't he there?'

'Disappeared without trace. He seems to have cleared everything out of his flat.'

'I see,' said Benson.

'I wish I did. Of course, he might have just gone on his holidays early. However, I do think it a bit irresponsible of him to leave without a word.'

'Yes. Mrs Jones, did Meryl say anything about what the matter is?'

'Yes, Martin, she told me everything. I think she's a

very brave girl to go through with the pregnancy. It'll be touch and go with the university authorities as to whether they'll let her stay on. A gutsy girl, that Meryl.'

Mrs Jones stopped speaking, expecting Benson to say something. But Benson couldn't. He stared at the receiver, then at the acoustic covering of the telephone booth and read Abergavenny 45423. How dare people write on public property like that!

'Are you still there, dear?'

'Yes, Mrs Jones,' he whispered.

'Anyway, we were all taken for a bit of a ride. Some worse than others,' she continued.

'Yes.'

'Meryl will come through it. She's a very game girl, Martin. She's very fond of you, by the way.'

'Is she?'

'Oh, yes. She was full of you last night. Terribly sorry for the trouble she'd caused.'

'She didn't cause any trouble.'

'You could do worse than get yourself fixed up with a girl like Meryl.'

'Er . . . Can I come and see her, Mrs Jones?'

'I think it's better if you don't, Martin. Leave it until after the holidays. By then things should have settled down a bit. Come to think of it, she could always take the flat here. Between you and me, I don't think that Enoch Mohammed will be back.'

'Don't you?'

'No. There are a few too many broken hearts round Aberystwyth, aren't there? We landladies notice a thing or two from behind our lace curtains.'

He hesitated, but there was something in Mrs Jones's voice which told him that she knew everything. He was the only one who knew nothing. 'Yes, I suppose so.'

'Look, give me your home address and I'll pass it on to Meryl. And I'll give you her London number.'

Benson dictated his address and phone number to Mrs Jones.

'I know people in West Kirby,' said Mrs Jones. Well, he thought, Mrs Jones *would* know people in West Kirby. West Kirby was full of big houses with Rovers in the drives and chiming clocks on every available horizontal surface. 'Meryl's London number is . . .'

Benson unclipped his pen and searched around frantically for a piece of paper. Finding none, he wrote the number on the acoustic board by the phone.

'Have a super Christmas. We'll get together in the New Year to plan that dinner-dance. Don't worry about anything, Martin.'

'No,' he said. 'Give my love to Meryl.'

'Of course I shall.'

'Bye, then.'

'Goodbye, Martin.'

He put down the receiver carefully, watching himself doing the action. The camera crew was busy behind him. Fyfe Robertson was saying: *This young man has many things on his mind. Why? What has happened? Well, it all goes back to one evening a mere two months ago when this same young man gave a little soirée in his room for Meryl – of whom more later – and two African students . . .*

Benson dismissed the camera crew with a look, then set about memorizing the seven digits he had written on the acoustic board by the phone. He walked purposefully back towards his room.

Meryl was still pregnant! How could she be? She had gone off for an abortion at the clinic of a friend of her dad's, hadn't she?

Pimping, boys. I do not mince my words. Oh, it looked like a friendly little student gathering, I'll grant you that. But not a bit of it! The lost sheep Benson has turned into a slavering wolf! Vice-President of the Overseas Students is he? VICE President, he is! He opened the door of his room and found a piece of paper but also found that in his confusion he had forgotten the number, and trailed back to the telephone booth, only to find it occupied by Shigo. He jiggled about waiting for Shigo to finish.

Of course, they had never discussed the operation in so many words. He had just assumed that she had gone through with it. Why hadn't she told him she hadn't? Perhaps she was just telling Mrs Jones she hadn't. Perhaps she just wished she hadn't and was pretending that the baby was still growing inside and had not been taken away and put in the bin. Yes, perhaps it was part of her breakdown that she needed to think the baby was still alive and not weeping somewhere in limbo in the form of a winged cherub for its little life cut off.

'Stop it!' he told himself out loud. No, it looked as if Meryl had decided to keep the baby. She could not have fooled Mrs Jones. Mrs Jones knew everything. It would not have surprised him if Mrs Jones had found out about his feelings for Enoch Mohammed. Yes, that was it! Meryl was still in love with him and had told him about the baby! That would definitely explain why she was in such a state and why Enoch Mohammed had beat a retreat. But perhaps he had gone because he knew about the funny business over the dinner-dance. But . . .

'It was very sad about the dinner-dance,' said Shigo to Benson.

Benson in his own peculiar world was not ready for the remark. 'Was it?' he asked.

Shigo gave him a funny look and walked away. Not giving Shigo a second thought, Benson made for the booth and copied down the number on the wall. Then he scribbled across it with his Bic, giving about as much thought to the mess on the board as he had given to Shigo.

He returned to his room and placed the number in his suitcase to make sure he would not forget to take it home. Then he wrote a note to Omar.

With no lectures to attend, no Meryl to meet, he wondered what to do next. It might be a good idea to keep a low profile and away from contact with overseas students. Well, he could walk down to Aberystwyth and deliver his note to Omar. Yes, he could do that, and on the way he could try to sort things out.

He kept his eyes wide open, searching for any dark faces that might look at him accusingly. He dropped the note in for Omar, telling him what time they should meet at the station the following day. Then he scouted about for something to do.

He walked aimlessly for a while, thinking about Meryl. Then he found himself thinking about the Man. He thought about the Man. Then he tried not to think of him. The Man had not got in touch with him, though many had been the times when Benson had lain on the bed hoping against hope that the door would open and there the Man would be. But probably the Man would be too shy to come into the hostel. No, he wouldn't. He would stride in with his flies open and humiliate Benson in front of everyone. The idea excited him. Then it humiliated him.

He was walking across the bridge over the Rheidol. The river – the same river that bubbled youthfully at Devil's Bridge – sighed sluggishly into the harbour to his right. He was walking out of Aberystwyth and he was walking toward the Man's cottage. Can I find it? Do I want to? Well, I do and I don't. Still, I've got to get out of Aberystwyth. There's no peace for me here.

An erection he felt would trip him up was growing under his anorak. He started to think about the afternoon he had spent with the Man, though this only caused the erection to pound more strongly. I am entertaining lascivious thoughts, he thought. Then he thought what a funny expression 'entertaining thoughts' was. 'Excuse me, Lord Benson, there's a dirty thought outside.' 'Show him in, will you, Moriarty.'

'Come this way. Lord Benson is ready to entertain you now.' The thought came in all bulges in crimson pants with its flies open. Benson entertained lavishly, limping down the Cardigan Road. But then other thoughts came, and they all confused him and he thought that thought was not always such a good thing. It might be nice to go for a day or two without thoughts. Perhaps very stupid people did. Perhaps really clever people just had one thought at a time. In-between people like him had thoughts that tumbled around like prizes wrapped in lots of layers of paper in a bran tub. You felt about and fumbled with each one in turn but never managed to really get to grips with one before your time was up. Anyway, even if things turned out well with regards Enoch Mohammed – and that was by no means guaranteed – Benson would at the very least have to offer his resignation from his post of Vice-President of the Overseas Students' Society. He was honour bound so to do, wasn't he? Harold Macmillan had, after all. If I can just get through the next twenty-four hours without being hounded, I'll be all right. It will all have sorted itself out by the New Year!

These thoughts were not at all entertaining, he thought, though they made walking easier. Traffic whizzed along the road. How strange it was that there was so much traffic. What on earth was there to do in Cardigan? What an odd name for a town!

After a couple of miles, Benson decided to hitch. It did not take him long to get a lift, but he was not sure where to tell the driver of the Cadbury's chocolate lorry that had picked him up to stop. When he thought he was getting near the turn off, he told the driver that he had come far enough.

'Good luck!' said the man as Benson got out.

The lorry driver had said that he did not like chocolate. Benson watched the lorry retreat into the distance. He shook his head at its rear. Fancy driving a Cadbury's chocolate lorry and not liking chocolate.

But perhaps Meryl would pursue Enoch Mohammed to the end of the earth. Maybe he should marry her. It would be nice to wheel a coffee-coloured baby around the place in a pram. People would think he'd adopted a poor orphan from Africa. It would cause quite a sensation in the More Utopia!

But then he thought that was no firm foundation for marriage. He'd end up like the thin chap watching Rita Tushingham lighting a sparkler at the end of *A Taste of Honey*. You had to be able to do the necessary for marriage and the idea of doing the necessary with Meryl just did not appeal. Even if he could manage something, she would quickly guess that his heart wasn't in it. She'd go off and find herself someone satisfactory, and he'd probably do the same. And what about the baby? It was a poor look out if both parents were adulterers. No, if he married Meryl for the sake of the child, he'd have to give up sex completely and just devote himself night and day to its care. 'Well, I might be able to,' he told the bald hedgerow on the Cardigan Road. Then he recognized the turn off to the Man's cottage.

Excited just by the erotic geography, Benson forgot about wheeling a pram and telling Aberystwyth ladies tales that rebounded to his credit and left them thinking: There goes a real Christian! He followed the narrow lane until it turned into the rough track he remembered and sat down on the verge, wondering if he ought to go any farther. He rolled himself a Sun Valley cigarette and while he smoked it he entertained thoughts about the Man again, which convinced him to proceed.

When he came within sight of the cottage, he could see smoke rising from the single chimney, but there was no dog barking in the yard as there had been when he had come before. Gingerly, he approached the cottage and went round to the back door. He knocked and waited, his heart pounding, imagining that at any minute the man would come to the door, leer, and open his flies.

But there was no reply. Part of him was greatly relieved, part greatly let down. He looked through the windows, recognizing the dim interior. He smiled at it, wondering if he would ever enter again.

He had almost reached the main road when he saw the man's car coming along it. The black and white sheep dog was sitting in the front seat. Benson made to blend with the verge to let the car pass. He did not want the man to assume that he had been looking for him. He planned to say that he had just happened to find himself in the neighbourhood.

The car stopped opposite him. The Man opened the nearside door and the dog growled, then barked at Benson. The man cuffed it over the head.

'Hello, I was just passing. I like long walks and . . .' said Benson.

'It's you, is it? I was wondering when you'd be back. Get in!' said the man.

The dog was pushed on to the back seat, where it crouched and growled resentfully.

Benson, ignoring the dog, blood pounding in his ears, got into the car.

'What kept you?' the Man asked.

Benson knew there were many answers to that, but his life's blood was pumping him up hard, removing the lubricating saliva of speech from his mouth, engorging his head with spectacular imagery of the disgraced ex-Vice-President of the Aberystwyth University Overseas Students' Society on his front, presenting the part of him which caused him most embarrassment, taking his punishment . . .

13

Two days later Benson arrived home with Omar. The trip had been unpleasant, the unheated train stopping for an hour on the single line track to Shrewsbury. Then they had had to wait a further hour on Shrewsbury Station for the arrival of the Liverpool train. Benson put a shivering Omar into the waiting-room near the coal fire, asking a vicar to remove his suitcase from the bench to make room. Omar seemed cheerful enough, but he did not talk much, and was not particularly enthusiastic about availing himself of Benson's Tabac-saturated handkerchief to revive himself with. Benson worried then that he was going to spend the Christmas holiday trying to make conversation.

But when they finally got home, Omar had proved himself a great asset. He effortlessly provided a shield between Benson and Dad and Alice. Finding the house warm, his hosts smiling and welcoming, Omar came out of himself and talked a lot more, definitely more than he ever had with Benson.

Alice asked Omar a few questions which Benson thought were a bit redundant. She sat in her police-woman's uniform, her legs crossed in Mum's favourite armchair, a cup of tea secured by a hand and her left thigh, asking him questions which five minutes with a Philip's Primary School Atlas would have rendered unnecessary. Omar answered her questions with great patience and good humour. He was definitely an excellent ambassador for the Sudan, Benson thought. He could see that Dad and Alice thought the same.

Alice asked Benson to help her make the tea and Dad was left alone with Omar. Benson had put Omar under strict instructions not to mention anything about the overseas students' Christmas dinner-dance. He did not want to panic them. No-one had managed to corner him about the incident. It was something which he would have to put into his drawer of worries, taking it out with a shaking hand in the New Year. It had not been his fault, had it? He had, after all, only been obeying orders.

Benson inspected Alice's attempts at sandwiches and cake all spread out on the trolley, ready to be wheeled into the lounge when the kettle boiled. The cups and saucers had been arranged in a decent manner. All the crockery matched. Mum had been very keen on that sort of thing. He did note, however, that there was no slop-bowl. There was jelly, but no trifle. The sandwiches were made of sliced bread, not the crusty split-tin that Mum walked a mile and a half to the best bakers to get. They were also cut in half, not the artistic triangles that Mum had made, always placing her hand flat on the top of the pile, saying: 'Say a prayer it works', before driving the bread knife down. It had always worked, just as it had always worked when her jellies came slurping out perfect from their rabbit moulds.

Alice had gone to the trouble of making a sponge-cake, even if it did have a sprinkling of petit bourgeois icing sugar on the top and not Mum's butter icing. She moved about the kitchen with great fluency, knowing how to close the cupboard in the kitchen cabinet that took a knack. She went straight to the cutlery drawer and the arrangement of cutlery was, he noted with relief, the same as it had always been in the Benson household. Left to right: forks, knives, spoons, soup spoons, teaspoons. But Alice warmed the teapot by placing it over the spout of the kettle. He frowned at that, but had to admit it was better than not warming it at all.

'You're very quiet, Martin.'

'Not really,' he said. 'I was thinking.'

'What were you thinking?'

'Oh, nothing.'

Alice placed the teapot on the trolley. Then she filled the kettle again and placed it on the stove. 'Now, is there anything I've forgotten?' she asked.

'Well . . .' He had been about to say that Mum would not have countenanced a teapot without a tea-cosy. There were two: one for every day, that looked like a grey cardigan and had holes in it for handle and spout and a grey and royal blue pom-pom on top, and one with embroidered flowers on it that fitted over the pot like a too-big hat. This one was used for best and, in less serious times, he had loved to wear it when it came off the pot all warm and rich with the aroma of tannin. 'No, I think we've got everything.'

'I've forgotten the tea-cosy!' said Alice and she made straight for the drawer to the right of the sink – as to the manner born – and took out the embroidered one. 'This is the one we use for best, isn't it?' she said, smiling as she placed it almost reverently over the steaming pot. 'There we are!'

Benson had to give her credit. Dad had taught her well. Alice had learnt domesticity surprisingly quickly. On the train he had feared that he and Omar might be greeted by mugs of tea with the tea-bag in it. Mum would not let a tea-bag in the house. She had always been of the opinion that the tea for tea-bags was swept up off unhygienic warehouse floors in Assam. A plate of Kit-Kats and a bowl of Smiths crisps had also inhabited his darkest premonitions. But such was not the case. Of course she still had to pass more difficult tests. He had not inspected the airing cupboard to see how the linens were kept. He had yet to sample a cooked meal, to run his finger across horizontal surfaces to see if dusting was being assiduously done. The real tests still lay ahead.

'I've got some good news for you, Martin,' said Alice

as Benson was about to wheel the trolley into the lounge. Alice did not look as if she were about to impart good news. She fiddled with the sugar spoon in the bowl.

'Your dad said I shouldn't tell you until I was absolutely positive. Well, I've been positive for a couple of weeks now, but then he said I should wait until you came home. But I can't wait any longer. I'm going to have a baby, Martin!'

'How do you mean?'

'I'm pregnant!'

'You mean you're going to have a baby?'

'Yes. It's due in July.'

Benson suddenly thought: Wormwood! Wormwood! But he said, after a pause: 'Well, this is a surprise! Congratulations!' and, frowning, bit his tongue hard.

'Wheel the trolley in then.'

Benson wheeled the trolley into the lounge thinking that what he needed was a good long walk along the prom to attempt to sort out what he had just heard.

Dad was talking to Omar about his time in the Middle East during the war.

'The Gippos led us a dance, I can tell you,' he said.

Benson looked at Dad disapprovingly. Then he looked at Omar concernedly. Omar wore a smile and said: 'Yes, the Egyptians are a cunning people. We in the Sudan have learnt not to trust them.'

'But you have to hand it to the Gippo,' continued Dad, 'they can make a lot out of very little. I can remember taking Land Rover axles to one of their workshops in the morning and coming away with half a dozen copies in the afternoon. Yet all they had to work with was a fire like the one in the grate here and a pair of bellows. Try getting that done round here. Impossible! I brought a lovely leather pouf back home with me. Do you remember the pouf, Martin?'

Benson nodded. Of course he remembered the pouf!

271

He had sat on it most days for the first ten years of life. Where had it gone? He could still see the gold outline of camels against precipitous pyramids. Everything passed.

'We had to throw it out a few years ago. Cracked all over. But we've still got a beaten tray with Arabic writing on it. Perhaps you'll be able to translate it for us, Omar. I've always wondered what it said.'

'I'll be glad to try.'

Benson poured the tea. Milk for everyone except Omar. Sugar for no-one but Omar. He distributed plates and offered sandwiches. And all the time he thought: She's going to have a baby! I am going to have a sibling!

Dad was giving Omar his impressions of Cairo during the war. It was a whole new world for Benson. He had never enquired about what Dad had done in the war. He knew he had been in the Army in the Middle East but it had been something he just took for granted. And Dad had never volunteered any information. Yet here he was telling all to Omar. It made him feel peculiar. Why had he not thought to ask? There he was weeping to War Requiem when all the time his dad had been moving people into the sun and having strange meetings.

Benson and Alice, sitting next to one another on the sofa, listened for a while. Then Alice said to Benson: 'We'll let them get on with their men's talk. Now tell me: how are you?'

Benson said that he was fine, thought the examinations had gone all right, was eating properly and had lots of friends at Aberystwyth. But he was thinking it odd that Alice should opt out of the other conversation to talk to him. It was a familiar happening in the old days. Couples would visit the Bensons and the man would talk to Dad about the garden while the woman talked with Mum about knitting patterns and Frances Parkinson Keyes books at the library. Why did Alice think that he would not want to be part of the men's talk? He found himself hardening himself against her, then softening. The idea of her having a baby hardened and softened him at one and the same time. It was all most confusing. Still, all in all, things weren't turning out as badly as he had thought.

'Will you stop work when you have the baby?' Benson asked.

'Oh, yes, I think so. For a while at any rate. Your dad has quite a few more years to put in before he can retire. Still, you never know, I may want to go back to work.'

Benson nodded.

'You are pleased about the baby, aren't you, Martin?'

Benson looked up at Alice and saw that she was looking over at Dad, who had stopped talking in mid-sentence and was looking at Benson, saying an elongated 'And . . . er . . .' to Omar as he did so.

'Yes, I'm very pleased for you. I've never had a sibling before.'

'A sibling?' asked Alice.

Benson was inordinately pleased to have an audience who would have to run to the dictionary, just as he had to run. 'A brother or sister.'

'My wife is going to have a baby, Omar,' said Dad.

'That's wonderful news!' said Omar, his face lighting up. 'Wonderful!'

Dad and Alice smiled, and Benson wished he had been able to heave spontaneous enthusiasm, haloed by a broad, pearly beam, over Dad and Alice.

Dad and Omar started talking about Omar's family. Alice listened intently. Benson thought of Mum looking down on the scene from heaven. In heaven there was no sadness. In heaven there could not be any conflict. Mum could not stomp around heaven in a mood because Alice was having a baby with Dad. If she could, then heaven wasn't heaven. But Bertrand Russell did not think there was such a thing as heaven. Where was Mum then? Nowhere? No, that was not

273

possible. Not possible. Mum was in heaven and was in ecstasy. Probably she was choosing the right cherub to put into the body of Alice's new baby. She would make sure that it was perfect, just right. The baby would be just as much Mum's as Alice's.

After tea, Alice asked Benson if he could take care of the washing up, as she had to get ready for work. Benson happily stacked the crockery and wheeled out the trolley, leaving Dad and Omar talking about irrigation methods. He wanted to be alone with his thoughts for a while. In the kitchen, he returned the Roberts from the Home Service to the Third Programme and listened to 'The Critics' as he washed up. He did not understand 'The Critics' most of the time, but it was a good litmus paper to test his intellectual development. He definitely understood more than he had done. They were talking about Alan Watts's *Beyond Theology: The Art of Godmanship.* The woman with the posh voice did not seem to think much of Alan Watts. He had, she thought, caused all sorts of trouble with his postured-Zen. The man with the high voice, whom Benson felt must be a homo, said that Alan Watts was a twentieth-century Vicar of Bray. Well, he knew about the Vicar of Bray, could sing the song. The Vicar of Bray had changed religion all the time. Is that what Alan Watts had done? Postured-Zen was a bit of a problem. He still had some way to go before he was an intellectual. He was relieved when the critics turned their attention to reviewing a production of *Hamlet.* Benson felt that their assessment was a little trite. How could they say that Polonius was a stupid old man? He had given excellent advice to Laertes. If only people had listened to Polonius the play might have ended on a much more cheerful note. No, Polonius was the only really sensible person in the play. A sage through and through.

Alice was going to have a baby! She was at least forty. Dad was at least fifty. He would be almost seventy by the time the child was Benson's age. How could he do such a thing and still sit there talking happily to Omar? Perhaps the implications hadn't sunk in on him yet. When they did, what would he do? If he had been Dad, he thought, he would have been happy to have finished with child-rearing. To start again at his age! Dad would not be able to listen to 'The Critics' in peace for years to come! He wouldn't even be able to get a good night's sleep! It wouldn't come easy for poor Dad, especially now that he was past his prime. And Benson felt a quote coming on: '"You cannot call it, love: for, at your age, the heyday in the blood is tame, it's humble, and waits upon the judgement; and what judgement would step from this to this?"' He held out the pan scourer in one hand, the dishcloth in the other, just as Hamlet had held out the picture of Claudius and his father. But answer came there none. What could have possessed Dad?

He decided to think about something else. Was Clitherow back for the holidays? Perhaps he could persuade Omar to walk with him to the Clitherows' house. They both needed a bit of exercise.

But Omar was already booked for the evening. Dad had told him while Benson was in the kitchen that he was going down to church for Novena. Omar had said that he would welcome the chance of seeing a Christian service, and Dad had offered to take him.

'Yes, well . . . I thought I'd go and call on the Clitherows.'

'You don't want to come with us?'

'Er . . . no thanks. Thanks, though.'

Dad nodded.

Clitherow had not returned. Mr and Mrs Clitherow did not know when or even if he would return for Christmas. They had had a card from him posted in Surrey. He was staying with Amanda. He was having a good time, he said.

'Still, you've come to see us,' said Mrs Clitherow, pouring Martin a sweet sherry. 'That's as good.'

'It's lovely to see you, Mrs Clitherow.'

'Call me Agnes, Martin. I know it doesn't come easy to call an old biddy like me by her Christian name, but I think you've just got to bite the bullet.'

'And call me Paddy,' said Dr Clitherow from behind his paper.

'All right, Agnes,' Benson told her. Then he told her everything about his term away, omitting only matters sexual.

'Well, I'm glad the old scallywag at least came for a visit,' said Mrs Clitherow. 'I've been a bit het up about him. Not writing. Not phoning. There were times when I would have got into the car and driven down to check up on him, but Patrick told me to leave well alone.'

'I told her to try and remember her own youth,' said Dr Clitherow.

'I can remember more about it than I've ever had a mind to tell you,' Mrs Clitherow informed the newspaper and the billowing pipe smoke that rose behind it. 'But I was always meticulous about writing home. And these are strange times young ones are living through.'

'Was there ever a time that wasn't a strange time?' asked the voice from behind the paper.

'Look you,' said Mrs Clitherow, 'I'm trying to talk to Martin! If you wish to join in our conversation, then come up here to the table with the rest of the human race.'

'I'm reading my paper!'

'Read your paper, so.' Then Mrs Clitherow turned back to Benson. 'Did he tell you about this Amanda girl?'

'Yes, he said he might be getting engaged.'

'Didn't you try to persuade him not to?'

'I did, yes. I didn't think he was sure of it himself.'

'Well, Martin, I have to tell you that he has gone ahead and got himself engaged. I wrote him a very ratty letter back after he had dropped his bombshell. Sure he's far too young. Much younger than he thinks. Younger in lots of ways than you are, Martin.'

'How do you mean?'

'Well – now what *do* I mean? – I think you've had a lot to cope with. Your mum dying and everything. God rest her. Your time in the monastery must have been an experience, I should think. No, you're a man of the world, Martin. Laurence has had a very easy passage through life. He's had everything on a plate.'

Benson felt immensely pleased to be so complimented by Mrs Clitherow – Agnes. A Man of the World, was he? Goodo. He thought for a while – as any Man of the World would – searching through the cornucopia of his considerable experience for a measured response full of wisdom.

'I would be very surprised if Laurence was completely sure that he wants to marry Amanda himself. But I'd say that you would be better not opposing it. If you try to stop him he'll probably go the other way. At least I think so anyway.'

'I think you're probably right, Martin. But it's going to be hard. I'm dead against people marrying so young.'

Benson nodded enthusiastically.

'How are you doing at home?'

'I don't mind so much now. Dad has his own life to lead. It was a bit selfish of me to think that he would be happy to live all alone.'

'You're a wise lad, Martin.'

'No, I'm not,' he answered with unusual certainty, thinking of his trudge round Aberystwyth collecting money from overseas students; hitching out to the remote Welsh cottage for a swift stab at excitement from the man who refused to like him. 'No, not at all. Life is so complicated.'

Mrs Clitherow nodded. 'Oh, you've got that far, have you? It had to happen, I suppose. I think you'd better have another sherry.'

'I don't mind if I do.'

Mrs Clitherow poured and Benson postponed saying 'when' until the glass was almost full.

'I've brought home an overseas student for Christmas. His name's Omar. He's from the Sudan.'

'Lord, you're up to your neck in overseas students, aren't you!'

'Yes, I like to be around them. I think they've got a lot to teach me.'

'You must bring your friend to see us.'

'Oh, yes, I will. I wanted to bring him tonight but Dad's taken him to Novena.'

'And him called Omar!' said Dr Clitherow.

'But you didn't go with them?' asked Mrs Clitherow.

'Er,' Benson was embarrassed. 'No, I still don't go to church, Agnes.'

Mrs Clitherow nodded. Then she said: 'You won't be going to Midnight Mass on Christmas Eve? Your Dad will be disappointed. Go on, it won't hurt that much will it?'

'I don't know,' said Benson. He felt it would hurt. He was his own man, wasn't he? A Man of the World with formidable integrity. He'd have to worry about that now. There was always something else to worry about. 'Did I tell you that Alice is going to have a baby?'

'She *isn't*?'

'She is,' said Benson, nodding, sipping his drink, revelling in revelation.

'Rather her than me!' said Dr Clitherow from behind his newspaper.

Mrs Clitherow gave the newspaper a stern look. Then she took Benson's hand. 'Look, that's great news! Great! Let's drink to the new baby, Martin!'

Benson left the Clitherows at half past ten. Dad and Omar were deep in conversation in the lounge when he arrived home. There was a bottle of whisky on the coffee table and Omar was drinking, which surprised Benson rather.

'Come and sit down, Martin!' said Dad. 'Bring a glass and have a drink.'

'I don't think I ought to, Dad. I've had two glasses of sherry at the Clitherows.' Dad had never asked him to have a drink before.

'Miss Stone at church asked after you,' said Dad.

'Yes? Is she all right?'

'Miss Stone doesn't change,' said Dad. 'If there's a bit of good needs doing within range of her old bike then Miss Stone will be doing it. She's in a flap about the crib at the moment. She and Omar really hit it off. Omar's been telling me what a lot of work you've been doing for the Overseas Students' Society.'

'Well, I don't do that much. Congratulations, by the way.'

'What on?'

'The baby.'

'Thank you, son. It came as a bit of a surprise. I didn't know I was capable of it!'

Another first. Benson looked at Dad as he winked at Omar and Omar laughed appreciatively, slapping his knee. It must be the alcohol, Benson thought. He's never talked like that before. Part of Benson was shocked, another part delighted. The two parts warred with one another.

Dad and Omar continued where they had left off before Benson came in. Gardens and animal-husbandry seemed to provide the common ground. Benson searched through the *Radio Times* but found nothing, wished Mum were there, wished Alice were there, yawned and said good night.

As he made for his bedroom, savouring the taste of Euthymol, he could hear Omar and Dad laughing in the lounge.

Benson smiled at the floor benignly, rather as he imagined Mum on better days smiling benignly down on him.

14

Standing between Dad and Omar, Benson sang carols lustily. It was five minutes before midnight; they had been singing since twenty past eleven. He was beginning to suffer from a dull pain in his knees and thighs, and noticed that quite a number of the congregation were either leaning heavily on the back of the pew in front or had sat down, unashamed to be seen to be giving in.

Singing 'Away in a Manger', and sharing his hymnal with Omar, he could see Mr and Mrs Clitherow three rows in front, Mrs Clitherow wearing a scarf on her head with pictures of mountains, chalets and fir trees, together with the word INNSBRUCK printed in German Gothic lettering. Before the carol started Mrs Clitherow had looked back at him, giving him and Omar a wonderful Christmas smile, followed by a wink just for him that had made the whole trip worthwhile.

The day of Christmas Eve he had eaten up in worrying about the approach of Midnight Mass. As he did his Christmas shopping, Benson fretted about whether he ought to go or not. He did not want to go, felt it would be somehow hypocritical to attend. But Mrs Clitherow's saying that Dad would be disappointed, together with the knowledge that Omar wanted to go, had finally brought him round to it. He would pick up his sceptical principles again in the New Year. Once more for old time's sake and for his dad wouldn't hurt too much.

Anyway, Benson felt that some thanks were due to the Wisdom and Spirit of the Universe. There was the baby growing inside Alice for a start, the idea of whom was growing on him daily, like bitter-sweet Guinness. Also, that morning he had gone into the local bank to cash a cheque for ten pounds in order to buy his Christmas presents. He knew that he was already £4 10s 6d in the red. His heart had been beating fast. The manager of the bank – who knew Dad – passed across the office space behind the counter and wished Benson good morning. Benson tried to reply but his dry mouth would not work. Still, the cashier had handed him the money without looking at his naughty red balance. Benson rushed off to do his shopping: a gardening book for Dad, a book by Dr Spock for Alice, a pair of leather gloves with string backs and a bottle of Mumm Rollette for Omar, a Cheshire Life calendar for Mr and Mrs Clitherow, a copy of *The Prophet* for Laurence.

All evening the Bensons' house had been filled with the aroma of slow-cooking turkey and boiling giblets. Alice had had to go off to work at eleven, but she prepared everything for the coming Christmas dinner in a manner which had pleased her critical stepson. After a sleep in the morning, she would be able to get up around one in the afternoon and simply boil the vegetables and make the gravy.

The carols ended at last, and the congregation sat down with audible sighs of relief. The altar looked beautiful. The Miss McCarthys had outdone themselves. Displays of flowers covered the back of the altar and all the statues to left and right of the nave. The six brass candlesticks were all aglow with fresh white candles.

'Are you all right, Omar? You aren't bored or anything are you?'

Omar shook his head and smiled a gentle smile. Benson looked to the front again, but the memory of the smile pulsed in front of his tired eyes. Gosh, maybe Omar would see the error of his ways and convert to Catholicism! That would be wonderful! I would have been partly responsible. No, it wouldn't. It would be terrible, and I would be partly responsible.

The priest and altar boys had come up to the altar to begin mass. The choir started singing the Kyrie. Everyone was standing again. Benson did not think much of the music, or the manner of its playing. It would be far better, all things considered, if they had borrowed Dr Leptos's piece of Schütz together with his stereo. The old biddies in the choir warbled flat and sharp, rather massacring the music. And Mrs Hopper the organist only seemed to manage to strike the odd right note.

It was soon time to sit down for the sermon. The priest, a new one to Benson, said that he hoped everyone would remember that Christmas was not only about the pleasures of the flesh. Benson wanted to interpose, to remark that no-one would have turned out at midnight on a freezing cold night if they had thought that. Really, he thought, there ought to be a right of reply during sermons. You should be able to put up your hand – or blow a whistle – and protest if you thought something the priest was saying was really silly. But it would never happen. Not as long as the Catholic Church believed itself to be the Guardian of All Truth. Next, the priest told the congregation about the second collection, and how it was all to go for the maintenance of the clergy. You'd think that the clergy were all in need of repair. Well, they were in a way, but it was such a silly expression. Why did they not just say that they wanted a Christmas Surprise like everyone else and that money would be the best thing because then they could buy what they wanted with it? Every week Dad gave an envelope in at the collection which had OUR GIFT TO GOD printed on the outside. That was silly and phony too. What need did God have of a policeman's coppers? No, it was the priests and the big buildings and the administration of the Vatican that they were collecting for. Well, he could see that somebody had to dust the *pietà* and shine up the marble. But why wrap it up in piety? Why bring God into it? It was insulting to Him. Blasphemous, almost.

Benson sat seething in like vein as the priest went from point to point like some boring financial columnist. At last they all stood up for the Creed. Nothing the cleric had said lifted his heart, cheered his soul, helped him answer his questions or conundrums. He was only thankful that for once leaks in the church roof had not been mentioned. But the Catholic Tombola Championships (North-West area) had been advertised and all loyal, God-fearing parishioners enjoined to participate. Yawn.

At the Consecration, Benson started to worry about whether he should take communion. He decided that he would. He had sinned. According to the Church his soul was maggoty and black. But Myvanway Roberts and Sean O'Malley seemed to think it might not be after all. He would go along with them in this, while trying to please his dad at the same time. He told the Wisdom and Spirit of the Universe that he was sorry for the sins he had committed that were really sins, but that he was a homo and if the Wisdom and Spirit of the Universe hadn't wanted him to be a homo then He shouldn't have made him a homo. But never would he confess his sins to a priest. Never.

Dad stood up when it came time for communion and started to ask Benson to let him pass. Instead Benson smiled and asked Omar to let both of them pass. He walked to the front of the church and knelt beside Dad at the altar rails. The Host approached, and for a moment he felt that damnation was approaching with It. He thought of Scobie in *The Heart of the Matter.* Scobie had tied himself up in all sorts of knots over sacriligious communions. It had driven him to suicide. Silly Scobie! The plate was passed to him. He put it under his chin and pushed his tongue out. Then, feeling the slightly bitter dry taste on his tongue, he passed the plate to Dad. Dad looked into his eyes as he received it from him. Before lowering his eyes, Benson was certain that he had seen the beginnings of a smile on Dad's lips. The Host softened. He swallowed, stood up and walked back to his pew, eyes cast down, hands joined in front of him, like in the old days.

After mass, Benson took Omar to see the crib. He had hoped that the black king would be there to make Omar feel more at home, but it would not be placed there until the Epiphany. Then he stood next to Omar and Dad in the cold dark as friends came up and wished them happy Christmas. Mr and Mrs Clitherow came over and Benson introduced them to Omar, who at once started talking to them as if he had known them all his life. They made Benson promise that he would bring Omar to visit them.

Mrs Clitherow gave Benson a kiss. Then she and Mr Clitherow continued chatting with Omar.

Benson looked suitably humble, but he felt as proud as could be, proud to have Omar standing near him, to be associated with him, to steal for himself some of Omar's exoticism. This is my African big brother! he thought, and his heart pounded with joy.

'Happy Christmas, Miss Stone!' he said. 'You did a wonderful job on the crib again.'

'It's a labour of love, love,' she replied. 'Happy Christmas, Martin. God bless.'

The bells in the tower of the church started to peal out, adding its sound – a much nicer one, Benson thought – to the ones tolling in the Anglican church half a mile up the road.

Dad had volunteered to give Mr and Mrs O'Neill a lift home, so Benson said that he would be quite happy to walk home alone. Omar offered to join him, but Benson said he might catch a cold, and anyway he quite fancied being alone.

The sky was clear, lamp-lit, but full of stars. Benson felt unutterably happy and at ease. He did not think that he had felt so peaceful for years. The feeling worried him. Perhaps, he thought, I am so deeply indoctrinated that I can only ever be happy as a good Catholic? If I follow my conscience and the dictates of love and desire, am I going to be forever dissatisfied and nervy?

He shook himself and trotted along the road towards home. At the top of his road, he looked to left and right and, finding that there was no-one about, he cupped his hands around his mouth and shouted at the stars and whatever was behind them, 'Happy Christmas, Mum!'

Then he returned his arms to his sides, still gazing upwards, staring out the stars.

The trip to Liverpool that Benson had been planning for Omar took place on the day after Boxing Day. Benson took Omar over on the ferry. He had remembered to bring some bread, which they threw at the seagulls following the wake of the boat.

Benson showed Omar the names of Arabs and Africans on the war memorial at the pier head. Omar stopped and read the black metal names, touching each one with his finger. 'It's a long list,' he said, turning to Benson. He moved along the columns of names. 'Look, on HMS *Anking*, Muslims, Chinese and English died.'

Benson nodded, thinking 'Mine ancient scars shall not be glorified, nor my titanic tears, the sea, be dried . . .' and followed Omar on to the main plinth of the memorial, where an old man sat on a seat huddled in a raincoat. Omar said hello to the man and the man nodded to him. Benson smiled. They read the inscription in silence.

The man stood up and Benson saw that he had a black rosary threaded through the fingers of his right hand. He took Omar by the arm and led him back to the list of the dead.

'I was on the HMS *Fiona*. We was sunk by A/C off Sidi Barrani, 18th July 1941. My thirty-seventh birthday. Not much of a present, eh? I got rescued, but those lads didn't. There's not a day goes by when I don't think of them. I knew every poor sod on that list. Their names are here all right but they're forgotten really. No-one here gives a toss,' said the man.

'God remembers them,' said Omar to the man, and he rested his black hand on the man's shoulder.

'They were good lads . . .' The man reached up and patted Omar's hand, then he turned away, returning to his seat on the monument.

'The old are wise, and their wisdom makes them sad,' said Omar as they walked away.

Benson thought about that.

They listened for a while to a flustered woman on the soapbox of the Catholic Evidence guild, gallantly trying to field questions from an assortment of Liverpool Bertrand Russells and Orangemen who shot her down in flames with their big guns of secular and Protestant rationality.

'She is very courageous,' Omar said.

Benson thought about that too, but could think of other words to describe her. He did not articulate them, though.

Then they visited the Anglican cathedral.

'They've been building it since the start of the century and won't finish it for ages,' Benson told Omar.

The dark red cathedral moved Benson still, made him prayerful and meditative. But he fought the feeling and led Omar into Liverpool 8 to see the wretched housing and rail against the insult to Liverpool's poor of having a huge cathedral while the people had so little. Omar said the people probably enjoyed having the cathedral so near. Benson said they would enjoy draught-free accommodation more.

He took Omar past the art school where John Lennon had studied, along by the Philharmonic Hall that had

murals of naked women on the walls that had made
Benson and his friends giggle when they had gone
there for schoolboy concerts. Then they had looked at
the construction site on which the Catholic Cathedral
was being erected. They went down into the crypt.
Benson said that the crypt would have done. They
hardly needed to build anything else. They also went
to The Cavern to see the exact spot where the Beatles
had played, but it was closed. So they looked at the
door for a while.

Though Omar was pleading tiredness, Benson
insisted on a five-minute visit to the Walker Art
Gallery. He led Omar up the stairs and straight into the
room where his favourite picture hung. '*Faithful Unto
Death*,' he announced proudly. 'You see the soldier is
about to die. The volcano is going to erupt. But he
doesn't move. He stays faithfully at his post. Look at
the way the artist has captured the reflection of the
glowing lava on the soldier's eye and armour.'

Omar nodded but didn't say much. He wandered off
to look at *A Summer Night*, a painting that showed
four nude women in a bedroom with a view over a
night sea. Benson apologized to his soldier and went
off in pursuit of Omar. He thought how strange it was
that the soldier never changed. Benson was changing,
but the soldier waited for imminent death year after
year. He'd been waiting ever since he was painted in
1896. Would he, Benson, come back one day when he
was a wise old man and find the soldier just the same?
He felt a pang of jealousy for the beautiful soldier. But
if he hobbled back after thirty years and found in the
picture only ash and rusty armour, would that be
consoling? Probably not, but . . .

Omar pointed to the body of one of the women in the
painting. She was stretching. He gazed at her and
whistled. Then he looked at the other figures, going
close as if he were inspecting the dishes in a help-
yourself café.

287

'Omar, people will think you like it!' whispered Benson.

He had not quite meant that, but had noticed that an attendant was approaching, looking stern.

'I do like it! They are so beautiful!'

On the way out Benson bought a postcard of *Faithful Unto Death*. He would send it to Gareth with the message: This is my favourite painting. Love, Martin. Yes, that is what he'd do.

Omar bought one of *A Summer Night* and put it in his wallet.

Thousands of starlings twittered alarmingly and swooped from tree to cornice to parapet around the city as they made their way to the ferry in the gathering dusk. Omar looked about him and Benson hoped he was feeling the magic of the city. The skyline of the place, so near home yet so far in some ways, still moved Benson. He wanted Omar to catch its atmosphere. He had played him Beatles records. There were not many places in the world where songs filled you up to the brim with a feeling for the place, were there? Liverpool's songs followed you about like a chirpy soundtrack to a comedy film. He wished he was from Liverpool and not from Wirral, where nothing momentous was happening, where nobody thought to celebrate Malcolm Lowry, where you could only gaze across the brown estuary to the centre of the cultural universe, feeling left out.

On the ferry returning to Wirral, crowded with shoppers returning from the sales, Benson caught sight of a figure he knew. He was not sure at first where he knew the man from, but then suddenly he did. Purple images of an evening among the Protestant dead in the cemetery next to the library returned. He turned away, but not fast enough, and, knowing he had not been fast enough, was not surprised when Andy's distinctive voice said: 'You haven't forgotten me, have you?'

'Er . . . no. Hello, Andy. Andy, this is Omar.'

Andy shook hands with Omar: 'Who's your friend?' he asked Benson, looking straight at Omar.

'Omar and I go to the same university. Aberystwyth. He's staying with me for the holidays.'

'That's nice,' said Andy to Omar.

The route home lay along the prom. Benson had been hoping that Andy would get the bus, but he just said, 'I'll join you,' and tagged along.

Andy asked Omar all the usual questions, making Benson feel a bit left out. He thought how bored Omar must be with all these English people without the least sense of geography asking him things about the surfaces of his life. But Omar never looked bored. There seemed to be nothing he liked better than engaging in idle chit-chat.

Andy was just the same as he remembered, though he had grown his hair longer. Thinking of the night in the cemetery over two years before still excited Benson a bit. He also recalled Andy's indifference to him later; how, though Benson had been desperate, Andy had not seemed to want to continue with him. That had hurt at the time. He wanted to ask him about it, about many things.

'I don't have to ask you how you're doing, dear!' said Andy to Benson.

Benson suddenly was aware that he had been a million miles away, not listening to the conversation.

'How do you mean?' asked Benson.

' "How do you mean?" she says!'

Benson looked daggers at Andy. Where were his manners? How dare he 'she' him in mixed company like that!

He walked on a few paces ahead to register his displeasure, but after a bit his pique diminished and he thought how odd it must appear to Omar. He allowed himself to walk more slowly until Andy and Omar were once again alongside him.

'Not married? And you twenty-seven? What do you *do*, dear?' Andy was asking Omar.

Omar laughed and replied that he was too busy working to do anything.

'What a sinful waste! Don't you think it's a sinful waste, John?'

Benson had forgotten that he had told Andy his name was John. It was true, he thought, your sin will find you out. There must be a whole office-full of angels spending their every waking minute in arranging fateful meetings like his with Andy. If my luck goes on like this the man from the farm will be knocking at the door at home asking for me with his thing out. But if Omar noticed he didn't say anything.

They turned off the prom. Andy was telling Omar about his new job as a furniture upholsterer. 'I stitch and I stitch and then I stuff the stuffing in until it's nice and hard, dear, and then they come and sit on it and if it's hard enough it's comfy and they buy it, if you get my meaning.'

And Omar did. He stopped in the road and laughed backwards and forwards like the laughing policeman at the indoor fairground in New Brighton. Benson had never heard him laugh like that, nor had he realized that Omar had a taste for vulgarity – at least when sober. He had consigned Omar to a very special, sexless place. Had he not had his strange experience with Enoch Mohammed he might have looked at Omar differently. But he was convinced that Africans just weren't. Omar, he had decided, was a cold African abroad who, when he had finished at university, would return to Africa and produce monster goats, grow flesh over rib-cages and remember Benson fondly as the one good white man when the Coca-Cola salesman came to town.

'I think we'd better go right when we get to the top of the hill,' Benson informed his erring companions.

'Aren't you going to see me home? It's not often I

get the chance to talk to a real live African, dear.'

Omar slapped Andy on the shoulder as if he thought he was the funniest thing in the world. Benson did not think Andy was funny. Had Omar not been with them he would have given him a piece of his mind. It was all very well Andy not caring a damn who knew he was a homo, but it was quite another thing to cover Benson with the same lurid make-up. He fumed away silently to himself as they followed the detour to Andy's house.

It was with feelings of no small relief that Benson bade goodbye to Andy at his front door. Omar was still laughing from the extravagant farewell when Benson said, 'He's not really a friend. Just someone I used to know.'

'Wonderful! He is a wonderful man! Very different from most people you meet.'

That was certainly true. Benson thought about that. The day had given him several things to think about and it was only half past five.

They arrived home to the news – left by Dad in the form of a note on the morning-room table – that Clitherow was home. Dad was out at work and Alice would be going to work at eleven that night.

Benson was overjoyed and asked Omar if he would like to come and meet Clitherow with him. But Omar said that the long walk had tired him out, and that he would like a quiet evening.

Benson bolted down his tea of turkey sandwiches, Christmas cake and jelly. He telephoned Meryl, but there was no answer. Still, he thought, in all probability Meryl was burning the candle at both ends. He made a mental note to try her number again later. He did not want to be accused of letting her down a second time.

He put on his coat, said goodbye to Alice and Omar, who were sitting in front of the television watching what looked to Benson like rubbish, and trotted round to the Clitherows.

There was a red Spitfire sports car in the drive. Benson could see Laurence's shape through the stained glass on the door, elongating and compacting as he walked towards it.

'So you've decided to pay us a visit!' Benson said.

'Thought I would. Christmassed in Surrey, don't you know. Those southerners really know how to put on a Christmas, I can tell you. We had pheasant *and* ham,' replied Laurence. 'I've brought Amanda up with me, by the way. We're engaged.'

'Are you? Congratulations,' said Benson, hoping his lack of enthusiasm showed in his voice. 'Is that her car? I've brought you a present. It's not much.'

'Thanks, I didn't get you anything, though.' Clitherow put the present on the hall-table next to the Sacred Heart, but he did not comment on the beautiful paper, nor the bow that had taken Benson ages to get right. 'Yes. I think congratulations are in order. Yes.' He took Benson round the shoulder and whispered into his ear: 'We sorted out our small temporary difficulties. You really ought to try it with a woman, Martin! All the rest is just a cheap substitute.'

'I thought you hadn't liked it much when you tried?'

'Well, things have happened since. I'll tell you later. Now come into the parlour and meet Amanda. And . . .' he postponed opening the sitting-room door, '. . . you won't mention any of the things I said to you when I visited, will you? And don't, for God's sake, say anything about, well, the rest.'

'What do you think I am?'

Clitherow winked, and went in ahead of him.

Benson pulled his pullover down over his hips, felt his hair to make sure not too much was sticking up, and walked into the Clitherows' big living-room with its bay windows looking out over the Mersey estuary. He was disappointed to see that the heavy curtains were tightly shut, depriving him of his favourite view. If he lived in this house, he thought, he would never close the curtains. Hang the draughts. Mr and Mrs Clitherow were sitting on either side of the fireplace, directing their attention to a girl with her back to Benson who was talking animatedly.

Mrs Clitherow got up when Benson came in. 'Did you have a good Christmas, son?' she asked him.

'Yes, I did, thank you very much, Agnes. It was lovely.'

'And this is Amanda,' said Clitherow.

Amanda turned on the sofa, smiled at Benson and said 'Hi!'

Benson had never met the daughter of a Conservative MP before and was most curious about Amanda. She had long straight, blonde hair, that looked like Mary's in Peter Paul and Mary. She was tall, taller than Clitherow by an inch or two, and was wearing a red leather trouser suit.

'You're Martin. I've heard such a lot about you. I feel I know you very well already.'

'I'm Martin,' said Benson. He mentally kicked himself.

Amanda smiled.

Benson tried to think of something witty to say, but couldn't. He felt foolish. Still, he thought, the daughter of a Conservative MP must be used to inarticulate yokels. They had to kiss babies round the council estates at election times. He had seen them doing it on the television. They talked ten to the dozen while the startled householder clung to the door and smiled foolishly. This never fazed the MP in the least. They were all talk.

'Congratulations on your engagement,' said Benson to Clitherow and Amanda.

Clitherow smiled and asked Benson what he would like to drink. Benson thought, then he said: 'A bitter or a Guinness if you've got one.' He would have preferred something sweet but he wanted to show Amanda that he drank Labour drinks. He wished he had a cloth cap sticking out of his pocket. Perhaps a ferret too.

'Mother and Father don't approve of what we've done,' said Clitherow to Benson.

Benson looked over at Mr and Mrs Clitherow.

'It's not that we disapprove, just that we think it's a bit early. You're both so young,' said Mrs Clitherow.

Benson was disappointed to see that Mrs Clitherow had not followed his advice not to oppose the marriage. But when he had given that advice he had not really expected that Clitherow would go through with it. He supped his Guinness, noticing that the atmosphere was not pleasant.

'Amanda's parents are delighted for us. I don't know why you should be so against it.'

'We really are deeply in love,' added Amanda.

'I don't think we doubt your feelings,' said Mrs Clitherow sternly, 'just that you should think about it a bit longer before you commit yourselves.'

'Well, it's too late now, mumsy!' said Clitherow.

'Don't call me that! I've told you once.'

Clitherow smirked and drank his wine.

'Er . . . Dad and . . . Alice are having a baby,' Benson tried to keep the conversation going.

'I've started knitting already,' said Mrs Clitherow. 'A matinée coat. It's pink and blue stripes, just to be on the safe side.'

'How far have you got?' Benson asked.

'Not very far. I went wrong quite early on – a bit out of practice, you see – but it'll be ready in good time, don't you fret.'

'Alice says she doesn't know you very well. I think she'd like to meet you.'

'I'll drop in on her, so. I can give her a few hints on childbirth, that I can.'

'I don't see why it's too late now,' said Dr Clitherow to Clitherow and Amanda. 'You're not marrying until you've finished at university. There's many a slip . . .'

294

Benson thought it was unfortunate that Dr Clitherow should bring the conversation back to Clitherow and Amanda.

'Yes, we won't be married for ages,' said Amanda. 'We've plenty of time to change our minds, though I doubt we shall.'

'Are you enjoying Oxford?' Benson asked Amanda.

'Yes, it's great fun,' replied Amanda.

'It's so much fun we're not getting much work done,' added Clitherow.

Hearing the couple speak at the same time, Benson was aware of how similar their accents were. Clitherow had become quite posh to match Amanda, but Amanda had that slightly American accent that sometimes showed up in Clitherow's speech too. It really irritated him. Why couldn't Amanda have learnt to speak like they did on Merseyside? Why did Clitherow have to follow her?

'What's your father's name, Amanda?' Benson asked.

'Duncan Petrie. He's an MP.'

Benson nodded. He had heard of Duncan Petrie. Duncan Petrie was in the forefront of backing for Rhodesia's unilateral declaration of independence.

'Yes, I've heard of him,' said Benson. Not only had he heard of Duncan Petrie, he had also had to defend the British against the charge that all British people were like Duncan Petrie. 'Do you agree with your father's views?'

'Most of the time, yes. I was brought up in Rhodesia, you see. Once you have lived in Africa you know what the whites are up against. It would be the height of folly to hand over to them now, or in the foreseeable future.'

'And South Africa?' Benson allowed himself to note that, beneath Amanda's thick make-up, her skin was acned.

'About the same as Rhodesia. If you could just *see*

the other African countries, Martin. They're all such a mess.'

'Yes, but that doesn't make it right!' exclaimed Benson.

'I think you've got to take a pragmatic and a long-term approach,' said Clitherow.

'What does that mean?'

'It seems clear enough to me.'

'So you agree with Amanda?'

'Yes.'

'You've changed in three months. Let's hope that when your head has stopped turning it will be facing to the front again,' rapped back Benson severely, quoting from *A Man for All Seasons*, his favourite play.

'Hear! Hear!' said Dr Clitherow.

Cheered and spurred by Dr Clitherow Benson asked, 'Are you learning how to play croquet and ride ponies too?'

'I've got a pony called Sugar-Lump,' said Amanda.

Mr and Mrs Clitherow and Benson stared at her.

'Come on, Martin, why didn't you bring your Sudanese chum to see us? We could have had a good argument then,' said Clitherow.

'I'm not bringing him near you. You'd probably put him in the kitchen to make the tea.'

'No, they tend to be clumsy,' said Amanda, joining in an argument which Clitherow and Benson had made their own. 'They can decimate a teaset in ten seconds flat, but we might get him to do a bit of gardening. They're good at gardening.' And she turned to Clitherow and they both laughed. Mr and Mrs Clitherow and Benson watched the mirth in front of them on the sofa in stony silence.

Benson thought of Omar's hand on the grimy raincoat of the man at the war memorial. Then he thought of the old man's hand patting Omar's. He felt like crying but looked at his hands instead. Amanda would probably be charming to Omar if he visited. Omar would leave saying what a wonderful girl she was, how lucky Clitherow was. But Benson knew better. He also knew that he could retrieve the situation. He knew that he did not have to do what he was about to do. No, he could sit on, go on to other topics, let the anger boiling inside him retreat to just one more ache. But he decided not to sit on. He stood up. He thought of *Faithful Unto Death*. He tried to remember why he had stood up. He remembered.

'I'm sorry,' he said to Mr and Mrs Clitherow, looking past Clitherow and Amanda, 'I've got to go.'

'Suit yourself!' said Clitherow, and he kissed Amanda.

Benson gave Clitherow a mournful look, then armed the look with daggers, sending them hurtling towards his ex-best friend.

Mrs Clitherow accompanied him to the porch.

'Good for you!' she said.

'I'm sorry, er . . . Agnes. I just leapt on any excuse to get at him. He's not the same fellow he was at all.'

'No, Martin. We must just say a prayer. Who's the patron saint of hopeless cases?'

'St Jude, also known as Thaddeus,' answered Benson mechanically.

Benson waved goodbye, saying he would come back to see her before he went back to Aberystwyth. He walked home the long way, along the prom. He aimed a prayer to St Jude at the heavy sky, wondering as he did so if there was a saint who specialized in humiliating prejudiced snobs.

15

When Benson arrived home, Alice was watching television in the lounge, wearing her policewoman's uniform. There was no sign of Omar.

'Where's Omar, Alice?' Benson asked.

'He went out for a walk half an hour ago. Your dad's still on duty.'

'I thought Omar said he was tired. He could have come with me to see the Clitherows. I hope he'll be all right.'

'How are they? I sometimes nod to them at church but I don't really know them.'

'Laurence has brought his fiancée home,' replied Benson as he threw himself down on the sofa.

'It does seem a bit fast. One term at university and ready to tie the knot. That Amanda sounds like a fast worker.'

Benson wasn't sure that it was quite appropriate for Alice to talk about fast workers, but he nodded anyway. 'I think she's used to getting what she wants. I can't say I thought much of her.'

'You haven't got a girlfriend yet?'

'Er, no.'

'Do you want one?'

He had not the slightest idea what to say. 'Er . . .'

'Well, it will come in time I should think. No sense in rushing into it.'

'That's what I think. There are plenty of fish in the sea. What's on the telly?'

'Some play. I haven't been taking much notice to tell you the truth. I don't get on with plays.'

'Mum and I used to like plays,' said Benson.

'I thought you'd stay longer at your friend's.'

'I stayed long enough,' replied Benson bitterly.

'What's up, son?' Alice asked, leaning over towards him.

'Nothing, I mean, well . . . I can't stand Amanda! I really hate . . . dislike her!' But as he chose Amanda for his ire he knew he was dodging what was really on his mind. That included Amanda too, of course, but there was more. 'Me and Clitherow were good friends. Best friends. Then in she comes and spoils everything! She's a horrible posh snob. She's got a pony called Sugar-Lump! She's made Clitherow really nasty too. He's so impressed by everything about her. Her dad is that Duncan Petrie who supports Ian Smith.'

'He'll get over it. He's not marrying her yet, is he?'

'No, but that's not the point, is it? It'll never be the same.'

'What won't?'

'Our friendship. I really don't think I like him any more. I hated the way he talked to his mother. I could have slapped him. And he just sat there and agreed with Amanda's nasty opinions.' And Benson thought: If I'd stayed on and talked it over perhaps things would be all right by now.

'But he was bound to get a girlfriend. If it hadn't been this Amanda, it would have been someone else.'

'I suppose so.' He looked at the television. 'Do you mind if I turn it over?'

'No, have what you like.'

They watched the end of a variety show. A group was singing.

'Isn't that the Swinging Blue Jeans?' Alice asked.

'No, I don't think so.'

'Who is it then?'

'I don't know but whoever it is they're miming.'

'They always mime,' said Alice in a way that showed she took it for granted that the world would always show her its depressing flip-side.

Benson nodded. 'It'll soon be over.' Then he thought that there was no reason in the world why he and Clitherow should not be on the programme. They could mime at least as well as the soppy group. He and Clitherow could be Martin and Laurence and sing songs with some guts to them and knock the silly smiles off Peter and Gordon's faces. But then he thought: We're not friends any more.

'It was the Moody Blues,' said Alice as the credits rolled.

'Was it?' Who cares? 'There's news now, I think.'

'There's never much news round Christmas,' observed Alice.

That was sound of Alice, Benson thought. She had noticed it too. The television people were just too lazy to hunt for real news round Christmas.

Benson watched the news with only mild interest. Then, quite suddenly, he was watching Myvanwy and Sean presiding over a carry-cot in a bus shelter. He could see the King's Hall in the background. Then he saw Meryl in a long, loose dress holding out a pound of Black Magic to Myvanwy, who smiled sweetly, just as she had when Benson had told her he was a homo.

'An unusual way of drawing attention to those who are poor and homeless at Christmas has been devised by some students at the University of Aberystwyth . . .'

'That's where you are!' cried Alice.

'Shh!'

'. . . who are living for the whole Christmas period in a bus-shelter. The police tried at first to move them on but the spirit of Christmas stayed the long arm of the law and the nativity scene has been allowed to proceed. The police even brought the holy couple blankets from the police cells to keep them warm. There is a shepherd . . .'

'I know her. That's Meryl!'

'. . . there's even a real live baby, but she is taken home for feeding and to sleep.'

The camera panned out to a distant view of the bus-shelter. Then Sean in Arab headgear and a false beard was talking to the camera. 'We wanted to show how the message of Christmas is relevant to our time. Christmas is not about shopping and getting drunk. It is about new life and the poor and loving one another.'

It was over. The newscaster said rather them than him and the weatherman came on and observed that it would probably snow on the Aberystwyth Nativity that night.

'It was nice what that chap said,' said Alice.

'Yes,' said Benson, burning up. It could have been me on the telly just now, he thought. I might even have been able to say something pithy about giving to those who are really in need. I bet Sean and Myvanwy knew they were going to be on! And what was Meryl doing there? Meryl was the last person who should be there. She should be living it up in Hampstead at some snobby party saying as she clinks champagne glasses with people like Amanda and Clitherow: 'Oh, yes, I'm pregnant! And I'm going to have it too! My dear, everyone is having abortions! I don't think it is quite the thing though, what!'

The weatherman was now forecasting snow for Merseyside.

'I hope it snows,' said Benson, thinking how much better he would have been as the shepherd. He could have turned to the camera and told the world how disgusting he thought Duncan Petrie was. 'I don't think Omar has ever seen snow.'

'I hope it doesn't. Fancy people you know being on the television!'

'The girl who gave Mary the Black Magic is one of my best friends at uni.'

'Funny thing to give Mary, a box of Black Magic?' observed Alice.

'Well, they're trying to be up-to-date. The symbolism

301

of the Black Magic is quite telling, if you think about it,' observed Benson, thinking of Ralph Wynne, and other things.

'Is it?'

'Yes.'

Alice got up, saying she had to think about going to work. As she was leaving the room she stopped, observing herself in the mirror. 'The baby doesn't show yet, does it?' she asked.

Benson looked. He thought that Alice was sticking out a bit around the waist. Still, most women did. He wondered if she was wearing a corset. If he felt her hips he might be able to feel the bits of whalebone and the bumps that had given Mum away. The thought brought tears to his eyes. 'No, not yet. Won't be long though.'

'No, it won't be long,' said Alice. She touched her curly hair and smiled at herself.

Alice had been gone half an hour when Omar rang the doorbell. Benson had turned off the television as soon as she left the room and started reading *Native Son*. He had been finding it difficult to concentrate because of Meryl's latest surprise and the unhappy events at the Clitherows. At last he had thrown aside the book and stood in front of the mirror so recently vacated by Alice.

Who does he think he is, boys? asked Brother Hooper. *The Brothers assigned him, quite rightly, to a B form. But Benson was not satisfied with that. Benson has aspirations if you please. He walks off in a huff because his best friend opts for rectitude. He thinks he has stuck to his principles. He thinks he is on the side of tolerance and racial harmony! But you and I know, boys, that filthy lusts propel thick Benson towards the oppressed. A pharisee, he is. Filthy lusts wrapped in virtuous packaging. He is merely miming virtue.*

There are some uncharitable people, said Fyfe Robertson, *who would accuse our hero of mixed motives. Well, let me tell you, viewers, that I have been around this naughty world long enough to wonder whether pure motives in the Platonic sense really exist at all! If you ask me, viewers, and I know Benson very well having interviewed him on many occasions, he is doing his very best in a damned difficult world. Well done, young man!*

Benson answered the door. Omar was standing on the step, his hair covered in a halo of snow. 'Look!' he exclaimed, gesturing to the snowfall caught in the porch-light.

'It's snowing,' said Benson.

'Wonderful! Wonderful!' said Omar.

Benson looked at Omar with his light covering of snow. He agreed with him that it was wonderful.

'Come in. You'll catch your death. I'll make you a Horlicks,' he said. 'Where did you go, Omar? I was starting to worry,' Benson told Omar after Omar had dried himself and been presented with a mug of Horlicks.

'I went for a walk and then I called in on Andy.'

Benson looked at Omar hard. 'Andy?'

'Yes. We had a drink. He is a very nice person. He's asked me to go and see him again.'

'That's nice,' said Benson, thinking it was anything but. He just hoped that Andy had behaved himself with Omar and hadn't let anything slip about what he and Benson had got up to in the distant past. Some hope, he thought. Hopeless case, that Andy.

'I would like to take a bath before I sleep,' said Omar.

'Yes, I'm sure the water is hot.'

Omar smiled, said good night and quietly closed the door of the lounge behind him.

A bath? He had a bath this morning! thought Benson, watching the dead television screen, once more smelling wormwood. Then he told himself to be more charitable. A bath was probably just what Omar needed to warm him up properly after his walk through the snow.

The next day it continued to snow, and Benson took Omar for a walk to the sandhills. He took delight in watching Omar's wonder. Omar kept opening his mouth wide to catch the curls of snow on his tongue, held out his hands, smiling as the snow landed on the unpigmented palms and turned to water in a moment.

Benson thought that every English family should have someone home for Christmas who had not seen snow. He had caught Omar's enthusiasm and knew he would always remember how his friend had reacted. Snow would trigger black and white images as poignant as those in Pasolini's *Gospel According to Matthew*, his favourite film.

The sand dunes were glorious white Himalayan peaks connected by majestic arêtes and corries. The brown sea behind them looked bereft, a real, dull world behind the magic whiteness. They had to rub their eyes at the brightness of it. And in the dark behind lids great whorls of colour drifted.

They slid down the dunes and were quickly covered in snow. Sir Martin Benson felt greatly reassured that he was in the company of Sherpa Omar. His other companions pleaded with him to return home to meet the Queen, but Sir Martin replied, 'I am going to live in a remote village in Nepal with my friend Sherpa Omar. Do not try to find us. Abominable snowmen guard each and every route. Adieu.' They left the dunes scarred, the surface a salt-and-pepper combination of snow and sand.

That night Omar informed Benson quite matter-of-factly that he was going to visit Andy. He did not ask Benson to accompany him, and Benson suspected the worst.

Could it be that Omar had fallen for Andy's wiles? He had taken it for granted that Omar would never do such a thing. Now it looked as if he might have. If Benson had told Omar how much he was attracted to him when he had visited him in Aberystwyth, would Omar have taken him to bed? Maybe he would have. It seemed at least possible. But did he want to? Did it help Friendship? Would he have liked Omar as much if he had? He was not sure.

Omar left for Andy's house. Benson, saying that he was going to get some cigarettes, left a few minutes afterwards and followed Omar's footprints in the snow. He was soon within sight of his friend, noting that Omar took paces about six inches longer than his. He tried to jump the gap, to step in Omar's footprints. He did not notice that there was any warmth in them.

It was still snowing. Millions of white dots arched past the sodium lights at a windblown angle. He was careful to keep out of sight, terrified that he would be discovered. It was such a silly thing to be doing. What did he hope to find out? Omar had been completely straightforward about where he was going. What would he learn when Omar finally arrived at his destination?

He saw Omar turn into the path to Andy's house. He held back and by the time he was opposite the house Omar had disappeared inside. The light in the attic was on. He stood next to a phone box looking at the light, half expecting that it would go off. That would indicate something. But it didn't go off. He retreated inside the phone box. Someone had left a piece of chewing gum in the ash-tray. Someone is going to have to clear that up. Do people have *any* consideration? Do they make the *least* attempt to place themselves in other people's shoes? No they don't. And he looked up at the attic window.

The cold got to him and he soon gave up, wandering back towards home. He went into a pub and bought half an ounce of Old Holborn, not being able to get his favourite Sun Valley. When the man came back with his change, Benson ordered a pint of Guinness, which he drank leaning against the bar. When he had finished that, he ordered another.

The black beer slipped down easily enough but it did not cheer him up. Rather he felt he wanted to cry. He thought of Clitherow. Goodbye Clitherow. Enoch Mohammed. No, he mustn't think of him. The Man. What was the Man doing now? He could not imagine the Man having a Christmas with a tree, a turkey, and friends. Rather he could see him getting drunk with his dog and waggling himself, lying on the couch.

He left the pub and made for the toilet by the cemetery. He wanted to go. He was not going for any other reason other than he wanted to go, was he? He walked down the pitch-dark winding path that led to the toilet.

Then suddenly he was reeling back, having banged his nose on something. He wondered for a split second if someone had hit him, held his arm out in front of him to protect himself and found that he had collided with the locked door of the toilet. The council must have closed it for Christmas, he thought as he rubbed his sore nose in the dark. That was typical of the council. No consideration.

He was drunk. He turned back towards the yellow sodium lights of the street but he was not ready to appear under their glare. Cars were passing and he knew he would feel guilty to be seen coming out. He would have to wait until it was quiet and he was ready.

He stood listening for the sound of cars, watching approaching headlights. The pain had abated and he thought of Andy. Their trysting place nearby would now be covered in snow. He imagined himself telling Andy what had happened to him, and Andy's response: 'Biffed by a fucking cottage door, dear!' And in the dark he began to giggle, then to laugh. Then, as quiet returned to left and right, he furtively darted back on to the pavement. As he walked like a good citizen

306

down the street towards home, rubbing his bruised nose, he began to cry. He lifted his face to the snow and tried to see past it into the blank, snow-white sky. He thought he had succeeded for a moment. In that split-second, the snow clouds parted and he thought he could see Andy again: 'You banged your nose on a fucking cottage door, you daft queen!' Then, quite suddenly, he was laughing again, surrounded by curled springs of winter blossom.

Yes, he thought. I am a man of the world, but Andy's right, I'm a bit of a daft queen too.

He frowned at this admission, then he swayed homewards, opening his mouth, sticking out his tongue – just as Omar had done that morning – to catch the white snowfall.

16

It was wonderful to open the door of his room at the hostel back in Aberystwyth. His Philips was just as he had left it, down to the record of 'The Times They Are A-Changin' on the turntable. It had been remiss of him to leave the record on. It would have to be dusted like mad to bring back the shine. He got out a cloth right away and cleaned the record-player carefully, rotating the turntable to do so. Then he set about rearranging the rest of the room. It was a new year after all. Time for changes. He imagined himself spending his second term at university in a room as tidy and simple as Shigo's. And the tidiness would mirror the tidiness inside him.

He left his room and called on Ianto first, the Wagner above his head alerting him to Ianto's return.

Ianto had got into trouble over the Christmas holidays for trying to write a Welsh Nationalist slogan on the dam at Lake Vernwy. He had been let off with a caution, but was vowing further escapades which boded little good. Benson counselled Ianto to seek the breaking down of barriers, rather than the building of new ones. But Ianto kept going on about the rapaciousness of the English.

'There are good and bad everywhere,' said Benson pacifically.

'Look,' said Ianto. 'I'm not going to get into any bloody queer rows with you this term. I'm going to have my time cut out campaigning for Welsh-speaking hostels.'

Benson did not like the sound of that. 'You mean no overseas students?'

'As many as want to come in – as long as they bloody speak Welsh. Anyway, I'm head of the organizing committee. We'll be having petitions and marches.'

'You do realize what you are advocating, don't you, Ianto?' said Benson solemnly.

'Go on, bloody tell me.'

'Cultural apartheid, that's what.'

Ianto guffawed. 'I bet you'd have a separate hostel for homos if you could find any to bloody join you.'

'I would not,' replied Benson because he felt he had to. Then he wondered if perhaps Ianto were right. A hostel for homos might be quite nice. Everyone could sit down in the tidy sitting-room, speak the same language and wonder what was going on on Planet X outside the window. Also he might have a friend as handy as Ianto was now.

'Well, I think it is a hazardous course you're embarking on. You got cautioned at Christmas . . .'

'By the judiciary of a bloody foreign power!' interrupted Ianto.

'Well, we won't quibble over details. They have the power and could make life miserable for you. Best that you keep your head down.'

'Look, I've already broken my New Year's resolution. I'm not supposed to speak English more than is absolutely essential for purposes of day-to-day bloody intercourse. This conversation does not come under that category.' Ianto started sorting through a pile of books and papers. Benson thought: I've won!

'Suit yourself, Ianto,' he said, and left the room.

On his way back to his room he thought about organizing an anti-Welsh-speaking-hostel demonstration. Then he saw Simeon disappearing into the shower-room. Perhaps a good shower is just what I need to wash off British Railways and Ianto, he thought. After that I'll have to trace the whereabouts of Meryl. He thought of her and the image in front of him was that of Meryl made up of black and white lines entering every lounge in the country. He seethed momentarily, then calmed down by thinking of babies.

The entire population of the More Utopia went silent and turned towards Benson and Meryl. Benson looked round at his fellow coffee-drinkers and smiled lamely, mouthing 'sorry' as he did so.

Then he turned back to Meryl, who was smiling a smile of galling sweetness at him. Benson looked at his empty coffee-cup, and the silver paper from a recently-devoured Penguin biscuit, separated with great care from its backing and flattened out on to the Formica. He frowned at it, wondered if anybody in Aberystwyth was collecting silver paper for charity, then chided himself for his falsetto outburst at Meryl. He tried to recall how he had said it. 'You! A Catholic!' he had said. Meryl had nodded and said: 'That's right,' quite serenely. Only then had the More Utopia gone all quiet. What was he going to say now? Perhaps he should say nothing. Perhaps he was still irked by the fact that Meryl had been on television. No, appearing on television was bourgeois. He'd convinced himself of that on the way down the hill. He should just say nothing. It was only Meryl trying to get him worked up, wasn't it?

But Benson could not manage silence for long.

'Why?' he asked Meryl quietly, relieved to hear that the low hum of normality had returned to the More Utopia.

'I need something to hold on to, Martin.'

'But you've got plenty to hold on to!' stated Benson. 'You've got friends, family, *literature*. What about literature? You said it held the key! What about that?'

Still Meryl was serene. 'It doesn't answer my need. I thought it would, but when this . . .' and Meryl pointed to her tummy, '. . . happened, nothing in literature gave me the least support. Couldn't find a single thing in Eliot that I could pin on the hood of a pram to cheer me up.'

'Myvanwy's behind this, isn't she? She's been getting at you.'

'Neither Sean nor Myvanwy "got at me". I pride myself on not being the sort of person who can be "got at", unlike some people not a million miles from where I'm sitting. I just watched them together at the hostel. They were always so full of *joie de vivre*. When I told Myvanwy I was pregnant she listened, then she hugged me. When I told her I was going to have an abortion, she did the same thing. No, she didn't get at me in the slightest.'

'But what about since? They must have got you to come back to play the shepherd in the happening.'

'No, Martin, you are in error again. They rang me at home in London to see how I was doing. I wasn't doing very well. Mother kept muttering darkly about how time was passing and it wasn't going to get any easier, referring to the abortion of course. My dear parents were thinking I had merely postponed it. Mother even confessed tearfully to taking a bottle of gin and a scalding bath while at Lady Margaret Hall back in the mists of time. I was at the end of my tether when Sean rang and mentioned that they were short of a shepherd, so I borrowed my mother's car and drove up. They were surprised to see me.'

'So when did you decide to become a Catholic?'

'It started when I went down to London for the abortion. I wasn't sure about it.'

'You seemed sure.'

'I *seemed* many things, Martin.'

Benson felt that Meryl was rebuilding her whole character in front of his eyes. It was an unnerving thing to witness, but horribly fascinating too, like the blob in *The Strange World of Planet X*. 'Go on,' he said.

'Thank you, I will,' said the old Meryl. She lit a Gold Leaf. An aunt had given her a box of a hundred for

Christmas. Benson had wished that his selection of aunts had been able to stretch to something so enjoyable and utilitarian. 'I went to the clinic for a preliminary chat. That didn't help. I wanted someone there to say: "Don't do it. Have your baby. You'll manage." But no-one did, of course. They just checked my blood pressure and asked me to come back the following day with my nightdress. I wandered out and through Covent Garden. The fruit and vegetable sellers had packed up and there was just a lot of litter everywhere.'

'*My Fair Lady*,' said Benson.

'Quite. Anyway, I walked into Maiden Lane and saw a Catholic church on the left. There was an absolutely grotesque statue in the doorway.'

'There usually is. And you went in?'

'Yes.'

'Fatal. You don't have to tell me what happens next,' said Benson, nodding confidently.

'What happened next?'

'A priest came up to you. He seemed dead concerned and you broke down and told him everything.'

'No, the place was empty. I just sat at the back and looked around. Then I started walking about and I thought: I could take those hymn books; I could help myself to those pamphlets, stuff the poor box in my handbag. There were some gold candlesticks on the altar. I thought: I could take them too and no-one would know. Then I sat down again. I could hear the traffic outside but inside it was silent. It was odd. I was aware of the noise but soothed by the silence. Noise and silence all very distinct.' Meryl gazed out of the window and exhaled smoke. 'Can you understand that? I could hear the city and yet the church itself was silent.'

'It's either silent or it isn't,' said Benson, though he knew what Meryl meant.

'I sat there a long time and I thought to myself: I want

312

the baby. I really don't have to be told. And I also thought how nice it was that the church was open and trusting.'

'Well, it isn't, believe me.'

Meryl sighed with exasperation. 'I was referring to the building rather than the institution. I'd been sitting there for about fifteen minutes when an old tramp wandered in. There were candles burning in front of several dreadful statues. The tramp went round and started blowing out the candles. He was swaying like mad—'

'So what did you do?'

'If you'll give me a chance, I'll tell you. I stood up, took my matches out of my bag and followed him round relighting them. The tramp saw what I was doing. He blew out a few of the ones I'd relit, then he swore and passed out in a pew. When I had relit them all I sat down again.'

'Yes?' Benson asked. 'What else?'

'Nothing else. When I came back Enoch Mohammed didn't want to know. I had thought he might be interested in at least continuing our relationship, but he wasn't. You know most of that. Anyway, to cut a long story short Martin, I decided to become a Catholic because at this point I need a fixed point. I'll still be my own person. I don't believe the Catholic Church is the depository of all truth. Far from it. But it will do for me. You can understand that, can't you? You always say you're looking for truth.'

He could understand it, but he could not heave into his mouth a yes. He made a compromise, half a nod, leaving him looking at the useless Penguin wrapper.

'When are you going to get the water torture?' he asked at last, with a grin.

'What's that?'

'Baptism.'

Meryl smiled. There's hope for her, he thought. She won't get swept up in the whole complicated game of

313

Catholicism. They didn't get her at the right time. She'll play the game according to her own rules, ignoring any nonsensical cards that turn up, 'Go to hell without passing Mary.' Meryl would mould the Church to suit her purposes rather than the other way round. That would be all right. It was like Omar really. 'Well, if you want any tips about morals, mortal and venial sins, which saint for which job, anything like that . . . you know where to come.'

'You must be joking. I'm keeping it all to myself from now on. I'm taking instruction with Myvanwy at the abbey. I tell you, Martin, learning about Catholicism certainly throws light on all sorts of things. I never really understood *Dr Faustus* before, but I am beginning to now. Definitely a good move for all sorts of reasons.'

'And the baby?'

'We'll cross that bridge. I'm going to take the flat at Mrs Jones's.'

'So Enoch Mohammed isn't coming back?'

Meryl pursed her lips, then shook her head mock-sorrowfully. 'I'm sorry, Martin,' she said.

'Sorry! Who for?'

'You. You'll never know now, will you?'

'Know what?'

'Quiescence and tumescence, with special regard to Enoch Mohammed. Father laughed like a drain when I told him about you!'

Benson was appalled on two counts. How could Meryl tell her dad that? How could he laugh at something so serious? But he did not protest. After all, he thought, I know something that Meryl doesn't. Well, she does know, but she doesn't know I do too.

He allowed himself an enigmatic smile.

Did you see that look, viewers? Such humility! You and I well know that Martin Benson knows whether there is any difference between tumescence and quiescence. He has the Secret Knowledge, viewers; the knowledge we seek to keep from the bairns. It is something I would like to know but being long in the tooth shall probably never know. Ask me about whether a Scotsman wears underpants, though, and I'm your man! said Fyfe Robertson.

'I'd like another coffee and a Wagon Wheel, Martin,' said Meryl.

'But you've already had two coffees and a Wagon Wheel!'

'I'm eating for two,' she said.

And I'm paying for two, Benson thought. Thank God I'm a homo. I'd never be able to afford a wife and child. Maybe that was what sent Enoch Mohammed running! No, he must have decided before. He knew he was going when he asked me to collect the money. He didn't know about Meryl then, did he? I must ask Meryl about that. He bought Meryl two Wagon Wheels.

'Why thank you, kind sir!' said Meryl, like Moll Flanders.

'You probably zapped me with a prayer to the patron saint of extra rations for unmarried mothers,' said Benson, noting that Wagon Wheels seemed to have decreased in size yet again. If this went on they'd be bite-sized. They already were if you were prepared to be accused of being a pig. 'Actually, St Gerard Majella might be a good saint for you. I'll see if I can find you a medal or a holy picture of him.'

'Stop it, Martin.'

'OK. Tell me, Meryl, Enoch Mohammed didn't know you were pregnant until just before he left, did he?'

'He still doesn't know.'

'How do you mean?'

Meryl's upturned eyes sought solace from the fishing-net. 'I never told him, Martin. I wanted to that day, but he told me he was going away to get married. There didn't seem a lot of point in telling him after that.'

'I see,' said Benson. 'So all the time I was collecting money for the dinner-dance I was really supplying funds to top up Enoch Mohammed's dowry.'

'It seems likely. What's happening about that, by the way?'

'Mrs Jones has made the British Council put on a dance for us next month. The 14th of February.'

'And are you still Vice-President of the Overseas Students' Society?'

'Yes, I think so. I offered my resignation, of course, but Mrs Jones refused to accept it. I'm all right.'

'Good. How did Christmas go with Omar?'

'My lips are sealed,' replied Benson, suddenly knowing what he would do that evening.

'It's like that, is it?'

Benson caved in. 'No, not really. But I have hope. The holiday went very well except I lost my best friend, Clitherow. He's become a real snob.'

'But you know what you're like, Martin. By next week you'll have changed your mind.'

'I don't think so.' He felt a sudden ache and changed the subject: 'What about you, Meryl? Will you be all right?'

'I think so. Mrs Jones is being wonderful. And I've got lots of friends.'

Benson saw Myvanwy, Sean and Meryl skipping along the street arm in arm, singing 'Faith of Our Fathers' while he stared after them from the doorway of a dirty bookshop. 'Am I one of them?' he asked.

Meryl pouted her lips, leaned across and kissed him on the mouth. He tasted her lipstick and wondered how she could stand it when she licked her own lips. Then she sat back and said, 'As long as you keep the Wagon Wheels rolling in.'

'I will,' he told her.

That evening he read *Waiting for Godot* until he thought it was about the right time to visit Omar. There was Gareth too. He had to make sure Gareth was all right and pick up effusive thanks for sending him a tasteful postcard from Liverpool while he was at it.

He was nervous as he passed the National Library, his thoughts centred on Omar. Would he be able to pluck up the courage to tell Omar that he was like Andy? Where would that get him? It could be that Omar and Andy had only talked. But Benson doubted that. He could not imagine Andy letting such a heaven-sent delicacy as Omar pass by unfelt, unstripped, unsucked. Neither could he imagine that Omar would visit Andy twice for the benefit of mere conversation. Perhaps now, knowing what he thought he knew, Benson would be able to make of Omar Dearest Him. Perhaps Omar's fling with Andy had been a good thing in disguise.

When he arrived outside Gareth's fish and chip shop he was foiled in his intention of making sure that Gareth was alone inside before going in. There was heavy condensation on the window. He could not see anything of the inside of the shop from across the road. He crossed and tried to find a part of the window that was clear. Mist had climbed the window like a rising tide. Drops dribbled down it. He remembered how he had often made two drops on the kitchen window at home and then seen which would win the race to the window sill. After that game, Mum had made him take a chamois leather to the whole window and dry it off. Still, now drops made the chip shop window trans-parent along their narrow valleys, and be bent down to look through. It should only take a second, he thought. He squinted. Yes, there was Gareth. He was standing talking to someone. He could not see who he was talking to, but he could see that Gareth was crying, his head bowed over the fryers. Benson moved to see what could be making Gareth weep there in the fish and chip shop. He stood up on tip-toe and peered over the condensation. Benson's mouth dropped open when he saw that it was the Man from the farmhouse who was leaning against Gareth's counter. He wasn't speaking, just looking at Gareth weeping, with the flat, cold, manly look that Benson knew well.

Benson lowered his head. Things slotted sickeningly into place like a guillotine against its baseboard. He turned away from the fish and chip shop and continued on his way to Omar's house. He crossed his fingers that everything would go well between him and Omar. It would be lovely to have a regular friend in Aberystwyth. And it could just happen. It could just happen tonight.

But he must return later to see Gareth. Yes, he would have to. Gareth would need a shoulder to cry on. Benson, like Plato, had broad shoulders, hadn't he? He and Gareth had a lot to talk about, a lot in common.

He stopped. Shouldn't he turn around and go back now? He should go into the shop, vault across the counter on to Gareth's side and comfort his friend against the attack of the Man. He should face the Man and accuse him of cruelty and thoughtlessness! Should he? He jiggled on the spot. Brother Hooper and Fyfe Robertson made their comments. He shooed them away. He was on his own. But why was everything in life so bloody complicated? Tissues of issues, tossed like playing cards into the sky, landed untidily, littering everything. People changed. Even God seemed to change. But Gareth needed a friend. That was as clear as a white dune against brown sea. But he had to see Omar. He had to see if Omar might be the One. The Man, for all his shocking chemistry, wasn't. That was certain.

Benson, walking towards Omar once again, started whistling 'Chimes of Freedom'. Thank God for Bob Dylan, he thought. Then Gareth weeping came back to mind. Yes, a friend was definitely what Gareth needed. On his way back from Omar's, he would try to be one.

But he stopped again, unhappy and dissatisfied,

feeling about in his pocket for a sixpence. What a fool I am! he thought. And he ran back along the Llanbadarn Road towards the chip shop, telling himself as he ran that it would not be a good thing to arrive at Omar's feeling empty.

THE END

A SELECTION OF FINE NOVELS
FROM BLACK SWAN

THE PRICES SHOWN BELOW WERE CORRECT AT THE TIME OF GOING TO PRESS. HOWEVER TRANSWORLD PUBLISHERS RESERVE THE RIGHT TO SHOW NEW RETAIL PRICES ON COVERS WHICH MAY DIFFER FROM THOSE PREVIOUSLY ADVERTISED IN THE TEXT OR ELSEWHERE.

☐	99421 9	COMING UP ROSES	Michael Carson	£4.99
☐	99380 8	FRIENDS AND INFIDELS	Michael Carson	£3.99
☐	99348 4	SUCKING SHERBET LEMONS	Michael Carson	£4.99
☐	99455 3	KINGDOM SWANN	Miles Gibson	£4.99
☐	99208 9	THE 158LB MARRIAGE	John Irving	£4.99
☐	99204 6	THE CIDER HOUSE RULES	John Irving	£6.99
☐	99209 7	THE HOTEL NEW HAMPSHIRE	John Irving	£5.99
☐	99369 7	A PRAYER FOR OWEN MEANY	John Irving	£5.99
☐	99206 2	SETTING FREE THE BEARS	John Irving	£4.99
☐	99207 0	THE WATER-METHOD MAN	John Irving	£4.99
☐	99205 4	THE WORLD ACCORDING TO GARP	John Irving	£6.99
☐	99141 4	PEEPING TOM	Howard Jacobson	£4.99
☐	99063 9	COMING FROM BEHIND	Howard Jacobson	£4.99
☐	99252 6	REDBACK	Howard Jacobson	£5.99
☐	99399 9	MIDNIGHT EXAMINER	William Kotzwinkle	£4.99
☐	99440 5	THE HOT JAZZ TRIO	William Kotzwinkle	£4.99
☐	99239 9	BABYCAKES	Armistead Maupin	£4.99
☐	99384 0	TALES OF THE CITY	Armistead Maupin	£4.99
☐	99086 8	MORE TALES OF THE CITY	Armistead Maupin	£4.99
☐	99106 6	FURTHER TALES OF THE CITY	Armistead Maupin	£4.99
☐	99383 2	SIGNIFICANT OTHERS	Armistead Maupin	£4.99
☐	99374 3	SURE OF YOU	Armistead Maupin	£4.99
☐	99408 1	THE COVER ARTIST	Paul Miccou	£4.99
☐	99461 8	THE DEATH OF DAVID DEBRIZZI	Paul Micou	£4.99
☐	99381 6	THE MUSIC PROGRAMME	Paul Micou	£4.99
☐	99403 0	DIARY OF A MISPLACED PHILOSOPHER	Joseph North	£3.99
☐	99389 1	THE PARTY AGENT	Nigel Pickford	£4.99
☐	99419 7	THE REDNECK BRIDE	John Fergus Ryan	£4.99
☐	99389 1	FLIES	Sadie Smith	£4.99

All Corgi/Bantam Books are available at your bookshop or newsagent, or can be ordered from the following address:

Corgi/Bantam Books,
Cash Sales Department,
P.O. Box 11, Falmouth, Cornwall TR10 9EN

UK and B.F.P.O. customers please send a cheque or postal order (no currency) and allow £1.00 for postage and packing for the first book plus 50p for the second book and 30p for each additional book to a maximum charge of £3.00 (7 books plus).

Overseas customers, including Eire, please allow £2.00 for postage and packing for the first book plus £1.00 for the second book and 50p for each subsequent title ordered.

NAME (Block Letters) ....

ADDRESS ....

....